Grissom

In the Company of Snipers

Book 26

Irish Winters

WINDY DAYS
PRESS

COPYRIGHT

Grissom; In the Company of Snipers, Book 26

Cover design: Kelli Ann Morgan, Inspire Creative Services
Cover image: Paul Henry Serres Photography
Interior book design: Bob Houston eBook Formatting
Editor: Linda Clarkson, Black Opal Editing

ISBN Paperback: 978-1-942895-16-9
ISBN eBook: 978-1-942895-17-6
Library of Congress Control Number: 2023920725

In the Company of Snipers

You can find Irish Winters

On Facebook:

https://www.facebook.com/author.irishwinters

IN THE COMPANY OF SNIPERS

This series revolves around former Marine scout sniper, Alex Stewart, and his covert surveillance company, The TEAM, home-based out of Alexandria, Virginia. An obsessive patriot and workaholic, he created the company to give former military snipers like him, a chance at returning to civilian life with a decent job, security, and a future.

This is not a serial with each book ending at a cliffhanger. *In the Company of Snipers* is a collection of passionate love stories involving strong women and men who are tough enough to take on the world alone. Each is a stand-alone read, complete in itself.

Spoiler alert: Every story contains adult scenes including sexual situations (some explicit), language, and violence. I don't write sweet romance, so be forewarned.

Book 1, *ALEX*, reveals how The TEAM came to be, as well as how Alex met Kelsey, how they fell in love and fought all odds to stay together. Each of the following books is a complete romance in itself, where, in the course of an active TEAM operation, one agent comes face to face with his or her demons. The men and women I write about are all patriots and warriors, dealing with what they've lived through or mistakes they've made.

It's my hope that you will come to realize along with my heroes...

Love changes everything.

Chapter One

"They won't let me leave. They keep giving me drugs. Why won't they let me go? I've got a job. I work for you. Get me out of here!" Grissom McCoy yelled from where he sat on the edge of his hospital bed, his gaze fixed on the floor between his feet.

Leaning forward from his chair at the foot of that bed, Murphy Finnegan studied the troubled agent fidgeting with the hem of the pale orange Shady Creek Asylum shirt he'd been wearing the past three days. If that ugly shirt hadn't told Grissom anything, the over-sized orange flip-flops on his feet should've.

"Why do you think you're here?" he asked gently.

Grissom shrugged. "I don't know. Did I take one to the head? Is it a TBI? Am I dying? That why they won't let me leave?"

"No, you don't have a traumatic brain injury. You're too tough to die, but you're not well, son. You asked me to find your boys, remember?"

Grissom nodded, then slowly, like every other time Murphy had tried to jog his memory, the nod changed into a head shake. "No. I… ah… don't remember asking… Shit. I don't remember anything." He scrubbed both hands over his bearded face, then up over his shaggy hair, as if searching for those elusive memories. "I think I got shot. Least, I know I was in a shootout or something… somewhere... But I can't find any points of entry. Did I take one to my skull? Is a bullet still in my brain?" The tenor of his voice rose even as he avoided looking at Murphy. "Is that why I'm here? Who did it? Who shot me?"

"You weren't shot, but—"

"Where's my damned kids?" Grissom cut Murphy off, peering past him to the closed and locked door of his room. "If I asked you to find them, they gotta be missing. Where are they?"

Murphy's chest lifted with anguish more than the relief he wished he were feeling. The wound Grissom remembered happened years ago, back when he'd been active duty before he'd joined The TEAM. It had nothing to do with this voluntary confinement. These newer wounds were inflicted by his wife, and they weren't going away soon. "We're still looking for them. You don't remember, but—"

"Pam took my boys, didn't she? She ran out on me and took Tanner and Luke and—"

"And half The TEAM's looking for them."

"Half's not good enough! Get me out of here. I'll find them. I will, and I'll find Pamela, and when I do—"

"You're not going to find her. Think, Grissom. Please, just stop and think. Try to remember what I've already told you."

Grissom's life had become a tragic rerun that wouldn't stop playing. As many times as Murphy'd explained what his wife had done, Grissom kept asking. Always the same questions. Always the same answers. The truth wasn't kind, and his brain wouldn't let him accept it anyway. It was protecting him and doing a bang-up job of keeping him confused.

As for Pamela, she'd done Grissom dirty on so many levels. First, by cheating on him whenever he'd been OCONUS, while still active duty. Now, by taking Tanner and Luke with her when she'd fled to Central America with her boyfriend, Mike Estes.

Unfortunately for her, karma was a sneaky bitch. Murphy now knew Estes had made his living providing guided tours in one of the three Cessna's he'd owned. *Had* being the key word. He was at the stick when his plane went down off Costa Rica's west coast. Fortunately, Grissom's boys hadn't been on that tour. The former Mrs. McCoy had ditched them somewhere. Murphy knew for sure because the Costa Rican Coast Guard only pulled six bodies out of the Pacific: Pamela, Estes, and his four paying tourists.

Murphy still had no idea where Tanner and Luke were, which was the real problem. Between him and TEAM One's top dog, Mark Houston, they had most TEAM agents working to locate the boys. Agent Leisha Warner had backtracked Pam's activities to the morning she'd left the States. Pam's neighbors had been helpful. The retired couple across the street from Grissom informed Leisha that every time he'd gone OCONUS, Estes had all but lived with Pam and his sons. The middle-aged couple who lived next to the McCoys confirmed the same ugly truth. Pamela had been a cheat and a liar. No surprise there.

Murphy could only hope those little boys were still alive. Pam couldn't have been vindictive enough to have killed them to spite Grissom, could she? Or worse, sold them into the noxious flood of human trafficking sweeping the planet? The sex trade. Made Murphy's gut tighten at the thought of how cruel that woman had been to Grissom. But was she cruel enough to destroy her own kids? Recent events told him, 'Hell yeah.' Was only months since Heston Contreras had ended the infamous Maeve Astor, with an assist from the well-known nature photographer, Miss Tuesday Smart. Astor hadn't had a problem killing her children. Had Pam sunk as low?

"Oh… Oh, yeah." Oddly, Grissom calmed as quickly as he'd escalated. "Sure. Robin's good. My boys love her. She babysits for us."

His breathing settled, which was great, but—us? Murphy had no idea who Grissom was talking about. "Robin…?"

"Yeah. My neighbor. Robin Singer. She's a real good girl. Lives with her parents. My boys love her. She babysits for us."

There was that 'us' word again.

Grissom pursed his lips as if forcing himself to breathe slowly, like a woman in labor. "I need to see 'em, Murph. You'll make sure they come see me as soon as they get here, won't you? Is Robin bringing them? That'd be nice." He swiped a hand over his hair again, as if he wanted to look good for whoever Robin was.

"You're injured." Murphy pressed a hand to his sternum. "Here." *Mostly.* "And you took quite a hit to the back of your skull, too."

Grissom had yet to make direct eye contact, and that was troubling. "You sure? Cuz I gotta tell you, my head don't hurt, and there's no hole in my chest or belly that's big enough to even stick my little finger in. I checked. I can't find any wounds anywhere. No entries. No exits. Christ sakes, don't you think I'd know if I was dying?" The longer he talked, the higher his voice crept back into hysteria.

This visit was going nowhere. It was time for Murphy to back off before Grissom lost what little equilibrium he had. Inhaling a gut full of regret, Murphy lifted to his feet.

Grissom jumped up, still staring at the door like he was waiting for someone to come save him. "Don't go. Not yet. This place is killing me. All they wanna do here is talk, and I'm sick of it. I… I got a wife and kids to get home to… two kids… two little boys… Err, ah, don't I? Pamela. That's her na-a-a-m-m-me…" The nervous tone in his voice rapped down low into slow gear, like a vinyl record on a turntable losing power. "Pam-e-la," he whispered, blinking. Still not facing Murphy. Not really seeing anything. "It's not me, is it?" he asked. "It's her. It's Pam. She's… she's gone. She's run off and took my boys and she…"

Died. Just say it, Grissom. Remember. That's the only way you're getting out of here.

Grissom's hazel eyes went blank. His lips thinned.

Murphy sucked in a breath, knowing what was coming next.

Sure enough. Grissom blinked and then yawned, as if his poor brain had just rebooted, and he woke up in the middle of the same nightmare. "Well, hey, Murph. You come to win back the cash you lost playing poker with me last night?"

Interestingly, he still wouldn't make eye contact. Murphy made a mental note to ask Grissom's doctor what was going on and what that lack of eye contact meant. If anything.

"Just came for a visit. How are they treating you here?"

"Here?" Grissom blinked once again, his gaze on the door of the room that'd be his home for as long as it took for him to remember who he was and why he was there. Four cream-colored walls and a comfortable bed with a navy-blue comforter, a mostly empty closet, a dresser, and a desk. A private bath and a single window framing bullet-proof, unbreakable, polycarbonate glass. No one could get in and Grissom couldn't get out. For now, the world was safe.

There were no pens or pencils on the desk. No paper clips either. The desk's legs were bolted to the floor and the dresser's drawers were painted on. The bed was bolted down as well, and the blinds on the windows were enclosed inside two more panes of polycarbonate. No drawstrings to hang himself with or to fashion a garrote. Nothing anywhere to fashion any sort of deadly weapon with. Which didn't mean squat when the man inside this room was a trained killer.

"Where am I?" Grissom asked, for what seemed like the hundredth time in the last thirty minutes.

Murphy sucked in a bellyful of patience and sat back down. Grissom's nerves were shot and his heart had been blown away with them. He just didn't know it yet, and there was no way to help him understand. He'd lost touch with reality when he'd rear-ended that FedEx truck, and judging by the way this visit was going, he wasn't coming back anytime soon.

But then…

I'll be damned…

Grissom did something he hadn't done since becoming a full-time resident of Shady Creek Asylum. His gaze scrolled from the door to Murphy. "She left me this time, didn't she? Pam ran off with that guy who's been hanging around my place. She doesn't think I know, but I do. That's what you're telling me, isn't it? She took my sons, and she dumped them somewhere in" —he closed his eyes and touched two fingertips to his right temple— "where, Murph?" His nostrils flared and his belly inflated with a deep breath.

Murphy could only guess that the pain of not knowing where his sons were had somehow gotten through. Grissom needed those boys. Good fathers always did. But the stark sadness in his voice was a knockout punch Murphy hadn't seen coming. Neither did he expect Grissom to lift to his feet, plant them like he was ready to fight, and declare, "Help me find my boys or get the hell out of my way. I'm leaving."

"Now hold on a minute." Murphy put both palms forward, but he knew better. There was no way he could stop or placate a man the size of Grissom. He stood a good foot over Murphy. He was as tall as Agent Shane Hayes, bulkier than Agent Beau Villanueva, and his hazel eyes were two pissed-off death rays, mean for the first time in days. He leaned over Murphy like a dragon over the knight he meant to chew up and spit out. "I said move, old man."

Murphy allowed a faint smile. Sass was a step in the right direction. Belligerence was better. "Call me old man again, and I won't sign-off on them letting you out of here."

"I don't need you signing anything for me. I sign my own shit. Get out of my way."

"You're not going anywhere—"

"The fuck I'm not!"

Grissom's roar blistered over the top of Murphy's wispy combover. But rules were rules, and he could bellow, too. "Back off, buster! If you'd shut up and listen for a guldarned minute, you'd understand that you can't go—" damned if this junior agent's hands didn't ball into fists "—ALONE! You big dummy!" Murphy yelled, before Grissom could cock that hammer-of-a-fist and knock him on his ass. "One is none and two is one! Remember? You've got to be smart about how you handle this. Take someone with you. Hell, take everyone. We're all on your side, and you know better!"

Grissom's chest heaved, and Murphy knew his time to reason with this bull moose of a man was running out. Either he got through to Grissom now, or he lost him for good. Righteous rage was one thing, but Grissom going rogue could get a lot of people killed. Including himself.

"Your mission, the one I'm giving you right now," Murphy added hurriedly, "is to locate your sons without killing anyone, you hear me? Yes, Pam took Tanner and Luke to Central America. We've tracked them that far."

An angry grunt was all he got for an answer. He kept talking, not sure if he should tell Grissom that Pam was dead or not. "Which agents do you want on your six?"

"Alex."

Murphy shook his head. "No. He just retired, this time for good. Who else?" Alex would only remain retired until this shit hit the fan, but Murphy refused to let Grissom punch that ticket.

"Leisha Warner."

"Not Leisha, sorry. She twisted her knee two nights ago. Can't walk. Might be looking at surgery. Who else?"

"Cassidy Dancer."

Murphy gulped at how Grissom's tone kept wrapping higher. Maybe not everyone could support him. "She's on maternity leave." He seemed focused on female operators, so Murphy offered, "Phoenix Bond and Jenna Bates are already in Costa Rica. So are Everlee Yeager-Hayes, Izza Maher, Camilla Garner, and—"

"I want Taylor Armstrong, Cord Shepherd, and Walker Judge."

At last, agents who were available. Murphy shrugged off the tension fisting the hell out of his shoulders. "They're yours. They've been working with Mother, but they'll be glad to go with you. Anyone else?"

Mother was the genius office assistant who managed all things technical, as well as most everyone's personal business when she could get into it. Or so she thought. Sasha Kennedy hadn't earned the moniker of Mother just because of her astute ability to hack federal and non-federal databases throughout the world. The woman was inherently nosy, but she was a genius, and, in her annoying way, she was motherly. Sort of.

"And Alex," Grissom barked. "I want Alex!"

"No!" Murphy bellowed back at his hard-headed agent. It was time to draw a hard line.

"Yeah, Murph! Alex!" Grissom bellowed back. "Call him! He'll come once he knows what I'm up against. He understands. I know he does!"

Of course, he would. Alex was a father and a hard-charging son of a gun who always—always—had his agents' backs. Which was why Murphy refused to dial that number. "Think, Grissom! Guldarn it, think! Kelsey just survived a gunshot to her head, and she damned near drowned. She needs Alex a helluva lot more than you do." *And I'm in charge of TEAM Two, damn it. Not Alex. Not anymore.*

Grissom shook his head, his brows furrowing into a dangerous V. Which told Murphy the man didn't remember how close Kelsey had recently come to dying, or what nearly losing her had cost Alex. Obviously, Grissom didn't recall that he'd been there the day both TEAMs had taken down the human trafficking ring of then-Secretary of State Tristan Obermeyer and his despicable buddies, Michael Keane, Lancaster Wirth, and his son, Miles Wirth.

It was Lancaster who'd put the hit on Kelsey; his son Miles who'd hired Ryan Malloy, Ireland's best sniper, to do the ugly deed and wound, not kill her. Of the three main players, Obermeyer, Lancaster, or Miles—no one knew which had offed Malloy, then hired a couple local tough guys to kidnap London Wilde, now Heston's fiancée. Heston had rescued London and, in the process, had righteously ended Obermeyer. With a heap of prejudice.

Murphy knew where that body was, but the FBI still considered Lancaster and Miles Wirth as missing. Not that Murphy cared what the Bureau thought. Even if he knew where the Wirths were buried, he'd never tell.

"You gotta call him," Grissom ordered more calmly. "Please. Alex is the best."

"Yes, he is, but if anyone's going with you, it's me, guldarn it." Murphy stabbed his thumb into his chest for emphasis. "Let me make a few calls—"

"Then step on it! I gotta get gone, Boss. My boys need me!"

Grissom finally said the right word. He'd acknowledged who his first-line supervisor was.

"Understood. Grab a shower while I work on getting you released. Once that's done, I'll have Mother line up an Air Force bird out of JBA." Joint Base Andrews. "Then I'll make sure Taylor, Cord, and Walker meet us there."

Most of the agents on both TEAMs were already searching for Grissom's boys, either online from TEAM HQ or physically, boots on the ground in Costa Rica. Except for those with permanent stateside workloads: Mark Houston, Mother, Axel Cho, Harley Mortimer, Zack Lennox, David Tao, Maverick Carson, Tripp McClane, Jake Weylin, Cord Shepherd, and Beckam Garner.

Grissom turned for the head. "Grab me some decent clothes and boots. I ain't wearing this orange shit. My go-bag and all my tactical gear, too. My vest. I need weapons, Murph. Get my knives and pistols. All of them."

Murphy watched the bathroom door close behind Grissom. With any luck, his brain was finally mending. If not? Murphy was in for a helluva long flight to Central America.

Chapter Two

Grissom scrubbed the tiny, sample-size bar of yellow soap over his head, down the back of his neck, and back around through his beard, which was too damned long. What the hell was going on? Why hadn't he shaved today? At least trimmed his beard like he usually did?

Most of what Murphy'd said made sense, but Kelsey had been shot? Since when? What fool with a death wish did that? Not being able to recall that sweet woman's near-death experience was one of many black holes eating at Grissom's brain, making him doubt himself and Murphy. Making him doubt everything. Like why was a tiny bar of soap he could barely hold in his big hand in this puny shower? Why'd he need Murphy to sign anything?

Grissom vaguely remembered being in a fight at some bar and the cops showing up. Tasering him. But the why, where, and when escaped him. And now he was—what? Incapable of making legal decisions? Under protective custody? Committed to a fucking asylum? Whose bright idea was that?

'*Yours,*' the tiny voice inside his head whispered. '*The night you crashed. You agreed with Murphy after he insisted you wouldn't want to scare your sons.*'

"How could I scare them? I don't even know where they are," he exclaimed out loud. To himself. Like talking and answering himself made sense? Maybe he was crazy.

'You'll find them. That's what you do. Protect the weak. Defend the powerless. Bring the lost lambs home. Never ever give up.'

Grissom nodded at the astute summary of the Army Ranger he used to be. "Yeah. That's what I do." *Did. Intend to do…*

The image of three children a world away shimmered between the misty spears sluicing from the showerhead. In a blurry flash, Grissom was back in Syria. To *that* day. Talk about a clusterfuck. He hadn't been distracted or angry back then. Not at all.

One of the local leaders had contacted their CO with an urgent, "Help us! We found a bomb! In our school! Hurry, come help." Which was pretty much the state of the entire war-torn country back then. At one time, Syria had been one of the most educated countries in the Middle East. The government had promoted literacy for all boys and girls. Close to one hundred percent of the country's children were enrolled. Education was free.

Not anymore. The war brought chaos, along with the cruelty of child soldiers and gender-based violence—aka, rape—the standard weapon for invading countries in the whole fucked-up world.

So Grissom's squad had hurried. Once in the village, they'd checked with the man who'd called. He'd claimed to be the teacher, that the school was the only normal thing left in the children's lives. So dutifully, Grissom and his men had combed through the two-room, four-by-four brick schoolhouse, but hadn't found squat. He recalled being thankful that there were no children present, that the town's people had, at least, protected their kids. Their boys. Parents in Syria didn't send girls to school anymore. Too many had already been kidnapped and exploited and—worse.

All six in Grissom's squad had followed their Military Working Dog, Thumper, as she'd cleared each dark, little room in the building. Corporals Karras and Barone, Thumper's handler Sergeant Halliway, and Grissom had been tight on the MWD's butt when she'd alerted and bolted out the only exit that faced west. They'd gone left and followed her to the rear of the building. Captain Hauser and Sergeant Anderson went right. The squad reconnected behind the building, by that time facing due east. Nothing there but dust, scrub brush, and acres of barren landscape. No trees or buildings. Nothing to hide behind. No rusted-out trucks. No broken-down homes.

Despite the lack of obvious threats, Grissom had taken a knee at one rear corner of the building, and covered his squad's backs, his M16 ready to spread suppressive fire in all directions if needed. Karras had assumed the same position at the opposite rear corner.

It wasn't until Thumper'd started digging and Halliway called her off, that a prickle of unease had slithered up Grissom's spine. Down on his hands and knees in the dirt with his rear end stuck in the air, Halliway had peered into the hole, then popped back up with a shit eating grin and said, "You guys gotta see this."

Grissom and Karras had stayed put while Hauser and Anderson squatted alongside Halliway. "A fuckin' French *drain?" had hissed out of Anderson. "Out here? In the desert?"*

Quietly, Captain Hauser had stuck a gloved hand deep into the hole up to his shoulder and jerked out one end of a twelve-inch-diameter plastic perforated pipe stuffed full of small arms, cell phones, and a tangled mess of—

Incoming! Suddenly, they were taking fire from somewhere in all that nothingness behind the schoolhouse. Thumper charged the attackers, who Grissom still couldn't see. They seemed to be shooting high and wide, not aiming to kill as much as to annihilate the schoolhouse. That was when a bullet slammed into his chest and knocked him on his ass. He'd assumed it had hit his tactical vest. He'd shaken it off. Kept covering Thumper's fluffy butt.

When another spray of bullets went wild over his head, years-worth of muscle training had taken over. Grissom had jumped to his feet and nailed the two-foot-high scrub bush where most of that wild-assed gunfire had been coming from. It didn't register until much later how small that bush was, or how narrow a grown man's shoulders had to be for him to hide behind a foot-wide sprig of dusty branches.

Karras took out the other shooter, and Thumper—poor, poor MWD Thumper—had earnestly ripped the third bastard apart.

Like the good attack-trained dog she was...

Had been...

Would never be again...

Everyone there saw the limp, bloodied, and too small to be a man's arm she'd dragged back to her handler, her tail held high like a flag. She'd done her due diligence—like she'd been trained. She'd ended the assailant, and she was proud.

She'd come back for the rubber ball in Halliway's pocket. Her reward for doing a good job…

For being a good girl…

Only then did Grissom realize the shooters were three malnourished ten-year-old boys, who'd looked more like they were seven. Three boys who'd been bullied into shooting American soldiers by Syrian terrorists who'd threatened to kill their mothers if they hadn't obeyed.

Intelligent, gun-smart Americans understood the difference between select-fire assault rifles and machine guns. But ten-year-old, frightened kids, armed with bump-stock modified AKs, only knew how to squeeze triggers. Three little boys, damn it. They'd gone down like pins in a bowling alley. No bravado. No belligerent screams of 'Infidel!" They'd just dropped, their tiny bodies torn apart by the best of America.

Caught up in the somber reverie, Grissom fantasized how, if he could go back in time, he wouldn't've returned fire that day. If he'd known who the shooters were, he would've shot to disable the AK, not to kill a child. But he couldn't turn back time, and he hadn't shot to disable anything. He'd returned fire to save his men, and bottom line, he'd do it again. He didn't need forgiveness for killing a kid. A mother's son. A father's pride and joy. Forgiveness would never be in the cards. He just needed to put the past behind him and move on.

Shaking his head at the utter injustice of war, Grissom knew he'd carry the grief from that tragedy the rest of his life. Thumper went home with Halliway when he'd processed out. She was living the life on his ranch in Texas, like a good WMD should. But Grissom had gone back to his life of hell with Pam, and he'd be damned if he'd carry the pain of losing his boys, too.

Lifting his face to the shower's spray, he ran the tiny bar over the rest of his body and wished the water could rinse the confusion out of his head, as quickly as it got rid of the soap suds. Cranking the tap as hot as it could turn, he let the stinging heat work his shoulder muscles, then turned and offered his back for the same harsh treatment. He was a rubber band stretched so damned tight that every muscle and bone in his body hurt. Had for days.

Absent-mindedly, he fingered the scar in his right pec, the puckered divot beneath the inky tattoo glaring out at the world, left by the bullet he'd received that day. Of all things, the debacle at the schoolhouse happened the same day Tanner was born…

The day Pamela had finally informed Grissom he was a father…

That what they'd done during the one and only alcohol-induced night they'd spent together had produced a child. Even though he knew for damned sure he'd used a condom…

That he'd better plan on marrying her, unless he didn't care if people called his kid a bastard. Her ugly word. Never his. Not for one second, not for the space of a breath, had Grissom ever regretted the births of either of his boys.

How was that for Karma?

Marrying Pamela was his greatest regret. A barfly who'd zeroed down on any guy in uniform, she was supposed to have been a one-and-done. He'd been drunk off his ass that night. She'd been particularly aggressive, and, okay, good-looking enough, if a guy liked a woman with long, stringy red hair, tight metallic stretch pants, and jugs that had more than filled his hands. Which apparently Grissom must've liked that night.

Hadn't taken much for Pam to get him out of his uniform and into her bed.

Waking up in that same bed the next morning was another mistake. He'd rolled out of there as quickly as he'd opened his eyes. He didn't do breakfasts or mornings after. The one thing he remembered wasn't the sex, only the condom, which was nowhere in sight the next morning, although he damned well knew he'd suited up the night before. He never went bare, not with barflies or hookers, not even with the occasional woman he might've cared for. Or liked. Which were damned few. Which made him wonder if she'd kept the condom. If she'd planned the whole thing.

Barflies and tag chasers were known to poke holes in rubbers to trap soldiers into marriage. Or to inseminate themselves with what a guy left behind in that latex trap—if he'd been smart enough to bring his own condom to the party. Either way, she'd gotten what she'd wanted. The first chance Grissom had, he'd flown back to the States and asked her to marry him. That was the day he'd finally met his firstborn. Pam hadn't given their tiny baby boy a name yet, hadn't even filled out the form for his birth certificate. So Grissom named the beautiful child in his hands after his Army buddy, Captain Tanner Eli Gunn. It was a strong name. Grissom took care of the paperwork that made Tanner legally his son, and then, like it or not, Grissom made Pamela his wife. God, he hated that word. She'd never been a wife. More like a soul-sucking leech who'd preyed on stupid, horny men like him.

Where are my boys? What'd she do with them before she died? To them?

A fierce breath of determination sent the steam in the stall billowing up to the vent in the ceiling. There was no curtain or shower door. No lock to the head. Not like Grissom cared. If some nurse or doctor needed to invade his privacy to make sure he wasn't hurting himself or jerking off, let them look. Dumb asses. What hurt was everyone treating him like an incompetent idiot, as if he ever had or would hurt himself. As if he were suicidal. A danger to himself and to others. To his boys.

Shaking his head at all the know-it-alls in the world, Grissom let the past stay where it belonged—behind him. He couldn't change what happened to those boys in Syria. Sure, it sucked. Always would. But so did his life. The only things keeping him going were his sons.

Turning the faucet off, he hurried through the rest of his abbreviated grooming routine. Towel dried. Raked his fingers over his wet head to keep his too-damned-long hair out of his eyes. Finger-combed his beard so it'd air-dry quicker. Used the tiny sample-sized deodorant standing on the counter by the sink. Because, hey, the damned drawers to the one and only cabinet in the room were painted on, and he had no idea where his jeans and boots were.

As a final salute to the almighty powers in this place, the ones who thought they knew better than him, Grissom ripped the wet towel off his hips and tore it into narrow strips, then braided the strips into a single rope. If the staff in this asylum thought they could, in any way, restrain a man like him, they needed a lesson in creativity. Twisting the rope into a tight, efficient noose, he left it hanging on the showerhead, where any damned fool could've hanged himself if he'd wanted to.

People didn't need height to hang, just gravity and something tight around their necks. From then on, all a person had to do was lean into the act and let gravity take over. Risk-takers who dabbled in the dubious pleasures of autoerotic asphyxiation found out the hard way. Lean into that noose too long and you ended up dead.

Not Grissom. He had two God-given reasons to live. He just needed to find them.

Jerking the unlocked door to the head nearly off its hinges, he charged back into his room, stark naked, and found Murphy there, along with some guy in gray scrubs. Must be the doctor, judging by the disapproval wrinkling his forehead and the way he held his hands on his hips, like he thought he was important.

"Mr. McCoy?"

The guy's voice sounded familiar. Grissom had the faintest notion he'd met him before. "I'm Grissom McCoy. What do you want?"

"A word with you if I may—"

"No, you may not. I've got work to do, and if you think you're gonna stop me—"

"I'm not, but I'd like to send you out of here with a bottle of—"

"I don't do drugs!"

"These are only to relieve anxiety. They'll help you focus and—"

"My focus is fine. I'm outta here and—"

"Your focus is shot to hell, Gris," Murphy interjected quietly, but with enough authority to shut Grissom down. "And you know it. Else you'd remember the brawl in that bar and punching the officer who tried to arrest you. You'd remember taking off on your bike and crashing into the rear end of that FedEx truck, which is why you ended up in here. And you'd remember to wear pants!"

'*Traitor!*' the nasty voice inside Grissom's head screamed, at the same time another calmer voice whispered, '*Murphy's only ever been on your side. He's not lying. Trust him.*'

Murphy tossed him a pair of gray sweat pants. Grissom obliged and covered up. He swallowed hard, wishing his mind would engage all the way, damn it, instead of throwing opposing arguments that felt like grenades at him. Wishing he could remember, while striving not to look as weak and confused as he felt.

Doc Whoever-He-Was held out a small, green plastic bottle, the kind with a white child-proof cap and arrows that told you which way to turn, which way was up, and which way was down, and… *Shit.* Accepting help went against everything Grissom was and knew to be true. Men didn't show weakness, damn it. They bucked up and carried on, and they—

Doc rattled the pills in that bottle, not impatiently, more like he was tempting Grissom.

"You don't take them, you won't be released," Murphy said, "and I'll make damned sure you take them if you're going with me."

Grissom snorted. "You're going with me."

Murphy shook his head. "No, Gris. *You*" —he pointed at Grissom's chest— "are going with *me*" —he stuck a thumb at his own chest— "and that's the only way this is going to work. You follow *my* rules, and we'll find your boys and bring them home."

A thousand questions whirred like an egg-beater gone wild inside Grissom's head. *What if we can't find them? What if they're hurt? What if their bitch of a mother sold them? How will I ever get them back then? What if I never find them? How can I live without them?!*

What started as a string of logical questions morphed quickly into panic-laden shrieks that bounced inside his skull. Until Murphy landed a solid smack on his shoulder. The sting and warmth of that old man's hand got through and… Grissom forced the frenzied panic back with a hard-earned swallow. It took everything he had to whisper, "Fine."

"I want it clear that I'm releasing you against medical advice, Mr. McCoy," Doc said. "Your friend here has already made several counseling appointments for you, and he promised you'll keep them. Will you?"

Grissom finally met Doc's gaze. The tag on his shirt said **DOCTOR WINDHALL**. He had bright, brown eyes. Caring eyes. Not cold, but warm brown eyes. Tanner's eyes were warm and brown and alive, just like Doc Windhall's. Maybe those pills in that bottle would keep him calm enough to once again be a good operator.

He took the bottle. "I promise," he told the man. "After my boys are home and I'm sure they're okay, then…" He sucked in a breath, needing a minute before he revealed that he might just need someone else's help after all. "Okay, yeah. I'll come see you."

The guy's chest heaved as if he'd been holding his breath. "Thank you, Grissom. Ms. Ashlee Peyton is our family counselor, and I know she'll love working with you and your boys. I imagine they'll need a little help when they get back home, don't you think?"

He extended his other hand, his right hand, and automatically, Grissom took it. Because that was what men did. Their word was their bond and a handshake sealed the deal. "You might be right. Yeah, sure."

"I look forward to working with you," Doc said. "I'm here for you and for your boys. All you have to do is call."

Grissom nodded. Yeah, sure. He'd come see this guy again, but only after Tanner and Luke were back where they belonged. At home. With him.

Chapter Three

The flight to Costa Rica was long and tiresome, typical when flying AF transport. Grissom and his team were last-minute hitchhikers, traveling on Uncle Sam's dime. The C-130J-30 Mother snagged their passage on, was the stretch version. A recent modification added 15 feet to its fuselage, increasing the bird's usable space. Most of that usable space was currently occupied by four dozen active-duty US Army and Air Force members, three helicopters, a shit load of palletized disaster and first-aid supplies, bottled water, and other rescue and medical equipment. All were deploying to southern Costa Rica's Peninsula de Osa, in response to extreme flooding and mudslides. While that unexpected disaster spiked Grissom's anxiety into the red zone, Murphy insisted Luke and Tanner weren't anywhere near there.

Grissom now knew Pam and Estes had gone down with his plane in the Pacific, twenty-some miles off the coast of Samara, a small village on the northwest coast, known for its palm-lined beach. Both were assumed dead, as well as the four tourists flying with them. According to the latest intel from Agents Shane Hayes and Beckam Garner, Luke and Tanner weren't in Samara, nor were they in any of the villages along the coast. All that astute intel did for Grissom was eliminate one possible location out of thousands. Not good enough.

The further south the AF bird flew, the more stifling the air inside the noisy transport became, and the shorter Grissom's temper. By the time they touched down in Puntarenas, he was half out of his mind. The aft loading ramp had no more than cracked far enough open to let in a rush of humidity when he was on the tarmac and antsy as hell. His boys needed him. He didn't have time to waste. It seemed like hours before Murphy, Taylor, Cord, and Walker joined him. Where the hell was their ride out of here?

Grissom commenced pacing. He'd been in Costa Rica before. At its widest, it was a hundred seventy miles. Transportation would be problematic. If his boys were hidden somewhere on the Pacific side, it could take hours—days!—before he could get to them—if he knew where to look. If not? *Fuck!*

Puntarenas itself was a port town situated on a long finger of land stretching west from the Costa Rican mainland into the Gulf of Nicoya, which in turn opened to the Pacific. The landmass of the conjoined Puntarenas and Guanacaste Provinces lay between the Gulf of Nicoya and the Pacific, putting Tanner and Luke yet farther away. Driving distance by bus, which would take Grissom and his team north and around the Gulf, would still, if all went well, waste close to eight hours. By POV, three to six. Murphy should've engaged a local helicopter, damn it. Why wasn't anyone waiting there to meet them? What was taking so long?

Damned if Shane Hayes and Beckam Garner didn't pull up in a fairly new passenger van, instead of the beater vehicle Grissom had expected. The van looked like it would accommodate everyone plus gear. But that meant Tanner and Luke were three to six hours away. Not acceptable. *Shit!*

His nerves were eating him alive and time was wasting. No one seemed to think finding his boys was important enough to hurry, damn it. *No one but me!*

Grissom bit his bottom lip to keep from blowing his cool and making a bigger ass of himself. Instead of opening his mouth and spewing the anxiety eating him alive, he stowed the gear he'd brought, err, make that, what Murphy'd brought *for* him. Murphy was not the enemy here. None of these men were, and Grissom knew it. So what if Murphy hadn't thought ahead and engaged better transportation—like an airplane or a helo? What if Shane and Beckam were wrong and Tanner and Luke were on the Pacific side of this damned country? On the coast?

Growling at the growing frustration he was holding back—barely—Grissom raked his fingers over his already mussed hair. The still tender scar at the back of his head, the one he had no idea where it came from, screamed at him to take it easy. Like hell! He had two little boys to find. He was not the important one here! Only Tanner and Luke!

"Let's hit the road," Shane said, as he climbed back into the driver's seat. Beckam ducked inside and claimed the farthest window seat in the middle row behind Shane. Wordlessly, Taylor, Cord, and Walker angled their wide bodies between the two middle seats and crammed themselves onto the rear bench. Murphy climbed up with Beckam and pulled the passenger door shut. Grissom launched his ass into the empty front passenger seat and buckled his seatbelt. His fingers commenced tapping the dash, needing to be gone.

Once headed away from the runway, Shane explained, "We're pretty sure your boys are being held on the west side of the peninsula. If all goes well, you'll be on the way home with them before sunset."

Grissom absorbed that info as calmly as possible, as if he hadn't just been pissed-off and nearly out of control. "This peninsula? They're that close? Really? Are you sure?"

Shane shot him a quick glance before his gaze returned to the road. "You look like shit," he said, slapping a hefty hand onto Grissom's shoulder. "But, yeah. Becker's gut's been talking to him, and he believes your wife left Tanner and Luke here, where Estes lived, not on the coast where they, umm, crashed. Mother's been looking over Jed McCormack's satellite images. Right, Murph?"

"Right," Murphy replied. "Mother, Axel, Beau, and Ember have all been working twenty-four-seven, scrutinizing every image taken of this area this month. She'll call if they find anything else. Just you wait and see."

If they find anything... Not anyone... Shit! Grissom shook off the profound negativity driving him. His boys had to be here, and he had to believe they were. There were no other options. He had to find them, and it had to be today. How could he live, ever breathe again, if—?

"Grissom," Shane said quietly, his hand still a brick on Grissom's left shoulder. "We *will* find them, buddy. Every available agent is right now searching for them, if not in this country, at home poring over those sat pics. We're all on your side. You're not alone."

"Yeah, but..." *I'm the only one who's going to lose his mind if I never see my boys again. I'm the only one who'll go home empty-handed. What if she sold them? Pam would do something like that. The woman's bitter to her core. She never wanted boys. Only little girls she could dress up and twist into mini-versions of herself. You guys have no idea what our life's been like!*

Instead of voicing his despair, Grissom cranked the window open and let the salty air blow in. There wasn't enough oxygen in this crammed-full van, and he had a gutful of adrenaline to burn. He ached. Every tiny nerve and muscle fiber in his body hurt, they'd been wound tight for so damned long. Too long. God, he'd been a mess since he'd married Pam. The only joy in his whole life was his two little guys. But he didn't know where they were! Or who they were with. And…!

No! Just no! The never-ending roller coaster ride he was on was killing him. Grissom knew he had to settle down and trust his fellow agents. He knew that, but shit! The thought that Tanner and Luke *might* be in a city of close to a hundred and thirty-five thousand… Did. Not. Help! What was he supposed to do? Start knocking on all those doors? Wait until Mother and her people *found something*? Not someone? Not—!

"Jesus!" he mentally blasted into the wide blue sky overhead. *"Help me find my boys, damn it! They need me. They don't even know their mother's dead, and I don't know where they are. I can't do this alone!"*

Another hand landed on his other shoulder, as if reminding him again that he wasn't alone, no matter how much he felt like he was. Had to be Murphy. Of course. The old codger dug his fingertips into Grissom's shoulder muscle and growled, "Swallow this and don't give me any crap."

Sure enough, Murphy's right hand was clenched into a fist between the door and Grissom. He looked down and the gnarled fist opened and revealed one of those tiny, damned pills he was supposed to take. "Now?" he asked, like a whiny brat.

"Take it!" Murphy snapped. His other hand released its hold on Grissom's shoulder and a dripping wet bottled water appeared out of nowhere. No sense arguing. Everyone in this van was on Murph's side.

'And yours,' the annoying voice in Grissom's head whispered.

Jesus, is that my conscience?

Shane seemed to know where he was going. He didn't need Grissom's help—or interference—so Grissom obeyed the order to self-medicate. It might work. He'd given his word, so, yeah. He swallowed the tiny pill, then chugged the entire bottle of water to make his boss happy. Someone in this van might as well be.

Shane hooked a right that took them to the other side of the narrow strip of land. Everywhere he looked, Grissom saw homes, apartments, and markets sandwiched between fishing or boating businesses. Boats bobbed along the shore, some along small, private docks, while some had been turned on their sides on the beach. Seabirds squawked overhead. The air smelled of salt and sea. Grissom could only pray. Nothing prepared a man to lose his children. Not all his years in the Army. Not any amount of well-honed training. It all came down to his boys being strong enough to survive this nightmare n their own. If they were okay, he'd be okay.

God, please let them be okay. Take care of my babies for me. Please!

It'd only been minutes since Shane pulled away from the airfield when he turned into a narrow alley. A three-story building that looked a lot like a hundred-year-old *Motel 6* faced the rear of an open-ended warehouse that stored boats. Lots of boats.

Shane maneuvered the van up against the warehouse wall, leaving Grissom just enough room to get out. Nobody moved. Nobody said anything. Everyone seemed to be waiting so…

"Are they here?" Grissom asked, his sharp eyes quartering the building on his right and the warehouse at his left. The warehouse looked empty of everything except storage racks filled with boats, which made sense. Nothing suspicious there. But the motel was oddly quiet, considering it was probably an apartment building now, not a motel. It was a long, weathered wooden structure that had once been painted white, with a red, clay-tiled roof. Walkways terraced each story, with stairs leading to ground level at both ends of the building. No maid service carts anywhere. No drapes on the windows. Someone's laundry draped over one end of the top-most banister.

"Yes," Beckam said with authority, from behind Grissom. "See the toys on the second level landing?" He stretched a long finger between Shane and him, pointing at what Grissom should've noticed. "Bright plastic trucks and cars, too."

"That's what you're basing your best guess on? Stupid toys?" Although Luke did sleep with toy trucks at home, and his boys were prone to fight over which toys were whose. But Grissom had no way to know whether those were really Luke's or not. It made sense Pam would've brought the boys' most treasured belongings with them, if only to keep them out of her hair and quiet, so she and—

A deadly growl percolated from deep inside Grissom's chest. Damn it. He shut down the thought of Pam and Estes acting like man and wife in front of his sons. Way down. This was a new day, and if his boys were in there—

"Besides," Beckam added. "That's the only room with its drapes pulled shut."

Oh, yeah. Grissom noticed that now, too. Opening his door, he put a boot on the ground. By the time he was upright, Murphy was standing on his right, Shane on his left, both with pistols drawn. Grissom blinked, and just that fast, Beckam, Taylor, Cord, and Walker were with him and also armed. He hadn't thought to pull his pistols. Honestly didn't need them if his boys were in that room.

The nightmare in Syria roared back to life, screaming a bloody vengeance that couldn't be ignored. "No," he growled, more at himself than at the men with him. "No weapons, guys. None. Not if my boys, hell, not if any kids are up there in that—"

He wasn't finished speaking when the six brave men with him holstered their weapons. Nothing had ever sounded as good as that metal sliding into leather or mesh pockets. It took a buttload of stress off his shoulders.

"Your call, Grissom," Shane whispered. "You lead."

"Second level?" he asked, his heart pounding at the possibility that finding Tanner and Luke could happen this easy. This soon. He hadn't been in country an hour yet.

"Yes," Beckam declared quietly. "You ready?"

Pushing a nervous breath through his chapped lips, Grissom swallowed hard and said, "Yeah. We go in soft. I'll knock and call out to my boys. If they're in there, they'll come running." Just like they used to do every night when he got home. God, could it really be this easy?

No one argued for a surprise attack or offered another method of B&E. Where Grissom led, they followed. Yet the moment he wrapped his fingers around the dirty metal doorknob on that second-story room, he faltered. He trusted these men with his life. He would trust them with Tanner's and Luke's lives, too. Right?

But shit still happens…

How well he knew… "Weapons up," he whispered at the still-closed door. "Just in case."

Again, the quiet sound of metal whispered against mesh and leather. All but his. He'd never lift a weapon against a child again.

Instead of barging in like he would've in Afghanistan or Syria, Grissom released the doorknob and knocked softly. He didn't want to frighten his sons. He called out a firm, "Tanner and Luke, are you in here? Can you hear me? It's me, Dad." *Please open the door, Whoever-you-are who's got my boys. Don't make me have to bust it down.*

The door sprang open inward, and the prettiest bombshell stood there, blinking her big, beautiful, absinthe-green eyes. Long, brown hair, parted down the center, cascaded over her shoulders in messy tangles. She looked exhausted, as if she hadn't slept, bathed, or brushed her hair in days.

Murphy shouldered past Grissom and stepped inside the motel room. "Tuesday?"

Tears filled her eyes as she opened her mouth to answer but—

"Daddy!" three-year-old Luke screamed from behind the partially closed bathroom door. "I here! Daddy, I here! Don't leave! I coming!"

Grissom dropped to his knees as both of his boys plowed into his arms, damned near knocking him on his butt in the open doorway.

Tanner burst into tears. "I'm sorry, Dad, but I" —he hung his head, choking on shame no boy should have to feel— "I peed my pants. I'm sorry!"

Luke cried and Grissom couldn't hold back the emotions drenching his cheeks and running into his beard. "Oh, my sons. My boys," he cried, his voice raw and hoarse. "I think I might just do the same thing, Tanner. It's okay. I don't care if you had an accident, and I'm not mad. I… I…" He couldn't begin to verbalize the emotional storm in his heart. All he could do was hold the most precious things in his life. His sons. The baby boys he hadn't been sure he'd ever see again. They were here. Shane and Beckam were right.

Grissom broke down and sobbed, unashamed to let his love show or to let his boys know how much they meant to him. Men cried, damn it. His boys needed to understand that showing love was not a weakness, and he loved these boys more than life.

While he held his crying boys in his arms, the guys chatted with the woman who had them. She was probably tight with Pam, damn her. Grissom struggled to listen to what she was telling Murph, but right then, he had what he'd come to Costa Rica for. That woman could go to hell, for all he cared. He just wanted to take his sons and go home.

Chapter Four

"That's the thing, Mr. Finnegan," Tuesday explained. "That woman literally threw her boys at me. I've never seen anything like her. She was rude and kept slapping that little guy's head. And the names she called him were awful. I couldn't say no, I just couldn't. Is this man really their father?"

Before Murphy could answer, Grissom lifted his bleary eyes and growled, "Damn straight, lady. I'm their biological father, not some joker with a hard—"

"He's my Daddy!" Luke bawled, his teary face buried in Grissom's chest. "And I wanna go home."

"Shush, little guy. She's just making sure I'm your dad." Grissom kissed Luke's sweaty forehead, then the top of Tanner's head. He had yet to loosen his grip on them, not the way both clung to him. Both traumatized. Both so damned upset, it was killing Murphy seeing them like this. Thank heavens for family reunions. Watching Grissom's relief made everything Murphy'd gone through to get him here worth it.

"What's that woman's name anyway?" Tuesday asked.

"Pamela McCoy," Murphy replied. "Sorry to barge in like we did, but those guys standing over there are TEAM Agents Hayes and Garner. Agents Armstrong, Shepherd, and Judge are at the window."

"Hey, Tuesday," Shane said. "What are you doing here?"

"Shane!" Tuesday shrieked as she launched herself at him.

He let her hold onto him. Let her break down and cry on his shoulder while he patted her back and murmured, "It's okay, Tuesday. You're okay. You're strong, remember? But damned if you don't show up in the worst places."

"I'm not okay," she whined into his neck.

Thank goodness he kept calming her down because Murphy had his hands full. "We all work for Alex Stewart, ma'am," Murphy explained. "I'm assuming you've been in touch with him?" It was possible. Alex tended to keep track of people who helped his agents in the course of them doing their jobs, and Tuesday had been involved in bringing down the infamous Maeve Astor not long ago.

Turning to Murphy with one arm still hooked around Shane's neck, Tuesday wiped her teary face and nodded. "Yes, Alex gave me his card the day Heston and I left for New York City."

"For that interview," Shane interrupted. "That's the only uppity TV program Everlee and I've ever recorded. You did great, by the way." His eyebrow spiked. "So what happened between you and Heston? Everlee and I kinda thought you two were… you know."

Pushing out of his arm, she smoothed a hand over her face. "Not Heston, sorry. We were just friends. Like I am with you and Everlee. I'm… I'm still living the dream." Didn't sound like that dream was working out for her anymore. "Still working with Robert, and right now, we should be filming the effects of global warming in Antarctica. I was supposed to meet him here, but our plans changed. He was filming the flooding in Peninsula de Osa instead. He might still be there, I don't know. I've been kind of busy."

Murphy didn't miss the tender glow that lit her pretty face when her eyes zeroed back to Grissom and his boys, all three still on the floor. At last, they were together again, and Murphy knew Grissom was finally on his way to a complete recovery. He looked at peace, as if his devils had been vanquished. Everyone knew how badly his wife had treated him since day one. Murphy'd met the woman, and the only word that described Pamela McCoy was *witch*. He didn't like to speak or think ill of the dead, but he wouldn't be surprised if she'd roofied Grissom the one night they'd been together. Murphy knew her type. Barflies and tag chasers only wanted the military benefits that came with marrying a soldier.

"What's your name?" Tuesday asked Grissom. "I mean, besides Daddy" —she winked at Luke— "which is actually enough proof for me. But I can't very well call you that, can I?"

"Grissom McCoy, ma'am," he answered gruffly, both arms still around his boys like unbreakable steel bands. "Tanner's six. Luke's—"

"I free" —Luke held up three fingers to Tuesday— "and I gonna be this many next time." He upped another digit, making him four on his next birthday. Sweet little guy.

Tuesday walked over to where Grissom had landed and knelt alongside him, in the middle of the open doorway. "I'm so sorry, Mr. McCoy. I knew they were tired, but we'd just gotten back from the beach, and I was going to take them to the market to get something to eat after they showered. Why didn't you ever answer your phone? I've been calling the number your wife gave me, but it goes straight to voicemail every time."

That answered one of Murphy's many questions. He didn't doubt Tuesday Smart for a minute. Not knowing how she and Heston Contreras had taken out Maeve Astor, one of the deadliest black widow killers Murphy had ever encountered. Tuesday and Heston had saved Everlee's life that night.

At last, Grissom relaxed enough to blow out a sigh. "Sorry, ma'am. My fault. All this is my fault."

"No, it's not," Tuesday said kindly. "It's that jerk's fault, the guy your wife's with. Who is that creep? I'd never let him near my children, if I ever have any."

Murphy cut in before Grissom could go ape-shit telling Tuesday just who the hell Estes was—err, had been. "Grissom's been in the hospital, ma'am. Dumbass got into a fight with a delivery truck, and the truck won. Probably when he lost his phone."

Tiny Luke pulled back far enough to put both hands on his father's bearded cheeks. "Did you get hurt, Daddy? Where's your owie? Let me see it so I kin kiss it better."

Grissom leaned forward enough to bump his forehead to Luke's. Murphy watched the muscles in his throat work as he struggled to tell his boy, "I'm okay, Short Stack. Fact is…" He choked. "I've never been better. What say we get out of here and go home?"

Tanner and Luke both declared, "Yeah!" at the same time.

But Murphy caught the narrowed brow Grissom flashed his way. Before Murphy could explain that yes, he had a plan, and that plan included them flying back to the States via commercial air, Tuesday cut in with, "Robert's private plane is still in San Jose, guys. Let me call it for you. It can land at the Puntarenas airstrip, no problem, and it'll get all you men home quicker and in more comfort. Okay?"

"Us too?" Tanner asked timidly. "Can we go home with Dad? Please, Miss Tuesday?"

Murphy looked away. Damn it, Tanner was hurting as much as his dad. All three of them had been through hell, and yes, Grissom was just another big kid in Murphy's opinion. He'd been taking care of young men like him since the guldarned Vietnam War.

"Yes, buddy," Tuesday replied patiently, her hand gently squeezing Tanner's shoulder. "You and Luke are the most important men in this room, right, Dad?" she asked pointedly.

"Yes, ma'am," Grissom replied gruffly, his eyes glistening after that heartbreaking plea from his oldest.

"And because you've been so much fun in the short time you've been with me, I'll ask the pilot to let you sit up front with him for a couple minutes during the flight home. Would you little tigers like that?"

Tanner simply nodded. He hadn't smiled yet, neither had he loosened the stranglehold he had on Grissom's neck. It was Luke who asked excitedly, "What's a pilot?"

Before she could explain, Grissom finally looked up and into Tuesday's glistening green eyes. "I… I think they like you."

Poor woman looked close to breaking down. "I kinda like them, too," she replied softly. "They've been perfect gentlemen. You should be proud of them."

"I am. Yes, ma'am, I sure am. Would you mind if we cleaned up in your bathroom before we head out?"

"Sure. Let me help." Tuesday shot to her feet, both hands extended to his boys. Like she'd probably done frequently over these last few days. But this time was different. Neither boy reciprocated. They both just sat there looking up at her, like they weren't ever letting go of their father again. Her hands dropped. Her chest heaved. She'd just realized her time with Tanner and Luke was over. She was a babysitter, not their mother, not even a blood relative who could drop in to visit them someday.

"Umm, never mind. Sure. I'll get their clothes and—" Pivoting on her heel, Tuesday stepped out of sight behind the closet's louvered door. It was heartbreaking to watch her shoulders quake even as her spine straightened. Poor kid. She was like so many disappointed soldiers. When things were tough, they still had a job to do, and Tuesday's job had nothing to do with mothering. She wasn't a soldier who'd eventually go back home to her family and forget the ugliness of the world. She didn't have a family.

Tuesday Smart wasn't going into any battle zones, either, not working with naturalist photographer Robert Freiburg. She was documenting climate change. If anything, her profession was showing people the magnificent beauty of the world. She was a teacher, helping others understand how to save their planet. Not that a rewarding career could ever replace the love of a brave man or a family, but what she did was still important.

Yet Murphy doubted her adventurous life could replace motherhood, which was precisely what he was looking at. One of the loneliest things he'd ever seen, a mother with no children. Tuesday needed a man in her life, one who could help her realize her dream of becoming more. Was that man

Grissom? Hardly. Grissom had a shit ton of issues to work through before he'd be ready for a relationship.

Good, healthy relationships weren't the norm in American culture anymore anyway, and Murphy wasn't sure they ever were. Look at him. He was pushing seventy and on his second marriage. Alex was on his fourth, although four seemed to be the magic number for him. Numbers two and three had simply been a desperate man's attempts to recreate the family he'd tragically lost. No way they could've lasted, and Murphy didn't blame Alex for trying. Every failed relationship had led him to Kelsey, and their marriage was something to be jealous of. One had only to glimpse those two kids together to believe in true love.

Murphy took a step in Tuesday's direction, to at least give her a fatherly hug, then thought twice and left her alone. There was nothing he could say to make the upcoming goodbyes easy. Grissom had his boys back. The mission was over. It was time to get the troops home where they belonged.

He turned to Shane and Beckam, Taylor, Walker, and Cord. Lastly, to Grissom, still on the floor, completely absorbed in his boys and totally oblivious to the woman breaking down behind that darned door. She had yet to duck away from the closet. Damn it, Grissom needed to at least acknowledge how tough this was going to be for her. But it was Shane who stepped to Tuesday's side and put an arm around her shoulders. When she leaned into him, Murphy told Grissom, "Get moving. We've got a plane to catch."

He lifted to his feet, both boys still in his arms. Luke giggled at the shift in position, but Tanner was holding onto his dad so tight that his fingertips were white. His eyes were squeezed shut and his face was wet with tears. He was embarrassed about his pants, poor damned kid. And Murphy no longer thought Grissom should be mindful of Tuesday. He was putting his boys first like a good father should. Tuesday'd have to walk her own path, and sadly, it didn't include the McCoys.

Murphy cleared his throat, "If you'll arrange our flight home, ma'am, I'd be much obliged."

She stepped away from Shane with a soft, "Tell Everlee I said hi, okay?"

"Yeah, sure. Stop by next time you're in Virginia."

She walked away from him to the nightstand, where she unplugged a cell phone from a charger and made the call. Looked like everyone was going home happy. Everyone except Tuesday.

Chapter Five

"What's your problem today?" Robert asked tersely.

Tuesday's head shot up at his tone. Sure, she was tired as all get out, covered in squishy filth, and she'd seen more trauma these last few days than she'd expected during a photo shoot. But this wasn't a normal assignment, and she'd never minded helping others. Robert had no reason to snipe at her. He was the one with a problem.

As often happened when covering natural disasters, instead of just taking photos, she and Robert were knees-deep in rescue efforts slash body recoveries slash offering first-aid and comfort to the poor people affected by the flood. The waters had subsided, but they'd left a ton of mud and debris in their wake, as well as death and destruction. American soldiers and airmen were there, assisting the Costa Rican Emergency Response teams, and recovery was going fairly well, considering how bad the flood could've been. Only two bodies had been found so far, and both were elderly men, not women or children.

Tuesday had never balked at any assignment Robert sent her on. She'd bucked up, packed up, and traveled alone more times than she could count. She was a freaking 'woman of the world'. Independent. Robert's proverbial Gal Friday. She could take care of herself. And she had, damn it. That was her life. She was reliable, intelligent, and a master at her craft.

Then why couldn't she stop the tears dripping out of her traitorous eyeballs and leaving telltales streaks running down her dirty face, huh? She shoved her muddy hair out of her eyes yet one more time. That was another thing. She'd lost the elastic tie she'd kept on her wrist, probably because it didn't want to be around her any more than she did. Who was she kidding? The only reason she was here was because Robert needed her. And he only needed her because she had a talent for lighting and perspective and, okay, so her photos ended up in natural history magazines and documentaries, and the public loved her work.

And now she was rambling. Hadn't yet answered the man who could fire her. Forcing her chin up, she turned and faced Robert. Tuesday took a second to formulate a passive, agreeable answer and replied, "I'm just tired. I'm taking a break. Can I get you another bottled water?"

"That all?"

He was either asking if the water was all she planned to bring him or if being dirty and tired were all that was wrong with her. She ducked the truth with a curt, "Yes, Robert. After twenty-four hours without a single break, I'm spent."

"Fine. Stick to capturing the human element on film when you're done resting. You're missing some great shots. Closeups. I want more closeups. How long do you think you'll be?"

Tuesday had never thought Robert could be as obtuse as he was right then. She shrugged, still keeping her feelings private. That was her. Cold, untouchable, and frigid, damn it. Let the world think what they wanted. They would anyway. "Depends if I get any sleep. How many bottled waters do you want?"

She'd no more than asked when an airman driving a frontend loader carrying a pallet of bottled waters arrived and bellowed, "Blue Light Special, people! Water's here! Come and get it!"

When she was sure that Robert heard the guy, Tuesday turned on the balls of her feet and headed for the massive OD green tent marked **WOMEN ONLY**. A hot shower and a decent meal, courtesy of Uncle Sam, were waiting for her. America had provided not only over-the-top disaster relief, but an extensive logistical trail of supplies and support personnel for the duration of the relief effort. Even for her, a nobody who took pictures and called it living.

Once inside the tent, which could've held a three-ring circus sans the trapeze act, she headed for the locker she'd been assigned. She'd previously stored a backpack of extra clothes and other essentials there, as well as the hardened case full of sensitive photography equipment she'd brought with her. The USA had provided every aid-worker with either a courtesy cosmetic bag or a shaving kit, full of enough necessities to get them through a couple days of nonstop volunteer work. But Tuesday wanted her own body wash, shampoo, and conditioner, not some generic products made by the lowest bidder.

Next, she claimed the shower stall at the farthest end of the tent and locked herself inside the plastic cubicle. Turning the spigot to hot, she stepped into the spray and let the heat wash her cares away. If only life worked like that. But with every dab of slimy mud sliding out of her hair and off her body, she thought about those two little boys and wondered what they were doing. Were Tanner and Luke McCoy eating enough? Were they safe with their father? Grissom McCoy seemed like a good man. He'd certainly broken down like a father who'd missed his kids should. But had poor Tanner had the nerve to tell that rough bear of a man what his mother did to him? And how did Mr. McCoy respond to the ugly truth that Pam McCoy, his wife, was a vicious troll? That she'd basically sicced the jerk she was with on that sweet little boy? That she'd belittled and embarrassed Tanner in the worst way possible? In public. Would Mr. McCoy have agreed with what his wife did? Was poor Tanner in for more abuse or was he finally safe?

With all her aching heart, Tuesday wanted to know. Mr. McCoy hadn't seemed anything like his wife, but Tuesday hadn't spent enough time with him to be sure. Thinking back, she wished she'd demanded those little guys stay with her until she knew for certain they would be well taken care of. She couldn't see their father hurting them, not the way they'd clung to him the moment they'd run into his arms.

The tortured look on Mr. McCoy's face… The tears that had leaked out of his tightly closed eyes… The way he'd crushed those little guys to his chest while he'd kissed their heads and faces and buried his nose in their hair…

Thinking about how he'd openly expressed his love for his boys still melted Tuesday's heart. The man's anguish at finally getting them back into his arms had turned her into a puddle of sappy goo in the closet where she'd hidden. What she wouldn't give to be loved like that again. To be wanted. To be, just once more, encircled in the arms of a man who'd search the world over for her if she'd gone missing. Who'd be willing to fight, to die for her. Just for her.

She had that once, so very long ago, in another lifetime. But her life had been turned upside down the day her parents died. One of her dad's friends had lovingly intervened and whisked her away from Duluth, Minnesota, to far-off New York City. Frederick Lamb could've been her grandfather, but he wasn't. And yes, he'd done all he could to ensure the rest of her life was comfortable. Including marrying her. Naturally, the press had attacked her for that. Bullying, slandering, and spreading lies were what they did best. Character assassination, too.

Without knowing anything about her or what she'd already lived through, they'd declared her a gold-digger and so much worse. At the time, she'd still been in shock from her parents' deaths. She'd been living both a dream and a nightmare and hadn't the faintest idea how to handle that kind of hostility. But never once had Freddie wavered in his devotion and protection. When he'd been murdered, Tuesday had found out how much he'd loved her. In his grandfatherly way, he'd left everything to her. His penthouse. His skyscrapers. His businesses. His shipping company and every acre of his prime NYC real estate. By then, she'd been viciously educated enough to know she'd be better off turning Freddie's successful business ventures over to his sons. She hadn't a clue how to manage the extensive Lamb empire anyway. It turned out to be a good decision. Jeff and Henry Lamb were her best friends. They kept in touch and included her in their family events. But as much as she knew they loved her, she was still, and would forever be, that orphaned rag girl standing in the wintry cold, outside Macy's lavish Christmas window display. Forever wishing Santa would bring Mom and Dad back. Forever on the outside, looking in.

Thank God, Tuesday was there the day Mike Estes dangled poor Tanner, by his ankle, off the three-story balcony of that high-priced hotel on the beach. The bully was berating Tanner, a six-year-old for the love of God, for the childhood offense of wetting the bed. What should've been a lazy day tanning in the sun ended with Tuesday screaming at Estes, from the parking lot below to, "Stop right this minute! Put that little boy down! Now!"

Madder than a hornet, she'd stomped up the stairs to that balcony and launched herself into Estes' ugly face. Of all things, the boy's mother had jumped to her sadistic boyfriend's aid. Like he'd needed help more than her son?

It still boiled Tuesday's blood. She hadn't known anyone's name when she'd launched herself into the heart of that dysfunctional-as-shit family, but she did now. When Pam McCoy told her to mind her own blankety-blank business, Tuesday attacked. Not physically. There was no way she could've taken on Estes or Tanner's mother by herself. Instead, she'd gotten into a screaming match. Names were traded, some of them informational, some not so nice. By then—thank God!—Tanner was back inside the room with his little brother. But that hadn't meant he was safe, and Tuesday wasn't dumb enough to assume he'd ever be safe with that woman.

When Pamela got snotty and screeched, "You want these little shits? Fine! Take 'em! They're yours! Keep 'em! I don't ever want to see 'em again!"

Tuesday barked back with a loud and clear, "Yes! You bet I'll take those boys! Give them to me. Now!" Immediately. As in right then and there, by heck. There was no doubt in her mind those frightened babies would be better off with her.

Pamela had stormed back into her room and returned, dragging the crying boys behind her in one hand, a shabby suitcase in the other. Which she'd promptly tossed over the railing, like the cruel, wicked *Witch of the West* she was. Shoving her sons at Tuesday, so hard that Tanner stumbled, she'd screeched, "There. You want 'em? They're yours. I don't ever want to see them again. They're nothing but a pain in my ass anyway."

"I'll make sure you don't." With her shaking hands on those frightened little guys' quaking shoulders, Tuesday had simply turned them toward the stairs and together they'd left their mother behind. At ground level, they'd stopped long enough to collect the damaged suitcase and pick up what clothes and toys lay scattered across the parking lot. Within the hour, Tuesday had moved those poor babies into her hotel room, where they all broke down and had a good, long cry.

Tanner had blamed himself for everything, and little Luke had just wanted his Daddy, whoever the hell that was. Not like it mattered then. Tuesday took charge of her poor, frightened charges, got them showered and dressed in dirty pajamas from their broken suitcase. Which she wouldn't have done if she'd had another choice. Everything in that suitcase had stunk to high heaven. The next morning, she'd taken them shopping for whatever those traumatized little guys had needed. But first, she'd fixed an All-American breakfast of pancakes and maple syrup and scrambled eggs in her room. Those boys ate as if they'd been starved. Tuesday guessed their thoughtless mother had simply ordered room service, which in Costa Rica meant Gallo Pinto, a dish of rice and beans topped off with chopped fresh vegetables and plantains—not the kind of breakfast most American children would appreciate.

But Tuesday wasn't their fairy godmother. She couldn't just wave a wand or crinkle her nose to solve their problems. But she could give them what they needed. She'd been through some crap in her life, but, until her parents died, all she'd known was love. Not these two little guys. No child should ever—EVER—have to endure the abuse Tanner had. Every time Tuesday thought of that ugly brute holding him upside-down over the railing, yelling at him, threatening to drop him…

Damn him! Damn Estes and damn Pamela, too! What a shrew!

Again and again, Tuesday had to fight to contain her anger that first night, for the boys' sakes. They'd been through enough, and she had no idea what their life had been like before then. But comforting them she could do and she did. She ordered dinner in, and after they ate, she and the boys spent the night eating snacks and watching a rented animated movie about a friendly giant. Tuesday couldn't recall the title; only how warm and sweet those two little bodies had felt snuggled against hers. Only how Tanner had cried during the first night for his dad. How he'd wet the bed, and it was no wonder. Who wouldn't pee themselves after being dangled upside down and threatened with death by an ogre ten times his size?

Tuesday had never wished evil on anyone in her life. Cursing others served no purpose, but she knew how to defend herself and her friends. Just ask Shane and Everlee. She had no problem taking out a threat, not the polar bear or the human asshole kind, pardon her French. Her fingertips fluttered over her lips at that dirty word. She almost sounded like Shane and his friend, Heston Contreras. Both had potty mouths, but not her. Not usually. Cussing was a slippery slope that led to worse profanity, and what kind of a mother would that make her? Only…

I'm not anybody's mother. Wasn't even in the ballpark. Motherhood started by falling in love with the right man. The only man in Tuesday's life at the moment was the crusty older fellow who sent her on assignments all over the world. Always alone. Most of the time to isolated climates where only penguins, seals, polar bears, or camels lived. Or to natural disasters and war zones, to catch the emotional cost of man's inhumanity to man.

What she wouldn't give to be back in that tiny hotel room in Costa Rica again, munching popcorn with two little boys who, for one brief moment, had thought she hung the moon. Those few days with them had been a glimpse of paradise. Sure, poor Tanner had been embarrassed by his lack of bladder control, but never once had Tuesday made him feel guilty. Poor sweet kid. If anything, she'd gone out of her way to keep him and Luke too busy to think about how they'd been treated. Or how quickly their mother had tossed them out. *What a witch!*

Tuesday slapped the faucet off and dried her tears along with her hair in the only absorbent towel she'd brought with her. Man, she was tired of her life. Or lack of it. She really was running on empty. Like it or not, she was done being Robert's trusty Gal Friday. It was time he found someone else to trek the world at his command. Something had to change, and that something was her.

Chapter Six

Grissom couldn't believe the elegant hotel suite Murphy had prepared for him and his boys after he'd found out Pam trashed their modest two-bedroom home in Silver Spring, Maryland, the night before she'd run off to Costa Rica. Which was just as well. That place had only been a quick buy and temporary solution after Grissom moved his family from Graham, Washington. He'd intended to take time finding something larger and closer to TEAM HQ in western Virginia. There was no going back now.

He didn't ask Murphy exactly how she'd trashed the house or his things. He had nothing of value. Neither did his boys. But he could imagine. Pamela could be pleasant, but that mood never lasted long. She'd never been a strong, resilient, capable, alpha-type of female, the kind of woman who'd take care of herself and her family when he deployed. Some wives were. Not Pam.

She'd always been more Jekyll and Hyde, one minute sweet and affectionate; the next, a jealous, insecure, name-calling she-wolf, who lashed out at everything and anyone who got in her way. He'd put up with her physical abuse for the past six years because he'd honestly thought that was what fathers of sons did. They endured to the end, damn it, and they kept that shit to themselves so they didn't scare their kids. Like his father had.

No. More.

Grissom was done ignoring the truth, or acting like an ostrich and burying his pain and humiliation the way his father had. His boys were hurting, and he was man enough to admit he needed help, too. Lots of help, given how long he'd put up with Pam's shit.

Both Tanner and Luke were exhausted, nervous wrecks by the time they got to the hotel. But while the flight into Virginia had been long and tiring, for the first time since Grissom had been stuck in the looney bin Murphy called a sanitarium, he could breathe. He'd even slept on the plane, but only after Tanner and Luke had fallen asleep, cuddled on his lap.

The pilot and flight attendants had all been gentle with the boys, which had helped Grissom relax. His overly protective tendency to lash out first and ask questions later hadn't manifested once on the long flight home. Not even when the pilot had invited both boys to join him in the cockpit. It had helped that the guy left the cockpit door open so Grissom could watch. He would've been fine with them staying up front for an hour if they'd wanted. But both boys had run back to him after a very brief visit.

During the time they'd been with the pilot, Grissom had watched his sons like an eagle watched over his eaglets. Luke had been excited, but he'd never suffered his mother's wrath like Tanner had. Luke had eagerly climbed into the co-pilot's seat, but Tanner had stood wooden, stiff, and unsmiling between the seats. He'd nodded when spoken to, but Grissom noticed he'd also stepped back when the pilot had reached for him, only intending to shake his hand. Luke had enjoyed the adventure, but Tanner had acted as if it were torture.

Worse, Tanner had no more than returned to Grissom's side when he'd urgently needed to use the bathroom. Grissom had paid extra-close attention to that simple act of his son relieving his bladder, and thank heavens the stream flowing out of Tanner wasn't red. Wasn't even pink. Still…

Grissom suspected the worst. Had Estes molested his son? Had Pam allowed it? Encouraged it? Too bad they were both deceased, because the need to kill them again was damned near uncontrollable. Just thinking that his little boys might have had to fend off an adult male was—

Shit! Shit! Shit!

As he lay there in the king-size hotel bed now, with both boys draped over him like two baby sloths, he knew damned well that Pamela hadn't just bullied and battered him. She'd mistreated his sons too, and he'd been a dumb, blind ass to have ever believed that a mother wouldn't hurt her own children.

A trickle of wet warmth seeped from his oldest son, over Grissom's thigh and onto his pajama bottoms. Instead of shoving Tanner aside and yelling at the sound-asleep child, Grissom calmly smoothed a hand down his boy's back and whispered, "Hey, bud. Time to get up."

Tanner was a dead-to-the-world kind of sleeper. Two bleary, brown eyes flickered open, but Grissom knew he wasn't quite yet conscious. First, he got a crooked, groggy smile. Then a wide-eyed shocked, "Oh, no! I gotta get up, Dad! No, no, no!"

Grissom kept his hand right where it was, holding his panic-stricken son to him as if nothing was wrong. "No worries, Scooter. You're okay. Just take it nice and slow."

"But I'm…" Tears replaced the shock as raw humiliation rolled over him. "I gotta go right now. I'm… I'm… Dad!"

Grissom leaned into his oldest son's panic-stricken face and placed a kiss on his now sweaty forehead. "Calm down, Tanner. It's okay. If you're getting up, I'm getting up with you. But don't you dare think anything's your fault, because it's not. It's natural, kiddo, especially after all the crap you've been through. So take a deep breath and don't stress over something you can't help. Just let it go and we'll clean up later, okay?" Releasing Tanner, Grissom climbed out of bed, then stopped at their shared dresser on his way to the ensuite head and grabbed clean underwear and pajamas for them both. Accidents happened. No. Big. Deal.

By the time Grissom quietly shut the door to the head behind him and Tanner, his poor kid was in front of the toilet, tears dripping off his chin, with his wet pajama bottoms circling his bare feet. "You want help or would you rather take care of things yourself?" he asked patiently.

That was all it took for Tanner to kick out of his bottoms and barrel head-first into his dad. "I'm sorry I peed on you," he cried into Grissom's belly. "I didn't mean to. I won't never do it again. I… I promise. Honest, Dad," he managed between hiccups.

Scooping his half-dressed six-year-old into his arms, Grissom sat on the edge of the tub and held Tanner's wet little bottom on his peed-on pajama-clad knee. Shaken to his core at the panic pouring out of this poor kid, Grissom reached for the thick, white towel hanging on the towel bar overhead and wrapped Tanner in it.

"Let me tell you a secret, kiddo," he whispered into Tanner's trembling head. "There isn't a man alive who hasn't peed on himself or his buddies when he's stressed or afraid or" —God, Grissom hoped not— "hurt. Trust me. Some things scare the crap out of all us guys. Sometimes we know what's scaring us, sometimes we don't. And pee washes off. Heck, it's mostly water, nothing to be ashamed of. But if something's scaring you, I'm here whenever you're ready to talk about it. Every time. Anytime. Don't think you have to hide any stuff from your old dad. If you're worried or frightened, bring it to me and we'll talk it out. I'll listen. Every time. Anytime. You already know I'll never hurt you, right?"

"Yeah," Tanner breathed shakily. "I know, Dad." His cheeks ballooned with a big puff of air before he asked on a long nervous breath, "Where's Mom? Is she here? You're not gonna tell her I peed on you, are you? Please don't. It'll just make her mad, and she'll... and she'll…"

Grissom didn't miss the outright terror in his son's innocent question. "How long has she been hitting you?" he asked, forcing calm into his tone, despite the violent rage percolating beneath the surface. Rage at his dead damned wife.

Tanner shrugged. "Forever, I guess. She likes Luke, but she hates me. She told me if I ever told you, she'd kill Luke and make me watch, and I really like Luke, Dad. I don't want her to hurt him, too!" He ended on a terrified whine that pierced Grissom's soul.

Damn her! Damn her to hell.

His jaw shifted to one side, a nervous tick he'd developed as a kid living with an abusive mother. Focusing on breathing, he needed to regain his control, for Tanner's sake. Poor kid didn't need to witness a full-grown male's temper tantrum. But damn. Grissom's mother had only hit his dad, not him.

She'd always laughed it off, as if her slaps and punches were nothing more than rough-natured jokes. But Grissom had seen the bleak stares from his dad after those unexpected strikes. How he'd taken every abusive hit or kick she'd dished out in stride. How he'd always made excuses for her. *'It's okay, son. She doesn't mean anything by it,'* or the old standby, *'It's just the way she is.'* They'd been Grissom's role models for parenthood, and for too long, he'd put up with Pam's abuse. Never again. He understood now. He was just like his dad.

Funny how it took sitting there with his traumatized son on his lap before Grissom realized he was the byproduct of a long line of spousal abuse. It had been passed from his mother's mother, his grandmother—to him. Well, it ended here. Right. Damned. Now.

Looking up to the ceiling, Grissom couldn't help it. He was damned thankful Pamela and her asshat boyfriend hadn't survived the crash. Made a man believe in the whole *'finger of God'* reckoning thing. That maybe He actually was watching over mankind, that He did reach down once in a while to interfere in people's lives. That maybe, He who had made blind men see and the lame walk, had finally opened Grissom's eyes.

"Your mother isn't here, Tanner," he murmured softly, "and I've never, ever told her anything you told me. Whatever happened when she wasn't around stayed between you and me, and that's a promise. She did some things on her vacation to Costa Rica that…" *Got her killed.* "… didn't work out so good for her. She's gone for good, kiddo. You'll never see her again."

"Really? She's never coming back?" Were those eyebrows raised with relief, and was that breathless little boy question tinged with hope?

"Never," Grissom confirmed solemnly. "Talk to me whenever you're ready, okay? About anything and everything you want. I'll listen because I love you, kiddo. Simple as that." As if he needed to prove what he said, Grissom snuggled Tanner under his chin. "Understand, Scooter?"

"Yeah," Tanner breathed shakily. His heart still pounded like a mother, though.

To change the subject, Grissom said, "Let's get you into the tub for a quick rinse, then into clean PJs, okay?"

"But Dad…" Tanner blew out a long, slow breath. "I want you to know that… that she… she hit me. A lot. Like every time I had a… a accident. She'd slap my head and yell at me, and it always hurt and…" The story this poor boy had kept to himself for too long spilled out between hiccups and tears. "The last time, the time Miss Tuesday fighted with Mom, Mom was screaming at Mr. Estes to… deal with me. She said she was sick of me, and he… and he…"

Grissom gritted his teeth so hard, he heard a molar crack. If there were any way possible, he'd march into Hell and kill Estes again. He'd wring the bastard's neck! Then Pam's!

"And he grabbed me and he made me go outside with him, and I was ascared, and then he… he hanged me upside down, D-Dad. Over the railing. He shaked me real hard, and he said if I… if I ever peed my bed again, he'd drop me on my big, dumb head down to the parking lot. I don't mean to, Dad. Honest. I can't help it. I try real hard, but when I'm asleep, I…" Tanner covered his eyes with both hands and burst into tears. "I can't help it," he sobbed, shaking with shame. "I'm a stupid kid just like Mom says."

How many times had Grissom been told the exact same thing by his mother? Too many.

Enough!

"Don't believe anything your mother ever said, son. You're not stupid; she is. You're smart and compassionate, and I'm so damned glad you were there to protect your little brother. Luke needed you, understood?"

"Uh-huh," Tanner murmured, as Grissom held his trembling boy flat against his heart, pissed at Pam for always being a bitch. He was as bad as his dad, and so damned grateful for that Tuesday woman, whose last name he couldn't recall. Wasn't sure he'd even heard it. His entire focus had been on his boys that day in Costa Rica, and once he'd found them, the rest of the world had disappeared. His ears had stopped working and his heart had taken over. Nothing and no one else had mattered. Still didn't. Just Tanner. Just Luke.

It might be nice to send her a sincere thank-you note or something, though. Maybe a small bouquet of flowers. Pam had never liked anything he'd given her, but maybe that Tuesday woman was different. Maybe she would like flowers. She'd already proven she was brave and strong enough to face two heartless bullies. The least he could do was send her a thank-you note. Make that a text. Thank-you notes required addresses and stamps and…

Yeah, no. He didn't need to start something with a woman he'd never see again.

"I know how hard you try, Tanner, and that's all anyone can do. You're a good boy. Don't let anyone tell you different, and don't worry if you still have accidents. One of these days, your body will mature, and your brain will wake you up in time and tell your muscles to hold on a little longer. You'll see. Some of us guys mature later than others. It's no big deal. It just is what it is." Grissom rocked his firstborn on his lap until the sobs and hiccups ceased. "No matter what happens, no matter how many times things don't go like you want them to, you'll always be safe with me. I'll never hurt you, scream at you, or scare you. Never. And who cares what Mr. Estes thinks? I sure don't. He's a big, fat jerk."

Grissom got a weak chuckle out of Tanner at that childish pronouncement.

Telling him about Pam's and that fat bastard's demises could wait for the day Tanner was more confident, maybe after he and Luke received the counseling help they needed. He might tell them their mom was dead then… But he might not. Grissom wasn't sure how to handle traumatic news like that, but he'd deal with it. Eventually. After he paid Murphy back for this outlandishly expensive hotel room. And for the days Grissom had spent in that asylum. And for his new cell phone. The new house Murphy had helped Grissom locate and buy. The boys' and his counseling. All of those things cost money Grissom didn't have and didn't see a way of accumulating in the near future, not with his kids living with him now. They came first. Debt would always come second.

Instead of feeling weighed down with responsibility, Grissom felt good for the first time in years. Pam was permanently out of his life. He and his boys might never be wealthy, but the three of them were going to be okay.

"You know what, Dad?" Tanner asked, his sweaty fingers fidgeting with the bottom strands of Grissom's shaggy beard.

"What, son?"

"I'm glad Mom isn't coming back."

"You know what, Tanner?"

"What, Dad?

"Me, too." *Fuckin' glad.*

Chapter Seven

Two Weeks Later

Tuesday unbuckled her seat belt and leaned forward, stretching her lower back muscles to get the kinks out after the flight north to New York City from Miami. She'd given Robert two-weeks' notice, although if he'd pressed, she'd still handle an occasional assignment from him. They'd worked together for years; it was what friends did, and their friendship was solid. He knew he could call her anytime and she'd answer. He also knew she'd been reassessing her priorities, since Maeve Astor's death in Little Rock, Arkansas.

Which was true. Tuesday needed to step back and take a good long look at the life she'd thought she'd chosen. It was time to reclaim the person she'd been before her friend and benefactor, Frederick Lamb died. Life on the road or stuck in the air for hours at a time was no longer good enough. It used to be. Once upon a time, she'd thrilled at the adulation heaped upon the photos her world travels and innate talent had wrought. She'd worked hard to achieve the pinnacle of success she'd never intended to reach. She'd been proud of her reputation, and she hadn't minded the isolation of her chosen career.

Until that day on the beach…

Until she'd faced off with that bitch and her sadistic boyfriend…

Until she'd felt a little boy's terror pounding like a steam engine against her heart…

Until she'd known the simple comfort of that same child's tender, freshly showered, sweet-smelling body aligned with hers on a bed in a hotel room...

Tuesday couldn't explain why those few days with the McCoy boys had affected her as deeply as they had. But standing up for them against those two narcissistic creeps had made her acutely aware how life had more to offer than just awards and adulation. For the first time in years, Tuesday felt hollow, as if she'd leaned the ladder of her life and every last one of her good intentions, dreams and plans against the wrong tree. Tanner and Luke had filled that hollowness, and now, she craved something besides the life she'd always thought she wanted.

After the last passenger had tromped by dragging a large rolling carry-on behind him, she stood in the aisle and reached into the overhead compartment for the hard-shelled, hybrid carry-on that housed her priceless cameras. Clothing, shoes, and everything else she traveled with were always checked at the gate. Never her cameras. They were expensive, sure, but their real value came from the grandfatherly man who'd given them to her.

Freddie's memory held a treasured place in her heart, along with her father. They were the standards, the benchmarks she judged all men against. The man who finally stole her heart would have to be like them. Thoughtful. Generous with his affection. Handsome would be nice, but it wasn't a deal breaker. She'd never been one to gush over pretty guys. Beauty was only skin deep, but ugly went all the way to the bone, and she wanted that undefinable something that Shane Hayes had with Everlee. What Mark Houston and Libby Houston had. That impossible dream called true love. *That*—she was a sucker for.

True love. Was it real? She believed so. She'd seen it from afar. She'd just never gotten close enough to experience it. She could've fallen for Shane and Heston Contreras. Both were honorable, courageous, handsome men with strength behind their convictions. But nothing had ever clicked with either of them. She considered them as friends, not boyfriends or manfriends. Just friends. Like Robert. Like Freddie.

Quickly, Tuesday double-checked to make sure her cell phone was in the inner pocket of her jacket, along with her chubby tube of cherry-flavored lip moisturizer. Not gloss. That crap made women look like they were trolling for easy hook-ups. Which. She. Would. Never. Good men were hard to find but they were out there.

The moment she stepped out of the breezy jetway into busy, noisy La Guardia Airport, she spotted Mark Houston in line next to her gate, boarding the flight to Paris. His beautiful blonde wife was with him. Weren't they the most adorable couple on the planet? Libby waved energetically, and Tuesday waved back. Imagine seeing them here, of all places, and in this hectic crowd. They were near the front of the line and would board soon, so she hurried over to say hi. She got a big hug from Libby and a joking, "My heck, woman, you travel as much as my agents," from Mark.

He was the tall, dark, and incredibly handsome type, a guy who worked out and was smitten with the boisterous, but diminutive, powerhouse blonde woman at his side. Mark and Libby were both in jeans, running shoes, and light jackets, with backpacks slung over their shoulders instead of carry-ons rolling behind them. They didn't look at all like the power couple Tuesday knew them to be. Mark was a full partner in the highly-touted, yet much-maligned, covert surveillance company out of Virginia, The TEAM. Firecracker Libby was the mother of five and a former RN, who'd gone back to school to trade her nurses cap for a physician's stethoscope. How these two managed all they did, yet stayed strong and were so obviously in love, was another positive sign that true love existed. They were what Tuesday wanted to be when she grew up. What she wouldn't give to handle a private photo shoot with them and their kids and—.

Lightbulb! A photo shoot with all TEAM agents and wives. And their children! Great idea! Family photo shoots. Was it possible? Or had they signed NDAs to keep The TEAM out of the public's very narrow eye? Judging by the way Tuesday's pulse raced at the concept, it was worth looking into. She still had Murphy Finnegan's and Alex Stewart's business cards somewhere.

Mental note to self: *Find those cards and call one of those guys the first chance you get.*

When the Houstons said quick goodbyes and stepped up to the gate to scan their boarding passes, Tuesday walked away with a bounce in her step. So what if she had no significant other in her life? Sure, she'd like to be in a solid relationship like the Houstons, but she didn't need a man to fulfill her. She wasn't the quivering bundle of tears and nerves she'd been after her parents' deaths, either. She could do this, and it'd be fun. If Mr. Finnegan or Mr. Stewart agreed.

Since she'd sold Freddie's condo after his untimely death, Tuesday had no reason to visit NYC. The city held nothing for her. She rented a car and headed for the Hamptons, home of the filthy rich and famous, also where Jeff Lamb lived with his family. She spent a day getting reacquainted with them, then backtracked the next morning and caught I-95 south to Baltimore. Her heart wasn't in the many historical sights of the city, so after spending a night in the birthplace of the *'Star Spangled Banner,'* she hooked back onto I-95 and headed for the District of Columbia. It wasn't long before she was cruising I-495 and crossing the Potomac River at the American Legion Memorial Bridge.

Tomorrow was Christmas Eve, and this adventure might prove futile. Most government offices were closed for the holiday season, and federal workers were already burning through their use-or-lose leave. But it might be the most opportune time, too. Managers had to stay and lock up, right? Surely Mr. Finnegan would still be in the office.

The weather was still fairly warm so Tuesday kept her windows down and her hopes up. The air flooding her vehicle was brisk and fragrant, precisely what she needed, Mother Nature's chilling energy wrapped around her. When a song she liked came on the radio, she cranked it up and let the music and wind, the healing properties of sensation and rhythm, get her heart pumping and her blood pounding. Before she knew it, the District was far behind, and she had a decision to make. The junction of I-495 South and I-66 West lay less than two miles ahead. Where was she going? Was she just out for a long, mind-cleansing, thought-provoking drive? Was that her plan? Did she even have a plan?

Answer: Not yet. Norfolk lay to the south, as did the Carolinas, Georgia, and Florida. The Keys and Cuba, if she were so inclined. But Murphy Finnegan's office lay west, in the shadow of the Shenandoahs, near Sperryville, Virginia.

The TEAM, that was where she needed to be. Sure those offices might be closed as well, but nothing ventured, nothing gained, right? What could it hurt to find out? Just a few more gallons of fuel and a pleasant drive.

Decision made. With a smile on her lips, Tuesday chose the exit and pulled into the first decent hotel on westbound I-66. Why not? She wanted to shoot a series of TEAM photos. What would it hurt to ask? In person?

Early the next morning, she loaded the address from Mr. Finnegan's business card into her navigation system and began again. Unfortunately, the coordinates had to be wrong. She didn't know what she'd expected from a company with the stellar reputation The TEAM had, but this place was not it. Couldn't be. The location she arrived at looked more like a ranch slash private airport, complete with two large olive-drab barns situated beyond acres of lush green pastures, framed by miles of pristine, white fencing. A tractor sat idle near one of the barns, and quite a few large, well-muscled horses with long elegant tails, full manes, and gleaming coats, grazed at her right. What on earth did a covert surveillance company do with so many horses? Parades?

At her left—*man, those things had to be expensive*—four high-tech helicopters sat on a short stretch of concrete, each sleek and as black as night. One was larger than the others, but none revealed any flashy logo or company name—which would've been helpful—only the required Federal Aviation Administration's identification.

A one-story building that appeared a tiny bit professional sat between the two diametrically opposed enterprises of air travel and ranching. No signage anywhere. No visitor parking, either. No **DO NOT TRESPASS** signs. If Tuesday hadn't had Mr. Finnegan's card, she'd think she was lost.

Okay then. Summoning her can-do attitude, she parked grill-first at the curb, in front of the steps leading to the double doors, at the center of what had to be an office building. The place looked deserted, which made sense, given the holiday. The entire face of the building was glass so dark, she couldn't see through it. Didn't slow Tuesday down. She'd faced off an enraged mama polar bear once, and she'd traveled the world alone too many times to worry about the Leave and Never Come Back vibe rolling off this no-name place.

She'd dressed in business casual today. Nothing fancy. Plain black boots with one-inch heels. Pressed denim jeans. A white, crisply ironed long-sleeve cotton blouse beneath her favorite navy-blue blazer. Which was well-worn and the cuffs a titch frayed, but it was warm enough for the season. She left her puffy down parka on the backseat for what would be a quick dash to those darkly-tinted glass doors. What were they, ten feet high? Twelve?

Sucking in another quick breath of courage, she stepped out of the rental, smoothed her hands over her backside in case her blazer had wrinkled during the drive, and shut the car door. With her head held high, she tossed her tousled mane over her shoulder and climbed the few steps to the entry. For the briefest moment, she regretted driving with all the windows down. If she wanted to make a good impression, her hair needed a good brushing. She let that split second of insecurity go with the light breeze still toying with her. Windblown was a good look for her, and Freddie had taught her never to back down. She was here to offer Mr. Finnegan an incredible offer of free publicity and… He. Would. Love. It.

A welcome sign would've been nice, though. Would've ensured she wasn't barking up the wrong tree. Even the moniker, The TEAM, etched into the vacant glass wall she was facing would've been nice. But the only thing staring back at her from that wall of black glass was her grimacing reflection. Which she instantly turned into a bright, eager smile. Grim was not how she faced the world. *Head up. Shoulders back. Never let 'em see you blink.*

Reaching for one of the flat-black metal handles running the width of each door, she'd barely curled her fingers around it when it swung noiselessly inward. Must have an automatic sensor. Okay then. *Look out world. Here I come.* Until—

"Too-day!" The high-pitched voice screaming from the pasture stopped her in her tracks.

Oh, my gosh! Is that Luke McCoy screaming bloody murder?

It is! The sweet little guy hadn't gotten her name right once during their short time together. Not that she'd ever cared what he called her. Instinct took over. To heck with meeting Mr. Finnegan. Forsaking her grand mission, once again Tuesday turned on her heels and ran to rescue that adorable little guy, her boots smacking the concrete lot like runaway castanets, and her legs pumping furiously. Faster! He was in the pasture, running between and around all those horses?

Oh. My goodness! They were so big. And wide. They might step on him. Her throat went dry at that very real threat. With one step, they could kill him. The tiny guy didn't stand a chance. She had to get to him. Now!

Her heart hammered, not from exertion, but a heart-pounding panic she'd known when Tanner McCoy had been dangled upside down and threatened with being dropped three stories onto an asphalt parking lot. She didn't pause to worry how she'd clear the sturdy pasture fence blocking her way. Just vaulted over the six-foot blockade without laying a finger on it. Luke was in danger. He was all she could see. *What's he doing here?*

"Luke!" she yelled hoarsely, scared to death for the little guy, even while all those monstrously huge animals shied away from her as she dodged between and around their hefty bodies. They'd better get out of her way! And they did. Some guy exited the barn and was walking among them, but she didn't care. She lost sight of him when the horses stepped in the way. They didn't seem aggressive. Most of them acted as if they were afraid of her. One kicked up its very impressive hooves and—

One giant hoof. One teensy kick. That was all it would take to kill her baby! Tuesday poured every ounce of willpower into reaching Luke before she lost him for good.

"Get back, wild horses! All of you!" she yelled at the few animals still in her way. "Don't you dare hurt him!"

Finally. There he was. Little Luke McCoy. Standing calmly between two beasts, an innocent child caught between giant hooves and bigger bodies. A big grin lit his pudgy little face. His arms wide open and—

What if one of those creatures decided to lay down? They'd crush him!

Full-blown panic pushed her harder. Faster!

"No! No! No!" Tuesday yelled. "Get away from my boy, you wild beasts!" Frantic to save that innocent child, she slid on her knees between those two huge animals, her arms wide open, and… *Oomph*! Finally! That blue-eyed, warm little boy was in her arms and Luke was safe.

These horses were so big, and he was so, so small. And chuckling. She didn't understand how he could laugh when he'd been in mortal danger, but it didn't matter. Kids didn't know any better. He was only three. But she had him, and God, how that mattered.

Tuesday had never known fear so desperate before, not ever. Not even when facing off with that mother polar bear. She could barely catch her breath. Her chest heaved for more oxygen than her lungs could pull in, and every bit of her was shaking. She was a Halloween skeleton coming undone. "Luke," she huffed, holding him tight against the jackhammer in her chest. "My sweet little guy, what… what are you doing out here?"

And where's your thoughtless father? How could he do this to you after all you've been through? I'll kill him!

For the first time, she noticed that the tiny red cowboy boots on Luke's feet matched the child-size felt cowboy hat on his strawberry-blond head. He was dressed like a miniature cowboy, in jeans and a long-sleeve, red-and-white checkered shirt with bright silver snaps in place of buttons. All of which she disregarded the instant he ducked his head under her chin. Like the baby he still was, Luke snuggled into her with his arms sandwiched between them. While most kids would've held on tightly, Luke seemed to want her arms all the way around him.

Tuesday obliged. She needed him right where he was. With her. Adrenaline was such an overwhelming force of nature. Only seconds ago, she'd been fresh as a daisy, clean-smelling, and dressed to impress. Not anymore. Her hair was not only windblown, but tangled, sweaty, and stuck to her skin, as was her shirt. Grass stains covered both knees from her less than impressive slide into home base—Luke. Her neck and face had to be scarlet. To top it off, she was emotional, scared at what could have been, and she needed a good cry. She no longer cared about TEAM photos. They weren't important. Luke was.

She had him, and this cute little guy was everything she hadn't realized she'd ever wanted. Luke and his brother, Tanner. They needed to be taken care of. Properly. They were important. Only them. Sure as heck not their neglectful father. Where was he?

Trying to slow her heart rate, she bowed her nose into Luke's baby-soft hair and breathed the essence of this little boy back into her heart. He'd knocked his silly hat off the moment he'd collided with her, but the last scent she expected to smell was the manly fragrance of smoky cedar, spice, and—alfalfa?

"I missed you, Too-day. A whole lot," he murmured against her breasts. He seemed content there and she surely was. It'd been awhile since she'd felt this grounded. Since those few days in Costa Rica. "And I wub you, Too-day."

Heartbreaking words from an angel. *Wub.* Her most favorite word in the world.

"And I love you, Luke," she replied honestly, closing her eyes at the intense mothering instinct sweeping her common sense aside. What she wouldn't give to have this little guy and his innocent words and hugs in her life every day. But he wasn't hers, and he had a father—somewhere—the jerk.

With her nose still in Luke's hair, Tuesday scanned the pasture, no longer afraid of anything or anyone. The horses all had their noses to the ground, grazing as they walked, and they weren't as threatening as she'd first thought. Despite their size, they were actually graceful and calm. Serene. A couple were black, one was totally white, but most were reddish-brown with black manes and tails. A few had drawn close to where she and Luke were sitting. A reddish-brown fellow with a white streak down his nose, snout, whatever that long face was called, ambled over and nipped at her hair with huge prehensile lips, as if he was tasting her.

"Buzz off," Tuesday told the too-friendly beast, leaning as far from it as she could get. Still angry at the worst case of child neglect—in the world!— she asked Luke, "Where's your father?" *Because I am so going to give him a piece of my mind. The nerve of that stupid, stupid man, to leave his son—his three-year-old baby—alone! Again! In a pasture of giant animals that could easily step on him and kill him! What is that man thinking? O-o-o-o, just you wait, Mr. Dumbass McCoy. You are going to get it!*

"There you are," a deep rumbling baritone voice exclaimed from behind the oversized rump of the reddish-brown horse with the white streak on his nose.

"Hi, Daddy," Luke chirped innocently. "Look! I finded Too-day!"

Had to be Mr. McCoy, the slacker. Tuesday attempted to glare up at the man, but the December sun was behind him, and all she could make out was a large black silhouette with a cowboy hat standing over her.

"I see that," he replied calmly. Too calmly. As if he hadn't just lost track of his tiny child. As if nothing was wrong with a three-year-old running through a pasture of elephant-sized animals… All. By. Himself!

The more Tuesday thought about what Mr. McCoy had and hadn't done, and what could've happened, the hotter her blood boiled.

"Whatcha doin' sitting down there, Miss Tuesday?" Tanner, ever the polite brother, asked from within the shadow his father cast.

Well, I'll tell you what I'm doing down here. "I'd just pulled up and parked when I heard Luke scream, Tanner," Tuesday replied as evenly as she could muster, lifting one hand from Luke's warm little body to shield her eyes so she could at least look Mr. McCoy in the eye while she let him have it. No such luck. The man cast a large shadow, but the sun behind him was so bright. "So I did what any responsible adult would do when they find an unattended three-year-old child in a field of wild horses. I ran as fast as I could to rescue Luke before one of them stepped on him." Tuesday put as much insinuation into her explanation as she could without frightening Tanner. He was as skittish as his little brother was affable.

"Aww, they weren't gonna step on Luke," Tanner chided. "They're just big kids."

"Kids? You call these monsters kids?" she nearly shrieked.

"Well, yeah. They wouldn't hurt anyone, Miss Tuesday. Maverick and China train 'em all to be real gentle, just like you."

Before she could protest being lumped into the same category as horses, Tanner stepped away from his negligent father and piled onto her and Luke, like the teddy bear he'd been in Costa Rica.

Tears sprang to Tuesday's eyes at the sweet bundles again in her arms. Man, she'd missed these boys. In an attempt to control her emotions, she blew out a breath and sat there with her eyes closed and her arms around them, soaking in the sublime sensation of being loved and needed. Once again, she had the McCoy boys on her lap and in her heart, where she wished they could stay. But they couldn't, and there wasn't a thing to be done about it. They had a father, and as careless as he was, Mr. McCoy was legally their keeper.

A gloved hand landed lightly on her shoulder, as the irresponsible jerk in question crouched casually beside her and said, "Sure good to see you again, ma'am."

"Ha! I'll just bet," she shot back at him. Would've packed more wallop if she hadn't had to blow her messy hair out of her eyes just to see him. And if he hadn't reached a gloved index finger into her face and tossed that stubborn chunk of snarls over her shoulder for her. That was—thoughtful. She could finally see him. *Wow.*

"There you are," he murmured, his eyes roaming over her hair, face, and lips. "I'm sorry I didn't thank you for taking care of my boys in Costa Rica, Miss Smart. I should have. Didn't mean to be a jerk, but everything happened so fast. I'd gone down there, thinking I'd have a long hard search ahead of me, and that I might never see them again. But the first place we looked, there they were. Safe and sound. With you. As soon as I finally had them in my arms, I kind of zoned out, and all I could do was…" He paused, seemingly at a loss for words.

It was hard to chew this guy out now that he'd gotten up close and personal. He didn't seem like a negligent father anymore, and there was too much pain in his eyes for Tuesday to cause more. "You did thank me," she reminded him tartly.

"I hate to admit it, but—"

"My Daddy's got a big owie," Luke informed the world loudly, reaching his hand around to point at the back of his own head. "It's right here. Don'tcha Daddy?"

Mr. McCoy chuckled. "Yes, I do, son. But it's mostly gone now, thanks to you boys." Despite his attempt at humor, a flash of something incredibly sad flickered in the wells of his gorgeous eyes.

Tuesday's heart thudded to a full stop. *This* was Tanner and Luke's dad? This handsome brooding male with a neatly trimmed beard and tiny gold sparkles in his warm hazel eyes? This Gerard Butler wannabe?

She remembered the angry, shaggy bear who'd collapsed in her hotel room's doorway the moment he'd had his boys. Not this dangerous-looking guy who still managed to give off a sexy vibe. My heck, he was as big, well, almost as big as the horse nuzzling the back of his neck like a great big puppy. An unbidden thought sprang to life in Tuesday's mind. What would it feel like to nuzzle his neck and stick her nose in his deep brown hair? What'd he smell like? His son, Luke? Was this where those delicious smoky cedar, spice, and alfalfa scents came from?

No. Just no. She shook off the ridiculous notion of getting close enough to nuzzle anyone. Way off. She didn't like Mr. McCoy. He wasn't anything like Freddie, and he certainly didn't measure up to her father.

But when he used that same gloved finger to tip the brim of his cowboy hat up and she caught the full effect of his smile, it was harder to breathe, this time for a different reason than anger. Luke and Tanner's father was a cowboy, through and through. He had the jeans. The hat. A western shirt with the same shiny silver snaps as both his sons' shirts. His hair was thick, lush, dark chocolate—hat hair that matched Tanner's, not Luke's adorable strawberry blond.

Worry lines etched his forehead, and the traces of silver at his temples accentuated the creases at the corners of his eyes. This man had known heartache and pain, but to see it written across his face and buried within his eyes connected him to Tuesday in a way she hadn't expected. She knew that kind of pain. It wasn't temporary, and it never went away. It was the deep, ugly kind a person had to learn to live with if they wanted any measure of peace in their life. The kind that devastated a person's soul, that left it wrecked and lost and… broken. Not just broken, but shattered into too many pieces to ever be put back together again. He was her, on the long ago morning that Frederick Lamb had found her after her parents' funeral.

Just then, that extra-large horse with the streak down his snout draped its long head over Mr. McCoy's shoulder and hugged him, like they were buddies. The horse was saddled. Without looking, Mr. McCoy reached a hand behind his head and stroked its giant head. The darned horse closed its eyes and moaned—or whinnied or nickered or—whatever big horses did. Or said. Because it sure looked like it was communicating nonverbally with Mr. McCoy, like guys with their chin nods and head bobs. She'd heard of pig Latin. Was this horse Latin?

The handsome smile made it obvious how much Mr. McCoy adored his boys. It showed in the easy way they were him. They'd been wound tight when Tuesday'd rescued them in Costa Rica. But now? They looked happy and healthy, like little boys should, and Mr. McCoy seemed genuinely okay with them traipsing through this herd of horses. And if he was okay with it…

Embarrassment squeezed Tuesday's eyes shut. *Darn. I've just made a fool of myself, haven't I?* Mr. McCoy had only let Luke out of his sight because he knew these horses wouldn't hurt his son. He'd been around them enough to trust them, and so did his sons. She was the problem, the hysterical lunatic who could've caused any one of these horses to panic, maybe even the whole herd to stampede. She could've gotten Luke hurt or—killed.

She bowed her head, sorry for every mean thought she'd harbored against Mr. McCoy. *How will I ever look him in the eye again?*

Chapter Eight

The first day of counseling went well. The horse therapy that followed did, too. As Maverik would say, this wasn't their first rodeo. Grissom had brought his boys horseback riding here at TEAM HQ stables before. Many times. Since he'd moved his family to the East Coast, riding Maverick's so-called 'kids' had been a regular guy-thing Grissom did with his boys. They'd don their cowboy duds and boots, and for a few hours each weekend, as many as they could get away with, they'd left the troubled McCoy household behind and pretended they were cowboys riding the range. He hadn't called it therapy back then, but he'd known about Maverick's *Everyone's a Cowboy* program when he'd still lived in Washington. If being outdoors with horses, fresh air, and most importantly, his boys, was therapy, they could call it whatever they wanted. He was done being stupid and proud. He didn't matter. Only Tanner and Luke did.

The first time riding these large animals, sure, they'd been leery of getting near, much less sitting on top of horses so high off the ground. Adult Percherons were not kid-size, not by a long shot. Averaging sixteen to eighteen hands high, they were intimidating beasts of burden with wide, muscular backs and big heads. But they were also enthusiastic workers with strong, intelligent personalities, known for their good dispositions and overall gentle natures. Because he was too young to ride alone, Luke still rode with Grissom. Not Tanner. Once he'd understood the nuances of communicating with Star, his favorite, through the gentle use of voice, reins, and the pressure of his knees and boots, shy Tanner had blossomed into a natural cowboy. It didn't hurt that he idolized Maverick or that Maverick kept a pint-size saddle on hand for the six-year-old Wyatt Earp now snuggling his face into Miss Smart's neck.

Damned if she wasn't a pretty sight for Grissom's sore eyes and his weary heart. He couldn't help smiling at the impressive pink blush creeping over her cheeks. She probably realized now that Luke had never been in real danger, and that she might've overreacted a little. But hearing her tell Star to, *"Buzz off!"* and hearing her call Luke, *'my sweet little boy,'* had nearly taken Grissom to his knees. There sat a complete stranger, on the ground, in a pasture full of horses, and, well, horse shit, which was definitely stuck to the bottoms of her boots, maybe even her backside. Yet there she stayed, seemingly content and loving on his boys like their mother had never, ever done.

Blowing a longer-than-normal breath to steady his frayed nerves and trying to figure out how not to make Miss Smart feel worse, he admitted, "I'm not really sure how it happened, but the police report claims I plowed my bike into the rear end of a FedEx delivery truck and—"

"And the truck won," she said softly. "I remember Mr. Finnegan saying that. When did it happen?"

He swallowed hard. "A few days before Costa Rica. I was, umm, hospitalized for a while." No way was he mentioning that, that... What was its name? Sugar Lane

Asylum? Walnut Creek Nut House? Why couldn't he remember?

"Are you okay now?"

"Ah, yeah. Sure. Why wouldn't I be?"

"No reason." And why did the sound of her voice soothe away his frustration at not being able to think straight?

Damn. Miss Smart was a good-looking woman, and he was a sucker for green eyes. Her brown hair was long enough it hung over her shoulders and into her face like a tangled jungle waterfall, its wispy fingertips caressing her full breasts. Didn't hurt that those tempting breasts were testing the tiny buttons on her shirt. The kill shot she couldn't possibly know she'd fired straight into his heart, was how gently she was holding his grubby, sweaty boys. Both of them. Like she'd truly missed Tanner and Luke and couldn't bear to let them go. Grissom couldn't make himself look away from the concern shining in her eyes—concern for him. Of all people, she seemed worried about him, too.

"Yes, ma'am," he replied hoarsely. "Little by little, I'm… I'm getting better." What the hell was wrong with his vocal chords? He sounded like a damned frog.

"Please, just Tuesday."

"Same here. Grissom. Not Mr. McCoy." *Because I am not my dad.*

"Too-Day!" Luke chirped. "Call her Too-Day, Daddy. Like I do!"

"Yeah, but you're saying it wrong," Tanner cut in. "You talk like a baby. It's Tues—"

"I not a baby. You are!"

"No, you are!"

"Boys," Mr. McCoy warned quietly. "How do we behave in the presence of company?"

"Like gentlemen with good manners," Tanner declared with his chin up. Right before he stuck his tongue at Luke and informed him, "See? I know how to treat ladies, but you don't."

"Do too!" Luke yelled, his face getting redder.

That's when it happened. Tuesday tipped her head back and laughed. Instead of being annoyed and swearing and hurting their feelings like Pam would have done, Tuesday let loose the most beautiful sound Grissom had ever heard. Full of joy and love and all those things a mother should shower over her children, it was as rare as a hummingbird lighting on his finger. He couldn't help it. He fell head over heels in love with this beautiful woman.

This had to be the first time she'd witnessed the competitive streaks both McCoy boys harbored. The sound coming from her throat was the sweet tinkling of stars falling from heaven, each touchdown a bright, crystal vibration striking Grissom's heart, pouring peace over him, maybe even into him. No one had ever—ever—loved or enjoyed his kids like this woman was. Other people's kids were annoying to most folks, tiny people to be endured, not enjoyed or valued. Many times, not even treated with any measure of respect. But Tuesday still had her nose in Luke's messy hair, and Tanner had his arm stretched around her shoulders as far as he could reach, and—

Grissom's eyes watered. What was in the air? He wasn't allergic to anything. But his brain had conjured up a picture of Tuesday Smart sitting on his couch in front of the large stone fireplace in his new house, reading to Tanner and Luke, both of them snuggled on her lap, in her warm arms, and—

The idyllic image morphed into Grissom with his head on her lap. Her fingertips in his hair, gently massaging his scalp, and—

Get a grip. He had no business lusting over this woman just because she'd saved his sons from their sadistic mother. Tuesday wasn't a plug-in-mom, and he wasn't in the market for a replacement for Pam. Hell no! He was no prize. Hell, he was barely coming to grips with the mess he'd made of his life. What could she possibly see in him? Nothing. Because there was nothing to see.

'Forget Tuesday, dumbass!' the childish memory forever stuck in his brain screamed. *'Last thing you need is a relationship. Any relationship, you shithead! You didn't even pass algebra!'*

Damned if the soft-spoken, counseled and healing part of his brain didn't whisper patiently, *'For now, Grissom. Forget her, but just for now…'*

He shook off the echo of his mother's nagging voice. Counseling had taught him to focus on the here and now, not the condemnation of Christmases past, nor the wishful thinking of Christmases future. Both were partially right, yet equally detrimental to healing and moving forward. One haunted a past he couldn't do anything about. The other taunted a future that might never exist. He now knew that he was prone to use what had happened in his past life to beat himself up. Once he'd realized he was in charge of either sabotaging or helping, he'd become a determined son of a bitch, intent on moving forward and giving his boys the best lives he could.

Tuning out the lady in question, he zeroed in on the lesson Tanner needed to remember. "Remember how some of us guys develop later in life?" he asked in a calm, reasonable, and, most of all, fatherly voice.

That brought Tanner's brown-eyed gaze up to his. "Oh, yeah. I… I do, Dad. Sorry. I forgot but I remember now, yeah, and I can be a nicer big brother," he replied quickly. Then, turning to Luke, he said, "I'm sorry. I love you and you're a good boy. Don't let anyone tell you different."

Wow. If that didn't put tears in Grissom's eyes, nothing could. He brushed a hand over his face before anyone saw. Kids. They did say the damnedest things. Before he could praise Tanner for using his exact words, Tanner asked Tuesday, "Wanna go to Cakes and Honey with us?"

Oh, shit. She looked to Grissom as if he were the decision-maker. The simple understanding he read in her eyes, the acknowledgement that she was the stranger and had eagerly deferred to him, took her up a couple more notches in his esteem. She respected him. That was new.

Like the lovesick idiot he'd turned into, Grissom explained. "Cakes and Honey's a local diner that serves breakfast all day. They're famous for their pancakes, but you can get lunch or dinner there, too. Everything they serve is homemade and it's all good. Us guys go there after we're done playing cowboy." He reached for her. "Need a hand up?"

Tanner and Luke bounced quickly to their feet, but the moment Grissom wrapped his fingers around Tuesday's much smaller, more slender, very feminine hand, his heart stuttered. Touching her felt as if he'd grabbed a live wire. She must've felt the shock too, the way her shoulder jerked. But he wasn't ready to let her go. His fingers tightened instinctively, as if losing this connection would hurt him worse than hanging on would. Most likely, whatever might happen between Tuesday and him would kill him. He was the weak link in this— whatever it was. First date? Only date? Not a date? He had no idea.

"Sounds good," she replied, relaxing her grip into a *'maybe,'* instead of the *'hell no!'* he thought he'd felt seconds ago.

Every last one of his misgivings evaporated in the light of her willing acceptance.

With a gentle tug, Grissom pulled Tuesday up off the ground. He didn't tug her into his arms and against him like he wanted, though. The urge was surely there. It was almost irresistible and he would have, until smarty pants Tanner announced, "There's no shit on her bum, Dad."

Which made Tuesday laugh even as she twisted to look at her backside.

"Geez, Tanner, thanks for telling the whole world," Grissom teased. "Ladies don't want everyone looking at their, umm…" *Butts.* Yet there he was, looking at said ass and appreciating the skinny jeans covering it and her long legs, like a coat of denim blue paint he wanted to scrape off with his teeth. Naturally, her gaze darted to his face at the same time his stupid male tongue ran a hungry lap around his lips. Both of them. Man, he was pathetic.

The only thing that dragged his mind out of the gutter where it had run—not wandered, not even strolled, the damned horny thing—was when Tuesday stuck her tongue out at him. The laughter dancing in those pretty eyes was rain falling in a desert that hadn't seen water in years. And he was that bone-dry desert. She wasn't mad or offended, wasn't the tiniest bit perturbed. Damned if she didn't turn to Luke and tell him, "You've got better eyes than me, little guy. Make sure I don't have a speck of horse shit on me, okay?"

Like the innocent child he was, Luke puckered his lips in all seriousness and looked her backside over before announcing, "I don't see no poop on your bum. Let's go! I hungry!"

"You're always hungry," Grissom said, as he hefted a boy into each arm.

"Uh-uh, you don't get them both," Tuesday protested. "Who do I get to carry?"

Immediately, both boys reached for her, and the fight was on.

"Me!" Tanner yelled. "Carry me! Ple-e-e-e-ease? I'm bigger than Luke, but I don't weigh much, and I promise I won't wiggle like he always does."

"No, me!" Luke yelled louder. "I smaller. Me, me, me!"

Grissom tipped back on his heels to keep from falling into Tuesday. "Hold on, guys!" He laughed, and wasn't that the oddest sound? Him? Laughing? He hadn't laughed in a long damned time, but there he was, happier than he could remember being—ever.

To end the argument, he tossed Tanner over his shoulder, then made sure Tuesday had a good grip on Luke before he let go of his youngest.

Tanner twisted around and complained, "Aw, Dad, that's not fair. He always gets his way."

And like the two-foot bully Luke could be, he crowed, "I winned! I winned! I a winner! Tanner's a loser!"

Instantly Grissom shifted into protective mode. Tanner wasn't a loser and those were Pam's mean words. He opened his mouth to correct the cute little bully, but by then, Tuesday had tossed him over her shoulder and a teasing grin spread over her face. "You think Cakes and Honey can use a couple more bags of potatoes, Grissom?"

Man, he loved hearing his name coming out of her mouth. And Luke was just a baby parrot at heart. He hadn't meant anything cruel. Grissom landed a gentle smack on Tanner's denim-padded backside. "One way to find out, ma'am."

Tuesday turned toward TEAM HQ with a bright, "I'll drive. My car's parked right over there."

"Nah, I'll drive. My truck's closer. It's in the barn. That way we can toss these bags of spuds in the back and be done with them."

"Yeah! Throw us! Throw us!" both boys yelled at the same time.

Grissom's cheeks were beginning to hurt. He hadn't smiled this much in years. And never, not once in his life, had he been drawn to a woman like he was to Tuesday. Was she for real or was she hiding an evil personality beneath the glam? Was he under a spell, like he had to have been under that one night with Pamela? Was Tuesday just another hard-earned lesson lurking in his future? God, he hoped not. Most of the guys on The TEAM were happily married. Happiness *was* possible. He'd seen it with his own eyes.

But he hadn't grown up trusting women, an early lesson his mother had taught, then enforced regularly. Looking back, he'd always known something was wrong with her, that not all moms had vicious streaks. The fact that he'd married a woman exactly like her didn't speak well of his ability to navigate the world of women. Not that he'd had a choice.

When it came to accepting responsibility for fathering his firstborn, he would gladly endure a dozen Pams. He would. For Tanner and Luke, he'd do anything. No child should ever have to learn how tough life was as a newborn. Or face it alone. Not a day went by he wasn't thankful for the two steady lights in his life, which brought him back to Tuesday. She wasn't anything like his mother or his deceased wife.

Damned if the evil witch sitting on his shoulder didn't whisper, '*So far, asshole. Just you wait and see.*'

Grissom brushed his mother's mean spirit away yet one more time. He'd read the newspaper accounts of the standoff in Little Rock, Arkansas. As pretty as she was, Tuesday seemed tougher and, at the same time, kinder than the two females in his past life. She'd had a shitty life, too, losing her parents like she had, then losing the older gentleman she'd married to that cold-blooded murderess, Maeve Astor. Among the long list of heinous atrocities Astor had committed, she'd poisoned Mr. Lamb. Those were damned hard blows for anyone to have to deal with, much less a teenager. They'd turned Tuesday into a recluse who preferred the far-off solitude of the Arctic and Antarctic. Or so the press said, not like they printed the truth anymore. Still…

He sensed a canyon of lonesomeness behind her cheery façade, and he had the strangest need to vanquish the demons causing that pain. If the bright light dancing out of her green eyes every time she spoke with Tanner or Luke was any indicator, she was not the hermit the press had portrayed her to be. She wasn't just talking *at* his boys. She was actively engaged *with* them. She was interested and listening. Hanging on every word. Enjoying them. Treating them with respect. Even now, with Luke riding high on her shoulder and giggling like a… a three-year-old. Damned if both his sons weren't acting like kids again. Grissom knew damned well he owed that positive change in their lives to the woman who'd taken them in when their mother had thrown them out.

Like the damned sullen cowboy he was, TEAM Agent Maverick Carson stood at the double-wide side door that led to the barn's inner sanctum. 'Least that was what his wife China called it. Maverick's one knee was bent, the heel of that dusty boot braced against the side of the barn. His black Stetson was low over his forehead. A scuffed, black leather holster hung low on his hips. Neither pistol strap was secured, which meant both weapons had a round in their chamber, common practice for people who always carried.

If Grissom didn't know better, he'd think he was looking at a gunslinger, not another victim of the war in Afghanistan. Maverick had lost his brother, another jarhead, in an operation where the intel had been flawed. Make that FUBAR, as in fucked up beyond all recognition. He'd been on the same hillside, in the same ambush, the day his life went to hell. That event and a later altercation with another TEAM agent over a woman, precipitated Maverick quitting The TEAM and walking all the way to Wyoming—just because.

Grissom knew damned well that, somewhere during that marathon journey, Maverick had intended to disappear himself off the face of the earth. Instead, he'd met China Wolfe, a well-known Wyoming horse breeder and the proud owner of the Wild Wolf Ranch. She gave him a job. He helped her out of an ugly situation with her sister. In the end, her sister committed suicide. China still owned the ranch and a sizable parcel of land in Wyoming, and their new ranch wasn't far from TEAM HQ. Maverick was once again a trusted TEAM agent, as well as China's husband and father to her adopted daughter, Kyrie.

He might not look the type, but Maverick was also the light at the end of Grissom's tunnel. If Maverick could put his life back together after all he'd lost—and he'd lost plenty—Grissom could do it, too. Losing Pam was no loss. He counted that a total plus. Good riddance. All she'd ever been was the biggest mistake of his life, and he was damned glad that chapter was over. But he'd die if anything happened to his boys.

"Hey, Grissom. Who's your girlfriend?" Maverick asked, sticking a finger into the brim of his hat and pushing it back.

Grissom set him straight. "She's not my girlfriend. Tuesday Smart, meet Maverick Carson. He and his wife own these horses."

Tuesday stepped forward, her right arm extended, the other still flat on Luke's wiggling rump. "Mr. Carson, good to meet you."

"Maverick," he grumbled, even as he straightened to attention and took her hand in his. "Likewise, Ms. Smart," he said more politely. The guy was tall, lean, and dark-haired. Damned if his brown eyes weren't attentive as hell now that he had a pretty lady in sight. The dog.

And damned if him touching Tuesday like she'd just said something fascinating—which she hadn't—didn't irk the shit out of Grissom. Maverick had big, capable hands that had gentled many a skittish horse or fearful rider. He had no business stepping in so close to Tuesday and touching her like he was. He was holding onto her hand too damned long.

Not like Grissom cared. He didn't. Didn't know why the sight of her slender fingers caught in Maverick's powerful paw bothered him, either. Grissom had no business worrying about Miss Smart. She was a professional. She didn't need him to interfere and could certainly handle Maverick on her own. She'd probably seen more of the world than he had, and she certainly knew how to handle a weapon, if Heston's yammering about her cool head and sharp shooting was fact, not fiction.

"Everyone's a Cowboy, huh?" Tuesday asked when Maverick finally released her. With a feminine grunt, she leaned over and set Luke's feet on the ground. "Brilliant concept, but isn't this breed a little large for most handicapped kids?" she asked once she was upright again.

"Nah," Maverick replied, staring over her head at Star, the nosey gelding who seemed to love human company more than he liked hanging out with his four-legged buddies. "First thing we do is let them handle and get to know the horse they'll be riding, from a loading ramp. Next, we teach 'em how to saddle up and mount, if they're physically able. Nothing to it once they're comfortable being around our kids. We start our severely handicapped clients with one of our miniature donkeys unless they insist on a horse. Percherons aren't all we breed. We've got a few quarter horses. Vanners, too. Hop up on Star, why don'tcha? He'll show you how good all my kids are."

"There's that word again, kids. Do you really see kids when you look at these" —she waved a hand at easy-going Star— "giants?"

A genuine grin cracked Maverick's ugly face. "Yes, ma'am, I do. Raising horses is no different than raising kids. It's not rocket science." He *was* flirting! The ass! "All you gotta do is love 'em and never let 'em down. You'll see soon as you git up on Star. He's a good kid to start with."

She cocked her head. "I don't think so."

"Sure!" Tanner exclaimed. "Dad! Let's go riding with Miss Tuesday. Please?"

Grissom coughed. He'd been so focused on Maverick's flirtation that he nearly forgot he had an audience.

"Yeah, Daddy! Pleeeezzzzeee," Luke asked, both pudgy hands clasped under his chin. Someone must've told him that pose made him look adorable. Which it did and he was, the little turkey.

If the way Tuesday's top teeth were worrying her bottom lip was any indication, she was tempted. "Your call," Grissom told her, puzzled at why his mouth was dry and his heart was thumping. Now was not the time for a panic attack, damn it.

"Your horses are still saddled" —Maverick aimed a spiked brow at Grissom— "because some guys ran out of the barn when they should've been brushing their rides down."

"Get over it, Carson," Grissom growled. "My kids'll always come first."

Luke giggled, and Tuesday did a funny thing with her face, making an upside-down 'oh, oh' smile that stretched the chords in her neck. "Oh, my. I haven't been on a horse in years."

By then, Tanner and Luke each had one of her hands and were pulling her deeper into the barn. "Please, please, please!" they chanted in unison.

"Might as well, ma'am," Maverick declared with the same cavalier tone he'd used when he'd said raising horses was as easy as raising kids. "Only takes a minute to saddle another horse, right, Grissom?"

Tuesday's shoulders lifted, and Grissom blinked, then blinked again. Talk about adorable. But another close encounter with Tuesday Smart might get him hurt and hurt bad. Could he risk his boys' hearts along with his? Because that was what he was doing. Taking a chance. On a woman. Again.

He opened his mouth to tell everyone, 'No,' when Tuesday murmured a timid, "Well, okay. A short ride wouldn't hurt, I guess. As long as you're sure?"

She directed the question at Grissom. Was he sure? Oh hell no. He had no idea how to answer or what she wanted him to say. But could he resist the trepidation shimmering in those glistening emerald eyes? Was she afraid of him hurting her or him getting too close? Did she honestly think he'd hurt her? Not happening. Not ever. Or was she just worried, like he was, where this one ride could lead? Going to lunch with his boys seemed innocent at first glance. She'd be on one side of the table. He'd sit with his boys across from her. No danger of touching, and they could part as friends. Nothing more.

But on a day like this? With Christmas Eve and all the emotions that went with it only hours away? Every shattered childhood dream? All those unrealized expectations? The nasty legacy of his mother screaming because his dad never did anything right? Of Pam screeching at frightened Tanner and Luke because they woke her too early?

This Christmas would be the first without What's-Her-Name. Grissom had their letters to Santa. He knew what they wanted, and every last item on those wish lists was already bought, paid for, wrapped, and hidden. The shrew who'd ruled their lives for the last seven years was gone. They were finally free to be themselves, just three happy-go-lucky guys who believed in Santa and elves and flying reindeer. They didn't need anyone else, certainly not someone as capricious as a… a woman as beautiful as… as Tuesday.

Masterfully, and despite his very reasonable misgivings, Grissom replied, "Sure. We'll ride the loop up to the border of the national park and have you on your way by suppertime."

There. That set a firm boundary. Tuesday could go for a ride with them, but he'd drawn a line. The McCoy boys didn't need her. Why take the chance? Why lead her on? He wasn't what she was looking for, and he didn't have it in him to sweet talk her and pretend he was. Life had been cruel enough for both of them. What could possibly come out of two damaged people getting together? If that was even what she wanted. Maybe she just wanted to spend another day with his boys. Yeah. That made more sense. What would one innocent horseback ride hurt?

"Smooth move, dickhead," Maverick muttered under his breath, loud enough Grissom caught it.

A nasty response came swiftly to his lips, but Grissom held it back. No sense returning tit for tat. Swallowing hard— or trying to—he followed his boys and Tuesday Smart into the barn. Apparently, he wasn't done playing cowboy yet, but this ride would be quick, sweet, dirty, and...

No. Not sweet and not dirty. Just quick, damn it.

Chapter Nine

She hadn't planned on running into Grissom and his boys today. Hadn't known they were here and would never dream of underhanded scheming like that. Hadn't planned to be riding a broad-backed horse with Tanner riding the bay, also known as Star, on one side, Grissom and Luke on her other. Hadn't expected she'd be with a man as hot, hot, hot as Grissom McCoy, either. Or as mercurial. One minute he seemed warm and approachable, downright affable, like Luke. But the next, he'd all but pushed her away.

Yet there she was. In the saddle, on a trail through a grove of bare-branched sugar maples, somewhere east of the Shenandoah National Forest. While the easterly breeze now blowing in promised icy rain or snow in the near future, the day was still sunny and the air was sweet with the scents of warmed, fallen leaves and the ruins of summer's bounty. Tuesday had no favorite season. She loved them all. Like the continents and countries of the world. Everywhere she'd photographed had its own history and appeal, and if forced to decide which country was better than the rest, she'd have to pick them all.

She wished she knew what she'd done, though. Grissom had definitely grown colder since they'd saddled up, and she hadn't missed the way he'd avoided looking at her when he'd finally agreed to this expedition. Grissom was a puzzle, licking his lips with lust one moment. Staring off into the distance the next.

While Tuesday chalked his change in temperament up to the traumatic events he'd lived through, she didn't deserve the evil eye he'd given her. The past year had been hard for her, too. She'd gotten caught up in Maeve Astor's evil web. The psychotic woman had killed anyone who got in her way, including her own children and Tuesday's greatest benefactor, Frederick Lamb. Since the moment she'd found herself wrongly accused of not only poisoning Freddie but burning Astor's husband and children alive, Tuesday's world had been turned upside-down.

She'd been slandered by the national press, hunted by the FBI, and finally caught by TEAM agents, Shane Hayes and Everlee Yeager. Mayhem and sorrow seemed to be the only constants in Tuesday's life. The old saying, *"If she didn't have bad luck, she'd have no luck at all,"* fit her to a T. Almost made her want to hide from the whole darn world. But she hadn't and she wouldn't. That wasn't how Freddie had taught her to deal with problems.

Being there to defend Shane and Everlee that night in Little Rock had been a privilege, no two ways about it. She'd shoot Maeve Astor again if she could. Astor's reign of unbridled hatred and terror had needed to end. As much as she'd terrorized Tuesday, it seemed fitting that she'd been there to help put the murderess down.

But then… Shane, Everlee, and Heston had left her to her noble causes and went back to their lives and jobs. Sure, documenting climate change across the planet was a worthwhile endeavor, but she'd been shocked at how much she'd missed them. For those few days, she'd had friends who'd cared about her. Who'd looked out for her. It was Heston's polite goodbye handshake at the end of their adventure in New York City that made Tuesday acutely aware of how empty her life was. It made her question her priorities. Her plans. Did she have any, other than to be at Robert's beck and call for the rest of her life? Was being sent to desolate places all she was good for? There was a time after Freddie's death when she'd craved isolation. But now?

She cast a sideways glance at Grissom. The brim of his cowboy hat was still down, keeping his face in shadow, not that his beard didn't already cover most of his face. But his hat kept him from making eye contact with her, which was disappointing. His shoulders were broad and his back was straight. Too straight. Like a wall, as if he meant to exclude her from everything, even just friendly conversation.

Neither Grissom nor his boys wore anything heavier than long sleeved shirts. Western shirts. Just like Maverick's. That was when Grissom's mood changed, when Maverick told him to saddle another horse. He must've felt trapped into doing something he hadn't wanted to do, which was her going horseback riding with him and his boys. Tuesday didn't blame him. She hadn't come here to ride horses and her idea of a TEAM photo shoot was ill-advised. Harebrained. Frivolous. Real warriors comprised The TEAM. A photo shoot like the one she'd envisioned would turn those warriors into clowns. Was that how she wanted the world to see them? Absolutely not.

"Shush, I'm still here," Grissom murmured to the sleeping boy in his arm.

Stiffening her legs, Tuesday leaned forward in her saddle to see around Grissom. Was Luke having a nightmare? Did he miss his mom or was he battling separation anxiety? Tuesday stole another quick glance, hoping to catch sight of Luke. She couldn't, not with that sweet baby boy cradled in Grissom's opposite arm.

The desperate, bearded, half-crazed man in Puntarenas had changed into a gorgeous alpha male who genuinely adored his boys. There was no more glorious sight on earth than a tough guy tenderly cradling his son. That alone made Tuesday's heart stall.

To get her flustered mind back on track, she told Tanner to, "Remind me the names of these horses. You're on Star, but who am I riding, and do they all have names?" She'd eagerly agreed to ride another horse when she'd learned that Star was Tanner's favorite.

"Yes, ma'am, they all get two names."

She had to lick her dry lips at the easy way Tanner called her ma'am. These boys had been taught to be respectful. Did they learn that from their mother? Tuesday knew better. No, the moody guy beside her was these boys' only teacher, and Grissom had done an admirable job.

"They get a legal name when Maverick registers them, but those are really long, and I can't never remember 'em. The horse you're riding is a mare. That means she already had a baby and her name's JeZabel. She's got a capital Z in the middle of her name, like Z. He named her cuz he wanted his name inside of hers cuz he was the only one with her the night she was born."

Tuesday cocked her head at Tanner. "Z is a person?"

"Ah-huh, Z and X are both persons," Tanner answered gleefully. "They're guys, and their real names are Xavier and Zeke, and they work for Miss China and Maverick. When I grow up, I'm gonna be a hired hand just like them. Maybe I'll change my name to just T!"

Tuesday grinned at the way his brows spiked. There was a day she'd wanted to be an astronaut, and why not? Childhood was the time for wild, crazy dreams. Heaven knew those dreams didn't last very long and, too often, they got trashed by what life threw at you. "Great job aspiration," she replied, encouraging Tanner to achieve whatever he set his heart on. "What horse is your dad riding?"

"Joker," Tanner answered. "He's a funny guy, but don't ever stand too close to him. He likes to step on people's feet, and I even seen him smile when he did it once!"

"Hmm, I never realized horses have personalities," she mused.

"Yup," Grissom said from her other side. "None of these horses are alike. The cattle in the back forty, either. Animals are the same as people. Snowflakes, each unique. Each special."

And there Tuesday was again, trying desperately not to be enamored with the indifferent man riding beside her, the reins loose in one hand, cradling his three-year-old in the other, and singing the praises of animals, as if they were people.

"And sons," she added quietly. "Your boys are as different as night and day."

"That they are."

"Can we gallop 'em, Dad?" Tanner interrupted, standing up tall in his much shorter stirrups to see around Tuesday. "Can we race, huh? I'll be real careful."

Grissom shook his head. "Not today. Lunch next, then chores are waiting at home. It's Saturday, remember?"

"Oh, yeah. Darn it." Tanner leaned back in his saddle. "I gotta clean the cat box every Saturday, and it's real stinky. Why do I always have to clean it?"

"Who owns Pixie?"

"Me…" Tanner sighed. "I know. I paid for her with my allowance, and I love her, so I'm the one who takes care of her because that's what good cat owners do."

Tuesday smiled. That last line sounded like something he'd heard a few times before.

"Besides," Grissom continued, "Luke has to pick up his toys and dust furniture in the family room. Company's coming over tonight. Walker and Persia."

"Oh, yeah!" Tanner exclaimed. "I forgot."

That cinched it. Grissom kept making it clear he had plans and those plans didn't include her. Tuesday got the point.

"Mind if I race Tanner back to the barn?" she asked Grissom, desperate to get away from this guy and the arrows he kept shooting into her heart. "Might even have the saddles off these big *'kids'* before you and Luke get there." It sounded like a good idea, as slow as Joker was ambling. Would've sounded better if her attempt at sarcasm hadn't sounded pitiful.

Tuesday was intent on leaving as soon as she could get this horse back to the barn and unsaddled. She had no business falling in love with these boys. They weren't hers, and who cared if their father looked like he'd just stepped off the pages of some high-powered cowboy magazine. Was there even such a thing as Cowboys GQ? Sheesh!

Grissom pulled back on the reins and Joker stopped walking. "You sure?" he asked, as if he was astonished that she had plans. She didn't. Not precisely. Didn't even know where she was sleeping tonight; only knew she had to get out of Virginia before dark.

The only thing Tuesday was sure about was how much it would hurt to tell these boys goodbye again. Last time had been hard enough. But now? She looked Grissom in the eye, intending this to be the last time. Some men simply weren't worth the trouble. "Yes," she whispered. Straightening her shoulders, she reinforced her plan with a loud and firm, "Might be a good idea to turn back now. I hate driving at night and the sun goes down early these days."

"You do?" Grissom asked. "Umm, hate driving at night?"

"You don't wanna go to Cakes and Honey with me no more?" Tanner asked, childish concern in his six-year-old voice.

Instead of answering his dad, she turned to the boy she loved with a lump in her throat. Tanner had that worried *'what'd I do wrong?'* look all over his face.

"I do, Tanner but… but…" She choked on the lie about to come out of her mouth. "I'm sorry, but I've got deadlines to keep, and schedules I've got to—"

"Bullshit," Grissom growled softly. "None of this is your fault. It's…it's mine. Please—"

"No." She put her head down, determined he not see the tears welling in her silly eyes. Wrong move. They fell anyway, like salty drops of rain out of a broken sky, straight from her foolish, shattered heart, to the tightly knotted fingers clutching the saddle horn.

She'd be okay. What choice did she have? Yet one more time, she'd pick up where everything went wrong and bury herself in the career she'd once loved. Maybe Robert still needed her. Calling him wouldn't be her first choice, but he'd keep her too busy to think about this sweet piece of heaven she'd found.

Some people were lucky. They met their true loves early in life, got married, and raised perfect families. They lived in peace and tranquility, went to PTA and Cub Scout meetings, took their sons and daughters to pediatricians, and they never, ever, knew despair, loneliness, or fear. Not her. Chaos was her life. Death her closest companion. She might as well get used to it.

"It's okay," she told the finely-tooled leather saddle. "Duty calls. Let's go back so I can leave. Then—"

She had no idea how Grissom made it happen. But one moment she was upright in her saddle, trying to get a grip on her messed-up life. The next, she was off the horse and in his arm, pressed under his chin beside a sleepy-eyed Luke. Unable to face one of the most perfect boys in the world, Tuesday closed her eyes. The gentleness of Grissom's hug meant nothing. He felt guilty, that was all. It was time to leave.

Chapter Ten

"I'm so damned sorry," Grissom whispered into the top of Tuesday's head, breathing in the lovely fragrance of roses wafting up the warm space between them.

"You squishin' me," Luke grumbled sleepily, shoving away from Tuesday. But then he must've opened his eyes, as quickly as he burrowed back into her and said, "Tuesday's cryin', Daddy. Why's she sad?" Damned if the tenderhearted little guy didn't start bawling along with her.

Great. Just great. Grissom had to get ahead of the mess he'd created before Tanner started crying, too.

"Because I hurt her feelings," Grissom admitted, shifting Luke higher up on his shoulder to make more room for Tuesday. She'd wormed her palms between him and her, and those hands were right then pushing him away. Grissom knew he'd never get another chance to, at least, be her friend if he let her go now.

"No, you didn't, Mr. McCoy," she protested, her voice tight and her hands firm on his chest. Which he wished were there because of something more than the sadness radiating off her. "I'm okay, Luke. I just… got something in my eye, and it's time I went h-home."

He was *Mr. McCoy* again. Damn it. What would've been so wrong with her coming on a simple horseback ride with him and his boys? Why'd he panic? It's not like that would've meant they were on their way to the altar or anything. Why had he screwed up a simple outing by thinking of himself instead of his boys? Or her? Grissom didn't fully understand why he'd freaked, but he needed to. Because, right then and there, with her in one arm and Luke in the other, he knew damned well that letting Tuesday go would be the biggest mistake of his life. He'd never be whole again, and for whatever reason, that was how he felt with her up close and personal like she currently was. Whole for the first time in his life. Not broken. Not even missing any pieces.

"What'd you do to her, Dad?" Tanner snapped. "Now she doesn't want to go to breakfast with us, and I'm hungry, and I…"

His bottom lip quivered and Grissom wanted to kick his own ass. These boys loved Tuesday. She'd been their sole refuge during the worst time in their lives, and they adored her. What would they have done without her? They'd been alone with two monsters until Tuesday showed up. He should've paid more attention, to that and to them and—

"And I love her more than you!" Tanner yelled, his eyes watering. "She's never been mean to me. Not once!"

"Tanner," Tuesday said gently, while she did precisely what Grissom was worried she'd do, shifted sideways and out of his grip. "Don't say that, honey. Your dad's not being mean to you. Look at him, sweetheart. He adores you and your brother, and he'd be lost without you guys."

Without glancing at his dad, Tanner tipped out of his saddle and fell into Tuesday's arms. "I don't wanna look at him. I'm mad at him," he cried, his arms a noose around her neck. "I don't want you to go. You just got here. Please, don't leave me again."

Shit. Tanner needed Tuesday more than he needed his dad? Didn't that make Grissom feel like a douchebag? Oh, yeah…

It was going to hurt like a mother, but he might as well tear the Band-Aid off and man up. "Tanner, you're right. I hate to admit it, but" —he finally caught Tuesday's eye— "I haven't been very polite today." *And I'm not really sure why. Am I scared? Hell yeah, I'm scared. Not of her but… Shit. I'm just worried, that's all. That's what I do best. I worry. And now I'm talking to myself…*

Tanner wiped his teary face and then smeared his wet fingers on his pant leg. "Is it PTSD, Dad? Did you have a panic attack like I do sometimes?" he asked between hiccups. "Is that why you thought you had to be mean?" Then to Tuesday, he said, "I get mean with Luke sometimes when I git attacks. I think I know what Dad's feeling."

Grissom's cheeks puffed with a heartfelt sigh. Weren't they a pair, him with his mixed-up memories, and poor Tanner with his mommy-induced panic attacks? Obviously, there were no secrets in the McCoy household, not since family counseling began. Not since Grissom decided the best way forward for him and his boys was to be totally honest with them. Not with the horrors or atrocities of war, they didn't need that crap in their little heads. But by admitting how worried he was sometimes, and that, yes, it was okay for guys to cry, and sometimes, even tough Army guys needed hugs. It was urgently important to Grissom that his sons understood why he woke up yelling in the middle of the night sometimes, and that when he did, it wasn't because they'd done anything wrong. Nothing that had happened in Costa Rica was their fault. If anyone was to blame, he was. And yes, Ms. Ashlee

Peyton, their family counselor, would surely argue with him over that. Grissom also knew he'd spend the rest of his life making it up to his boys for staying married to their mother as long as he had.

"Say you're sorry, Daddy," the baby tyrant in the family demanded, from high on Grissom's shoulder.

Setting Luke's feet on the ground, Grissom winked at his youngest, then did as he was told and took a step toward Tuesday and Tanner. "I made a mistake," he admitted. "I… I did panic, that's true, and I made you feel bad." He drew in a belly full of air and continued. "My boys have Post Traumatic Stress Disorder and so do I. There are things I may never remember, and some shit I'll never forget. I have triggers, and living with me is tough on Tanner and Luke. Nothing about me is easy, but I'm doing everything I can for them, and for me, too. And today…" He drew in a deep breath. "I don't really know you, and, shit, I'm not good with women."

"Ask me anything," Tuesday said quietly. "I've been in the press enough. I have no secrets."

He nodded at her, like the big dumb ox he was. "Yeah, but the press never gets anything right."

"And they invent stories. After all, lies sell more newspapers, not truth."

She had him there. Grissom ran a hand over his scruffy chin, not sure what to do or say next.

"I love you, Dad," Tanner said tearfully, "and I'm sorry I said I didn't."

Thank heaven for his sons. Grissom walked over to Tuesday and ruffled his fingers through his son's dark hair. "I know you love me, and it's okay to get mad. We've talked about that. It's better to vent instead of holding everything in until we explode, huh? Just remember that what we say when we're angry can be hurtful, too."

"I know, Dad. Like what Mom used to… to say to me," Tanner's voice cracked.

The poor kid stretched both arms out for his dad, and Grissom pulled him carefully away from Tuesday. He didn't want to make her feel bad, but the moment Tanner was in his arms again, a sigh of contentment groaned out of him. "Your mom was sick, kiddo. Sick and mean and bitter, and nothing she did was ever your fault. Stick with me. We might say things we don't mean sometimes, but we're going to get through this, I promise. I've got your six, and I know you've got mine, buddy. We're going to be okay."

Tanner wiped his face again, then lifted his eyes back to Tuesday. Grissom had to give her credit for not leaving. The McCoy family was a mess. They might look like dapper cowboys on the outside, especially dressed like they were today. But inside, he and his boys were dealing with a shit-ton of crap and would be for months, maybe years. Yet there she stood waiting and, if the expression on her face was an indication, she wasn't going anywhere.

"I have triggers too, Tuesday, but Dad doesn't never get mad when I… when I…" Poor Tanner paled at what he'd nearly admitted.

Grissom's gaze narrowed down on Tuesday. Surely, she already knew Tanner wet the bed. He was getting better, but night terrors still ravaged his self-esteem and accidents still happened.

Damned if she didn't step in close enough to cup Tanner's quivering jaw. "We all have secrets, sweetheart," she said softly, "and I'll keep yours forever. They'll always be locked up safe in my heart, and I wouldn't trade a second of our time together for anything. Deal?"

Just that fast, all that pent-up tension melted out of Tanner. "Thank you," he whispered. "You always been so nice to me and Luke, and if you hafta go now, I'll be sad, but I'll never, ever forget you."

"She's not going anywhere," Grissom declared, facing the woman his boys loved. "The McCoy family is a work in progress. We're men, not girls. We argue and fight, but I hope you'll join us for breakfast. Let me make it up to you?"

"Dad's right. We're getting better every day," Tanner said fiercely. "And before long, we're gonna be better than we ever, ever were."

"Yeah, and we're really hungry," Luke reminded everyone from where he stood at Tuesday's knee, looking up at her. Damned if his grubby little hand wasn't already tucked inside hers.

Drawing in a much calmer breath, Grissom looked into her clear green eyes and said, "I messed up. I'm sorry. Can you forgive me for being a… a guy?"

Two little faces pivoted from Grissom back to Tuesday. "There's nothing to forgive, Mr. McCoy," she said as she took a step toward Grissom with Luke following. "You were concerned for your boys. I respect that."

"Please call me Grissom," he asked her again.

She dipped her head. "Okay. Grissom."

He couldn't understand why his name sounded different on her lips than when others said it, but it did. "Breakfast?" he asked, encouraged by how easily she was forgiving him. "Please say yes, or I'm going to have a fight on my hands."

He gave her his best puppy dog eyes and hoped he looked a little adorable.

There was nothing, absolutely no hint of Pam's ugly nature in Tuesday. Why he'd thrown up those chicken shit walls between her and his sons, Grissom didn't know. Except deep down he did. Tuesday was too good to be true. She was everything his mother and Pamela had never been. She was kind and caring. She'd rescued his boys when she could've looked the other way and left poor Tanner in Estes' filthy hands. But she hadn't. She'd gone toe-to-toe with that pig, and then she'd faced Pam and succeeded in rescuing Tanner and Luke. She'd taken them in and treated them like they were hers. She'd loved them, and—

She loved them still.

Grissom's eyes finally opened. He *saw* Tuesday Smart, truly saw her for who she was and how much she genuinely loved his boys. Damned if the still small voice in his heart didn't whisper, '*Duh.*' Tuesday's love showed in the tenderly possessive way she held Luke's grubby hand. It beamed out of her eyes at Tanner like bright, golden rays of encouragement. She shared his worst secret, yet there he was, in love with the woman who was not his mother. Who would never be anything like Pam.

The enormity of what he was finally looking st struck Grissom like a jagged bolt of lightning out of the clear blue sky. He was treading new territory. If this went wrong, his sons would become collateral damage again. They wer the primary reason behind him establishing those boundaries. Only… his boys were the ones showing him the way. They'd both run headlong through those stupid, imaginary limitations he'd set and embraced Tuesday.

Grissom took another step toward her. "Just to be clear…" He cleared his throat. "You're too young for me." It sounded like he was setting another boundary, but it was the first thing that popped into his head, and, of course, it came right out of his mouth. Damn it, he'd blown it again, and another panic attack crawled like fire ants beneath his skin.

Until the corners of her pretty mouth tweaked upward, as if she knew he hadn't meant to be as rude as he'd sounded. Which made one of them. He was still standing there, wishing he could call that lame come-on line back.

"Gosh, how old *are* you?" Tuesday teased.

The tense fingers of panic relinquished their forward march as her smile spilled over him. Him, of all people. Was it possible? Could she like a guy like him? Not that he was in love with her. He honestly didn't know what genuine, honest, feminine love felt like. He'd never had it in his life. He wasn't in love with her now, damn it. But he could be. He could at least admit that much. He did like Tuesday, and he had kind of fallen for her when she was sitting with Luke on her lap, back in the pasture surrounded by all those "giant" horses.

"Twenty-nine," he declared boldly. Twenty-nine damned hard years of learning how to survive.

"Wow, that's really old, huh, guys?" she asked his sons.

"Yeah!" Luke squealed. "Daddy's older than everybody I know!"

"He is!" Tanner agreed enthusiastically. "He's real old."

Grissom shrugged off those playful jabs, wondering how old Tuesday was. Not that he'd ask. But someday he might. Maybe.

"I'm glad I'm not *that* old," she said as if she'd read his mind.

That was good enough for Grissom. With Tanner still in one arm, he reached for her free hand. "I'm buying breakfast. Let's ride."

The sun picked that precise moment to break between the clouds, spotlighting her in a shaft of golden light. WTF? Coincidence? Fate? Or—dare he hope—destiny? Grissom grinned at the sheer stupidity of that third option. She might be the angel who'd rescued his boys—and she was. But he was the nerdy guy in that movie, *"Back to the Future,"* the guy who'd mispronounced destiny and said, *"Density,"* instead.

Grissom didn't believe in destiny. But density? His mother had always said he was as dense as a brick. *That*—he could wrap his hard head around. Density it was and density was good enough. Look where it got that guy in the movie.

Chapter Eleven

With Luke on her left and Tanner on her right in one of several 1950s style booths at Cakes and Honey, Tuesday felt more alive than she had in a long time. Grissom had taken his sons into the restroom as soon as they'd arrived. But now, he sat by himself on the bench seat opposite them. His boys were wedged in, so tight against her that she had to lift her arms over their heads when she needed to reach anything on the table. Even though he was alone on his side of the booth, Grissom's handsome face was a mixture of pride and an emotion Tuesday couldn't quite put her finger on.

She nearly laughed out loud at the quandary she was in. There she sat, hugging his sons, nearly unable to put *her hands* on the table, yet neither could she put *a finger* on the emotion behind their father's expression. The moment was utterly, ridiculously sublime. She was surrounded by men, but did she understand them? Actually, yes. The boys were easy. But Grissom? The jury was still out on him.

After riding back to the barn, unsaddling their horses, brushing them down, and then watering them, Grissom, Tuesday, and the boys had climbed into his well-used, rusted Silverado. The poor thing looked like it'd seen better days— a long time ago. Once Grissom had strapped his boys into their booster seats on the rear bench, he'd helped Tuesday climb aboard. Thank heavens for running boards. She didn't want a boost up or his hands on her backside, and he didn't assume she did, like some guys would have. If anything, he'd been very careful to cup her elbow for that boost up. Between his assist and the suicide strap, she'd managed.

As good as Grissom's hug had felt during their ride, and as much as Tuesday was attracted to him, the truth remained. His sons weren't hers, and his feelings towards her were conflicted. So much so that he'd tried to sabotage the last hours of their short time together.

Tuesday honestly wasn't sure how she felt about him. Tanner and Luke, yes. But their troubled father? For a few moments back in the pasture, she'd enjoyed the evil eye he'd given Maverick. Grissom had been jealous. For no reason, true, but Tuesday noticing he seemed to care about her then, had warmed her like nothing had before. But somewhere between then and now he'd turned to ice. Made excuses. Wouldn't make eye contact. Until his boys forced his hand. Yes, Grissom had apologized, but only when he'd had no choice.

As much as his arms around her had grounded Tuesday…

As delicious as he smelled… (Alfalfa and cedar were her new favorite scents.)

As comforting as his broad, heavily muscled chest had felt beneath her cheek…

As much as she was attracted to Grissom McCoy, and she was. It was hard not to be. The man was kryptonite, but minus Superman's magnetic personality. Okay, so he was rough around the edges and unpredictable, but she could see the man of steel beneath the insecurity, if that was where his reticence came from. She didn't blame him. She wouldn't be eager to share her children after everything they'd gone through, either.

My gosh, it'd only been weeks since that fiasco in Costa Rica. He and his boys had to have moved out of the place they'd lived in with his wife during that time. Tuesday certainly would have. And they were in counseling. Family counseling. That was a tremendous number of really big changes crammed into a very short amount of time. Of course Grissom was overly cautious. She would be, too. If she had children.

But Tuesday wasn't even sure she and he had anything in common, other than their love for his boys. When he'd intermittently seemed to care and turn on what little charm he had, it'd felt like sunshine breaking through the frigid, starless Arctic night. But then, he'd turned to ice. What he'd just warmed became dark and empty again.

Tuesday Smart understood Post-Traumatic Stress Syndrome. She'd dealt with her share of it after her parents died, so much so she could be the PTSD poster girl. She'd had nightmares, depression, bulimia, you name it. At one time, she'd been suicidal. Her losses had been utterly devastating, and she'd been a kid. An orphan. A grieving, hurting child.

Nothing, absolutely nothing, could've prepared her for the police coming to her door that night—her parents' door—with the ungodly notification that they were dead. Freddie was the one who'd made sure she got the help she'd desperately needed. Not her minister. Not any neighbors nor a friend's parents. Not even a semi-interested social worker had shown up after the shock of that double death and funeral. Only her dad's business associate, some guy she'd barely remembered meeting, and he'd come all the way from New York City, just for her. The rest was history.

Freddie had never been her lover, and that was what and who was missing in Tuesday's life. Her soul mate. The man who'd always put her first. Who'd treasure her. Not the random guy with lies in his eyes and greed behind all the right words. Those were male versions of Pam, opportunistic users. The only treasure they wanted was the estate Freddie had left Tuesday.

Which made the world's far-off reaches seem safer. At least, preferable. Predators there weren't dressed in sheepskin. They came at you head-on, with obvious intent to kill. If they came at you at all. Truthfully, Tuesday had encountered more hate, deceit, and betrayal in America than she had from the wild animals and various peoples of the world she'd photographed. Greed was the real killer, and that sin was alive and well in the States.

Was Grissom the man of her dreams? Not likely. Was she attracted to him? Simple answer, yes. Complicated, thoughtful answer? Probably not. The spark between them was nothing more than her biological clock ticking down. Reminding her that her time was running out. That she'd better jump at the first man who came along if she wanted any kind of a family. Not happening. She deserved to be treasured like Shane treasured Everlee, and like Heston treasured London. That was her impossible dream, to have what they had. She could wait.

Sure, Grissom was handsome, in a brooding, unpredictably distant way. She'd always been attracted to tall, dark, and handsome, and Grissom had that in spades. His dark brown hair was straight, not wavy. Short on the sides, but long enough on top that fingers of it occasionally flopped into his eyes. His hazel eyes turned dark as quickly as his mood swings. He was thick through his chest, neck, shoulders, and arms. Slender at his waist and hips. Must work out a lot, maybe every day, as solidly as he was built. Did he have a workout gym at home? That made sense. She couldn't see him dropping his boys off with a babysitter.

Tuesday's fingers curled into fists thinking about his wife. And therein lay the problem. Tuesday refused to fall for a man because she loved his kids. She wanted to love the man of her dreams for who he was, and she wanted him to love her the same way. Not because his children needed a mother. Not because he wanted her money. Just because he couldn't live without her.

"You going to eat that?"

She blinked, not sure what Grissom was asking, until he aimed his fork at her untouched blueberry pancake. "Yes, I am," she declared, as if her mind hadn't wandered a thousand miles away. To prove it, she cut a small portion of the pancake with the side of her fork, lifted the syrupy triangle to her mouth. and opened wide. "Yum," she mumbled with her mouth full.

His pupils turned big and black. Suddenly, eating one of Aunt Jemima's finest turned into an exquisitely carnal act. Grissom made it worse when he reached across the table and, with the pad of his thumb, caught the drop of syrup on her chin. Tuesday closed her eyes, savoring the sweet sensation. It was a small thing, but no man had ever touched her like that before.

She'd been too broken to care about boys after her parents' deaths. Still numb with grief when she became a wife, then too soon, a widow. On the heels of those nightmares came being one of the FBI's ten most wanted criminals, and since then, it'd been easier to go along with Robert's travel plans. That, she knew. Air travel, international and domestic, how to handle an assortment of weapons. She had a concealed carry permit, and had faced off with a few predators in her time. But what she knew about intimacy between a man and a woman would fit in a thimble and still have room left over.

Her head was spinning at the mere thought of intimacy with Grissom. Thank goodness Tanner and Luke were too busy eating to notice how hard she was breathing or that the fork in her hand was shaking. One touch. That's all it took and her good intentions to keep this man at arm's length evaporated. Where had her bravado gone?

Chapter Twelve

'She's just like me,' Grissom thought as he'd captured that single drop of syrup and popped his thumb in his mouth. *She's afraid to fall in love. She's been hurt too many times to trust her instincts. Her gut.*

Tuesday's eyes tracked the movement. She was as turned on by that presumptuous touch as he was. Her nostrils flared when he'd put his thumb in his mouth and sucked the syrup from it. Her eyes were suddenly bright crystal emeralds as he let the maple sweetness roll over his tongue. They weren't just green, but had deepened into spectacularly dark emerald jewels, glimmering with a fire that came from somewhere deep inside. When her chest heaved, Grissom's gaze fell to the fluttering pulse in the hollow between her collarbones. She felt it too, the hum of sexual tension between them. He'd bet money she'd taste sweeter than any syrup.

Such a simple thing, touch. He'd never known the tenderness of it, only the absence of it in his life. His boys always gave it to him unconditionally, without reserve or judgment. But Pam's constant complaining about his lack of finesse during lovemaking drove his mother's point home. Through birth, he'd been cursed to repeat his mistakes. Through marriage, he'd been damned.

But how to make Tuesday want to stay? That was worth considering. He refused to use his boys as lures. Not like he needed one. If anything, they were already snagged and looked happy as clams, snuggled beside her with her arms around them. What male, no matter how old, wouldn't be happy? If anything, he was the outsider, sitting opposite the contented threesome, watching his sons soak up the light that radiated from Tuesday. Was it wrong for a father to be jealous of his children?

"So what'd ya think, Daddy?" Luke chirped. "Can she?"

Grissom blinked to get his wandering brain back on track. He'd been caught daydreaming about the lovely woman his sons were already enamored with, and he'd missed the conversation at the table. "Uh, what?"

Tanner giggled. "Stop looking at Miss Tuesday like that, Dad. I said I wanna show her my combat jet picture collection. Can she come home with us? Please?"

Grissom's internal self-defense mechanisms kicked in. He barely reined in the panic that sharing his sons induced when an instant "No!" burst out of his mouth. Allowing anyone inside his new house—into his sons' one safe place— risked everything. Their peace of mind. The daily routines he'd established to help them recover from their trauma. Tanner and Luke were all Grissom lived for, and they needed to feel completely secure before he allowed anyone—

"It's okay. Another time maybe," Tuesday said quietly.

Grissom saw it then. She thought she was the problem. She was only pulling away because—he was pushing her away. The 'No' came easier this time. "No, Tuesday. I mean, yes. Please come home with us. I think you'll be impressed with what Tanner's done. It's the best collection of F-16 fighter jet art I've ever seen." Because it was the only art collection compiled by a six-year-old Grissom had ever seen.

Her lips pursed into a small O, as if she couldn't decide. Grissom didn't blame her. He was having a hard time keeping up with his panicky-self as well. A woman had to be nuts to want to be anywhere near a nutcase like him. But there she was, considering doing just that.

"Okay, but I can't stay long," she replied, her voice soft and hesitant. "I still have… things to do today."

Damn it, Grissom had put that uncertainty in her head. He was the problem here, not Tuesday. He needed to turn this around. He'd goofed up, again. If he could only get his brain to stop throwing him off the cliff of despair every time he had second thoughts. Being paranoid was exhausting.

His mind went back to his original realization: *She's just like me.* Afraid to trust. Afraid to fall in love. No sooner had that epiphany swept over him when something in his head clicked. Tuesday Smart wasn't the threat here, and neither was he. They were both fighting the same dragon: Emotional Trauma.

The weight of the world lifted off his shoulders. Something that felt a lot like his old confident self, surged to the surface of his psyche, as if it were fighting for air. He could breathe again. Okay then. Grissom reached his right hand across the table, the palm up and open in invitation. "Can you stay long enough to have dinner with us? I grill a pretty mean steak." He shrugged both shoulders. "I mean, I am a guy, and that's what us guys do."

Talk about lame.

"Yes!" Tanner shrieked, bouncing his butt on the bench beside Tuesday. "Please, oh please, say yes. It'll be our very first picnic in our brand-new house!"

"And I got Tonka trucks," Luke proudly announced, as he climbed to his feet and squeezed her neck. Damned if the little guy didn't press his sticky face into her cheek and plant a sloppy, syrupy kiss on Tuesday.

Grissom's eyes teared up. There he sat, looking at the woman who'd jumped at the chance to save his sons. Yet they weren't worried Tuesday might hurt them. Not at all. They already knew she wouldn't. If anything, they loved her because she'd loved them first. She might not have said the words, but she'd surely proved it. Over and over again. Just look at her. Sitting there with her arms full of—*my boys.*

He coughed, then closed his eyes. He couldn't see anyway, not through the tears about to run down his face. That was when he felt it, Tuesday's delicate hand in his palm, skin against skin, squeezing some of her special kind of warmth into him. His fingers circled hers carefully. Getting close to a woman again was a dangerous thing. He didn't want to mess this up.

"Please say yes," he begged, sounding a lot like Tanner. "I know we just ate, but stay long enough for me to fix dinner for you. It's the least I can do." *Stay with me. With us. Please, just for one evening.*

"I'd love to," she replied.

Before he knew what he was saying, Grissom blurted, "That's my girl."

Tuesday winked at him, as if she really, truly was his girl.

Chapter Thirteen

It felt strange to be sitting beside Grissom again, in his truck, his boys jabbering on the rear bench seat behind them. It felt—domestic. Natural. As if Tuesday had traveled back in time to days when family meant familiarity and rules and acceptance and—love.

It felt like déjà vu had metaphorically reached across the universe and slapped the back of her head when he'd said what he'd said. *"That's my girl."* Her father's words. Freddie's words, too. Simple words of encouragement spoken by men from the generation before the plague of political correctness strangled the life out of every innocent little thing. Just because the all-knowing, anonymous *"they"* thought *"they"* knew better than everyone else. Comfort Tuesday hadn't heard in so, so long, she hadn't realized how much those words meant or how much she'd missed them. Fresh out of Grissom's mouth, they'd tunneled into her heart.

Once again, he'd taken his boys to the restroom before they'd climbed back into his truck and hit the road. They'd just passed The TEAM's property and were on their way from Cakes and Honey to the McCoy household, which was somewhere north of TEAM Headquarters. Striving to keep her heart locked up, she turned both shoulders toward Grissom and asked, "What exactly does The TEAM do?"

He shot a quick glance her way before looking back at the road. "We're a group of mostly veterans trying to make a difference in the world. At least, that's what I'm trying to do. Sometimes, we go into other countries to retrieve kidnapped victims or to take out HVTs, high-value targets. Alex has a group in Southeast Asia that rescues children from the rampant human trafficking trade over there, another in Florida that deals with the same shitty business coming north out of Cuba and South America."

Tuesday brought her left knee up on the seat and turned more fully toward Grissom. Making herself more comfortable, she rested her elbow on the console between them. "And Alex Stewart? I tried to find information on him, but he has no social networking sites. The only things I found were a couple old newspaper articles and some really slanderous press stories that don't match the man I met."

Grissom grunted. "Yeah, he hates reporters. Won't give interviews, not even to the big-shot national agencies. They're all owned by billionaires with political agendas anyway, and covert surveillance companies don't do politics and they don't advertise. At least, they shouldn't. You know, covert means invisible. So yeah, he keeps a low profile."

"Hmm. Then I guess he wouldn't consider letting me do a photo shoot of you guys and your families."

That brought Grissom's full attention to her. "That why you're here this morning?" he asked, his voice taut. "To do a photo shoot or… or did Alex tell you it was okay?"

"Not yet." Tuesday put her hand on his forearm. "Like I said, I guess he wouldn't even consider it, would he?"

"Oh, yeah. You did say that, huh?"

"But I did come here to ask Mr. Finnegan if I could." Man, this guy was tense again. That muscular forearm felt like it was carved out of granite and pulsing molten lava instead of blood.

"Why would you want to?"

"The idea came to me at La Guardia when I saw Mark and Libby, that's all, and" —she shrugged both shoulders— "I don't know. They're the perfect couple, and yet they're both busy professionals and manage a large family. I guess because they seem so much in love, I thought it'd be good to let the world see what I see. So here I am, still thinking it's a great idea, but—"

"How do you know Mark and Libby?"

"I spent a day with them and the Stewarts after that shooting in Little Rock. Everlee was still in the hospital, and Heston and Shane were working on some kind of reports—"

"AARs. After action reports. Yeah, okay."

"And I needed to thank Alex for believing in me when nobody else did. I tracked him down through Mr. Finnegan. Alex was so kind, and he listened to my version of everything that happened, so—"

"He's relentless when it comes to details. He can be a real asshole. Go on."

Tuesday nodded, trying hard not to smile. Grissom might not realize it, but he was a lot like Alex. Focused and a little pushy. A bit of an asshole. "What do you think about me doing a photo shoot of you guys with your families? Would Mr. Finnegan ever—?"

"Nope. Not me and my boys. Uh-uh. Not gonna happen."

"Oka-a-a-a-y…" Tuesday drew out the word. "I guess you've probably all signed NDAs anyway, huh?"

"No NDAs. Alex isn't like that. I'm just… Most of us guys are just…"

She gave that tense bulky arm another squeeze. "You don't want the publicity, I get it."

"No, it's just that…Well, yeah, but…" The cords in his muscular neck tightened and his Adam's apple bobbed, as if talking was suddenly a chore.

"It was only an idea," she said soothingly.

"And in any other profession, it'd be a great idea. I mean, look at all the firemen and male stripper calendars. Chicks eat that stuff up, but The TEAM… The TEAM… Us guys…" The muscles in his forearm turned harder, like that was possible. "We're not… It's just that…"

"No worries," she murmured to get him to relax. "Forget I asked."

"It's just that… a lot of us aren't proud of everything we did while we served our country. We made mistakes and some of those mistakes…" He drew in a bellyful of air. "Yeah, we have to work out and keep in shape, sure. That's one of the conditions of signing on with Alex. He's got an on-site gym, swimming pool, parkour course, and… hell. He's got everything anyone needs to keep fit. But we're not heroes, Tuesday. We might be fit and muscular and all that crap, but mostly, we're just guys and gals who came home alive and…" His chest heaved with an obvious internal struggle. "We're not heroes. We just want to be left alone to raise our families and live in peace. Is that asking too much?"

Tuesday ran her palm over his shirtsleeve, down the rigid muscles to his wrist in an attempt to comfort him. At his wrist, she slipped her hand under his and interlocked their fingers.

"I'm sorry I didn't think of that, and I should have. I wouldn't appreciate anyone using me like a trophy, either."

Grissom's fingers tightened between hers, something she wasn't expecting. "Yeah, right. And don't ever thank me for my service. I hate that. Most people who say it don't have a clue what they're saying or what's going on in the world. It's just the latest catch phrase. Hell, most people don't even mean it. They don't really care, and most politicians think all soldiers are stupid, like we flunked college so the only thing we were good for is getting sent to war. Assholes. They conveniently forget it's a volunteer army, for fuck sakes. We didn't *have to do* anything. We *chose* to defend our country, and the whole damned world would be smart if, for once— just once!—they thought about what that service really means. We volunteered, gawddamnit. We didn't *have* to do anything!"

"Noted," she replied easily. Grissom was very good at setting boundaries, and he was passionately patriotic, a quality missing in too many Americans these days.

"And another thing." His fingers tightened on hers. "I really am too old for you. I'm twenty-nine, for hell's sake."

"So you said," she answered just as calmly. "Would you like to know how old I am?"

"Well, err, yeah. Okay."

She couldn't hold back a smile at his obvious discomfort. He'd wanted to ask before but probably hadn't been brave or audacious enough to take the risk. "I'm twenty-five. Old, huh?"

His nostrils flared as a breath sighed out of him. "Twenty-five? Really? Nope, not old at all."

"So you were twenty-three when Tanner was born."

"Yeah. I was in Syria, deployed, when she called and told me I was a… I was a…" He cast a furtive glance over his shoulder at his boys. "Nevermind. Yeah, umm…" He cleared his throat and did what he did best. He changed the subject. "I'd sure like a family portrait of me and the boys, but only if you've got time to take one before you go. Maybe in our backyard. Today?"

"Of course. I'd love to do that for you, but I thought you guys had plans for tonight."

"Oh, yeah. Walker and Persia. Damn, I forgot they're coming over. Well, umm…" He glanced at her as if looking for a safe way out of what he probably thought was a dilemma, but to her, was nothing more than a simple mistake made on a busy day. "It'll be okay. You'll like them, and I know they'll like you. I'll still feed you."

Tuesday laughed. As if dinner was all she had on her mind. "Darn straight, you'll feed me, mister. Why else do you think I left my car in your parking lot? Just to ride in this old truck? I don't think so."

Darned if a genuine grin didn't crack Grissom's face. "Hey, don't knock my truck. She might be old, but *she's* never let me down." The way he emphasized that one word declared he'd been let down plenty.

She looked down at their hands, their fingers still entwined. He noticed and followed the direction of her eyes. Instead of pulling back and untangling his from hers, he lifted them to his mouth and kissed her knuckles. She couldn't believe he did that in front of his boys.

Tuesday glanced over her shoulder at Tanner and Luke. "Aw… They're asleep. How adorable."

Grissom leaned into the rearview mirror and grinned. "Yeah. They're the best of me, and they sure like you. Hell, I like you, Tuesday Smart." He pressed her hand against his thigh. "How about we play tonight by ear? You're busy. You've got schedules to keep, and when you need to go, Walker and Persia won't mind staying with my boys while I drive you back to your car. It'll work out, you'll see."

"Yeah, about that…" It was her turn to cough. Or choke. "I might've exaggerated about having things to do later." She wrinkled her nose at him. "I'm not working for Robert anymore and it just so happens, I'm free tonight."

The emotions that flickered across Grissom's face danced from surprised to concerned, before they dived into joyful. "You are? Really?"

She lifted her free hand to scratch the prickly heat rising up her neck. "Sorry I fibbed, but I didn't want to put you on the spot. You know, the boys were so excited, and they're really good at goading you into doing what they want. Like Cakes and Honey. Then me visiting to see Tanner's photo collection. You're a sucker for them, aren't you?"

"Yes, ma'am, I sure am."

Tuesday tipped the side of her head against her seatback, content to watch Grissom for the rest of the drive. He was handsome in a ruggedly beautiful way. Even his profile told a story of strength and determination, but also of pain and her old nemesis, survivor's guilt. She wanted to know everything about him. Where he was born. What his parents were like. What his favorite subjects in school had been. But mostly, how on earth he'd met Pamela, and why he'd married a nasty woman like her. Why he'd stayed with a woman who'd abused the boys he loved. Judging by how abruptly he'd changed subjects when he'd mentioned Pam calling while he'd been in Syria, Tuesday guessed that was when he'd found out he was a father. How could a man not know his wife was pregnant? Unless he and Pam hadn't been married then. And what about that head wound little Luke mentioned? So yes, Tuesday had questions.

He turned and caught her looking at him. "You're so damned beautiful," whispered out of him.

"No, you are," she said, mimicking his boys' style of arguing.

Grissom caught on fast. "No, you are. I said so first, and I'm older, and what I say goes."

There it was again, the feeling of familiarity, as if she'd known Grissom in some other lifetime. "I like you, too," she told him as he turned his truck into a long dirt driveway that led to an older, stark-white, craftsman-style home, sitting by itself in the middle of a field.

He squeezed her fingers again, and she could've stayed in the truck and sat there for as long as it took for his boys to wake up. But too soon, Grissom released her hand, reached over his seat, tapped Tanner's knee, and whispered, "Time to wake up, Scooter."

Tanner jolted, his eyes wide, the whites showing around his pupils. "No! Did I—? Dad, did I—?" His voice cranked high with anguish.

"No son, you didn't," Grissom replied patiently. "We're just home, that's all. No worries, kiddo. Take a minute to wake up, okay? You're with me and Tuesday. You're safe."

"Oh," he huffed, his cheeks red and ballooned with breaths of relief. "Sorry, I… I…"

"You have a nice home, Tanner," Tuesday interrupted his panic attack softly. There was no need for him to explain or apologize for anything. "I can't wait to see your fighter jet collection. Do you have your own bedroom?"

"No," he replied, still breathing hard and still waking up. "Me and Dad and Luke all sleep together. It's okay though, cuz he don't mind us sleepin' with him. We're gonna get real bunk beds someday when we're, umm, all better. Aren't we, Dad?"

Grissom hadn't stopped rubbing his fingers comfortingly over his son's thigh. "That's right. Bunk beds just like X and Z sleep in over at Maverick's bunkhouse. The cowboy kind, made of sturdy pine logs, along with two footlockers so a couple rowdy guys can stow their gear after a long day riding the range."

"Tonka trucks are important stuff," a drowsy Luke muttered. "I gotta go, Daddy. Hurry."

That changed the tempo from slow and easy to gotta get to the bathroom fast. Before she knew it, Grissom opened his home with a code he tapped into the sophisticated panel to the right of the door. And Tuesday was alone in the McCoy family room, gazing at a rear enclosed porch that overlooked acres of wildflowers and hundreds of small pines. Grissom owned a tree farm? How cool was that? It had to be his, as no fence divided the weedy backyard, and Tuesday couldn't tell where his property ended and the neighbor's—if there was a neighbor close by—began. But look at those pines. Beautiful, green pines, every last one of them.

A cozy kitchen stocked with industrial-size appliances stretched to her left. The room's retro, black-and-white tile floor contrasted well with its stark white walls, gleaming porcelain sinks, glossy white cabinets, and black granite countertops. Had Grissom chosen these options? If so, he had a talent for interior design.

Since Grissom and his boys had hurried through the doorway to the left of the fireplace at her right, she guessed that's where the bathroom was. Their quiet chatter still came from that direction, so she grabbed the opportunity to wander and explore.

But first… Tuesday paused behind the sturdy brown leather couch facing the red-stone fireplace. Two easy chairs flanked the couch. A large coffee table dominated the grouping. It wasn't hard to picture herself sitting on that couch while a fire glowed behind those glass doors. Maybe reading a story to Tanner and Luke.

A wooden box marked TOYS sat on one side of the hearth; a cast iron set of fireplace tools on the other. But the mantle… She walked around the furniture, needing a closer look at the framed pictures there. One of Grissom with an older man, might be his father. Two others, one a younger version of Tanner with a stern looking man in an OD green uniform. Oh, wait. That man was—Grissom? My, oh my, what was it about seeing him in uniform that quickened her pulse? He was ruggedly handsome, standing there as straight and grim as he was, his hands on a grinning Tanner's shoulders and a silver fighter jet parked behind them. No wonder Tanner had a picture collection of fighter jets.

The other photo was nearly the same, except Grissom was older and holding an infant, which had to be Luke. Again Tanner stood with him, one arm wrapped around his dad's leg. A pang of longing struck Tuesday. They were so handsome, and Tanner looked just like his dad. Why wasn't Pam in these pictures? How could she have thrown these boys away like she had?

Tuesday leaned in closer. Interestingly, Grissom wasn't smiling in either shot. Maybe Pam wasn't in those pictures because she was behind the camera.

Instead of waiting for him and his sons to return, Tuesday wandered into their kitchen. A cozy breakfast nook sat under the window to her right, a butcher block island with bar stools to her left. Not her idea of a well-organized kitchen. She preferred windows over the sinks instead of the antique brick that extended over the built-in range/oven combination on the far wall. She did like the sliding barn doors that closed the entry off from the family room, but Grissom's kitchen needed large, expansive, ceiling-high windows so a woman could seize the day while she lingered over her first cup of coffee. Although…

Why Tuesday cared about the windows in Grissom's kitchen was beyond her. It wasn't her problem.

The doorway with a hidden pocket door at her right led her into a wide hallway with the laundry/mudroom to her left, as well as a closed steel door that Tuesday guessed led to the garage. Three clothes baskets labeled boldly in caps: DAD, TANNER, and LUKE sat on the floor opposite the door. That made her smile. Grissom was organized. At her other side were two sets of stairs, one leading up and the other leading down, probably into the attic and basement.

Back in the family room again, Tuesday faced the entry she'd walked through just moments earlier and was wowed all over again. Instead of an empty, useless, waste-of-space cathedral ceiling overhead, Grissom had a loft. Its half-wall faced the rear of the home, which meant the dormer over the wraparound front porch provided the bright light streaming down and through the family room. There were no stairs, no way to get up there that she could see. But what a view anyone looking over that half-wall would have. If a person didn't know it was there, it'd make a great hiding place—or a library.

Grissom's home wasn't what she expected from a guy living with two boys, who all had some level of PTSD. She'd thought it'd be a messy, atypical bachelor pad, with mounds of dirty dishes in the kitchen sink, dirty clothes and smelly shoes scattered throughout the rooms, and fast-food garbage littering, well, everywhere. He'd clearly displayed signs of disorganized thinking earlier. Yet there she was, standing in the middle of a very tidy home.

Since he was still busy with his boys, Tuesday stepped up to the slider that led to his covered back porch. There was no need to open the door. She didn't know the code for his security system, but she could imagine being out there. Outside. With nothing but a clear blue sky overhead and the crisp wintry freshness of pine in her nose. Placing her palms to the cool window glass, she whispered a quick prayer. "Please, Father, can I have a happy ending this time? Somehow? I couldn't have been wicked in all my past lives, was I? Haven't I been alone long enough? Couldn't you give me a family like everyone else has? Just this once?"

She bowed her head, afraid if she kept praying she'd break down and cry, and what good would crying do? It'd just upset Tanner and Luke, the last thing she wanted. So she stiffened her spine and prepared for the moment when she'd have to leave them behind. Because the sun was setting and tomorrow was Christmas Eve. Santa was coming, and she needed to be gone before he arrived. Tuesday couldn't spend that special day in this house. She just couldn't.

It would kill her.

Chapter Fourteen

Grissom froze where he stood at the entry to the hallway, struck dumb by the quietly spoken words that had just poured out of Tuesday. After making sure his boys were doing their chores, he'd been quietly admiring the view. Her taut ass in those skinny jeans. How they made her mile-long legs look longer. The burnished tangles tumbling down her back, tangles he wanted to wrap around his fist. But the words she'd whispered were a no-kidding prayer, and he didn't want to intrude. *'But God, she's not wicked. She's pure and innocent and... and... You know it.'*

And she deserved to be wrapped up safe and sound inside the best family in the world. Maybe Mark and Libby's. They could use a nanny with all their kids. Surely Tuesday would love working for them. Or David and Nancy Tao. They were good people and had six or seven kids, most of them boys. Surely Nancy could use an extra hand around the house. Although, now that Grissom thought of it, the Tao boys were extremely protective of their little sister, and they might not like a nanny bossing them around. Not that Tuesday was bossy. Hell, Grissom wasn't even sure why his brain had decided she'd make a great nanny. She'd never said she wanted to be one, had she?

The loneliness pouring out of Tuesday killed. He understood every last one of those broken parts of her. The despair. The stinging sorrow for sins she hadn't committed. Survivor's guilt for losing people she loved. They had so damned much in common yet were still so different. She was the image of sophistication; he was a train wreck. She had brains, beauty, and friends in high places. He had a mortgage from hell, two children he treasured more than anything else, and enough debt to keep him in the poorhouse for the rest of his life. There was no way to sugarcoat it. He made good money working for Alex, but a decent life with him would still be damned near impossible.

Scrubbing a hand over his head, Grissom didn't know how to ease the sorrow leaking out of the beauty at the sliders. Okay, so Tuesday being anyone's nanny was a stretch. She was over-qualified. Frustrated he couldn't easily fix her problem, he walked quietly up behind Tuesday and wrapped his arms around her shoulders. He intended that hug to be nothing more than friendly.

But the moment her body stiffened at the contact, everything changed. This embrace was a mistake. He'd gotten too close, and now his nose was in her hair. She smelled like roses and Tuesday and—thank you, Lord—her lush, womanly body melted against him. Lifting her arms, she latched onto the forearms he'd crossed over her upper chest. Just her chest, not her breasts. Oh hell, no. He'd stayed clear of those luscious pillows. At least, he'd tried.

Because he was the father of two impressionable boys, damn it. Who were right then scrambling to get their chores done before game night. Single fathers had tremendous responsibilities that excluded dating, chasing women, and thinking just of themselves. Fathers didn't do randy stuff like that. Tanner and Luke needed him to be present, to be there for them, every minute of every day. Not gadding about town, trolling for hook-ups. Not trying, in any way, to satisfy his carnal needs instead of taking care of them. No way. They deserved the best, and by hell, the best was what he'd give them. If it took forever, he'd be the father Tanner and Luke deserved. He would.

Only… The woman gathered in his arms was a lovely bouquet of delicate flowers. A heady combination of roses and fresh air and—Tuesday. Her slender fingers tightened on his arms, and he fell in love with her all over again. How could he let her go now that he knew what it was like to hold her? He was just a man, and men were weaker than shit. Everyone knew that and…

This had to end. Right now. He couldn't let himself be trapped again. *No. Just, no.*

But… Caught in the rapture of simply holding her, of nearly surrounding her much smaller frame inside the study shelter of his larger body, Grissom inhaled the essence of the fragile, yet stronger-than-shit woman in his arms. The professional who'd loved his boys before she'd known them. Was that reason enough to entice her to stay? Grissom answered his own question by whispering, "How do you like your steak? Well done, medium, medium rare, or—"

"Just take me back to my car after I see Tanner's pictures, please."

"No," he answered, keeping his tone neutral but his answer sure. "You're as bad as me, Tuesday, setting boundaries that keep everyone away. But I see you. I mean, I see me in you. That might not make sense, but I can tell you're scared. Well, I'm scared, too, but like I tell my boys, it's okay to be scared, and it's okay to cry, and it's okay to…"

Jesus, where was I going with this?

"I am scared," she admitted quietly, still not facing him. "I fell in love at first sight with your sons, but that's why I have to leave. If I stay here any longer, I'm afraid—"

"That you might fall in love with me?" As conceited as it made him sound, Grissom had to know.

Tuesday didn't answer. Instead, she relinquished her ten-point grip on his arms and twisted around until she was facing him, looking up at him. Her fingers were now splayed softly over his chest, and she was so beautiful. Her green eyes were red-rimmed and glistening, and he could feel her pounding heart against his. He'd never felt so alive. There he stood, heart-to-heart, with the angel who'd dashed to his sons' rescue, instead of the manipulative, malicious troll who'd only ever seen dollar signs when she'd looked at him.

Tuesday wasn't Pam. Why couldn't he get that through his hard head? Not all women were evil. He knew that. She didn't fit the paradigm, not at all. Looking down into her delicate features, her pert turned-up nose, and the tiny freckles scattered over it like cinnamon sprinkles, was like diving head-first off that eighty-five-foot-high cliff in Hawaii. The one his Army buddy had called the Leap of Faith.

Grissom had been an arrogant, headstrong fool that day, cowed into a dangerous, risky dive by his pride. But when his buddy, Wade Kekoa, had explained how his last name meant *'warrior'* in native Hawaiian, well, Grissom couldn't NOT jump. He was a warrior, too, damn it, and he'd had to prove it. His reputation came down to a few foolish seconds of dive-or-die. So he'd dived.

The rush of that headlong dive from a ragged lava ledge was still the damnedest ten-second thrill of his life. The heart-stopping sensation of falling to his death, then fighting the ruthless undertow once he'd survived that fall and resurfaced, had nearly done him in. But after the success of living through the fall, came the first gulp of fresh air and the euphoria of being a no-kidding winner. Along with that realization came a powerful surge of invincibility and confidence.

For the first time in his life, Grissom had faced death and spit in its eye, and he'd won, damn it. High on that ledge, alone in the moment, he'd conquered fear and cowardice and a slew of the other negative shit in his life. By hell, yeah, he'd jumped. He'd literally taken that Leap of Faith dive by the balls and...

Speaking of leaping...

Grissom knew he'd lose Tuesday forever if he let her push away now. Very gently, ever so carefully, he pulled her tiny body flush against his chest and his damned randy cock. The belligerent thing thought it had a chance of seeing daylight the way it was twitching for attention. Couldn't have been more embarrassing if it screamed, *'Here I am! Pick me, me, me, me, me!'*

Shut the hell up!

"Grissom," Tuesday whispered, her chin up and her head tipped back to maintain eye contact. "I refuse to trap you like Pam did. That's why she called when you were deployed to Syria, wasn't it? I can only imagine how she worded it, but that's when she told you that you were a father, right?"

He tossed a quick glance over his shoulder to make sure his sons weren't within range of hearing. Not that they'd understand, but kids were smarter than people gave them credit for. Thankfully, Tuesday kept her voice low too because...

Duh. She cares about your boys as much as you do.

"True," Grissom admitted quietly. He opened his mouth to explain how he believed Pam had gotten herself pregnant, but he clapped it shut. Loose lips still sunk ships, and he didn't want to sink the McCoy ship now that it was actually afloat again. So he nodded, then wondered if Tuesday could read his mind.

"I can't do that to you. Yes, I care for you." Those intelligent, alert, ever watchful, green eyes maintained contact with his. "You've endured unimaginable betrayal, Grissom. You're almost as good a father as my dad was, and you say all the right things, but—"

"Forget about everything and everybody else." Damned if he didn't sound like his family counselor. Which was unfathomably weird. Him, imparting wisdom? Did. Not. Compute. But there he was. Willing to do anything to keep Tuesday, at least for the night. "Focus on what you feel right now, not yesterday, not even this morning. You feel it, too, the electricity buzzing between us. Don't you?"

She blinked, and he saw it then. The young woman in his arms was afraid of him. Not that he'd hurt her, but because...

Oh, my God! Grissom nearly smacked his forehead when his messed-up brain solved the biggest riddle in his life.

Tuesday, the ballsy woman who'd taken down Maeve Astor...

Tuesday Smart, the savvy, sophisticated, world-renowned photographer...

The woman who'd captured some of the planet's most amazing, powerful images of different peoples, animals, and the effects of changing climates across the Earth...

The barely out of high school young lady who'd made headlines when she'd married that older-than-dirt guy from New York City…

Oh, my God! Grissom should've known! He should've guessed! Or something. But at last, he was finally seeing past the very mature woman in his arms to the little girl behind that sophisticated mask, pressed against his bigger, stronger, definitely, all-male body. He got it. He finally got it.

Taking a full step back, he crouched to her eye level to see into those intelligent green depths when she answered his next question. "You've never been with a man, have you?"

One of her hands knifed up, shielding her face from his scrutiny. "No, I, uh…"

He knew it! He was right, and it made sense, given her messed-up history. She'd gone from being an average high school girl to an orphan, and from there, she'd been sucked into a phony marriage with that billionaire dude. Most recently, she'd worked for yet another older man, who'd sent her to the farthest, most isolated parts of the world. Where she'd had a gnat's chance in hell of meeting a man of her caliber, much less dating anyone. Much less experiencing… *that.*

Oh, my God. Oh, my God. Oh, my God.

"Tuesday, look at me," Grissom urged, gently cupping her jaw and using the soft pressure of his thumbs to tilt her chin up. "Please, love. Take a chance on me. I don't bite."

It took a few seconds before she blew out a soft breath and summoned the strength to do what he asked. By then, she was a leaf fluttering in the wind, her mask gone and tears on the verge of streaming down her cheeks. She knew that he knew her deepest, darkest secret. The sweet knowledge of who and what he had in his arms was inexplicably, magnificently, all Grissom had ever wanted. He could barely make out the details of her pretty face through the blur brimming his own eyes. God, he was a sap, crying like a two-year-old in front of this woman. But the idea that, here stood the most remarkable person he'd ever met, and that she was untouched and pure, floored the hell out of him. He should have run the other way and never looked back. He was still who he was, and Tuesday Smart deserved so much better.

But there he stood, once again looking over the edge of the biggest drop-off of his life, facing another Leap of Faith. Was he brave enough to take the jump and encourage Tuesday to jump with him? To stay with him, maybe forever? Oh, hell, yes. If a simple, frightening plunge off some cliff in Hawaii could fill him with euphoria like it had, he could only imagine what falling in love with Tuesday would bring.

He'd already fallen several times today. Now, he just needed her to fall with him.

Cautiously, trying his damnedest not to frighten her, Grissom pulled Tuesday under his chin and wrapped his arms around the sweetest woman he'd ever met. "Don't cry, love. I've got no resistance, and my boys will think you hurt me, if they see me bawling like a little baby, and—"

"They adore you, Grissom."

"I think they actually adore you more. Me, they just *endure* because I feed them," he murmured into the top of her head. "You wouldn't mind hanging around a little longer to find out what this feeling between us is, would you?" He felt like his boys when they begged, 'Please, oh please.'

"I don't think that's a good idea," she whispered into his neck, her breath a warm balm that threatened to unman

Grissom. "It'll give Tanner and Luke the wrong impression, and they've been through enough. They deserve better than us leading them on."

He played the only card he had left, simply lowered his head and placed a whisper of a kiss on her forehead. Keeping his mouth there, he begged, "Stay with us, Tuesday. Just for one night. Please. I've got extra beds. You'll be safe and sound. I'll stay in my room, or better yet, you can sleep in there. The bed's bigger and my boys will love sleeping with you. We'll tell them it's too late for you to leave so we're having a sleepover. It'll be a good way to end their day. What have you got to lose?"

Tuesday looked up at him then, blinking hard, trying to keep her tears from falling. "My heart," she whispered in a soft, tired voice. "I've only ever given it to my dad. What if…?"

And Grissom melted. Tipping into her, he pressed his lips to her forehead again and asked, "You didn't love that older guy you married, did you?"

"Not like that, no. He was good to me, but Freddie was more like a grandfather. He spoiled me and he took care of me. He paid for me to attend the best university and he… he kept me safe."

Thank God. "I'm not asking for forever, love. Just one night. After Walker and Persia go home, and once the boys fall asleep, we'll talk. Just talk. I think once we get a few things out in the open, you'll feel better, at least, more at ease. Okay? Give me a chance to prove I'm not always the idiot I was earlier."

Her chest heaved with a silent chuckle. "I never thought you were an idiot."

"Well, I am," he declared. "What do you think? Stay a little longer? It'd sure make Tanner and Luke happy. Err, damn it. I'm sorry. I wasn't going to use them to get you to stay, but I just did that. Shit." He raked his fingers over his head.

"Shush," she soothed, her fingers intertwined with his, in his hair, massaging the scalp he'd just scraped.

"Fu-u-u-u-ck…" whispered out of his mouth. "Don't stop." *Please, for the love of God, don't stop.*

With one touch of Tuesday's gentle fingers, Grissom's eyes rolled back in his head, and he became the ugly dog that hadn't been petted in years. Maybe never, sure not the way she was touching him. And just that fast, he knew why dogs' rear legs thumped when someone finally stooped down to talk to them and pet them. To reach out, take a chance, and touch them. His inner dog's leg wasn't the only thing twitching.

"You like that?" she asked, her breath warm and moist on his chin.

"Not as much as I like this," he replied huskily, his mouth hovering over hers, not quite touching, but giving her the chance to decide for herself. When her chin tipped up, Grissom lowered his mouth to hers and kissed her as chastely as she deserved. Thoroughly, yet gently. Not a hint of tongue against her tightly-sealed lips. Could this be her first kiss? How was that possible? But a man could hope.

"They're here!" Luke announced at the top of his lungs, damn it, breaking what for Grissom, had been a life-changing moment.

Most guys would've panicked and jerked away from Tuesday, distancing themselves to protect their manly image at the cost of hers. Grissom stayed where he was, facing her with his arms around her. One glance at his boys told him all he needed to know. Luke was focused on getting to the front door before his brother did, but Tanner's eyes were wide with surprise. He'd seen his dad kissing Tuesday, and the kid was grinning like a lunatic. Precisely what Grissom needed—encouragement from the six-year-old little man in his life.

He pressed a more casual kiss to Tuesday's temple and whispered, "Looks like we just got caught, love. Do you mind?"

She gave her head a slight shake and whispered back, "Not at all. I love your boys with all my heart, Grissom. I think they saved me at the same time I saved them."

He had to agree. "Funny how love works. They've been saving me for years."

Luke was at the door by then, not quite able to reach the knob and half turned around to make sure he beat Tanner. Reluctantly, Grissom released the miracle in his arms and told his youngest son, "You know the rule, Short Stack. I answer doors."

"Yeah, only Dad," Tanner taunted in his know-it-all, big brother voice.

"But I wanna see Uncle Walker first!" Luke squealed, bouncing at the still-closed door. "I know it's him! I already seen Aunt Persia! I don't hafta look out that teeny hole like Daddy does. I seen them out the window, and they wanna come in and play with me!"

Grissom made short work of that argument, swinging Luke off the floor and onto his shoulder. "What's the rule?"

Luke growled. "You hafta look out that stupid, tiny little old hole before anyone kin even open the door and come in, even when I already seen who's out there."

"And why do we follow rules in this house?"

Another grumpy growl percolated out of Luke. "So nobody can never steal me or Tanner again. Not never."

"Very good," Grissom praised his youngest troublemaker. "Hey, since you're sitting high enough to see, why don't you look through the peephole and tell me if Walker and Persia are still there. Look carefully. We don't want to let any trolls inside."

Luke and Tanner both giggled, but Luke tipped obediently forward, slapped both hands beside the peephole, stuck his nose to the door, and grumbled, "I don't see nothing. Oh, wait! Yeah, I kin see Uncle Walker, but not Aunt Persia now, and—Oh, Daddy! Uncle Harley's hairy eyeball's staring at me. He's here, too. Let me down! I wanna get down!"

Swinging his excited youngest over the top of his head but then tucking him under his arm before Luke could wiggle away, Grissom entered the security code into the panel behind the door and opened his home to his friends. Sure enough, not only Uncle Walker and Aunt Persia were there, but Uncle Harley, Aunt Judy, cousins Alex and Georgie, as well as Uncle Maverick, Aunt China, and cousin Kyrie. All TEAM members were called aunts or uncles, and Grissom made sure his boys addressed them respectfully.

"Come on in," he told his visitors. "Got someone I want you to meet."

As soon as he cleared the door, Maverick spied Tuesday standing back from the now-crowded entry. Off came his Stetson, he nodded politely and said, "Sure good seeing you here, ma'am."

She shrugged almost apologetically. But when Maverik headed toward her, Grissom made short work of the distance between that tall, lanky cowboy and his woman. *His woman*, damn it. "Folks, meet Tuesday Smart," he said, marching to her side and snagging her by her waist. "Tuesday, you already met Maverick, and—"

"And I'm China, his wife, and this is Kyrie, our daughter." China was dressed in her usual, western shirt over jeans and cowboy boots. Kyrie sported jeans, boots, and a t-shirt advertising her kitten sanctuary. They both had the same long hair trailing like ebony ribbons down their backs.

The lanky guy with the Texas twang followed the Carsons with, "Harley, ma'am." He tipped two fingertips to his forehead in respect. "This pretty lady here's my better half, Judy, and those two monsters are Little A and Georgie. Boys, hats off, and remember to use your inside voices, understood?"

Both boys doffed their cowboy hats and answered, "Yes, Dad."

Oh, yeah. Little A. That was Harley's son's nickname, not just Alex. That'd be too confusing, and Grissom didn't need to be more confused than he was. Little A was the quieter twin who'd answered politely. Georgie was the opposite, prone to cause trouble, just as prone to roughhouse no matter where he was. He'd said the right words, but his answer carried a ton of mischievous sarcasm.

Judy's dark red hair was pulled back in a no-nonsense bun at the nape of her neck. Of the four Mortimers, she was the boss and Harley knew it. Within seconds of his introductions, Tuesday found herself surrounded by Persia, China, and Judy, all jabbering at once, like women do. Made Grissom's heart swell seeing how quickly these wives accepted her.

She might not realize it yet, but she'd just been adopted into the highest order of sisterhood. TEAM sisterhood. Nothing stronger in the world.

Chapter Fifteen

Tuesday hadn't felt this much at home in a very long time. Not because Grissom's house was filled to the brim, though it was. He and the men were on the porch, no doubt talking about work, sports, or other guy things. Tanner and Luke had run for the master bedroom with Maverick's daughter and Harley's boys, where they were no doubt absorbed in some video game. Harley and Judy's boys were fraternal twins, one named after Harley's father, the other after Alex Stewart, which told Tuesday how close Harley and his boss were.

Tuesday felt at home simply because the wives had migrated with her into Grissom's kitchen. She'd overheard Harley ordering pizzas as soon as he'd arrived, with extra-large everything. She'd only intended to fix a vegetable tray to go along with all that greasy, cheesy sausage and pepperoni. But China, Judy, and Persia had taken over, and now a fruit tray was also in progress, and steaks were definitely off the menu.

While China washed the bags of carrots she'd pulled from Grissom's refrigerator, she explained how Persia used to work for the CIA, DEA, and a couple other federal agencies, before she'd wised up and joined The TEAM.

"Which is why she's so quiet," Judy teased, slicing two bunches of celery into petite finger lengths on a bamboo cutting board. "She's afraid she'll spill top-secrets if she starts talking."

"Then she'll have to kill us," China stage-whispered.

Persia smiled from the sink where she was rinsing the bag of red and golden delicious apples she'd found in Grissom's well-stocked pantry.

"I'm impressed with this guy," Judy declared, as she lopped off the root end of a celery bunch. "If I'd sent Maverick to the store to get something for dinner, he'd come back with a ten-pound slab of bacon and half a beef. But Grissom's kitchen is stocked full of healthy things. Did you see his pantry? The man has a bin of Yukon potatoes in there, and, get this, yams. Real yams. Not canned."

Tuesday instantly rose to Grissom's defense, "Of course. He's a dad. Grissom takes especially good care of his boys, that's all." She wanted to add, *'So what?'* But figured that might come off snarky, and she didn't want to offend Grissom's friends.

Now slicing the carrots she'd lined up on the countertop into finger-sized sticks, China went on about how Judy had first met Harley at Mark and Libby's wedding. How she'd met Maverick when he'd shown up, out of the blue, one day in Wyoming, and saved her and her horse.

She reminded Tuesday of an over-confident girl from her soccer playing days, that one from an opposing team. Jenny was as much a tomboy as Tuesday had once been, and she'd loved their games together. Jenny was all about the sport, the rivalry, and the competition, which meant they were evenly matched. Other teenage girls had pictures of movie stars or boy-bands taped up on their bedroom walls. Tuesday had eight-by-twelve glossies of Lionel Messi of Barcelona.

Cristiano Ronaldo of Real Madrid, and Manuel Neuer of Bayern Munich. Real men. Famous soccer players who played and worked hard. Not pretty boys. She'd never been attracted to a guy's looks as much as his strength, skill, and that elusive something that Shane, Heston, and Alex had. That Grissom had in spades. That innate male quality that told the world to 'shove it' with just a glance. That told weaker men and women to step up, man up, and amount to something. Tuesday could almost hear Grissom's favorite F-bombs interspersed in that description.

"Yup, that cowboy just showed up out of nowhere and started digging Star and me out of that landslide," China mumbled around the thin slice of carrot she was taste-testing. "We had torrential rain that spring and the hillsides were saturated. You know Star, the handsome gelding you thought was going to devour Luke this morning? Maverick's quite taken with you, girlfriend."

Tuesday jolted out of her head and back into the kitchen. A definite glimmer of mischief sparkled in China's deep blue eyes, but Tuesday didn't rise to the challenge. "Star's a very handsome, umm, kid. Tanner sure likes him."

"Yeah, well, Tanner likes all my kids, and they like Grissom's boys. Those three are regulars. They ride a couple times each week. You should join them."

"Mmmm," was all Tuesday would say on that subject. Horseback riding with Grissom and his boys on a regular basis meant staying, and staying meant putting down roots, at the least, renting an apartment. That wasn't happening. Her feelings for Grissom didn't equate to a future with him and his sons, and it'd be presumptuous to think they did. It'd be better if she left before this "thing" between them turned sour or—worse.

Liking a man, any man, would make him a target for the relentless tragedy stalking her, and she knew better than to hold onto anyone too tightly or for too long. Grissom had just found his lost boys; he needed them more than he needed her. She'd get through dinner, but that was it. She loved Tanner and Luke enough to let them go. Love hurt, but sometimes, it killed. She refused to take the chance.

Jolting out of the depressing plans for her future, Tuesday found herself in the middle of Judy telling how Harley'd been in a massive accident outside DC a few years ago. How his Jeep had gotten totaled, and he'd suffered a serious head injury. How he'd returned to the apartment they'd shared while she was at work and taken his weapons and enough ammunition to start a small war. Once she'd gotten home and couldn't raise him on his cell phone, she'd gone to her least favorite TEAM member for help—the Boss, as his employees still called Alex Stewart—whom she'd intensely disliked at the time.

"Why didn't you like Alex?" Tuesday asked. "I've met him. He's harmless. In fact, he was quite the gentleman when I visited him and Kelsey." Since the other women had taken over the vegetable and fruit trays, she was carefully spreading thin layers of cream cheese over ham slices. Who didn't like ham roll-ups?

"He was so darned bossy then, and he thought he knew better than everyone else, including me. Besides—"

"Harley kind of had a thing for Alex's wife back then," China cut in nonchalantly, as if she'd just mentioned a change in the weather instead of what sounded like Judy's husband's infidelity. "Not like he'd ever acted on it. Harley would never, but you have to understand that before Judy met him, he'd been dealing with an extreme case of PTSD, made worse by him self-medicating with some hardcore drugs and—"

"Who's telling this story?" Judy bit out, the knife in her hand now pointed at China. "Me or you?"

China tipped her head back and laughed. "You are, Miss Touchy Pants," she said, aiming a dripping wet carrot at Tuesday in return. "Before you get any more involved with Grissom, you need to understand that every single one of us TEAM wives are as bad-assed as our husbands."

Tuesday set China straight. "I'm not involved with Grissom."

"We have to be bad-assed," Persia interjected quietly, slicing each peeled and cored apple into petite wedges. "We can't help it. We're attracted to strong men, to alphas. Not to mention we've all been through some bad shit ourselves, and some of us just turned out a little meaner because of it."

China hip-checked Judy. "And kinder. At least, I'm kinder. Not sure about the rest of you."

"Did you happen to see any caramel dip in the refrigerator?" Persia asked China.

"Sure. Two tubs. You want both?"

"Yes, please. I've got enough apples for two trays."

"Here you go."

"Thanks."

"Sheesh!" Judy hissed, "Do you ladies mind if I finish telling my story?"

Both China and Persia laughed. It was easy to see that, despite their rowdy version of sisterly comradery, these women cared for each other. Judy hadn't sounded angry as much as flustered with the persistent interruptions. She started again with, "Anyway—"

"Anyway, that was only misplaced affection on Harley's part," China cut in with a mischievous sparkle in her eyes, "for the woman whose life he saved. It happens between doctors and patients all the time."

"Or nurses and patients," quiet Persia added.

"Wait." Tuesday cocked her head to make sure she'd heard right. "Harley saved Kelsey's life? When?" This she had to hear.

"And here we go again," Judy grumbled, aiming an exaggerated huff at the ceiling. "Yes, my husband had a thing for Kelsey. Yes, he saved her life before Alex finally married her. Alex and Kelsey were in the Pacific Northwest when everything went bad. He was in critical shape that night, so he sent Harley to find her. To save her. Her worthless ex kidnapped her after that worthless scum and his White Supremist buddies nearly beat Alex to death. When Harley finally located Kelsey, the first thing he did was snipe that asshole ex of hers and the jerks with him. Don't get me wrong. It's not like they weren't armed to the teeth. They were, but Harley took them out before they knew what was happening.

Judy's pride in her husband was easy to read.

"By then, poor Kelsey was in a bad way. Harley was afraid she wouldn't live to make it back to the Search and Rescue team. Alex had already been life-flighted to the nearest hospital, and… damn it!" Judy threw up both hands at the ceiling. "I know it was displaced affection! I know he loves me and his sons more than he loves anyone else! But just once, just once—!"

"You wish I'd shut my big mouth and leave Kelsey out of it, right?" China asked, leaning into Judy and wrapping an arm around her shoulder.

Judy didn't answer. The cords in her neck were tight and her face was red. Which for a redhead, meant she was scarlet.

"But leaving out the Harley and Kelsey connection isn't telling the whole story, sweetheart," China murmured. "He was pretty messed up when you fell in love with him, just like Grissom is now."

"I know. Except Grissom never did drugs like Harley did," Judy admitted surly.

That perked up Tuesday's ears. "Excuse me? Grissom isn't messed up. He just went through a lot of crap, that's all. So did his boys. And he doesn't do drugs. They're all getting better. But healing from abuse takes time, and his boys are happy again. He's the best father I've ever known, well, except for my dad. Surely you can all see that."

Grinning, China hip-checked Judy again. "What'd I tell you?"

Persia's big brown eyes were now fixed on Tuesday. "Damn, you're right. It's about time."

Judy just grinned.

Tuesday tossed her head, embarrassed she'd snapped at them for no reason other than they were discussing Grissom and his boys, and that needed to stop. The McCoy men were off-limits.

China chuckled. "You're not going to stand there and tell us you don't care for Grissom, are you?"

Tuesday's mouth went dry. That was exactly what she'd already done and intended to do again. "Umm…"

"I knew it!" Judy crowed. "You like him. A lot. I'm so happy. That man needs a real woman in his life for once. Talk, girlfriend. We want the deets."

But talking about Grissom behind his back was the last thing Tuesday would do. "Of course I like him; I like everybody. This is the first day we've had a chance to talk since Costa Rica, and he's been more concerned with his boys than me. As he should be, and…" She was rambling and suddenly as flustered as Judy'd been minutes ago. Judy, whose beautiful, piercing green eyes were right then looking straight through Tuesday.

A wave of prickly, warm embarrassment swept up her neck, and too soon her face would be as flushed as Judy's. Darn it. There was no way out, so Tuesday plowed through like Freddie had taught her. Swallowing hard, she admitted, "Yes, okay. I've liked Grissom since I first saw him. He was so gentle with his boys, and they were so traumatized. It was hard not to fall in—"

Screech! Hold the phone. You're not—in—love. You. Just. Met. Him.

"Stop it," Persia said, her voice commandingly soft. "Stop interrogating Tuesday. Don't mind us, honey. We're just nosy old women who talk too much" —she glared at Judy when she said that— "and we've all stood right where you're standing now. Just know that, no matter how things turn out between you and Grissom, you'll always have us. I, for one, am happy to finally meet the woman who took out that bitch, Maeve Astor. Heston brags all the time about how calm you were during that encounter in Little Rock. Do you believe in destiny?"

That question came out of left field. "No," Tuesday answered cautiously, not sure where Persia was headed. "Not after the life I've had. If that's destiny, you can keep it."

"I believe in destiny," Judy admitted softly. "Destiny's what brought Harley back home to me after that awful wreck nearly destroyed our lives. For a while, he didn't know who I was. Do you have any idea how awful that felt?"

Tuesday nodded. But at least Harley had remembered. Her mom and dad and Freddie weren't coming back. Couldn't.

"It sure as hell was destiny that brought Maverick all the way from Virginia to my ranch in Wyoming, on what could've been a very, very bad day," China said, her tone tender for the first time tonight. "I never would've been able to dig Star out of that landslide by myself. I had no cell service, not as high up on the hill as we were. It was steep and, once that hill let loose, it was muddy and…" It took a long moment before she added, "Yup. I believe in destiny. Star and I wouldn't be here today if Maverick hadn't been there to rescue us. That exact morning. On that exact hill. Jesus!" China dashed a hand at her eyes. "I owe that man in there everything."

Tuesday had no idea what to say, so she said nothing.

"I'm just as sure it was destiny that brought Walker to my beach in Florida," Persia whispered. "He'd just swum all the way from Cuba, alone, without back-up or a swim buddy. He was exhausted, and he could've chosen any strip of sand to land on, but he… he chose my beach. And I just happened to be there that day. Normally, I would've been in Washington, D.C. If that isn't destiny, I don't know what is."

Tuesday had nothing to contribute. She didn't know these women well enough to call them girlfriends. Sure, they were amicable enough, and their husbands were hotties, each an outstanding definition of hunk all by himself. But she could never believe in the abstract called destiny. Her life hadn't been easy, and everything she'd lived through hadn't been fair. She'd lost her parents too early in life and then Freddie. She'd been slandered by the press and hunted by the FBI, both because Astor had framed her for murders she'd committed out of her insane jealousy. If destiny was the driving force behind the horrors that were her life, Tuesday wanted nothing to do with it. Destiny was as bad as love. Not worth the risk.

Chapter Sixteen

Grissom stood half-in, half outside the kitchen door, like a stalker, listening to the wives discuss destiny. His boys were on his bedroom floor, happily playing Minecraft with Harley's boys. Grissom had split the game into four windows on the big screen. Kyrie and Luke were teamed up, hunting frogs, pigs, and sheep, while Little A was studiously building a mancave to survive the monsters that came out at night. Tanner and Georgie were going after the Sculk Shriekers, in order to summon and fight the Warden, or die, which was what usually happened. Each kid had a plate of pizza and a bottled water—with the lids loosened, not off. Grissom had just peeked in and left a barrel of popcorn for when the pizza ran out.

Now, he'd just overheard what Tuesday said about destiny: *"Not after the life I've had. If that's destiny, you can keep it."*

He agreed with her. Believing in destiny was, at best, a fool's gambit, a dangerous risk, and a dare. It was nothing more than believing in predetermination, that the gods or fates—or some other omniscient being—had set mankind on a course over which he had no say or control. Made a guy sound like a brainless marionette, stupidly dancing his heart out, at the end of someone else's string. Not Grissom.

He made his own decisions, damn it, and to prove it, he strode into his kitchen, snagged Tuesday by her waist, dipped her over his arm, and planted his lips on hers. Not passionately or rudely, like a sloppy jerk in a bar might, but softly and sweetly, which she deserved. Tuesday's history was as bad as his, and he refused to add to her feeling like she didn't belong anywhere. She did belong, by hell. With him. To him. And he wanted the world to know and the TEAM wives to see. Because these women would talk to their husbands, who'd talk among themselves, and before you know it, everyone at TEAM HQ would understand where Tuesday belonged. Did that make him a caveman? Grissom didn't care. He'd cared about the wrong shit for too long. Not anymore.

This chaste kiss was the start of something he and she could work on and work out. No one could ever treat her as good as he and his sons would, and he intended to prove it. This was the beginning of their life together. He'd been duped into a loveless marriage, and she'd been battered by the wicked hands of fate or destiny or, shit, whatever. Grissom didn't need destiny—or *density*—to tell him what to do. The self-demeaning crap that had defined his entire life stopped now. He wanted Tuesday, and together, they'd make their own way in this messed-up world, and it'd be good. Make that great. Damned great.

But this kiss… Her sigh… The feel of her delicate body laid back in his arm. It took Grissom a helluva lot longer to pull back from Tuesday's sweet mouth than he'd planned. He swore he could smell roses even as he tasted strawberries. Plush, juicy strawberries he wanted to bite into and savor. His tongue pressed the seam of her lips, asking for entry. Daring to at least try, to coax her into giving in to him. Just enough to let him know she was feeling the same electrical current he was.

The wives were still out there somewhere, watching and whispering, but he couldn't bear to end the sweetest kiss of his life. Not as limp as Tuesday had gone in his arm. Not as easily as she'd just sighed. The taste of her was temptation defined. A man could get addicted to the delectable, slippery sensation of her tongue tentatively tasting his bottom lip. Was she asking permission to explore?

Oh, yes, ma'am, permission granted. He opened his mouth and was instantly lost in the timid inquisition of the tip of her tongue tasting his. Of her trembling. Of her heart pounding so hard he could hear it. Of his bigger, stronger muscles flexing to reassure her that she could trust him, that he'd never let her fall.

"Ahem," someone behind him murmured.

Tuesday gasped into his mouth, and Grissom couldn't help but grin, like a little boy caught with his hand in the cookie jar. He'd finally done it, found the only woman he wanted to let into his life. Into his boys' lives. Barely pulling back, he refused the slippery panic inching up his spine. He didn't care if he'd made the wives uncomfortable. He couldn't release Tuesday, wouldn't dream of it. Not now. Damned if the confounded relentless panic pounding in his head didn't cease the moment he whispered into her awe-struck face, "No worries, love. I've got you. Trust me, I won't ever let you fall."

It hadn't been a no-holds-barred kiss. If anything, it'd been damned tame. Yet she lay there dazed, quiet as a mouse, blinking up at him through hooded eyes, her lips glistening from his mouth, and the prettiest pink glow on her face.

"Grissom," she answered breathily—softly, almost reverently—making it sound like a prayer. Not that she was praying to him, oh, hell no. He could never compete with the Man Upstairs, but maybe her prayer had been *about* him? *For* him? Maybe because she wanted him to kiss her again? That much was written on her face, and the light shining out of her startled green eyes made him want to beat his chest like Tarzan.

The noose his mother had been strangling him with for years fell away. His diaphragm expanded, then contracted. His lungs finally had enough room to breathe. As they filled again, Grissom knew—he just knew—he would marry this woman someday soon. This time, he wouldn't need to be drunk to do it. Now was not the time to ask, but—fuck! How many times in one day could he fall for this woman? Didn't matter. He'd keep falling as long as Tuesday kept catching him. What they had was a two-way thing called trust. He'd never let her fall, and if he messed up, she'd catch him. They'd survive. Somehow. Together.

Manfully, and with great care, he settled Tuesday onto her feet, then pulled her under his arm before she could get away. Not that she tried. No way she could fall now. Tuesday was breathing hard, and he knew he'd embarrassed her. He might've ruined his chance with her, but—

"Oh, my," purred out of her pretty mouth. "Let's do that again."

Not a nasty word. Not a hint of the crushing disgust that would've poured out of his wife's ugly mouth. But that word—*wife*—would soon apply to Tuesday. Until this claiming kiss, it'd been nothing but an anchor around his neck. A curse. But now? Grissom knew he'd never mean it the way he'd meant it with the witch who would forevermore be known as *What's-Her-Name*. Or—better yet—*What's-Her-Fuckin' Name*. Yeah. That fit better.

"You liked that?" he asked quietly.

"Yes," she breathed, her fingertips on her swollen lips. "I did."

When he finally pulled his gaze from Tuesday, Grissom found China, Judy, and Persia blocking the doorway to the kitchen, as if keeping others from intruding. China and Judy were smiling, but Persia's eyes glistened. "That was beautiful, Grissom," she whispered, her fingers fluttering over her heart. "There's nothing sexier than a man who isn't afraid to show how much he loves his woman."

"You have no idea," Grissom muttered, his voice gravelly and his eyes as misty as hers.

"Yes, I do, and I'm glad I was here to see it. Walker's been so worried about you. Do you have any idea how much you mean to us? To all of us? How important you are?"

"Well, ahh, err…" He didn't want to make this moment about him, not after he'd just admitted he loved Tuesday—before he'd told her. "No."

"Well, you are, you big dumb ox," China grouched. "It's about time you pulled your head out of your ass and realized how much everyone cares about you. And if you ever try that stunt again—"

"What stunt?"

"Driving drunk and slamming into the rear end of a truck!" China had a soft touch for her horses. Not so much with people. "How do you think you got that knot on your head?"

He ran his free hand up the back of his neck, to the ever-present bump on the back of his skull. He knew he'd hit a FedEx truck when he'd crashed. Also knew the bump wasn't as big or as tender today as it had been weeks ago. His skull was slowly healing, but Doc said the knot on that bone might never disappear completely. Come to think of it, he vaguely recalled being tasered by a cop that same night. Also knew the shock-and-awe of getting stunned hadn't slowed him down, which was telling. The only people who didn't go down when hit with a modulated electrical current designed to incapacitate a person's neuromuscular reflexes, were meth heads. Idiots who were so wired, they were out of their minds.

"You don't remember anything about the night you wrecked, do you?" China's voice softened.

"No, but that's why my bike's in the shop," he replied. Walker had told him that much during a quiet come-to-Jesus moment on the flight home from Central America. If he played this right, China might tell him everything else that happened that night. Like why he'd been drunk in the first place. What had kicked off the night of mayhem that ended with him incarcerated in Shady Hell Sanitarium, or whatever the place was called. And why hadn't that taser knocked him flat on his ass? Or out?

"But we're working on getting those memories back, aren't we, Grissom?" Tuesday interrupted his nefarious plan to bait China, her palm soft and sweet on his jaw. It felt like an angel had reached from heaven and was touching him.

Grissom looked down at the prettiest woman in the world. Tuesday didn't seem to care who was watching, just kept stroking his jaw, as if she knew how much he needed her hand on him. He pressed her other hand to his mouth and kissed the middle of her palm. He didn't need any answers from China. Not anymore.

"Knock, knock," Walker announced from behind the ladies. "This a private party or can anyone join?"

Persia turned into him, and the moment Walker looked at his wife, a colder-than-shit threat arrowed across the room at Grissom. "What did you do?" he hissed.

"Grissom didn't do anything," Persia murmured. "He and Tuesday just had a moment, honey, and I… I'm…" She stalled. Her chin tilted up to Walker. "I'm pregnant," she stage-whispered.

He wrapped her inside his well-muscled arms. "I know, sweetheart."

"Well, I didn't!" Judy snapped. "You are? Really, Persia? No wine for you."

"Finally!" China declared triumphantly. "That's why you're so quiet tonight."

Which made Tuesday laugh, and damned if her plump breasts mashing against Grissom's ribs didn't turn him hard. It was good everyone's attention was now focused on someone else. It gave him time to adjust the spike in his pants. Just that fast, his brain threw out a picture of Tuesday with her belly big and round with his child—their child—up on the flat screen inside his head. Was he crazy? Definitely. But the image of a possible future with her was incentive enough. His swimmers were powerful. He could knock her up in no time.

Shaking that crazy notion off, Grissom closed the short distance to Walker and Persia with Tuesday still under his arm. He stuck out his hand and declared, "Congrats, brother. I'm happy for you."

"*We're* happy for both of you," Tuesday corrected, her hand outstretched to Persia.

We're. Grissom loved the way that dripped off Tuesday's tongue.

"You should've been sitting down instead of standing at the sink," she scolded Persia. "I could've sliced those apples. Are you feeling okay? Does your back hurt?"

Persia grinned as she squeezed Tuesday's fingers. "I'm fine, really. I'm just three months along, but we figured tonight I could safely spill the beans."

Grumbling like the over-attentive watchdog he was, Walker splayed his fingers over her barely-there belly. "No spilling beans, babe. Baby Bean needs to stay where he is for two more trimesters. At least."

Chuckling, Persia leaned into Tuesday and said, "Morning sickness isn't for the weak of heart. If I'd known how much vomiting I'd be doing, all day, every day, I would've—"

"It's a boy!" Walker interrupted. "We're having a boy!"

"A baby boy," Tuesday whispered. The tremor of want inside those three words had Grissom pulling her in tighter. He knew how to make boys. What if—?

No. Impossible. No. Just no.

By then, Maverick and Harley were at the counter nibbling veggie sticks and fruit slices. Maverick pointed a carrot stick at his wife. "Don't you have something to share with these women, also known as your sisters by other mothers?"

China turned into a red-faced teenager with G U I L T Y stamped across her forehead. Her shoulders lifted with an I-don't-care, it's-not-important shrug. Until she said, "Me, too,

Persia. And Judy. And Tuesday. Only two months, but yeah—
"

"You're both prego and neither of you told me?" Judy shrieked. "What am I? Chopped liver?"

"No, babe, you're prime rib, all the way," Harley spouted, as if calling his wife a cut of beef was in any way romantic.

Tuesday giggled.

Judy told Harley to, "Shut up! These are my girlfriends, Harley. Do not objectify—!"

Just that fast, he was off the stool and kissing his wife, too. She melted into him the same way Persia had with Walker.

Grissom turned to Walker, grinning while the Mortimers mugged each other. "Sorry I've been an ass."

"You've been through a ton of shit, I get it. I'm sorry we couldn't find your boys sooner. That would've been a better way for you to come to, after the hit you took."

"Yeah, about that, why was I drunk that night?" Grissom asked, needing to know.

Walker's entire body flexed with a huge sigh. His chin sank into his petite wife's shoulder, whose eyes were on Grissom when Walker finally answered, "You were always drunk between operations. Guess that's how you coped with the disaster your life used to be. I'm not supposed to tell you what happened. None of us are. Doc Windhall would rather you figure it out yourself, but what the hell. The night you hit that FedEx truck, you were drunk as shit. You'd just been in a fight at Junior's and were running from Metro PDs' finest. They'd tasered your ass at the pub, but you were out of control and didn't go down. Instead, you ran out the door, grabbed your bike, and hauled ass down the GW Parkway. That's where you hit the delivery truck. Its taillights weren't working, so no wonder. But, yeah. You piled into its rear end, and your bike slid under the rear bumper. Probably would've killed you if your bike had been a piece-of-shit import. One of the arresting officers knew Murphy so he contacted him. Once Murph arrived, he decided to put you someplace where you'd be medically treated, as well as protected from yourself. You agreed."

Grissom grunted. "So that's how I ended up at Shady… umm…" He could never recall the name of that asylum. "So I committed myself?"

"Shady Creek Asylum, and yes, with Murphy's advice, you committed yourself," Persia finished for him. "They handle high-risk trauma cases there, and Doctor Windhall is the best. Which is why you're seeing a family counselor, instead of a warden. Doctor Windhall went to bat for you the night you arrived. So did Murphy and Alex. I have no idea what was in your system. You'll have to ask Doc Windhall about that. But once he spoke with the arresting officers, they said they'd talk to some judge and get back to him. They never did. That alone should tell you what you mean to The TEAM."

"They wanted to arrest Grissom?" Tuesday asked indignantly, one hand possessively gripping the nape of his neck, her fingernails dug in like tiny grappling hooks.

He leaned his head into hers, loving that she defended him. No one had ever done that.

Walker nodded. "Yes, ma'am. He tore up Junior's Pub, assaulted two DC police officers, evaded arrest, and a shit ton of other offenses."

"Well, that's only because he's been dealing with a shit ton of, well, shit," she declared, with a cocky head swagger. Her other hand was now flat in the center of Grissom's chest, as if telling him to keep quiet, that she was in charge and would fight this battle for him. Which was just plain crazy. Walker was former Navy, a damned SEAL, and more than capable of knocking Tuesday on her ass. Yet, there she stood, her shoulders squared, and sassing back as if she could take him.

Grissom knew he should've been paying better attention to what Walker and Persia were telling Tuesday, but damn. Her tiny, delicate hands on him and her snarky words on his behalf were like honey to a dehydrated baby bee. He was basking—simply—utterly—basking in the radiant light of this woman defending him. Of finally being good enough to maybe even be loved. She didn't have to say it. Tuesday Smart loved him, that was what the warm light beaming out of her was. It was love. Her love. This bright, intelligent, generous woman loved him as much as she loved his boys, and she was fighting for him like no one else ever had. Just like she'd squared off with Estes. She hadn't stood a chance then, either.

He could hardly see through the blur in his eyes. What was it about Tuesday that turned him into just another unwanted little boy?

"Relax, ma'am," Maverick said quietly, from behind where Grissom stood with Tuesday. "Murphy straightened everything out. Your man isn't going anywhere."

There was the confirmation Grissom craved. *Your man.* She hadn't said it yet, but Maverick did. That helped. Maverick knew Grissom belonged to Tuesday, and he was *her man*. Her only man. Damned if the threat of tears weren't turning him to mush. It was too soon, way too soon to speak the word he'd never once uttered during his entire marriage, surely not during his childhood. The L word was a precious, delicate thing. A sacred promise and a lifetime commitment. He used it with his boys every day, but for the first time in all of his years, he wanted to say it to a woman. To this woman. Tuesday.

Instead, he asked his team members, "Did I really agree to commit myself?"

Walker nodded. "Yeah, man, you did. But you hadn't yet known the scope of your wife's treachery then. None of us did, not until Murphy tried to notify Pam and couldn't reach her. He asked Leisha to check with your neighbors to see if they knew where she was. That's how we found out she'd destroyed your house and left with Estes, and… that he stayed at your house whenever you went OCONUS. Leisha dug into your wife's financials like a badger after that, and discovered Pam took your boys out of the country."

"And Estes, too," Harley added, from the barstool where he sat with Judy on his lap. "She paid for that bastard's ticket, too."

"On your dime," Maverick growled. China had one arm around his waist, and the cowboy looked as mellow as Grissom had ever seen him.

"Y'all know how Alex is," Harley drawled. "He knows people. Once Murphy told him what went down and what the police were gonna charge you with, he made a few calls."

"It's not like this was his first time dealing with a drug addict," Judy added.

"Grissom's not a drug addict," Tuesday snapped.

And once again Grissom was falling, so damned hard in love, with the sexy woman who still had her hands on him. He couldn't concentrate on what the guys were saying, until Walker slugged his arm and ordered, "Talk to Doc Windhall. If you have any regrets about what happened off the coast of Costa Rica, you won't after you check with him."

"What happened?" Tuesday growled, apparently ready to take on everyone in the room.

"Karma bitch-slapped that bitch, that's what happened," Judy replied testily.

China shot Judy a high five. "Yeah, you could say her *three-hour tour* ended with a bang."

Tuesday looked up at Grissom, the question burning bright in her green eyes.

He tightened his hold on her, loving how easily she molded her tiny frame against his bulk. "You don't know?"

Her brows furrowed into the cutest V. She shook her head, sending her chestnut hair tumbling over her shoulder. "I guess not. Is she okay? What happened?"

"No, ma'am, Pamela McCoy is not okay, not that she ever was to begin with," Walker drawled from where he stood behind Persia with both arms around her waist. "Turned out Mikey owned a couple planes. The day you rescued Grissom's sons is the same day he and Pam flew several tourists out over the Pacific."

A tiny "No" escaped Tuesday's lips.

"The plane went down," Grissom told her as gently as possible, which was difficult since he harbored no pain or regret at Pam's death. She deserved what she got. "I thought you knew."

"No, I… Oh, my God." The tip of Tuesday's tongue slicked over her bottom lip. Her chest heaved as if she were going to be sick. "Grissom," she whispered, her fingers fluttering over both sides of his face, and her green eyes bright. "If I hadn't been there… If she'd taken Tanner and Luke with her… Grissom, oh, God, they would've been… They could've been…" A set of ragged hiccups cut her short.

"Breathe," Grissom ordered, tugging her under his arm. "She didn't take them to her watery grave, and you *were* there, and my boys *are* safe and sound, and…" Shit. He was tearing up again. "She got exactly what she deserved, and you know it."

"But Grissom. She must've been scared, and the ocean's so cold, and what if—? What if I hadn't been there? Grissom!" Tuesday broke, just shattered there in front of everyone. "You could have lost everything. Your boys could've died! You could've—"

"See?" Persia interrupted quietly. "Destiny is real."

All at once, Grissom was surrounded by three pushy TEAM wives, wrapping their arms and bodies around Tuesday and, by default, him, because he was in their way.

"That's because you didn't go to Costa Rica just to take pictures, sweetheart," Persia, the wife who'd gotten in closest and now had both arms around Tuesday, crooned. "Destiny sent you to rescue Grissom's boys from that awful witch of a mother. Don't you get it? Destiny sent you to keep them safe for Grissom until he could get there."

"Which means you saved me, too," he murmured into Tuesday's temple.

She whimpered, and, one by one, the wives stepped back from the huddle and left them alone with her face buried in his shirt. It was pretty wet, but he didn't mind. He'd been peed on by the best. A few salty tears wouldn't hurt. Grissom had finally found the reason behind all he'd endured in his life, and he wasn't letting Tuesday Smart go.

Overcome with humility for the gift in his arms, he buried his nose in her fragrant hair and breathed in the loveliness that was Tuesday. "Destiny might be real after all," he murmured. "Because something put you in Costa Rica, on that exact beach, in that specific hotel in Puntarenas, on the precise day my kids needed you."

"Not destiny, Grissom. God," Harley cut in with certainty. "He knew what you needed, so He sent the best person for the job. He sent someone who wasn't afraid to stand up against polar bears, bullies, or black widow spiders. He sent Tuesday Smart."

Leave it to Harley to bring God into the picture. The only recovering alcoholic slash drug addict on The TEAM, he'd gone through his own personal hell back when Alex had first hung out The TEAM's shingle. Harley was still known to gift one of his dog-eared, scribbled-in Bibles to other struggling agents. Like Beau Villanueva. Like Renner Graves. And yeah, like Grissom. That was what they'd been talking about on the porch earlier. Harley'd handed over a well-worn Bible and the offer of one of his comfort dogs. Grissom accepted the Bible, but the dog was a discussion for another day. Not like that'd stop Harley. The guy was generous with his pedigreed pups, all of them trained service dogs. Which meant most agents now owned at least one, sometimes two.

"Okay, yeah, God," Grissom agreed. Believing in God made more sense than believing in destiny. He was, after all, the best, most loving Father in the universe. Destiny, on the other hand, sounded like a capricious wind that might blow in your favor, but not always, and never when you needed a good stiff breeze. But God? Grissom chose to be like Harley—a believer.

"Doc Windhall's on your side, Grissom," Walker said quietly. "We all are."

"Amen, brother," Harley added somberly.

"Ditto," Maverick declared.

"Me, too," Tuesday breathed against his heart.

Grissom followed those confidence builders up with, "Thanks, guys. I'll stop in and talk to him."

But whatever Doc Windhall might say, and even knowing these men still valued him as a competent operator, couldn't compare with what Tuesday whispered. Her honest, *'me, too,'* told him she'd never back stab or cheat on him. She wasn't made that way. Tuesday Smart was the warm, nurturing ray of sunlight he'd lived without most of his life. She loved him, and right then, her love was brightening the darkest hidden corners in his gnarly heart. Her love was lighting the place where he'd buried his soul a long time ago.

"Daddy!" Luke shrieked from the faraway master bedroom. "Georgie's cheating!"

"Again?" Judy whispered. "That boy is going to be the death of me."

"Figures it'd be Georgie," Harley grumbled as she slid off his lap.

"Kyrie's with them," Maverick said. "Give her a minute to get things under control and—"

"He's squishing Tanner!" Luke screamed. "Daddy, help!"

While Harley and Judy hurried to rescue Tanner, Grissom stayed put. "You know what I finally figured out?" he asked Tuesday, as the hubbub in his bedroom died down.

Sniffling, she gave her head a shake. "What?"

He slid his palms up her back and beneath her hair, cradling her head and so damned much in love. "That even messed-up guys deserve a happily-ever-after."

"Of course they do. Everyone does."

"Not everyone, but you and me sure do. Stay and talk once everyone leaves?"

"Okay, sure, but would you mind taking me back to get my car first?"

"Love, I'll do anything you ask. Anything at all."

Chapter Seventeen

At last, this emotionally draining day was drawing to an end. Game night turned out to be endless video games for the kids and conversation with adults. It was easy to see the respect these tough, warrior-types had for their women. The soft glow from the fireplace added a touch of romance, but it was the real friendships on display that saturated the air and conversation.

Unfortunately, all that comradery also worked against Tuesday. Seeing Maverick with China, both strong personalities who seemed to read the other's mind, as often as they'd finished each other's sentences. Seeing big, tough Walker Judge, so tender with Persia wrapped up in his arms since they'd drifted into the family room. And Harley. Man, Harley. Tuesday could've spent all night watching him with Judy. The way he teased her, incited her temper, and turned her creamy complexion nearly as fiery red as her hair. Which was often. How her sharp green eyes softened when she snapped back at him. They were the embodiment of opposites attracting, Harley being the carefree jokester and Judy his practical, no-nonsense other half.

Witnessing the love these couples shared made Tuesday think twice. Grissom had flip-flopped often today. How could she trust that being cozy with him now, wouldn't end with him pushing her away the minute everyone left? She was the fraud, allowing the illusion of being a happy couple to continue, when they weren't really anything at all. Not even friends. Merely acquaintances who'd shared a kiss or two. If anything, she was an empty-headed Disney princess. One kiss did not a future make, and there was no such thing as happily-ever-after. It was a fairytale and a lie, a risk she refused to take.

She'd feel better once she found a motel or nearby bed-and-breakfast, after she showered and had a good night's sleep. Things would make better sense in the morning. All too soon, this time with Grissom, Tanner, and Luke would be just another memory to revisit when times got tough, which they always did. As if any time in her life hadn't been difficult. But she'd known plenty of people who'd dealt with worse catastrophes than she had, so she wouldn't complain. Not as wealthy as she was, another thing that stood between her and Grissom. She wondered how much he knew. If he knew anything at all. Other than she was the woman who'd rescued his boys.

At the moment, her comfy boots were leaned beside the leather couch. She couldn't remember where she'd set her blazer, but it had to be somewhere in this fabulous house. She'd taken the corner of the couch opposite Grissom, going for distance instead of too much, too soon. Her legs were extended out straight, and he'd corralled her feet the moment she'd sat down. They were talking. Just talking. But his fingers massaging the bottoms of her weary feet were working wonders on her frayed nerves.

It was easy to see how much Harley, Maverick, and Walker respected Grissom. Judy, China, and Persia were just as generous when they'd invited her to Kelsey Stewart's place for their regular girls' night out before they'd left. Tuesday wasn't sure she was staying in Virginia long enough to make that happen, but the invitation was kind and the concept of having girlfriends again was tempting. She'd been on her own for so much of her adult life that, honestly, the drama between the TEAM wives tonight wore her out. She wasn't part of their intimate circle. Didn't know if she'd ever belong anywhere again.

The Tuesday Smart the world knew was a world traveler, used to the hubbub and chaos of international airports and flights, as well as the isolation of a hundred private landing strips and destinations the world over. She knew the pinch of having stayed too long in some of those places, after her food supply ran out, all for the sake of getting the perfect shot. She'd faced down a few wild animals, and she'd even eaten a rodent or two, when roasting their little bodies over a can of Sterno meant the difference between living and dying, waiting for the bush plane to take her home. Tuesday excelled at her craft, that much was true. She was worth every penny Robert paid her, and she'd received more than her share of awards and notoriety.

But in the end, she was still, and always would be, alone. That was her lot in life and she'd accepted it. Most photo assignments were tiresome bag-drags, getting herself and her gear from one airport to the next and then back again. Since her parents' and Freddie's deaths, she preferred silence in the middle of nowhere than sitting in any theater packed with today's self-absorbed fans. At the end of the day, she'd rather sit by herself while the colors of the sky changed from clear bright blues to inky pitch blacks, listening to the whistles, warbles, and chatter of birds searching out places to roost for the night. Mother Nature was the same the world over, gracing all living things with the same lights of day and of night, the same sun, moon, and stars. One had only to look up to appreciate how insignificant one was in the grand scope of creation. Tuesday was feeling every bit of that insignificance tonight.

The world of men was not her specialty, certainly not her strength. If anything, she put everyone she touched in danger. Being with all of these people emphasized everything she lacked. Grissom had his sons. The TEAM wives had their husbands and children. And there she sat, caught like an itty-bitty fly in a sticky trap of honey, the honey being the handsome man rubbing her feet with his magic fingers. The danger being the threat of falling in love with the gentle side of Grissom, then being pushed away the moment his anxiety took over. Or worse, of getting him killed, too.

This was as close as she'd been with any man since she'd traveled with Shane Hayes and Heston Contreras. But being with them hadn't been intimate. They'd never kissed her or made passes. They were friends. Guy friends. Grissom was something else. A large brooding beast one moment, then so kind and sweet the next she couldn't keep up. Being with him was like being the ball in a ping-pong match. Tuesday refused to waste the rest of her life being pulled in close one minute, only to be batted away and sent flying the next. And she'd never risk the life he had with his boys.

Tonight, he'd opened a bottle of white wine and turned the gas log in the fireplace on, then asked her to sit with him. The only light in the family room came from the orange glow cast by the flames. Tanner and Luke were asleep in his bedroom. Grissom had left his door cracked, then turned on the baby monitor sitting on the mantle, saying, "I need to be able to hear them. Usually us guys go to bed at the same time, but they're really tired tonight, and" —he'd shrugged— "who knows what the night will bring?"

He hadn't said that suggestively, just poured two glasses and handed one to Tuesday. He set his wine glass on the coffee table between the couch and fireplace, then reached for her ankles and slipped her socks off. Now they were playing a version of truth or dare, but had yet to come up with questions the other couldn't or wouldn't answer. She knew his favorite color, his birthday, where he was born, and that his parents still lived in his hometown, Portland, Oregon. He knew the same minutia about her. They'd talked about her role in taking Maeve Astor down, and everything that demented woman had done to frame Tuesday for several murders. Grissom knew Tuesday went to college in New York City. She knew he hadn't graduated high school, but had his GED and nearly enough credits for the business degree he was working on.

"The problem with attending college full-time is soldiers deploy a lot. Statistics is the next class on my to-do list, though. It'll happen."

"What then? Will you stay with The TEAM or do you have other plans once you have that degree under your belt?"

"Not sure. It's been a tough year, between me being in that wreck and almost losing my boys. Plus, Pam trashed our old house before she fled the States. Murphy took care of the mess and selling it, and my buddy Taylor found this home for us. All the furniture's second hand. I sure couldn't afford buying new stuff. Maybe once the boys are back in school and things settle down, I'll know what I should do. Until then…" He tipped his glass to his lips, emptied it in one swallow, and set it back on the table.

Tuesday watched the muscles in his neck flex with that manly swallow. Grissom's beard and sideburns were neatly trimmed. She had no idea what style it was, but it was more manicured than shaggy. His neck was clean-shaven, and he'd recently splashed on some brand of heavenly fragrance, maybe when he'd put the boys to bed.

He tapped her kneecap and teased, "Am I boring you?"

Startled out of her fanciful wondering, she chuckled. "I was just wondering if beards have styles and what style yours is."

He scratched his fingers over the shadow on his chin. "Don't know about style, just know it itches if I let it grow too long. So… boyfriends? Girlfriends?"

Tuesday scoffed. "Who, me? Not hardly. I was married before college, remember, so no boyfriends. No girlfriends." No friends at all. This was where Grissom found out what a pathetic loser she was. To forestall the inevitable, she focused on swirling the fruity Moscato in her wine glass, coating as much of the bowl as she could without spilling a drop.

"I don't have any girlfriends, either," Grissom said, with just enough tease behind his words that Tuesday's head came up. His hazel eyes were bright. The joker was grinning.

But this was a serious subject, and he'd already figured her out, so Tuesday admitted her biggest secret. "No college kid, male or female, wants to hang out with married women, much less one whose bodyguard stands ten feet behind her wherever she goes, and yes, even to class. I was a media target even back then. I was toxic. Me, a girl with no class, from Duluth, Minnesota, all because of my famous husband. Trust me, the paparazzi's worse than a pack of starving hyenas.

They don't mind spilling blood or tearing you apart if it gets them a photo and story."

"No significant other?"

She met his frank stare. "No, Grissom. Nobody but Robert Freiburg in my life, and he's fifty-something and married. I did have a lot of fun with Heston when he accompanied me to New York City for that interview, though."

Grissom's head canted. "Oh?"

Tuesday knew what she was doing was dangerous, but she was doing it anyway. "Yes!" She feigned gushing excitement. "He took me dancing at a club and then to a Broadway play. We ate at the best restaurant in China-Town, and he tracked down the most delicious New York cheesecake in the city. We even saw the Naked Cowboy! Heston took me on a wonderful river tour, bought us delicious Gray's Papaya hotdogs, and—"

Oomph! The glass was out of her hand, and Tuesday found herself pulled away from the armrest and flat on her back, staring up into Grissom's handsome face. Her legs were now trapped between his knees. His hazel eyes were dark, and, oh, so dangerous.

His thighs were thick and powerful. He was a beast, a bull, the heft of his body weighing her down, holding her in place, and she was a quivering caged rabbit beneath him. There was no escape. She'd never felt so small before. Or so alive.

A scorching wave of heat swept through her like a hurricane. Tuesday tried to swallow but settled for licking her suddenly dry lips. A gush released between her legs. Her mouth seemed parched, yet she was overly wet in other places. How'd that work?

Oh my, my, my. All the naughty things, those nasty, compromising things she'd been taught in school that good girls never, ever did, wouldn't think of doing, she wanted to do with the beast breathing his heavenly wine-scented breath over her face. Something strange and wonderful was happening to her body. She was on fire, burning with fever and want and—lust. Her. An untried virgin who had no idea what lust felt like until now. Or what to do with it now that it was burning her. What to do next.

Stay perfectly still? She could do that; she'd done it often enough before—if she could get her nerves to settle down and her body to stop quivering.

Should she take a risk? Reach out and pet the fierce animal gazing down at her through thick, black velvet lashes? Her arms and hands weren't caged. She could do that. Maybe. If her heart would stop pounding like the entire percussion section in her high school band.

Be brave? Throw caution to the wind and kiss him?

The perfect question.

Cautiously. Slowly. Terribly afraid she was wrong and that he might ridicule her, Tuesday reached one hand up to Grissom's face and nervously cupped that prickly masculine chin. His eyes closed. He growled, the deep bass vibrating through his body into hers. His eyes shuttered. Lines of pain stretched out from their corners and etched his brow. He was a mountain and she was a tiny mouse. Everywhere their bodies touched became a flame, a burning, glowing brand soaking into her skin. Insanely intoxicating. Downright indescribably tempting.

"You're a New Yorker. Hadn't you already done all those things?" he bit out, his voice husky and threateningly deep.

"N-not with anyone my age. Freddie was high-class. He took me to operas and charity affairs. B-b-ut Heston was fun-class."

"And…?" Grissom growled. "What else was Heston?"

Tuesday knew she'd poked the bear and now she had to deal with it. Him. "Are you going to kiss me or what?" she asked breathlessly. "Because if you aren't—"

She'd no more than finished when his mouth was on hers, and the tip of his tongue was ardently testing the seam of her lips, and…

Yikes. Trembling like the damned virgin she was, Tuesday licked Grissom's lips the same way he was licking hers. His whiskers rubbing her chin were softer than she'd expected, but those lips of his tasted like wine, only better. Sweeter. Full of dark magic she'd never experienced. With trepidation, she opened her mouth, intending to, at least, act like she knew what she was doing. How hard could it be?

The moment his tongue swept inside her mouth, lightning struck. Her eyes rolled back in her head at the decadent taste of his mouth. Her body tingled. Her toes. Her belly. The suddenly dripping wet place between her legs. While Grissom licked, nibbled, and devoured her, like she had that messy New York hotdog, a fire sprang to wiggling, twisting life inside of Tuesday. With every warm, wet caress of his tongue, the flame leaped higher and burned hotter. Her head buzzed. A muscle deep inside tightened with extraordinary tingles that felt a lot like pain and pleasure combined. Her heart pounded. Her breath came quicker. Before she could control her terribly unexpected, feral response to this man, that inner muscle snapped, unleashing a warm flood.

Grissom pulled her upright, then rolled over until she was straddling his hips, her knees digging into the couch. His hands still cupped her jaws, and he was French kissing the daylights out of her.

She dug her fingers into his bulky shoulders while his impressive erection pressed—right there. Between her spread legs. *Oh my, oh my.* Grissom, err, *it* was no small thing. Her body unleashed another embarrassing flood at the mere thought of what that long, thick organ would feel like inside of her.

"I'm just a man, Tuesday, and men are pigs and…" He growled, his fingers slipping down her ribs.

Lost in the fog of decadent sensations, Tuesday had no idea what he meant. Did he want her to move?

Grissom's back arched when she tipped away from him. "No, no, no! God, no. Don't move, Love. Please. Hold still. Give me a minute." That pained expression was back on his face.

Tuesday stilled, not understanding what he wanted, her to stay or go, but for sure not going to hurt him again. Everything was wrong. Not like in the movies. She'd ruined what could've been a romantic evening. Pursing her lips, she bowed her head and tried slowing her breathing and heart rate. When confronted or challenged by wild animals, not moving usually worked. She'd played dead often enough. She knew a few things about surviving in the wild. But she couldn't very well do that now or here, could she?

"Sorry I frightened you, love," Grissom whispered hotly against her lips. "I got carried away. I went too far and too fast, too soon. But you've never done this before, and I should've taken better care of you, and… Shit!" His eyes slammed shut and his body turned to steel beneath hers. His handsome face contorted. His heartbeat hammered beneath her fingertips. The veins up his neck and forehead bulged. He was in pain again.

What have I done? "I don't know how to do this," she cried, squeezing her eyes shut tight, so damned embarrassed. *'It'* was twitching like a beast between her legs, but he seemed angry and—

"No, no, it's truly not you, it's me. I've… I've…" Shuddering, he raked a hand over his head and whispered throatily, "I'll be right back. Don't go anywhere." With that, he gently set her against the back of the couch, and all but ran to the hallway. Maybe he just really had to go?

Tuesday didn't have much time, not if she'd somehow hurt him. Hurriedly, she shoved into her boots, sans socks. She had no idea where those socks or her blazer were, and she didn't care. But keys? Them, she needed. Patting her pockets down, she tried to remember where she'd put them after Grissom and Walker had retrieved her rental for her. She had to leave. It had been a long day and her poor brain was scrambled. Would he ever forgive her?

"Where are you going?" Grissom asked, surprising her from the hall.

Man, he was quick.

"Ahh…" Her heart climbed up her throat, as he walked back to where she stood at the opposite end of the couch. There was no easy way out of this.

Grissom held a hand out to her, the features in his face softer and his gaze so darned tender. Just like it had been when he'd dropped to the floor of that ratty hotel room in Puntarenas before his boys had run to him.

Tuesday stayed where she was, not sure what to do. "I have to leave."

He didn't grab her, didn't touch her. Just held out that great big, callused hand of his and cocked his head, as if coaxing her to give him a second chance. Him, when she was the one who'd spoiled what had been an incredible evening.

His beautiful hazel eyes glistened as if his heart were breaking. That couldn't be right. He was a man. He knew how sex worked. All men did. He'd had a wife, and they'd had two kids together. But Tuesday was still a teenage girl at heart. Didn't matter how old she was or that she'd been educated in the best schools. She was still dumb to the most important thing in the world, the goings-on between men and women. She never should've watched all those stupid Disney movies.

"Please stay," Grissom said quietly. "I got carried away and I frightened you, I know and I'm sorry. I messed up. I knew you'd never been with a man before, and, God, I can't believe I'm going to tell you this, but…" He'd gotten too close, and the grip she hadn't realized he had on her hips gentled. "Trust me, love. I want you more than I've ever wanted a woman in my life. Stay. I promise to be the gentle man you deserve. Give me another chance."

It was hard to relax, especially since she'd been close to bolting and never coming back. "I…" She huffed, needing to admit her mistake, too, but needing more air to do it. "I, umm" —deep breath— "made a mess of things." There. That said enough, didn't it?

"Is that why you put your boots on?"

Darn. There was no way out of this disastrous night, so Tuesday plowed through. Again. Like Freddie'd taught her. "Can we just talk?"

Stepping aside, Grissom gestured her to join him on the couch again. "Deal. More wine?"

Falling in love shouldn't be so hard! But what did she know about it? Nothing. She had no experience, no finesse, and no clue what was happening with her own body. Shaking like a ninny, she settled back onto the couch but kept her boots on. Just in case.

"Sure." *Because I need a drink!*

She'd learned about sex in high school biology. Who hadn't? But after her life fell apart and she'd gone so quickly from being plain Tuesday Smart to the infamous Mrs. Frederick Lamb, she'd set aside any thoughts of physical romance, dating, and sex. Why wouldn't she? She'd never been in the backseat of a car with a guy. She'd been earnestly into sports, not into jocks like most other girls her age. She hadn't dated. She'd been competitive, and, long story short, traumatized teenage girls didn't think about sex. All she'd wanted then was her parents back, and since that wasn't happening, she'd sunk into a depression that Freddie'd recognized and addressed. She'd seen her share of counselors, but nothing could bring her parents back. Or Freddie. He was just as gone as everyone else she'd ever loved.

Reading about the biology between men and women was one thing. Practicing it? Experimenting? Something else. She'd never, not once, bought a sex toy or practiced pretending. Because why? The only men who'd wanted her since Freddie's death were con artists and liars. They'd never wanted her, just her for herself. They'd only wanted her money and the notoriety of being seen with Frederick Lamb's young widow on their arms.

But Grissom was different, and that was a large part of his appeal. He seemed to have no idea how wealthy she was, and he'd only ever seen her as the woman who'd rescued his boys.

Okay then. Feeling a tiny bit more confident, Tuesday lifted her shoulders and sucked in a breath. She was no dummy. She'd faced down bossy male elephant seals, protective mother camels, and a few rowdy bears in her life. Even a pesky African lioness once. She knew what she wanted, and she wanted the tense gentleman sitting by the fire. The man she'd almost run away from.

Sure, Grissom was moody and damaged, but she was, too. Scrubbing her sweaty palms down the sides of her jeans, she prepared to stare down another kind of beast. The horny male she'd turned on. If she did it once, she could do it again.

Chapter Eighteen

"That's the crux of the debacle I made of tonight," Grissom explained. "I've never truly been in love before, at least not until my boys were born. Them, I love with my whole heart. Always will. Don't have a clue how not to. Have you ever, umm, been in love?"

He'd stepped over the line with Tuesday the way he'd gone caveman on her before. He'd damned near lost his mind once he'd had her soft, compliant body strapped over his hips. He'd embarrassed himself, like an inexperienced teenage boy after his first wet dream.

There was no excuse. Nothing that happened today was her fault, and he'd never blame her for his lack of control. The problem was all him. His experience with women had always been a contest of wills, of will she or won't she? Does she or doesn't she? And honestly, most of them wouldn't and didn't. There was always something wrong and it was usually him. Which was why he avoided women, except for the occasional hooker or tag chaser. He'd never been with a genuinely classy lady like Tuesday. Not only was she smart and capable of taking care of herself, she was drop-dead gorgeous, and he was weak. Damned weak.

"Just my dad," she croaked, licking her lips.

Grissom's cock noticed those succulent lips, the horny bugger. Strawberries. That was what they were, juicy, sweet strawberries he wanted to taste, lick, and bite. Her lips were slick from her tongue, but bruised from his kisses. It was hard not to stare at the delicate Cupid's bow of her top lip, perfectly matched against the plump cushion of her swollen bottom lip. One taste of her was all it took. He was thoroughly, impossibly addicted to this amazing woman.

But Tuesday was tired and nervous, still not making solid eye contact. He wanted to kick his own ass for frightening her, so he turned his head and faced the fire instead. Shoving the heel of one hand against his zipper to adjust himself, he hoped she didn't notice how tight his pants were.

Tuesday hadn't a clue what simply licking her lips was doing to him, and that was part of her charm. Inexperienced and innocent American women her age were unheard of these days. She'd seemed more confident before, but that illusion had faded. Now, she sat at the opposite end of the couch. Away from him. He didn't blame her.

Grissom stayed at his end. "Please, d-d-don't take this the wrong way, but you've got to stop licking your lips," he told the fireplace. "Because right now, I'm as close to losing it as I was before."

"Losing what?"

He closed his eyes. That right there—her complete lack of sophistication—killed him. It was unfathomable. Obviously, she didn't watch much television, not like that was a surprise. Nothing on American TV was family-oriented anymore anyway, and don't get him started on those trashy reality shows.

"Of losing control." Grissom turned to face Tuesday, his eyes tracking her reaction. "Every time your tongue sweeps over your bottom lip, I have a vision of you and me mashed together, and" —he raked his fingers over his beard— "you know biology, right? The physical differences between men and women?"

"Sure, I know that. I'm not stupid."

"I never thought you were. But there are different ways a man shows a woman he loves her, and for a woman to express her love in return... if she wants to, sometimes, mouths and lips and tongues get involved in different places and…" This was a conversation for the records. One Grissom thought he'd have one day in the far, far-off future. With Tanner. Maybe.

He did have Tuesday's undivided attention, though. The cords in her throat tightened as she swallowed. "You mean, men and women kiss each other… down there?"

"Yes, down there," he explained, gentling his voice even more. "Love between a man and woman is sacred. Whatever they want to do is no one else's business. You never watched, um, porn?" He let that question trail away, hoping he wasn't embarrassing her. Also hoping she wasn't into porn because it was a far cry from anything sacred. Hoping he'd get to be the man who taught her about sex. Wouldn't that be a miracle? A loser like him, blessed to love, honor, and protect a treasure like her? To teach her the finer points of marital bliss? Not that he had any experience in the bliss department. He was no virgin. He'd watched his share of porn as a teenager, and God knew what a mess his marriage had been.

Tuesday blinked those big, beautiful green eyes at him. "No, never. Why would I? It didn't seem smart to play around with something I'd never, umm, have." Her answer was full of worry as if he'd asked if she'd ever murdered anyone.

And Grissom fell in love with her all over again. What had he ever done to deserve a woman as sweet and pure as Tuesday?

"Play is the perfect word for what should go on between a man and woman if they truly care for each other," he answered nervously. He'd never actually played during sex, not like he might with Tuesday. Until tonight, he hadn't thought making love could be anything more than duty, especially after his shotgun marriage with *What's-Her-Name*. All she'd wanted at the beginning was *'Slam, bam, thank you, ma'am,'* and all she got afterward was nothing. She'd tricked him into marriage; he'd never loved her, and she'd sure as shit never liked him. Well, except for that first night. She must've liked him enough to keep the condom.

"I'll be honest," Grissom continued, thinking carefully how best to speak with this woman without making her feel more insecure. "Us guys get turned on by just about everything the woman we love does, with her hips, her lips, her eyelashes, hell, even if she flips her hair over her shoulder a certain way. By the way she walks and the shape of her lips when she talks. Hell, sometimes all she's got to do is breathe, and we're revved up and ready to go. As for me? Well" —he cleared his throat— "it's been years since any woman turned me on, and for sure, it wasn't my wife. Because you're so sweet and, okay, innocent and the most genuine woman I've ever met, I lost control before, and I scared you. I'm sorry."

"You want to… to play with me?" Her eyes narrowed like she was trying to understand.

Grissom nodded, hoping he was making his intentions clear. "Yes, I do. I've fallen in love with you at least a dozen times today. And every time, it's because of how your eyes shine when you looked at me or my sons. How kindly you told Persia you would've sliced those apples for her. How you let me kiss you in the kitchen. It's a hundred little things. You're something else, Tuesday Smart."

Lifting her index finger, she scratched her chin. "You love me?"

"Yes. I know it's too soon, but I can't hold it in any longer. Honest. If this wild, crazy, bubbly feeling in my gut is love, I want more of it. I want all of it, all of you. Only you. Would you… Would you mind if I… if I… Would you at least let me hold you while we talk?" He hoped so. Grissom extended an open hand, fully expecting rejection.

Tuesday's head bobbed. "Okay." Not *'I guess, if I have to.'* Not *'Hell, no, never, you creep.'* Just that one sweet little word: *'Okay.'*

A chestnut cascade rippled over her shoulders when, at last, she was back in his arms. The moment her body sank against his and her legs stretched across the cushions, the tension in Grissom's world evaporated. Tuesday snuggled under his chin, as if she hadn't been planning to leave him only moments earlier. Her poor heart still fluttered like she'd swallowed a butterfly. A big butterfly.

Grissom leaned back into the corner of the couch, taking her with him, keeping her tucked in close. Dipping his nose to the top of her head, he closed his eyes and swallowed a deep breath of roses in-bloom. Maybe she'd feel better if she knew his story. "I was never one of the popular kids in school. My mom…" His chest heaved. "Which is why I married a woman just like her, I guess. Role models and all that crap."

"It might be best if you start at the beginning," she murmured.

So he did. He told Tuesday how badly his mother had always treated his dad, how she'd slap, punch, and kick him, then laugh it off like it was fun and games. "She had no problem cuffing Dad in public, and whatever she dished out, he always took. Oh, he'd flinch because Mom knew where and how to hurt him, but, yeah…" Grissom's cheeks puffed with the years' worth of pent-up abuses he'd witnessed at home. "Growing up, I thought all mothers treated their husbands and kids like crap. I thought it was normal."

"Sure you'd think that. That was all you knew. You had nothing to compare her with. Assuming you had no grandparents."

Grissom shook his head. "She hated Dad's family, so no, we never visited them, and they weren't allowed to visit us. Her mom was tougher and meaner than Mom, though. It took me getting Tanner back home to realize I'm the product of generations of spousal abuse." He held a hand up to silence whatever Tuesday might say next. "But also, to decide, once and for all, that shit ends here and now with me."

"Sounds like your wife and Maeve Astor were wicked twin sisters."

"Wicked's a good word for them. Tanner finally told me how Pam slapped him behind my back or when I was gone. She made sure he knew she liked Luke, but she hated him. She threatened that if he ever told me what she said or did, she'd kill Luke and make him watch. I'm glad she's gone. Only wish I'd pulled my head out of my ass sooner and—"

"Shhhhh, don't say that," Tuesday whispered, gathering his fisted hand into her lap. Carefully, she straightened his fingers and interlaced them with hers. "We don't want to wake your boys, and honestly, we only know what we know, when we know it. You're not responsible for what your mother did to you or to your dad. That's on her and, in the end, she'll pay for it, just like Pam did. Your mother's abuse triggered your survival instincts, that's all. Even a tiny baby will turn away from pain, and you had to learn very early how to live around everything she dished out. How could you have known otherwise? Unfortunately, early role models establish our benchmark for normalcy, and those hard lessons become the lenses we view the world through from then on."

"Yeah, well…" Grissom lifted their joined hands to his mouth and kissed her knuckles. "If it takes the rest of my life, I'll make it up to my boys. They're everything to me."

"As they should be. But Grissom—?" Tuesday's delicate frame froze, a sign he was beginning to realize meant she was worried, frightened, or thinking too hard.

"What? Ask me anything." Using his softest voice, he continued with, "Honest, I've got nothing to hide. I'm an open book, and if we have the slightest chance of staying together after the mess I made of tonight, we need to communicate. True?"

She took a deep breath. "True, but this is happening awfully fast. Do you want me to stay?"

He pulled her closer. "Yes. Unless I've scared you and you'd rather not. You came into my boys' lives like an angel, and I'm not willing to let you go back to heaven yet. Not just because of my boys, but because… Honestly? I'm a selfish bastard. I want to keep you."

With the softest sigh, she leaned into his side and whispered, "Grissom."

That was all—just his name—and tears sprang to his damned eyes. Striving for control and unable to speak, he pressed his lips to her temple and simply breathed in the sweet feminine essence that was Tuesday. Tanner's birth had been the first ray of sunshine in his life, Luke, the second, and now, this incredible woman. She didn't have to say she loved him, just speaking his name was enough for now.

"I'm not leaving," she whispered, "not tonight. I had misgivings earlier. I didn't want to do or say anything that might remind you of your wife. I didn't know what to do with you. Sometimes you say all the right words, but then you clam up and shut me out."

"I did do that," he admitted without hesitation. "It's a defense mechanism. I throw up walls and set boundaries when I panic, at least, that's what my counselor says I'm doing."

"Because you refuse to get hurt again."

"Well, yeah, that and because my sons—"

"Because *your sons*, the same boys *I rescued*, are the best things in your life. Well, news flash. Tanner and Luke are the best things in my life, too."

And there it was. Truth and confirmation laid out in perfect simplicity, by the woman who loved his sons, maybe as much as he did. The harsh, nasty hiss of his mother's whispers in Grissom's head vanished at the absolute purity in Tuesday's words. "I can change," he declared, meaning it with every beat of his heart.

"I don't want you to change. I just want you to believe that I'll never hurt you or your boys. Not even Pixie, who I still haven't met."

"I know," he whispered, so damned hard in love with this woman he didn't want to breathe without her. "I'll give you a tour of the house tomorrow. You'll see the cat then, but I am getting better. And I promise, I can change."

"I like you the way you are," she murmured against his lips. "You're already perfect. But…"

He slid a hand beneath her hair to the nape of her neck. "But what? Spit it out. What are you afraid of?"

"Are your mom and dad still together?"

"Yeah, so?"

"So, I was wondering if…"

Cocking his head, he rubbed tiny circles on the back of her neck to let her know there was nothing she could say or do that would change his feelings for her.

Tuesday's throat muscles worked as she swallowed hard. Poor thing was still so nervous. "If your dad needs rescuing, too."

Not what Grissom expected. "You mean… a way to get away from my mom?"

"At least a safe place to go where she can't get at him. Somewhere he can have time to think, maybe get counseling and legal advice. Maybe learn how to defend himself."

"I never thought about that. I mean, Dad's had plenty of chances to leave Mom, at least, to press charges. He certainly has enough scars, but not once has he done anything to stop her. That's a great idea, though. We could open a safe house for men like him and me. Only we'll have to give it a manly name. Us guys don't like to admit the little missus beats the shit out of us. We've got to remember that. Guys' egos are important, but they're also part of the problem. I never would've admitted it if—"

"If Pam hadn't disappeared with your boys."

Grissom licked his lips. His heart rate kicked into overdrive as that night in the asylum with Murphy, the night he'd finally realized everything he lost, came back to him.

"Yeah, that. My head got scrambled pretty bad in that crash. Still don't know why I was so drunk."

"Walker said that's how you coped with life."

"Yeah, but…" Grissom slid his hand down Tuesday's spine and let it rest on her hip. He pressed his chin to the top of her head, trying to remember. "I can hold my liquor. Always could. Been drinking since I was a teen and got my first taste of forgetfulness. No, I think someone slipped me a mickey, you know, a knockout drug or something."

"When did you start drinking that day?"

"I honestly don't know. Probably as soon as I got home from work." He inhaled slowly, letting his lungs fill with the sweet perfume of Tuesday's roses. Most of what Walker'd told him about that night, he couldn't recall.

Tuesday's tiny hand slid over Grissom's chest, warming him. "What do you usually drink?"

"Bourbon. Cheap bourbon. Junior knows what I like. He takes care of me. Only I don't think I got drunk at Junior's."

"Tell me what you do remember."

"Good idea. Junior's is in the District near the Potomac River. My place back then was in Silver Spring. I don't recall being at Junior's, not even riding my bike to get there. Can't remember fighting the police or hitting that FedEx truck or… Hell, I don't remember anything until I came to in that asylum. Murphy was there. I remember him." Lifting his free hand up to his face, Grissom pinched the bridge of his nose. Trying to remember hurt.

"Shady Creek Asylum." Tuesday supplied the name he couldn't ever seem to come up with. "Sounds like whatever triggered you happened before you left home." With that, she wiggled off his lap and straddled his thighs again. "Maybe some kind of distraction would help your brain work better."

Grissom's blood supply fled south like a flood of snow melting in the Rockies.

Tuesday tipped forward, laced her tiny hands around the back of his neck, her fingers stretching up into his hair, and those luscious, plump breasts flattened against his chest.

He closed his eyes as the decadent warmth of her touch sent shivers up his spine. This woman wanted another chance. Thank God. Gripping her hips, he shifted her core over his stiff-as-a-plank cock, focused on keeping control as long as he could. If he could.

The heat spilling out of her body was already nuclear, and damn. Tuesday Smart was a damned fast learner.

Chapter Nineteen

Tuesday had no experience with men, but the best lesson she'd learned early in life was simple: *'If there's a will, there's a way.'* And she was plenty willful. Hopeful, too. The only way to get the experience she desired with Grissom would be by practice, and practice made perfect. So…

Positioning herself over his lap with her legs spread did the trick. Grissom's brown eyes were hooded again and his fingertips were digging into the cheeks of her backside, his thumbs into the tight crease between her thighs and abdomen. Her heart was seriously running one heck of a marathon, and she was nervous. But Grissom needed to know she was in this—whatever it was—with him, all the way.

A fiery line of tension ran down her centerline, joining her pounding heart to the heat pooling between her legs. If this was what it took to take their relationship to the next step, *dayam,* she was ready. She wanted Grissom, and whatever he needed or wanted to do with her. To her. If only she could stop shaking like a freaking virgin.

"I… I don't know what comes next," she murmured, afraid to look him in the eye, studying the shiny snaps on his shirt instead. "Show me?"

"Yes, ma'am." With a grunt, he was on his feet, his fingers splayed over her ass, and walking swiftly into the hall. Nudging the door to his guest bedroom open, he elbowed the light switch on before setting her on the bed across the room. Returning to the door, he closed it, twisted the lock in the knob, and asked, "Lights on or off?"

"On," she whispered, watching Grissom strip, needing to see him uncover every last part of the hard corded, all-male body she'd been secretly eying all day. She licked her lips at the thought of being with a behemoth like him. Being beneath him with his full weight spread over her. Hungrily. Eagerly waiting for the first sex of her life.

At last, she was on her first Grissom tour. He'd already popped the snaps on his shirt. It was open and untucked while his fingers deftly unbuckled his belt, and he toed off his boots. Rolling a hefty, tattooed shoulder, he tossed his shirt and then his pants aside. But not before he revealed the pocket pistol tucked into an ankle holster and the wicked blade sheathed and strapped behind his back.

"You were armed today?" she asked, her eyes scrolling over that fortress of a chest. The much-touted six-pack, comprising at least six tendons, sometimes more, stretched from left to right across his well-developed rectus abdominis. That was another tempting sight to behold. As was the black-as-sin tattoo running down his arm.

"I'm always armed, darling," he replied, his voice husky and his eyes bright, more black than hazel. Man, were they bright. Not sparkling with mischief, but glowering like barely banked coals with lust, strength, and a toe-tingling, sizzling energy that had long ago turned her nipples into diamonds.

In no way was he metrosexual, one of those suave, urban males who shaved everywhere, every day, sometimes twice a day. Who'd never be seen with a hair out of place, and would *'just die'* if they missed an appointment with their nail tech.

Dark, crisp hairs covered Grissom's arms and legs. An even smattering of scruff graced his chest, and Tuesday couldn't help blushing at the sexy trail running down his belly to the bulge in his briefs. Grissom was no inexperienced boy, no cocky, know-it-all college kid, either. He was all male, every last bulky muscle, every smoldering ridge and furrow, carved into his Mount Olympus physique.

Remembering what he'd told her about mouths being involved when men and women played together, Tuesday wondered where else her tongue and lips could wander over that rugged male physique. To those dusky, flat man-nipples? To the rigid rift between his hefty pecs? Down that tempting trail to his belly button to… there?

But would he like her mouth on him *there*? Was he ticklish? She needed to know these things, not just wonder about them. Her palms itched to run through the trimmed beard on his chin. Grissom was a real-life cowboy. Rough and ready. A little ragged and worn, but… So. Damned. Hot.

She couldn't control how her eyes instantly tracked the way his biceps expanded and flexed with every move, even when all he'd done was undress. Not only his biceps, but his triceps and pecs. His abdominals. His thighs and calves. His cock. That was what she most wanted to see. All of him at the same time. Naked. Grissom in all his primal glory.

Instinctively, her body arched at the thought of that handsome body pressed over hers. She needed to feel him, play with him. With *it*. Now. *It* looked damned impressive and long beneath his underwear. Thick. Hard. To heck with reading about sex, she wanted to play with every last part of the male biology lesson standing over her. Maybe he wanted her to get naked, too? She could do that.

Tuesday had barely touched the top button of her jeans when Grissom snapped out, "No," and was on her. Angling his knees between her legs, he nudged them farther apart than her skinny jeans could allow.

"First time, I get to unwrap my present." Impossibly, his already deep baritone turned deeper. So damned low and sexy, her core vibrated and her toes tingled, as if they were expecting an orgasm, too.

Grissom's fingers moved to her buttons, but her shirt didn't come all the way off. He unbuttoned it and just spread it open, then anchored it to the mattress with his palms. Open-mouthed, he stared down at what he'd bared. The tops of her breasts, her bra, and all her clenching, nervous stomach. His tongue ran a circle over his lips. "Fuck, you're beautiful, Tuesday."

She didn't move. Didn't dare, not as entranced as she was by the stark hunger glowering on his face. She liked that he used her name. Calling her 'love' was nice, but using her given name made this epic moment more intimate. More personal. A ton more special. He'd already declared he loved her, which seemed odd, considering how little they knew about each other. Using her name assured her that, whatever happened next, would be just between them. Just for Grissom and Tuesday. That the sight of her bare body turned him speechless? Frosting on the whole day.

When he lowered his head, her breath caught at the intense heat from his open mouth fanning her chest. His warm, wet tongue slipped over the tops of her breasts, tasting and licking, kissing, and…

Something very good was happening deep inside. She couldn't help it, couldn't stop it. Didn't want to. Her back arched by itself, as if begging Grissom to lick her here, there, and everywhere. "Oh, oh, oh, man! More!" breathed out of her in a wild frenzy of stars and pleasure and… wow. She had no idea kissing could feel so good.

"We'll take it slow," he murmured, scraping his beard up her neck and her chin, his mouth ending on hers. Deftly, his tongue arrowed between her lips and tangled with her tongue, encouraging her to explore and play. To be brave.

So Tuesday decided, yes. She'd been brave before. This was no different. Anything worth doing was worth doing well, and… *What is it with the freaking idioms? Enough already!*

Determined to get this show on the road, and to act like she knew what she was doing, she relaxed her jaw and opened her mouth wider. Giving back as good as Grissom was giving her. Using her tongue as a pointer while that unusual, but very pleasant pressure built inside of her again. Loving every nibble of his whiskered lips over her breasts. Luxuriating in the warmth of his massive body rubbing against hers. Stabbing her tongue into his wine-flavored mouth as far as she could. Sucking his lips and then his tongue, loving wine-flavored Grissom. In no way did she feel diminished, put upon, or prudish. Not as great as he was making her feel. Which was—

Happening again. "Oh, oh, oh! Oh, no! Grissom!" She growled like a wanton female dog in heat. If this was just her body getting ready for his, she wanted more.

His breath fanned over her with a sultry, "But oh yes, my love."

With practiced ease, he slipped off her shirt and her bra, and she had no idea where they went. All she could see were flames of desire in his eyes. The heat of his breath on her bare breasts was gasoline on fire. Tuesday had never before been so turned on nor so frantic for physical relief from the intense pleasure taking her body by storm. These feelings, these crazy, wild, wonderfully erotic, almost painfully pleasant feelings, were lightning bolts sparkling up the insides of her thighs, sparking back and forth between her nipples, and then down to her core and back up her stomach again.

He'd turned her into a writhing, moaning woman. A needy, feral animal made of muscle and electricity. A ferocious hungry woman who wanted more than just to lie still and be a good girl while he explored at his leisure. Every part of her ached for more. The added suspense of wondering what he'd make her feel next was powerfully arousing. Her thighs widened, granting him more access to the secret parts of her bare body. Like Grissom needed permission, given how tightly he'd locked his still-clothed pelvis into hers. If only they were skin to skin.

"Underpants," she growled into the busy mouth covering hers, her tongue jousting with his to get that command out. Simply pressing against him wasn't enough. The fiery heat consuming her was part of the whole Grissom package, as were his eager mouth and the work-roughened hands mapping her body. And she wanted the whole deal. All of him. More. Now!

Activated by instinct and running on lust, Tuesday lifted her hands from where she'd pressed them meekly at her sides. Giving herself permission to touch, she ran her fingers over his ribs, to his powerfully muscled back, and to… There. Down the dip at the small of his back. Over the rigidly flexing tendons and muscles pumping eagerly against her nakedness. Under the waistband of his briefs. Over gloriously taut, smooth, muscular buttocks. Just thinking about getting him naked and inside of her had Tuesday primed and burning for the next step that was—taking too long to get there!

Licking his way out of her mouth, Grissom rumbled, "Ah, ah, ah, tonight's not about me. Only you."

Whatever that meant. She couldn't get him out of his underwear, though, darn it.

His briefs still covered too much, but his hands were holding her head in a vise while he tenderly sipped at her lips. Too soon, yet not soon enough, his sipping turned to lapping, then…

He was making a meal of her mouth, their teeth clashing, their slippery tongues tangling together, everything in her driven by the need to mate. So strong it brought tears to her eyes and a flash-flood to her core. Swiftly, Grissom linked her hands in his fist above her head and kissed a path down the center of her body, feasting once again on her tender, aching breasts.

Releasing her wrists, he alternated suckling one swollen nipple while he tugged, pinched, and rolled the other. Then worked them over again. And again. Turning the tips into wet, hard, little beggars. Swirling his warm, wet tongue over and around each nipple as if it were his favorite popsicle. Gently biting, then full-mouthed suckling her breasts until every atom in her body was tuned to him. Only him. She'd never felt so adored. So loved. So horny!

The invisible line of electricity between her breasts and core was strung so, so tight, that it hurt. Not that he should stop. Oh, no, no, no. Back and forth he went, his hair skimming her chin and tickling her nose. The brush of his beard and his hot breath on her wet nipples turned them into ice. The steamy cave of his mouth warmed them just enough to burn and—

Another tsunami of hot, fierce pleasure broke loose from deep inside. A frantic, needy wave ripped up over her belly and breasts like wildfire. "Ahhhhh! Darn!" Tuesday growled, earnestly shoving her upward into Grissom's partially clothed body, needing more friction. Needing him naked. All of him. Every hard-corded muscle, every scrape from those crisp, manly chest hairs. She was on fire, burning from the inside out, and… "Ah! More! Grissom, I need more!"

"Shush," he murmured, covering her mouth with his hand. Too late. The wave rolling over her was large and way too hot to contain. Too much! The world turned Fourth of July fireworks bright, and she was lost, screaming in its throes. An overwhelmingly erotic need had Tuesday striving to clamp her legs back together. Too much! The sensation barely receded when another wave swelled low and deep. Her fingers clenched before she realized her nails were dug into Grissom's shoulders.

"I'm… I'm sorry," she murmured, dazed by the strength of foreplay, if that was what this was. But *dayam*. If this was foreplay, what would an orgasm force her to do? Hurt Grissom? Never. She pulled her hands away from him.

"No, love. Don't stop. Don't let go, just feel," he ordered, as if he'd read her mind. Which maybe he could. He was the teacher here, the man with tons more experience. "I'm tough; I can take whatever you dish out. Feel, Tuesday, just feel. Shut your mind down and let your body go. Don't be afraid to get wild, to fly. Go crazy. I'm here for you. I'll catch you when you fall."

"Was that…? Did I...?" She had no idea how or what to ask.

"Yes, those wonderful feelings you had were orgasms. Three orgasms. You're one helluva firecracker in bed."

Three? Did not compute. That phenomenal pleasure was pulsing through her again, blocking logic. Like those lightning storms, pushing her up high, into light so intense and warm and wanton, another scream begged for release.

Every flick of his talented fingers created more sparks, and every spark, the need to scream and hold on tight. Her blood was running hot. She was out of control—flying like he'd told her to do. While his teeth and lips feasted on her tenderized nipples and aching breasts, slathering sloppy wet circles, nipping and sucking, and—

It was happening again. Her hips gyrated as that lovely, wicked storm built higher and higher until... "Grissom. Too much! I can't. Too…!" It broke loose like a hurricane. Wicked, crazy lightning sizzled behind her closed eyes. Her hips bucked, desperately seeking the coarse friction of Grissom's massive male body. Wanting him inside. Every last rugged inch of him. Their bodies slammed together. The only thing between them ? That darn cotton Hanes chastity belt he was so determined to wear.

Darn it! Tuesday wanted his underwear gone and him naked. The thought that too much sex could kill her flitted through her semi-conscious state of euphoria, even as her fingers crawled between them, down his belly, frantically seeking the overheated missile still in his underwear. But what a way to die. Burning together, in love and lust—just him and her. Only Tuesday and Grissom. Forever and ever.

At last. She found what she wanted, pumping him—just once—before he clamped a hand over hers and ended her willful exploration of his magnificent body.

"Please, don't. Stop love. Hold still. You're responsive as hell, and if you keep that up, I'm going to come," he growled, his voice gruff and tight, his face pressed into the corner of her shoulder and neck.

Him coming sounded like a bad thing. "What's coming?" she had to ask. "Will it hurt?"

"I've lost count," Grissom huffed, his chest heaving like he'd just run a marathon. "How many orgasms have you had?"

"I have no idea," she replied stupidly, still trying to catch her breath and not sure why he was counting. Must be a guy thing. She'd lost count at three, after he'd told her what those glorious feelings were. If they were orgasms, then… "Is coming having orgasms?"

"You're so tight" —he pressed his monstrous erection, still completely covered by that darn Hanes barrier, between her legs— "Feel that? I'm so hard for you, I could pound railroad spikes. We need to slow things down. And yeah, coming's another word for orgasm."

"Slow things down?" she asked, loving the heat and girth of the lightning rod still pressing against her. Out of breath and panting, as tiny aftershocks lit up receptors she never knew her body had, she asked, "W-why slow down? I'm just getting started." To prove it, she slid a sneaky hand down his taut belly, under that darned waistband, and back inside his briefs.

His smile turned delightfully tender the second her fingers circled the girth and thickness of him again. With lovely ridges and bulging veins. She wanted to look at it, darn it. At him. At all of him.

"Because you've never done this before, and I don't want to hurt you. I'm not a small guy, and—" his shoulders lifted "—us going all the way tonight will hurt. But trust me, I'll take it slow and easy, and we'll work on it together."

"Has anyone ever died of too many orgasms?" He was still hard as a spike, yet velvety soft and so, so hot. Made her want to put her lips on him—there. Maybe more than just her lips. Maybe her whole mouth. *Bet he'd like that.*

As if he'd read her mind again, Grissom's entire face brightened even while he pulled her hand out of his briefs. *Darn it.* She'd lost her chance to fondle him.

"You keep saying stuff like that, love, and my head's gonna swell."

"Well? Has anyone?"

"If they did, they died happy," he teased.

"I believe it." Sweat trickled into her eyes, but Grissom captured her fingers before she could wipe it away.

"No hiding. Please, not anything from me. Ever," he told her gently. Earnestly. The top of his fingers smoothing over her damp forehead. "Not your tears, your sweat, or your blood. Not your passion or lust, your pain or your rapture. Not your curiosity, your questions, or your fears. Never, ever hide from me, Tuesday, and don't be ashamed of anything we do together. You want to try something new, tell me. Don't ask. You'll discover what you like and don't like soon enough. We've got time. We'll figure things out as we go. I'm just so damned honored to be the first man who's been with you like this. But I had to stop you. If you'd kept squeezing me like you were, things would've gotten messy, and I don't think you're ready for that."

A fiery blush stormed over her face, no doubt leaving bright red splotches in its wake and watering her eyes. "Okay, I guess. Agreed, no secrets. Only trust and honesty. That's a good rule. But Grissom, honey."

Impossibly, his eyes grew darker. Lust still glittered there, but—were those tears?

Sliding both hands up and over his rounded shoulders, Tuesday cupped that rugged, bristly jaw and stared into the worried gaze of the gentle giant breathing down on her. Grissom might look fierce and angry to people who didn't know him, but beneath that give-no-quarter, rough-and-tumble gunslinger, was a pure-hearted man earnestly fighting the world, and sometimes, fighting himself, too. She'd witnessed his panic attacks too many times today to pretend she hadn't seen the cracks in that handsome façade. But she also knew this beautiful, damaged man wouldn't give up; that he'd fight to the death for his boys, and now, for her, too.

Running the pads of her thumbs under his eyes, collecting those rare, precious male tears, Tuesday gave back to Grissom what he'd given her. "You aren't just the *first man*. You're my *only man*." She bumped her forehead to his. "You've made me—"

What could she say? There were no words for what Grissom had given her tonight. No one word could capture the range of emotions he'd ignited in the lonely stretches of her soul. For the first time in years, the hollowed-out pit in her heart was full. He'd changed her. Might've healed her. Right here, right now, in this bed.

"I've made you my woman, love," he finished for her.

"And you're my one and only," she whispered, her hands curled around the back of his neck, her fingers threaded into his hair. "All. Mine."

Chapter Twenty

They lay quietly on the guestroom bed, catching their breaths, their arms and legs tangled, and their heartbeats in sync while the overhead light bathed them in soft LED. Tuesday's warm breath fanned over his chest. Grissom wasn't in a hurry. They still needed to have a talk about birth control, but that could wait. What she'd just given him, allowing him to be the first man to explore her exquisite body, knocked the wind out of him. But when she said he was all hers? He'd damned near bawled like a baby.

The only honest love he'd ever known hadn't come until Tanner was born. His dad used to say the right words. He was good at talking about how much he loved Grissom, but not once had he proved it by being brave enough to save his son by leaving his wife. That would've been hard, sure. But real men protected their children from bullies and the chaos they eagerly inflicted on everyone around them. Even when those bullies were family and standing up to them was hard. Especially then.

Grissom couldn't help wondering what kind of man he'd be if his dad had, even once, manned up and stood up to his mother. If he'd ever protected his only child from witnessing the cruelty that woman had dished out. What she was probably still dishing out.

Instead of growing up carefree and innocent, playing baseball during summer break, like those kids in that *"Sandlot"* movie, he'd been stuck at home every winter, spring, and summer break doing chores. Every day. Scrubbing floors and toilets on his hands and knees—because that's how his mom's mother always did it. Washing dishes by hand for the same dumb reason. Fixing meals, breakfasts, lunches, and dinners. Dusting like a damned maid. Every day. He'd been his mother's slave, while his spineless dad had been the whipping boy for any and everything that didn't go like his mom wanted.

Even when the toilet backed up because she flushed her *'feminine products.'* Another rule from Grand-Mommy-Dearest: Those damned *'feminine products'* had to be called that and only that, not tampons, pads, or napkins. Hell no, every damned thing in that hell house had to be said or done *'the right way.'* Grand-Mommy-Dearest's way.

Grissom now knew how sick his grandmother and her daughter were, and that the best things for his dad would be plenty of distance and counseling. He might be weak, but he'd also taken the brunt of Grissom's mom's physical and verbal abuse long enough.

Tuesday was right. A safe house for abused men was an incredibly smart, thoughtful, and compassionate idea. His old man did need a way out, and Grissom meant to give it to him. To at least offer a way out. Funding was a huge obstacle, though, and Grissom would never hit up his boss for a cent. Alex Stewart was a well-known philanthropist in these parts. He could fund the entire project and not think twice about it, but Grissom needed to do this for his dad on his own.

Just like this over-priced house. There might've been more affordable options on the market. But Tanner and Luke had needed a home fast and his buddy, TEAM Agent Taylor Armstrong had one available.

Grissom had never carried this much debt before, but after Costa Rica, giving his sons a fresh start quickly, had been important. Fortunately, Taylor had recently finished building his latest house and it ended up being a mere two miles from TEAM HQ. It'd never been a priority to live close to his job, but Grissom was fine with the location. Taylor knew construction, and given his side gig, restoring aged Victorian mansions throughout northern Virginia, Grissom grabbed onto the once-in-a-lifetime opportunity with both hands.

After a frenzied week of dealing with the bank, shopping for food and other necessities, and moving in, Grissom and his boys went back to the place they'd once called home. He'd wanted Tanner and Luke to grab the few things they treasured, toys and such. But stepping inside and seeing the nasty violence Pam had wreaked on all they'd once held dear, was a wake-up call for both boys. It was a tough day that brought a shit-ton of closure. The boys cried while they'd dug through the debris in their shared room for their toys. Fortunately, Pam hadn't known Tanner kept his art supplies in an old box in the garage.

Thankfully, Murphy stepped in with TEAM muscle then. The house in Crystal Spring was now repainted, re-carpeted, and on the market. Good riddance. The TEAM stepped in again with used furniture and free labor, while the TEAM wives kept everyone fed during the moving-in process. His new mortgage was a killer, but once he went back to work and after the old house sold, things would even out. Somehow.

For now, he was one contented man. Whatever Tuesday wanted, he'd get it for her. The pleasure of being hers made him smile. She'd humbled the hell out of him with that simple, "Me, too," back in the kitchen. Then she'd made a man out of him by letting him love on her sexy body. She loved him like his boys did. Freely. Without reserve. Without qualification. She just—she just loved him. And she didn't have to say it. He knew. He could tell.

"You awake?"

Grissom knew she was smiling by the glow in her question. Quickly, he brushed a hand over his face and manned up before she saw the tears leaking out of the corners of his eyes. "Yup. You ready for round two?"

"As a matter of fact… yes." Pushing up from the bed, she slid one leg over his stomach and straddled him.

Grissom settled her over his hips. Cupping her jaw, he kissed and nibbled while he stretched his legs between hers. "I think we've done enough for your first time," he whispered. "I'm a big guy. It will hurt."

She squirmed beneath him. "But Grissom…"

He loved when she whined like a little girl not getting her way. "It'll hurt, so no. We'll wait until you're rested and ready."

"Awww. How long will that take?" Again with that adorable whine from a woman who should be on the cover of every high-class fashion magazine. A woman who should've been a helluva lot more experienced with men, not stuck in desolate climes by herself. What was up with that, anyway? No woman, especially one as young as Tuesday, should ever work alone or travel unaccompanied to far-off places, some of them warzones. Not that Grissom wasn't thankful for the solitude that had saved her for him. Maybe he was a greedy pig after all. But the question begged answering. Who was Robert Freiburg and what was he up to?

"You were right before," he answered, licking a circle around one diamond-hard tip, his palms pushing both breasts together so he could play with them at the same time. Forsaking that nipple, he turned his head and slurped the other. "This thing between us is happening awfully fast." *Suck. Kiss. Nibble. Nibble. Tease.* "I want you to be absolutely sure of what you're agreeing to before we take the next step."

Tuesday's chest lifted in his hands with her petulant sigh. "But I *am* sure."

Wasn't that the greatest? Her, a spoiled brat. Him, the reasonable one. Him? The crazy guy with no impulse control, who usually panicked, and until now, had messed up everything?

Stepping back and analyzing the pros and cons of situations before jumping to conclusions wasn't a new concept. It was an Army-taught life skill he'd forgotten and had to relearn in counseling, how to control himself in order to better manage life with his boys. To be the adult in every situation, never the aggressor, just because he was bigger. To never engage in power struggles with children, but to stay true to what he knew was right for them. To be gentle, kind, and empathetic. To put others first, no matter how old or small they were. To believe in his kids so they could learn to believe in themselves. That was how boys became men instead of bullies, perverts, and pedophiles. With plenty of parental trust and the right kind of teaching. With love. Always with love. Like he told his boys: *Every time. Anytime.*

Popping her nipple free from the suction of his hot mouth, Grissom pressed his chin between her breasts. "This is play, love. This, right here. What we're doing with each other now."

"I like naked play," she purred, rubbing her sweet-smelling flesh against his face, her neck flushed the prettiest pink.

"Have I created a sex maniac?" Hey, a man could wish.

Her deep breath encompassed his cheeks in a lush, warm fragrance. One part roses. The rest all Tuesday. Delicate fingers gently massaged the knots he'd never realized had all but locked his neck muscles into stiff ridges. Or maybe, those muscles relaxed because her touch was magic.

"I only know I like the here and now we've created," she murmured, her green eyes soft and hazy. "I'm not afraid of you, Grissom. I believe in you. I trust you."

She. Trusts. Me.

"Fuck," he hissed, so damned raw, but mostly proud as shit. "I wish I'd met you years ago. My life would've been so different." He knew, even after just one day, that Tuesday had never manipulated anyone in her life. She didn't know how. She simply was who she was, kind and honest with a heart as big as the great outdoors. And she'd just given him the power to break her heart—or die protecting it.

Her fingers smoothed around his head to cup his jaws. "That would've been perfect. Maybe we should invent a time machine, go back and do things differently," she whispered, her torso curled forward as she kissed the tip of his nose. "But then you wouldn't have Tanner and Luke, and I'm sorry, that's just not acceptable. I love those kids."

Grissom squeezed his eyes shut. It was either that or bawl like a baby, which he seemed to be doing a lot since he'd met Tuesday. What she said explained a helluva lot, and once again, she was right. Every single mistake he'd ever made, every wrong turn and stinking deployment, had brought him to her. They were two magnets, drawn through time and circumstance to each other. To love. Was that destiny or density? He no longer cared, as long as he ended up with Tuesday.

"There are no do-overs in life." Lifting her chin, she pressed her lips between his brows. "There's only us four kids, and we're doing the best we can with what we've got. And right now, I've got everything I ever wanted. I've got you."

The flowery scent of her hair floating over his face caressed Grissom like irresistible angel wings. It was time to change the subject before he broke down.

"So, umm…" He hugged her tight, giving himself time to breathe and calm down. He'd only ever been this emotional when his boys were born, and these feelings were wearing on his good intention to not roll her over and rut like a caveman.

"Umm" —*what was I going to say? Oh, yeah*— "I've been thinking about your idea. Thought I'd call Dad tomorrow and get a feel for how things are back home. You know, see if I can get an honest answer out of him. See if he'd be interested in making a change, maybe moving into a safe house, maybe even helping us put one together."

"Why don't you just invite your parents for a visit? You have a big house. Maybe then, you and your dad could talk, while me and your mom—"

"No," snapped out of Grissom before he could stop it. He shook his head. "Sorry, didn't mean that how it sounded, but

I don't want Mom inside this house. It's Tanner's and Luke's safe place. I can't let her take over, like I know she will."

Tuesday's fingers never missed a beat as they soothed over his suddenly tense scalp and neck. "Okay, no problem. Whatever you decide. You know them better than I do, and honestly, I'm afraid I'd hurt your mom if she made even one teensy mean comment about you or your boys."

"Which she would the second she arrived."

"Which would get her smacked, trust me."

Grissom chuckled. "You smack many people in your life?"

Still lying on her back, Tuesday smiled shyly. "No, but I've put down a couple of belligerent bullies before, and I know how to stand my ground, Mr. McCoy. What are your parents' names? You just call them Mom and Dad. Want to share?"

Oh, fuck, did he want to share. Just. Not. Them. But Tuesday deserved to know so Grissom settled for a terse, "Randy and Vivian McCoy. Dad's a janitor at a private hospital between Portland and Vancouver, and my mom's a, a housewife." If that was what you called being a prima donna who did nothing all day but expect everyone to kiss her ass.

"Which is a noble career choice, motherhood. A full-time mom is better than an army of babysitters. She's never worked outside the home?"

"Nope." Grissom let the P pop. "That's Dad's job, according to the Book of Mom."

"Then…" Tuesday ran her fingers down Grissom's neck to his collarbones, and he shivered like that ugly, three-legged ugly dog again. He was caught in the gentlest snare, one he savored instead of fought. One he craved. She was breathing on him and her eyes sparkled like green fireflies in the middle of a dark night. If he didn't know better, he'd swear there was magic in the air.

"Then what?" he asked, striving to keep from pushing her legs apart and shoving deep into her body.

"Then what's she do all day?"

"Nothing, as far as I know. But I haven't kept in touch." He didn't want to explain how rotten his mother was. There. That did it. Just thinking about his mom halted the blood supply to his cock.

"Okay then, call your dad whenever you're ready. I'll support whatever you decide. In the meantime…" Tuesday yawned. "Mind if I sleep over? Just tonight? Then tomorrow, I'll—"

"You'll stay right here, woman. In my house."

"But the boys—"

"The boys will be thrilled when they wake up and find you're still here."

"Well, okay." She burrowed under his arm, her head on his shoulder. "If you insist."

Grissom's hand smoothed down her back to her warm, plump ass. "I insist. I finally found you; I'm not letting you go."

"Hmmm," she whispered, her fingers fluttering over his like tiny angel wings asking to come inside. Tipping forward, she pressed a kiss to his sternum, her lips so damned soft against his skin that tears brimmed again. He'd never wanted a woman as much as he wanted the one with him now, and it wasn't just for sex. He'd watched Tuesday work her gentle, loving kind of magic on his boys, and she'd sprinkled it on him. He was a goner. Standing, not falling. He was totally in love.

Threading his fingers into her hair, he closed his eyes and whispered, "Stay as long as you want, love." Was it too soon to ask for forever?

"I will," she murmured through a sleepy sigh.

"Promise me."

"One more day, yeah, I can do that," she whispered.

Grissom knew he was grasping at the only gold ring he'd ever stumble across in his life, but he wasn't letting Tuesday go. Somehow, he'd convince her to stay tomorrow, the day after, and every day after that.

Chapter Twenty-One

Tuesday woke slowly, comfortably sore and astonishingly mellow after last night's adventure with Grissom. This morning was the beginning of Christmas Eve. She'd originally planned to be gone, but then last night happened, and there she was. In Grissom's house and not going anywhere. The bed beneath her was comfy and soft, and her entire body still thrilled at the seductive brush of what had to be expensive bedsheets over her Grissom-sensitized skin.

He wasn't there snuggling with her, yet he was. She could smell him in the masculine, smoky, cedar scent caught between the sheets. In the tingles of pleasure still rippling over her bare skin. At her wicked thoughts of him. In the marks they'd stamped onto each other. In just thinking how his big hands had gripped her backside, when she'd come her very first time. The weight of his magnificent body pressing her into the mattress, anchoring her for another spine-tingling attack. The roughness of his chest hairs against her sensitized breasts and nipples. His confidence. His strength. But he'd never lost his underwear. That had to change.

Pulling to the side of the bed, Tuesday wiggled her toes into the plush silvery-gray bedroom carpet and let a few happy tears fall. That grumpy, brooding male with the tender heart loved her, and he'd spent most of the night proving it, well, not proving it per se. She wasn't sure what the juvenile slang was for how far they'd gone. Second base? Third? Couldn't be a home run. That was reserved for 'doing it.' 'Going all the way.' And a bunch of disgusting descriptors for what Grissom called a sacred thing between a man and a woman.

How had he become the honorable, caring, and insightful male he was today, especially after living through a mother like Vivian and a wife like Pam? Somewhere along the line, Grissom had to have been exposed to at least one honorable, honest male who'd made an impression on him. She knew from experience it only took one good person to reach out and save a lost child, to change that child's entire world. To make a difference. Freddie had saved her. Who'd saved Grissom?

Alex surely fit the bill, but so did most men on The TEAM. Maybe Murphy? That made better sense. Mr. Finnegan had hired Grissom and introduced him to the tightly-knit band of former warriors, The TEAM family. The simple tag, The TEAM, made Tuesday smile. Instead of the lackluster, totally generic moniker, Alex should've called his business The FAMILY. Might've made it sound like part of the Mafia, but it'd be a better fit for what Alex had created. Tuesday saw the results in both Shane and Heston. In handsome Mark Houston. Even Alex. They *were* family, and their wives were the glue that made that family work.

But enough of that. Tuesday needed to get moving. She'd promised Grissom she'd stay one day and she had, but it'd soon be time to get back to reality.

Her clothes were somewhere in the room. She hadn't cared where they landed last night, wasn't sure she cared now. If not for Tanner and Luke, she'd be brave and march up to Grissom in her birthday suit, and she'd tempt that handsome Grizzly Bear back into her bed. As it was, she was afraid

Tanner and Luke might've heard too much last night. She doubted Grissom had females sleep over. Darn, she should've been quiet. But honestly? She'd lost her mind once he'd taken over. Her, a virgin with no experience. Wiping her tears, Tuesday giggled. Freddie'd always urged her to tackle whatever scared her the most. But holy cow, she might've scared Grissom last night.

Oh, that man. That big, warm, hairy, wonderful man. She couldn't believe the emotions being with him like that stirred in her brain and heart, and okay, her body and soul, too. They'd been frantic heathens last night, and she'd loved every minute of it. Okay, so maybe she might need to stay another night, you know, just to tempt the beast again. To make sure Grissom taught her everything. How many stayovers would it take to learn all there was to know about biology?

"He loves me," she whispered, reaching behind, intending to wrap the Grissom-scented bedsheet around her. To pull the masculine-scented sheet to her nose and inhale every last scintillating male pheromone he'd left behind. As if there could ever be enough.

Instead, her fingers tangled with a lump of soft fur that purred. Must be Tanner's cat. Tuesday had wondered last night where Pixie was. Now, she knew. The chubby black and white cat stopped purring and glared at her with half-shuttered amber eyes daring her to touch it again.

"Hello, Miss Pixie," she said, letting Pixie sniff her fingertips. "Aren't you a pretty girl?"

With a stretch of her fluffy neck, Pixie accepted the gesture, then closed her eyes, kicked her internal motorboat into high gear, and resumed purring. Like a pretentious queen on her throne. As if Tuesday were merely staff.

Stroking Pixie's long, sleek fur was a good way to wake up. Not the best. That would've been petting Grissom, but these few minutes alone gave Tuesday time to take stock of her new surroundings.

The room was painted white. The carpet was a muted, silvery gray, same as the headboard, both nightstands, and the six-drawer dresser beside the door to the ensuite bathroom. Twisting around told her the neutral tones throughout the room would make the perfect backdrop to the family portraits she intended to take today. Photos in rustic red, barn wood frames. The largest, a ginormous family shot of the McCoy family would cover the wall facing the foot of the bed. It'd be the perfect thing for anyone to wake up to each morning. Just not her. This wasn't her home and a guest knew when to leave.

"Sorry, Pixie, but you'll have to scoot over. I'm getting up," she said, rolling the chubby cat to the other side of the bed. She got a hiss for that slight, but Madam Pixie stayed put once she was paws down again.

Tuesday spotted her luggage next to the bathroom door. Grissom must've found her keys and brought it in for her. Perfect. In no time, she was showered and dressed in fresh clothes that didn't smell like horses. She'd barely packed her dirty clothes into her suitcase when a quiet knock sent her hurrying to answer. There stood shy Tanner in his stocking feet, clean jeans, a plain white t-shirt, and a timid smile.

"Dad says tell you breakfast is ready. Pixie!" He ran for the unmade bed and scrambled up beside his cat. "You been sleeping with Miss Tuesday all night?"

Tuesday stayed at the door, listening to Luke chattering with Grissom in the kitchen beyond, while she gazed at Tanner. "Do we have enough time to look at your amazing combat jet pictures before breakfast?" She hadn't forgotten her promise, but suspected he might have with all the commotion last night.

"Sure!" he replied, easily scooping Pixie into his arms and sliding to the floor. "Come on, kitty cat. You come, too."

Tuesday followed Tanner into the hall leading to the master bedroom at the opposite end. The guest bathroom and a linen closet were on her left. It helped knowing the guest room was far from the master bedroom. His boys might not have heard her after all.

The moment Tanner opened the master bedroom door, Tuesday knew she was finally seeing the real McCoy family room. It was a disaster. She chuckled at the clutter from the night, maybe the week, before. The king size bed didn't look like it'd ever been made up, not with half its tangled blankets on the floor, the other half balled on the mattress.

Several device chargers decorated both nightstands, along with lamps with mismatched shades. The mirror over the long, twelve-drawer dresser was too foggy to make out her reflection, and dozens of video games and game covers still scattered the floor in front of the big screen over the dresser, where the boys had camped out with their company. Candy wrappers, an empty popcorn tub on its side, half-empty water bottles, and several pairs of boy's tennis shoes were scattered, well, everywhere. The closed lid of the hamper beside the open bathroom door belied the truth—that no males had ever used them—as did the smelly pile of clothes next to the hamper. The entire place smelled of man and boy, Tuesday's favorite scents. Yup, this was where the McCoys really lived, all three of them. This was their hole-in-the-wall hideout, and they truly were desperados, apparently on the run from picking up after themselves. What were those tidy but empty hampers in the laundry room for? Show?

Tanner dropped to his knees, opening the lowest center drawers of the dresser. He'd already set Pixie down, and she was peering into the drawer, her ears perked forward like everything Tanner did fascinated her. "This here's my drawer," he grunted as it tipped forward onto the carpet. "Just mine. Nobody else can take nothing out of it but me. Dad said."

Tuesday expected a tablet, maybe a sketch pad. Anything but a professionally bound twelve-by-twelve scrapbook.

Settling to his butt, he flipped past the first few pictures, each preserved in a document protector. "This one's the best one I ever did. Here, look."

Dropping to her knees at his other side, Tuesday shifted until she was cross-legged, looking in wonder at a six-year-old's artwork. It wasn't what she expected. The eight-by-eleven photograph of a red, white, and blue F-16, one of the famous USAF Thunderbirds demonstration team gracing the left document protector, was good. But the colored-pencil sketch at its right was excellent. Six manly signatures, probably from those F-16 pilots, decorated the photo. Only one decorated the sketch. *Tanner McCoy* had been carefully penciled lengthwise along the right margin.

"You're quite the budding artist. How'd you copy it, with onion skin or tracing paper?"

"I don't know what that stuff is, I just drawed it. With one of these." Tipping forward, Tanner pulled out a plastic zip-lock bag of stubby, well-used colored pencils, a tiny plastic sharpener, and a white eraser from the drawer. An almost empty, hundred-sheet pack of drawing papers came next.

"You drew this freehand?" *Unbelievable.*

His shoulders lifted. "Yeah, I guess so. Does that mean I didn't cheat and copy it?"

She bumped her biceps against his. "No, it means you have a very steady hand if you traced a photo as precisely as you did this. You should be proud."

"Hmmm. Okay. But I didn't trace it. I just drawed it."

Tuesday had to look twice. "By sight?" *Seriously?*

"Yeah, 'course. Dad got a picture for me and Luke at the air show he took us to. I got to talk to the pilots, Miss Tuesday. The real guys who fly them T-birds. You should see them! Them guys are cool!"

"I'd love to," she murmured, more excited at the attention to detail revealed in Tanner's artwork than meeting any pilot. "Have you had classes?" *Did six-year-olds even take art classes?*

His shoulders lifted like it was no big deal. "No, I just like to draw." Reaching past her, he flipped back to the beginning page in his scrapbook. "This is the first one I ever did. It's kinda messy, but Dad fixed it for me."

"Why'd he have to fix it? From…" *Who?* Tuesday couldn't finish the question. She knew what she was looking at, possibly a gifted child's first foray into the world of art. A beautifully sketched hummingbird in flight, its emerald green throat, its wings a masterful blur of sapphire blues and grays, and a bright white sparkle in its eye. The paper had been torn into eight ragged pieces, those pieces now carefully taped—from the backside—back together. The repair had been done so well, it was difficult to see where it'd been torn. Grissom had carefully matched his son's pencil strokes, every penciled line, curve, and shadow. He'd even recaptured the iridescence in the tiny bird's smudged throat.

"He saved it from Mom," Tanner whispered, as if saying her name could make the witch appear out of nowhere. "She said it was stupid, and I was stupid, too. She always said mean stuff to me, and she's who teared it up, not Luke. Luke would never do anything like that, cuz, cuz he knows I just like to draw sometimes. It makes me feel good, like on really bad days and…" His shoulders lifted as if his *really bad days* weren't worth talking about. "Anyway" —he huffed— "she threw it in the garbage, but I…"

Tanner was breathing hard by then so Tuesday pulled him into her side, angry at Pam all over again. "It's okay," she breathed into the side of his sweaty head. "Your mother can't hurt you anymore, and she isn't ever coming back. I wouldn't let her near you if she did."

"That's what Dad says, b-but…" Tanner's skinny little boy body jerked with a hiccup. Tears breached his hazel eyes. "I still have all them bad dreams, Miss Tuesday. She's screaming and being mean to me, and I can't make her stop. She just keeps yelling and calling me names."

"Aw, sweetheart." Tuesday pulled him onto her lap, scrapbook and all. "Some people are just mean. They get pleasure from hurting others, but just you wait. They'll all get what's coming to them." And Pam surely had, at the hand of the mighty Pacific Ocean.

"They do? P-promise?"

"I promise, sweetheart. We reap what we sow, and if all we sow is hate and cruelty, that's what the universe sends back to us."

He snuggled under Tuesday's chin, his ear against her heart. Right here he belonged. "What's it mean to sow?"

Of course, a six-year-old wouldn't understand that little/big word. "Sow means to plant seeds, like the good habits I see your dad planting in you boys. Your mom thought she could plant ugly seeds that would turn you kids into big, mean, thorny thistles like her. But your dad's planted seeds of honesty, kindness, and love, and you and Luke have grown into perfect little men."

Carefully, Tanner shoved his open scrapbook to the floor and pointed at the man-size fingerprint in the lower left corner of the hummingbird drawing. "Dad came home early that night, and he saved my picture for me. See? That's his thumbprint. My picture was wet when he found it cuz Mom threw it in the garbage, and his hands got dirty, but, yeah. Dad's my best friend. He don't ever hit me."

Tuesday couldn't help the sigh that breathed out of her. "Your dad is the best, isn't he?"

"Yeah. He never hits me or Luke, not even once. I don't have to be ascared anymore."

Tears blurred her eyes. This poor kid was still suffering from his mother's cruelty. No wonder Grissom hadn't shown any remorse at his wife's untimely death. Divorce would've kept that awful woman in these boys' lives forever. Pam might've even gotten custody.

"And he bought me this cool book to keep my pictures in, and these plastic sheets keep them safe and dry and clean. Wanna see some more?"

"I sure do," she replied as Tanner pulled the scrapbook back onto his lap and flipped to the second page.

That was where Grissom found them, looking over Tanner's collection of jet fighters. Tuesday hadn't heard him until he sat on the bed behind her and asked, "Are you kids hungry? I made pancakes, bacon, and scrambles."

Twisting her neck, Tuesday looked up at him through blurry eyes. "How long have you been sitting there?" How much had he heard?

"Not long." But she could tell he'd heard enough by the sheen in those hazel eyes.

"You have quite a talented young artist on your hands." She wiped a hand across her face.

Tugging her between his knees, he nodded. "Know that, love. Pastels. That's what he wants for Christmas. Right, Scooter?"

"Yeah, and maybe an easel, but mostly pastels, cuz they're cheaper, and Santa can't afford to bring everything us guys want. Right, Dad?" Tanner answered brightly.

Geez, this kid was killing her. He didn't ask for much, and he wasn't as pumped as she'd been as a kid on Christmas Eve. Back then, she would've been climbing the walls by now at his age. There was no childish, holiday energy in this house, and that was because of that witch-mother of his. Tuesday brushed a quick hand over her face at the harsh reality she saw in his hazel eyes. All this little guy had ever wanted was his mother's love. Wasn't that a desolate thought on the day before the holiest night of the year?

"Right, son. Need a hug?" Grissom asked, his voice so darned tender.

Without a word, Tanner scrambled out of Tuesday's embrace and fell into his father's. Grissom's burly arm wrapped around him, as he extended his other arm for

Tuesday to join the huddle. By then, she truly detested Pam for what she'd done to this fragile child. Her first-born son, for the love of God. What made some people so mean?

Grissom murmured into Tanner's hair, "You're safe, kiddo. No one can ever hurt you again. They'll have to go through me and Tuesday first, and that just plain isn't happening."

Darned if Tuesday didn't whisper, "I know," at the exact same moment Tanner did.

Embarrassed, she leaned away, but Grissom's grip held her still. "You're safe, too," he said. "Now, let's eat. We've got a Christmas tree to chop down today."

That broke the evil spell that had seeped into the morning. With a mighty sniff, Tanner wiggled out of Grissom's arms and dropped to the floor. Very carefully, not even the littlest bit excited at the idea of chopping down a tree, he returned his scrapbook and supplies to *his* drawer. Tuesday would've distanced herself from his father while Tanner was occupied, but Grissom pulled her onto his lap by the time Tanner was back on his feet.

"Son," he said evenly. "I like Tuesday and I want her to stay with us for Christmas. Is that okay with you?"

The toothy grin on Tanner's pale face was more than Tuesday expected. But when he squealed, "I love Miss Tuesday, Dad! Please say yes, Miss Tuesday. Say you'll stay forever. Please!"

Wow. He was excited but—over her? It was all she could do not to bawl her eyes out at all the bleak Christmases he must've lived through, to make her staying one more night seem like it was all he'd ever wanted.

She didn't want to disappoint him, but she hated the holiday. The blessed, infamous day had only ever swamped her with lost, painful memories and the ghosts that went with them. Her mom. Her dad. Her dearest friend, Freddie. The tiny kids Maeve Astor had murdered. Their poor dead father, the unsuspecting man Astor had married solely to give birth to the children she'd intended to murder in order to frame Tuesday. All because Freddie had saved a broken little girl from Duluth, then married her to cement her standing as his sole legal heir. Which seemed totally bizarre, since neither of his sons would've contested his will in the first place. But that was a mystery Tuesday suspected would rear its ugly head soon enough. Not today.

Before her heart had time to wander farther down her depressing memory lane, Grissom's big hand captured her cheek and turned her to face him. "We've all got ghosts," he whispered. "Me. Tanner. You. Luke, too. Help us guys remember what Christmas is supposed to be about. I want this to be their best one ever. Please stay?"

Not fair. How could she refuse these adorable beggars? Tuesday swallowed hard, not sure of anything but the sweet glow in this man's and his darling boy's hazel eyes.

Freddie had also taught her the most important rule of negotiation: *Always ask for one more thing.* So she did. "I'll stay if I get to pick the tree."

"Yessssss!" Tanner yelled, jumping up and down as if his legs were made of springs. Then he was out the door, screaming, "Luke! Tuesday's gonna stay with us! Luke! Luke! Tuesday's staying for the whole day and then all night!"

She burrowed into Grissom's arms as Tanner's voice faded down the hall. "Notice he didn't say I'm just staying for

Christmas? Are you sure about this?" she asked, frightened this was another lapse for Grissom. Worried he'd throw up those prickly fortress walls without warning and block her out, like he had so many times yesterday. "Are we running when we should be walking? Taking it slow? At least, slower? For your boys' sakes?"

He growled, burying his nose into the sensitive spot behind her ear. "We're the same, you and me, remember? Both afraid to take chances. Afraid to let ourselves be happy. You had a family once. You actually know what real Christmases are supposed to feel like. I don't and neither do my boys. Help me make this one a Christmas to remember."

"And then what?" She could feel his lips curve into a smile against her skin.

"And then, I'll persuade you to stay and show us how to celebrate New Year's Eve. Groundhog Day. Valentine's Day. Saint Patrick's Day. Umm…"

"Easter?" she asked, suppressing the giggle working its way out of her heart.

Grissom leaned back, his hand smoothing over her backside. "Mardi Gras."

"That's not a holiday."

"It is in New Orleans." By then that massive hand was in the back of her pants, his callused fingers squeezing her butt.

"Boys. Breakfast," she reminded him, before they went crazy on each other. Not that she'd mind, but not with his boys waiting for them in the kitchen.

"Ah, yes. Right. Boys." He pulled his hand out of her pants. "Duty first, huh?"

"Not duty. Love. Your boys will always come first." She blew into his ear. "Then play."

Grissom laughed, his heart full of so much joy, that he sounded like Tanner. Guess falling in love was contagious because Tuesday was falling too. For the entire McCoy family. Even the cat. And she was falling hard. But that couldn't be. It might be time to think about them instead of herself. It might be time to get up, pack up, and leave. For their sakes.

Chapter Twenty-Two

"It's so pretty!" Luke squealed, clapping. His eyes filled with excitement at the imminent lighting of thousands of multi-colored lights now strung on the ten-foot noble pine Tuesday insisted was the perfect tree.

It was Christmas Eve and the four of them were in the loft, its ceiling high enough to accommodate Tuesday's tree. The lady in question sat cross-legged on the floor, her eyes lifted to what would soon, hopefully, be the bright golden star Grissom was installing on the damned tip of this big damned tall tree. Why he hadn't wired that star on top of the tree before he'd stood the damned thing in its stand was beyond him.

'Memo to self: Don't forget to do that first next year, dumbass!' Which he immediately revised to, *'Don't forget to wire the star on before you stand the tree up next year, buddy.'* Not dumbass. Never again would he demean himself, just because his mother did. What she'd done to him was wrong. He refused to let her legacy live.

Little by little, forcing himself to recognize his mother's snarky programming when it popped up like it just did, Grissom was rewriting his childhood history. And it was working, just like his counselor said it would. He just had to keep at it, the same way he often reminded Tanner to do the same, to combat Pam's toxic mothering. The McCoy boys were all works in progress, but it was a job worth doing and doing well.

"A little to the left, honey," Tuesday advised sweetly from below. "Not too far. Just a titch more—"

"Perfect! You did it! You done really good, Dad! It's beautiful!" And there was Tanner, offering encouragement and praise, another lesson in overcoming toxic mothering.

"Yeah!" Luke yelled, as if his father were on top of the Himalayas, instead of on the twenty-foot ladder in the same room.

"Inside voices," he reminded his rowdy boys.

"Let's sing something!" Luke yelled again.

"Would it be okay if I put the ladder away first, maybe climbed down before we start singing Christmas carols?"

"Well, a'course, Dad," Tanner chuffed. "Everyone knows you hafta get off a ladder before you can put it away."

Sarcasm? That was new.

"Duh," Luke chirped cheekily.

"Smart ankles," Grissom growled as he climbed down backward.

"Lights. Action. Camera," Tuesday said as—click. She pressed the master switch on the surge suppressor and turned on all those lights.

"Oh, wow. Miss Tuesday, look. It's so pretty! I wub it!" Luke again, still clapping, his screaming, childish exuberance a thing of noisy beauty. Made a tough guy's eyes water, seeing his boys excited over a damned tree. Not what Grissom needed as he levered the ladder's legs back to release the tension on the spreaders, keeping it from folding.

"Be back in a minute," he muttered, his voice husky, the ladder now collapsed and balanced on his shoulder, on its way back down to the garage.

"Hold up. I'll help," Tuesday offered, her taut ass already lifting up from the floor.

"No, stay here with my guys. I got this." Well, kind of. At least, he managed to finagle the extra-long thing through the loft door and down the back stairs without marring the wall board like he did on its way up. Tonight was Christmas Eve and the first ever McCoy Christmas tree was up, lit, and no doubt visible from the dark side of the moon. Maybe from the East Coast, the thing had enough lights. But it was what the boys wanted, and Grissom was making sure they'd have the brightest tree in the world. To hell with Happy Holidays. This year, the McCoys were having the best *Merry Christmas* ever.

Back in the loft again, he lowered his ass to the floor and sat beside Tuesday. She tipped into his side with a quick kiss on his cheek. He wrapped an arm around her and held on tight. Tanner was sprawled under the tree with Luke, both on their backs, their legs kicked out, and giggling like two little bank robbers, staring up into pine branches.

"I saw him kiss her." That was Luke, all giggles, shrugs, and whispers too loud for keeping secrets.

"She's staying here tonight. With us. All night," Tanner whispered back. "Dad likes her."

"Me does, too." Luke giggled, like the mischief-maker he could be. "I like her a lot."

"I showed her my picture book and she liked it." It was good to hear Tanner talking about his artwork again. She might not know it, but little by little, Tuesday was pulling him out of his funk.

Would he ever be the carefree toddler he'd been before? Grissom doubted it, and that weighed heavy on his mind. He'd failed the two people he loved most, the ones he should've protected. He blamed Pam for the harm she'd caused, sure, but he was responsible, too. He should've paid closer attention to what was going on at home when he was gone, and he never should've trusted her with the two most precious things in his life in the first place. Never should've believed a word out of her lying mouth. Hell, he never should've gotten himself into that jam in the first place. Not like he would change those mistakes now, but shit. He was the world's biggest dumbass for falling into that age-old trap of getting drunk to forget, which had also made him too drunk to remember. Her stealing that used condom was on him, and Grissom refused to deny it. He had no business condemning his dad for not standing up to his mother, either, not when he'd stayed in a loveless marriage as long as he had.

But shit, accepting Ms. Ashlee Peyton's counsel to let the past go and forgive himself so he could move on, was akin to climbing Mount Everest with a ton of crap strapped to his back. He was no better than a recovering alcoholic, had to talk to himself every day, remind himself that the only things that mattered now were his boys' happiness and safety. That he couldn't go back in time and change anything, and the only way forward was by focusing on the future. That children were resilient, and his boys were more prone to follow Ashlee's advice and good counsel than he was. That he needed to stay positive, open, and never avoid answering Tanner and Luke's questions. Which so far, hadn't been difficult. The only difficult question yet to be answered had to do with Pam's death. Grissom sighed. He dreaded the day Tanner asked what happened to his mother and why she wasn't ever coming back. Maybe Tuesday could help with that?

Which made sense. The only time he felt like he'd finally crested the summit of all that guilt, was in bed last night with her warmth wrapped around him. Being with her like that had felt like his greatest accomplishment since his sons were born.

Leaning into her, Grissom kissed her temple. They were still in uncharted waters, both of them damaged in their own messed-up ways. But she was no timid damsel in distress. As feminine and beautiful as she was, Tuesday was also a force to be reckoned with. Damned if she hadn't asserted herself plenty last night. At least, she'd tried.

"You hungry?" he breathed into her ear.

Her shoulders lifted. "For you," she whispered back.

Tipping to his back, Grissom took Tuesday with him, then rolled until he had her pressed into the carpet.

"The boys," she whispered, the tree's lights reflected in her green eyes.

"The boys already know I love you," he whispered back, then asked louder, "Hey, guys. Do you like Miss Tuesday as much as I do?"

That brought Tanner and Luke scrambling from under the tree and climbing on his back. Luke was laughing, but it was Tanner who declared over his dad's shoulder, "I love her, Dad. Can we keep her?"

Luke finally made it on top of Tanner's back, making this a three-layer McCoy sandwich with Tuesday pressed beneath them. "Yeah, Daddy, can we keep her?"

Grissom flexed his arms to keep the additional weight from crushing her. "What say you?" he asked the lady with shimmering green pools for eyes. "May we keep you, at least a while longer, Miss Tuesday Smart? Will you stay with us guys?"

The room stilled as if everyone was holding their breath, well, except for Luke who had a case of giggles. "Say yes, Miss Tuesday!" he yelled like everyone was deaf. "Hurry up! You gotta say yes! Me and Tanner wub you and we want you to stay!"

That kid.

"Inside voice," Grissom growled.

But Tanner wasn't breathing, and that was concerning. As much as Luke was jittery with excitement, Tanner had gone stock still.

Grissom studied his most traumatized child. "You okay, Scooter?"

Tanner's gaze zeroed past Grissom, his hazel eyes riveted on Tuesday. "You said you were gonna stay. Did you change your mind?" he asked quietly, his lower lip quivering.

Damn. Tanner had just made it intensely personal. Now Grissom's eyes were betraying him.

Reaching past him, Tuesday cupped the trembling boy's chin, like a real mother who loved her children would. "I'll stay as long as I can, as long as it's okay with your dad."

"It's okay," Grissom answered quickly.

"I got a ring!" *Jesus, did that boy only know how to yell?*

After Luke ran off to who knew where, Tanner whispered, "We don't need a ring if you say yes, Miss Tuesday. Dad says we only need to love each other and never be mean to each other and… and…"

Tuesday pulled Tanner over Grissom's shoulder and into her arms. Her eyes welled with tears as she covered his pale face with tiny kisses. "I loved you the second I saw you. You made my heart sing, sweet baby of mine."

Grissom lay there beside the tender scene, wiping his face with his free hand and so damned proud of the woman holding his firstborn like a treasure instead of a weapon to be used against him. Tanner needed Tuesday in his life as much as Grissom did. He wiped his face again. Damned tears! They kept running down his face. Which didn't really matter, not as hard as Tanner and Tuesday were crying all over each other. She kept murmuring sweet nothings into his face and hair, her hands smoothing over his head and shoulders, his back, then over his dripping wet face again. And like the selfish, spoiled brat he'd never been in his life, Grissom wanted her hands and every one of her kisses on him.

"I love you, Tanner," she murmured, her voice soft and sweet and so damned motherly. "I will always love you."

Grissom lifted an arm over his eyes to hide his tears. "Merry Christmas," he whispered, hoping he hadn't sabotaged the day and the rest of his boys' lives by being so damned emotional and asking that particular question. Tuesday wasn't ready to move in with him, much less marry him. They'd only met, really met, a couple days ago. They didn't know each other well enough to commit to each other. What the hell was wrong with him, putting the moves on her like he had? Normal people dated. They courted. They grew together. Over. Time. Significant amounts of time, not just twenty-four or forty-eight hours or however long it'd been.

When would he learn? He'd damned near asked Tuesday to marry him, to spend the rest of her extraordinary life with a loser like him. Did he want her to stay? Absolutely, but he needed to take it slow. To at least give her enough time to understand what she'd be getting into if she stayed more than one or two nights. Not scare the bejesus out of her.

Asking her to stay like he had, in front of his boys, was one for the books—the psycho books. He couldn't help wondering what his counselor would say about what he'd done. That he had no impulse control? *Well, duh.* He hadn't always been this impetuous, had accomplished a string of successful missions while active duty. Had he hit his head so hard in the crash that he could no longer control his big mouth?

Sure seemed like it. Lost in the dismal swamp he'd made of his life, he didn't see Luke running at him until… *Ooomph!* His wild child landed square in the middle of his chest with a breathless, "I got it, Daddy!"

Grissom coughed out a grumpy, "Got what?"

Luke pushed a circular, shiny thing into his face. "A ring, Daddy! I got a ring so you and Miss Tuesday can get married now!"

Tanner lifted up from Tuesday's chest long enough to say, "That ain't a ring. It's a nut."

"It ain't a nut. You are!" Luke tossed back, defiant to the end.

Tuesday diffused the squabble by singing, "Silent night. Holy night," which was all it took to get the boys singing along.

Marriage proposal disaster averted. Adding his voice to the age-old song, Grissom reached across the space between them and intertwined his fingers with Tuesday's. Tanner still hugged her like he'd never let her go, and Luke had settled flat on Grissom's chest, that shiny silver nut tight between his pudgy fingers.

"Thanks for finding the ring, Short Stack," he told his youngest quietly.

"It'll fit. I just know it," Luke stage-whispered back.

"It might," Grissom murmured, his lips against Luke's ear to keep Tuesday from overhearing. Nuts and bolts were made of stainless steel and polymers that, combined, resisted chemicals and corrosion. "But if it doesn't fit, I know a guy who can make it the right size."

"You do?" Luke asked with bright-eyed innocence. "Wow. That's really nice."

Yes, wow. Grissom clenched Tuesday's hand tighter as he took the nut from Luke and stuck it in his jeans pocket. Christmas began bright and early tomorrow. His boys didn't need presents from Santa. Destiny had already provided their hearts' desires.

Or, like Harley thought, God was behind Tuesday's sudden reappearance in Grissom's life. A man could hope.

Chapter Twenty-Three

Tuesday was up early the next morning, dressed in jeans, a simple white t-shirt, and her baby-blue bedroom slippers. Until last night, she'd slept in Grissom's guest room. But after he put the boys to bed, then waited until well after midnight to make sure they were sound asleep, she'd helped assemble the bunk beds in the empty room between the guest room and master suite. Bunk beds with wagon wheels for the head and footboards, as well as two sturdy wooden footlockers with the boys' names burned into each lid.

Setting their new bedroom up hadn't taken long. After that, she and Grissom had brought several bags of toys and stuff in from the garage. A big yellow dump truck for Luke, plus other small cars, racing tracks, and trucks. A set of pastels, an easel, and more drawing paper for Tanner. As well as new clothes, boots, jackets, and, of all things, cartoon underwear for both.

"Hey, don't knock underwear," Grissom warned. "Santa's a smart guy. They'll get what they asked for, but they're also going to get what they need."

Tuesday nearly laughed at the Santa's Toy Shop now spread under the tree in the loft. Grissom was up there, setting a timer for the festive lights. The boys were still asleep, though Tuesday doubted that would last much longer. Not with music wafting down from on high while their father was feverishly making sure this first McCoy Christmas was perfect. How could it not be? Tanner and Luke were too young to be jaded by the noisy yammering of the commercial world. They'd be thrilled with whatever Santa brought.

She only wished she'd had time to run and buy a few presents. The only thing she had to give was the spinach and bacon quiche she'd thrown together. Nutritious, sure, but nothing fancy. Not even special. And the bacon was Grissom bought. But a few spontaneous family photos? That she could do.

But she'd better hurry. The boys would be up soon. By the time the bacon finished, she'd set up a tripod with one of her digital video cameras in the loft. The memories captured today would be priceless.

Back in the kitchen, she set the quiche on the built-in warming plate on the kitchen nook table. Clever idea, that. Then she'd set the table, including glasses of cold orange juice all around, and had just enough time to wash her hands when—

"It's Christmas!" Tanner exclaimed, as he ran through the kitchen to the back hall leading to the loft where Grissom was still tinkering away. Making sure the oven and stove were turned off, she followed the boys with another camera, intent on capturing this, the first of many happy McCoy Christmases to come, for posterity. He'd changed into jeans and a black t-shirt that stretched deliciously over all those glorious muscles in the very best ways.

Never had she seen such sweet, smiling, goofy faces. And the toys! By the end of the mad dash through wrapping paper, which was a surprise all by itself. Really, a man who wrapped presents? Yet there they were, every last pencil set and mini-truck set, wrapped perfectly and tied with ribbons, bows, and hand-written name tags.

Tuesday had set up her video camera near the tree, but it was the personal up-close, once-in-a-lifetime still-shots that tore at her heart. Like the moment shy little Tanner offered Grissom the gift of his drawing, a portrait of his dad in his cowboy hat. That one choked up Grissom as much as it did Tuesday.

Spurred on by his rowdy, competitive nature, Luke ran downstairs to his dad's bedroom and all the way back up to the loft again with his gift to his dad: a brightly decorated piece of red construction paper full of a three-year-old's tiny green finger-painted handprints and…

Oh my, is that a footprint? Sure is. Tuesday kept snapping up every last memory. She stopped long enough to swipe a quick hand over her eyes, though, when Luke told his father in his loud little inside voice, "I made this pitcher just for you, and Tanner helped!"

"Luke made a frame for it, too," Tanner whisper-hinted. Which sent Luke running back downstairs and into his father's bedroom again with a frantic "Oh, yeah!"

By the time he returned, his face was red, and his blond hair was sweaty and stuck to his forehead. Making him look all the more angelic, the little scamp. "Here, Daddy," he huffed, his chest pumping hard under his green footie pajamas, both hands clutching a limp, black construction paper frame. "It…" *Deep breath.* "Goes…" *Another great big breath.* "Around my… my fingers pitcher I made just for you."

"Handprint picture," Tanner corrected quietly.

Which earned him a spiked strawberry-blond eyebrow and a glare, but oddly, not a single cross word. Only a breathy, "Yeah, Daddy. Tanner helped me make it last night. It's for you."

Grissom was cross-legged near the tree, the perfect backdrop for this magnificent teary-eyed father fighting his emotions. "For me?" he growled in his tough-as-nails way. What a sight, the love shining in those hazel eyes. Wordless. Fighting to contain his feelings and losing the battle. His dark hair tousled. His beard was somehow darker and thicker this morning. This man was so breathtakingly sexy, she ached to touch him, hold him close, and comfort him. But not now. The pain he was feeling was the good kind, and those tiny crystals beaded on his lashes were diamonds of the purest happiness.

Tuesday caught it all in her viewfinder, her fingertip recording one spectacular shot after another, as her digital CCD and CMOS image sensors perfected the resolution of every last pixel. She mentally cataloged which shots would make the best portraits for the walls of this, the McCoy boys' Christmas room. She was in her element, finally giving back for all Grissom's kindnesses. Finally feeling like she just might belong somewhere again. That she really should stay. Not afraid to celebrate Christmas for the first time in years.

Grissom pulled both of his tired, pajama-clad boys onto his lap and kissed their heads. "Thanks, Scooter. Thanks, Short Stack. You two are the best." He coughed and cleared his throat. "Did Santa bring you guys everything you wanted?"

Both nodded, but darned if Luke didn't yell, "Wait! I got something for Miss Tuesday, too!" And away he went. Back downstairs. In minutes, the poor kid returned huffing, puffing, and sweaty with another finger-painted masterpiece of their very glittery tree.

The moment he handed it to Tuesday, his eyes bright and innocent, full of childish love, Tanner lifted to his feet. "I didn't forget," he whispered. Pulling a silver locket out of his pajama pocket, he handed it to her. "Dad helped me buy this on our way home from South America. It's for you."

Aww. What a sweetheart. A falling star was inscribed on the face of the tiny locket, and she had a feeling there was a story behind the symbol. But she'd wait for the day Tanner was ready to share that story. For now, Tuesday knelt and gathered both boys into her arms. Her heart was breaking. Overflowing. Bursting out of her eyes. There was no sense holding back, so why try? She let her emotions run down her face while she held two of the most important people in her life. "Guys," she breathed, swallowing hard. "Thank you both. You've made this my best Christmas ever."

"We did?" Luke asked with enough enthusiasm to power a small town.

"You both sure did," she replied, pressing kisses to their heads while bawling her eyes out. This was what she'd been missing, intangible, inexpressible childish wonder, acceptance, and love. It'd been a long time since she'd felt like she belonged.

Tanner didn't move. Neither did Luke. Grissom leaned over and wrapped his arms around all three of them. "Best. Christmas. Ever."

Closing her eyes, Tuesday gave him her weight, just leaned back and decided to stay where she'd landed.

Grissom asked again, "Guys, did Santa bring everything you asked for?"

"Almost," Tanner answered evenly, snuggling deeper into Tuesday's arm. "But I got what I wanted most. I got Tuesday."

"No, I got Tuesday," Luke grumped, digging his elbow into Tanner.

"Yeah, Luke, you got Tuesday, too," Tanner replied easily, not arguing. "We're both really lucky, huh?"

That did the trick. Luke stopped shoving and instead, grabbed Tanner's arm and pulled him in close again. "Yeah. We're lucky bastards, huh, Daddy?"

Grissom sputtered, "Luke! We don't say things like that."

Tuesday grinned. Yup, these boys were definitely his.

"But *you* say bastard all the time," Luke replied without guile.

"Yeah, Dad. You even say the F-word a lot, and it ain't fart," Tanner added.

"Boy! Boys! Okay. Enough already." Tuesday could tell Grissom was laughing inside. "And you're right. I've got a potty mouth, but that doesn't mean you should. How about we all clean up our acts? I'll stop dropping F-bombs—"

"And saying shit and gawddamn and all that other stuff," Tanner murmured.

"And yelling," Luke shrieked, his voice loud enough to wake the dead.

"What will you boys do?" Tuesday asked quietly.

"Well, I won't never say bastard again," Luke declared, crossing his heart with his index finger as he added, "unless I'm really, really pissed."

Tuesday looked up at the ceiling, fighting hard not to laugh out loud. These boys. "While you guys decide on family rules, I'll take the garbage bag out. Where are your trash cans?"

Grissom looked up at her from where he sat with one boy straddling each thigh, both facing him like they were prepared for high-stakes bargaining. "Leave it. I'll take it out later."

"It's no big deal. Meet you in the breakfast nook, guys." She breezed out, the over-sized garbage bag filled with paper and bows over her shoulder.

"You'll need the code or you'll set off the alarm," Grissom called after her.

"So what is it?"

"Texting you right now. Got your phone?"

"Nope," she yelled over her shoulder. "Give me a hint."

That brought him to the stairway, and Grissom told her the code to silence his alarm. "Don't be long."

"Don't eat breakfast without me."

"Then hurry," he ordered.

So Tuesday did. He hadn't told her where the cans were, but how hard could they be to find? She ran downstairs and into the garage, planning to be back in time to hear Grissom tell his boys about their beds. That was why he'd kept asking if they'd gotten everything they wanted. Wouldn't they be tickled when they saw those bunk beds?

Tuesday couldn't help whistling a corny Christmas jingle from some commercial, as she walked through the garage to the outside door. She'd be back inside before those handsome guys made it downstairs. She wished she hadn't left her cell phone charging in her bedroom, though. That wasn't like her. Living alone most of her adult life had made her very aware of how important that one link could be.

But again, no big deal. Tuesday didn't plan to stay outside long enough to need it. She stepped into a crisp, cloudy day that smelled like winter. There was snow inside those fluffy, dark gray clouds barreling in from the east. *Brrr.*

Tossing the bag into the industrial-size green trash receptacle next to the garage door, she turned on her heel, ready to get back inside where it was warm, as quickly as she could. Until—

She ran face-first into a brick. The sharp-edged blow dropped her to her knees. For one blinding, head-throbbing moment, she saw stars whirling over the tips of two round-toed boots. She shook the hit off, ready to get back on her feet, at least on her knees. But the hit was too hard. Too mean. The world shook, turning her around and around until she wanted to vomit. Vicious buzzing swarmed up her spine. Her head turned into a noisy beehive. The last thing she heard before everything went dark was, "You bitch!"

Chapter Twenty-Four

Grissom cocked his head, watching for Tuesday through the stairway that had taken her down to the garage. The one she'd walked through just a few moments earlier with trash slung over her shoulder like she was one of Santa's helpers. Tiny hairs prickled up the back of his neck. Something was wrong. He could feel it. He could taste it. She'd only been gone minutes, but he couldn't shake the feeling that someone was watching over his shoulder. That time was not on his side.

Muscle training ordered him to get up off his ass and run after Tuesday. His spine stiffened to do just that, but taking off like an idiot, when she might return any second…

When this was more likely just another sneaky panic attack…

When he knew damned well Tuesday was capable of taking care of herself…

Would frighten his boys. Probably unnecessarily. She'd faced down and ended the psycho Maeve Astor. She'd been stuck in many of the most dangerous parts of the globe, all for the sake of some almighty important photographs, and she'd done well. She was a loner used to taking care of herself. She didn't need him to fight her battles. She was just like him. Never surrender was their motto. Maybe unspoken, but something they'd recognized in each other.

But his boys? This house was their sanctuary. They had to believe it was safe, no matter what happened to Tuesday. If she were in trouble.

So many ifs.

Pushing to his feet, Grissom slapped a hand over his rear pocket, making sure he had his cell phone. There was no way he could just sit and do nothing, but he needed to handle his exit gently. "Boys, that bag might've been too heavy for Tuesday. Stay here by the tree until I get back. Tanner, maybe you could share your pastels and help Luke make another surprise for her, okay?"

"Sure, Dad," Tanner answered, his nose in his pastels, "but I think he'll like my new colored pencils better. They're already sharp and not so messy. Luke, wanna make a couple new pictures for Miss Tuesday?"

"Yeah, sure!" Luke chirped like a noisy little magpie, already scooting over to where Tanner sat on his butt, readily giving up on his new *Hot Wheels* racetrack to draw a 'pitcher' for the lady who'd snagged his heart, too.

That went better than Grissom expected. Nonetheless, he took time to tousle both his sons' heads before he all but ran for the garage, hurriedly sliding in his stocking feet down the carpeted steps and hurtling across the cold concrete floor to the side exit. Frightened by the adrenaline dump burning through his system, he prayed his anxiety and this panic attack were nothing more than his overactive imagination. It stood to reason. Things had been going smoothly. What could go wrong?

But in case his gut was right, he reminded the Man Upstairs, "I can't lose her, and You know it."

Clearing the top of the riding mower parked at the side exit, like one of the *Dukes of Hazzard* boys, Grissom verified the double-wide garage doors hadn't been activated. Of course not. He would've heard them from the loft.

But something was definitely wrong. Tuesday wouldn't have dawdled. She would've returned quickly, simply because she wanted to spend Christmas with him and his boys. She said she'd be right back. She told him not to eat breakfast without her.

Pulling his pistol from the ankle holster hidden under his pant leg, he was thankful for every redundant session of military training he'd ever endured. He stomped into his work boots, then, pistol first, he cleared the exit and scanned the immediate area, the extra-large driveway and parking pad.

Just snow, damn it. It must've barely started falling, as fine a dusting as covered everything.

No sign of Tuesday. The bag of trash lay beside the trash bin, and—

Shit! A small pool of bright red blood. Boot tracks and a long bloody trail from the parking pad, through the snow to—where? Someone had taken Tuesday. Hurt her. Dragged her away!

Pissed out of his mind, Grissom ran for his mini-forest, following the smooth, blood splotched trail, dodging pine branches, his eyes on the ground. Who'd do this? Why Tuesday? Who'd dare? On Christmas!

Two women sprang to mind. It couldn't be them. One was dead. The other lived on the opposite side of the country. So who the fuck assaulted and kidnapped Tuesday?

Chapter Twenty-Five

Tuesday came to beneath a thin blanket of snow with a blinding headache. Snowflakes fell into her eyes and on her face, enough that ice crystals had welled in her eye sockets. Tiny icicles coated her lashes. She wasn't cold, though. Cold in Virginia was nothing compared to far-off Resolute Bay, Nunavut, Canada, the coldest inhabited place in the world. She'd gone there once, to photograph the Haughton impact crater on nearby Devon Island. Now that—was cold.

Blinking as more frosty goodness crashed silently over her, she elbowed her torso up and off the ground, then flopped back when she couldn't maintain her balance long enough to sit. What on earth? She was laid out like the letter L, beneath what had to be the only deciduous tree in Grissom's tree farm. At least, she hoped that was where she was. Her ankles were tied together. Her thighs and butt were positioned flat against the trunk. The soles of her slippers faced skyward.

By now, Grissom, Tanner, and Luke had to be worried out of their minds. Forcing herself to stay calm and to think, to analyze her predicament, she took quick stock of her surroundings. Plenty of tracks littered the thin layer of snow around her. Good. They weren't deep. Neither was the snow. Which meant she hadn't been unconscious very long, just long enough to be dragged into the trees and leashed to a really big tree by some jerk.

Her brain connected the dots quickly. Whoever'd done this came prepared. Only one rope restrained her, one end tied to her ankles, the other end slung over a very high branch, then wrapped around the trunk of a nearby pine. Too bad that nearby tree was too far away to reach.

A brick, probably the one she'd been hit with, lay a good yard away. That explained how the jerk got the rope over that high branch. Whoever he was, he'd pulled the rope tight enough she couldn't sit up far enough to reach the knots at her ankles.

Yet. The fool didn't know who he was dealing with. It was times like this when Freddie's staunch counsel came to mind. *Head up. Shoulders back. Never let 'em see you blink. Never back down.*

Tuesday knew what she was up against—an idiot. The rope was just rope. Nylon, not invincible, and that knot was nothing a kindergartener who knew how to tie his shoes couldn't untie. And she was the one and only Tuesday Smart, making this kidnapping just one of many obstacles life had thrown at her. Okay then.

Summoning her willpower and every last bit of her strength, Tuesday crossed her arms over her chest, curled her torso upward, and began the arduous process of lifting her stiff body and clenched butt off the ground and into a reverse Uttanasana yoga pose. Her thighs burned when, at last, she touched her nose to her knees. Flattened upside down and against the trunk like she was, and if she stretched, her fingers could, at last, reach the simpleton's knots.

If she wanted to. Instead, she wrapped her fingers around the stretch of rope above her feet, and, inch by inch, with her biceps flexing and every strand of muscle on fire, with her lungs burning and the taste of blood on her tongue, she pulled her body straight up that tree. Keeping her legs stiff. While upside down. Shaking, because upside down was not how she'd ever trained. Like a crazy ninja in the most bizarre full-body press of her life. Not bending her knees. Not giving up—ever.

Tuesday hadn't overcome the crap life had continually dished out by sniveling, crying herself to sleep, or by quitting. But by keeping her eyes forward and working her hardest to survive. To overcome.

At last, her slippered feet, then her knocking knees, passed the sturdy branch the rope now hung loosely over, its slack looping down beside her in thin air. The goal was not simply to escape, but to escape with style. To always—always!—go above and beyond expectations. To show that jerk how much better than him she would always be.

Sucking in a gut full of *'I can do this!'* at the same time her endurance began to falter, she levered the leg closest to the branch over and—finally—hooked her trembling knee over the sturdy branch. Lifting her other leg over the branch came easier, since her full weight was already fully supported.

A last. Whew! She pulled herself upright and sat *on* the branch. Looking down at the ground, Tuesday sucked in a deep breath of wintry air, then searched the surrounding landscape for Grissom's house. Whoa. It was farther away than she expected.

Dropping her hands and arms to her sides, Tuesday let them swing loose until the adrenaline that had powered her escape eased up and her jackhammering heart rate settled closer to normal rhythm. Didn't take long, which was good because there wasn't time to waste. She blew out another gut full of determination, breathing hard and dizzy, but successful. And mindful.

Whoever'd accomplished this kidnapping was no mastermind. They'd just gotten lucky. First by unexpectedly running into her with that darn brick. Secondly, by the weather. The snow made moving her easy. Well, she was awake now and she was pissed.

It took mere seconds to undo the childish knots binding her ankles. Jumping back to Earth, she landed on both feet and one clenched fist. Three points. Like a *Marvel* superhero.

The kidnapper hadn't really wanted her, or he wouldn't have left her behind. Her kidnapping was a sham, a hastily planned, poorly executed attempt to pull Grissom away from his house. The only reasons that came to mind were Tanner and Luke.

Worried for their safety now, Tuesday followed the compressed, smooth trail back toward the house, until she realized those bright red dots in the snow were not lady bugs. Surprised, make that shocked, she lifted a hand and gently touched two fingers to her aching forehead. Her fingertips came away wet and bloody. She had a deep gash above her eye. *Ouch. That hurt.*

Another slice trailed down her cheekbone, cutting into her lower jaw. Bricks were sharp. *Ow.* It was no wonder her head was buzzing and her footsteps, that should've crunched the frozen ground, were muffled, as if she were walking underwater. Darn. She might have a concussion. Shocked she hadn't felt any pain until then, Tuesday ran the rest of the slick trail, back to the boys she adored.

Where was Grissom? Surely he'd be searching for her by now.

At last, the rear of his house came into view. Darned if someone wasn't standing at the deck's sliders. She was nearly on the top step when Grissom's alarm shrieked one painfully long blast. She faltered, clapping both hands over her ears to keep her poor head from splitting apart. Didn't matter that the sliders were now ajar or that the guy had gone inside. She didn't care how big or mean he thought he was. She would go through him to save those boys. She had to. Who cared if she didn't have a weapon? She didn't. But she did need that blasted siren to cease and desist. Sound waves at the right decibel were destructive, and her aching head was feeling every last bit of those fierce waves now.

That short, squatty guy in black was inside Grissom's house, facing Tanner and Luke, both still in their red and green Christmas pajamas. Luke held a small plastic bag in his hand. His eyes were squeezed tight, probably from the alarm. His cheeks were puffed and red. Something gooey dripped down his chin. Tanner was reaching around Luke to get the bag. Luke had the hand with that bag stretched away from Tanner, while he held his other arm stiff behind him, keeping Tanner at bay.

And that person in black was…

Tuesday borrowed Grissom's favorite cuss word. "Fuck!"

Chapter Twenty-Six

The blood on the trail grew lighter the farther Grissom tracked into the trees. Instead of taking a direct route, which would've been smart, whoever had abducted Tuesday had veered west before turning eastward, into the trees. He wanted to scream her name, desperate for Tuesday to answer. But he couldn't risk alerting her attacker. Not willing to wait until the trail ran out, he jerked his cell phone out of his pocket, and called Alex, like he'd wanted to do at the start of this shitshow.

"B-boss. Sorry, I know it's Christmas, and you're with your family, but—"

"What do you need?" Alex barked like the Rottweiler he could be.

"Someone's kidnapped Tuesday. She's bleeding, Boss. There's blood on my driveway and more heading into the trees behind my place and—"

"On my way. Call Mother. Tell her to pull footage from every security camera within twenty miles." The phone went dead.

Grissom shook it to reactivate the screen, in case he'd accidentally disconnected Alex. But no. His screen flashed *call ended*. Knowing Alex, he'd be on site within minutes. Heading deeper into his trees, Grissom wondered who else Alex might call. Not a good day for anyone to be asked to leave their families, but damned if Grissom cared.

He was deep within his twenty-acre tree farm when Alex caught up with him. The guy was dressed in a USMC t-shirt and jeans. No jacket. He must've driven right over, then tracked Grissom. Tossing a set of earbuds as he passed by, Alex ordered, "Tell me what you know."

Grissom caught the earbuds and inserted them deep in his ear canal, where they'd keep him in contact with everyone on the same frequency. "She didn't come back after she took the garbage out. I found blood near the trash receptacle, then the tracks I'm following now. Whoever grabbed her—"

"Dragged her, understood. Which means she's not fighting back, and she's hurt. Who's with your boys?"

"No one. They know better than to open any outside doors while I'm gone."

"This might take a while. You sure about that?"

Damned good question. The bloody smears on the snow faded the further into the trees Grissom went, but the drag marks hadn't. "I had no choice. Have to find Tuesday."

He was shoulder to shoulder with Alex as they dodged dozens of six-foot, then eight-foot saplings. Then nine-footers. They were nearly to the other side of his land, when the trail ran out and—

"Shit," he hissed, his mouth dry. There was no sign of Tuesday. Just a mixed-up mess of boot tracks, and a long, nylon rope dangling from the eighty-foot tall shagbark hickory that straddled the property line he shared with his neighbor to the north.

Grissom knelt and studied the assailant's prints. "We're looking for a guy. One set of tracks. Size thirteen boots. Light tactical, military, all-terrain. Rounded toe. Anti-skid soles."

Just like mine. Panic flared. Had someone been inside his house and taken his old boots to frame him? He looked closer, making sure these tracks didn't carry the same tell-tale slice across the left heel, evidence of a different day and another shitstorm a world away. Thank God. These tread marks were sharp and clear. The soles had to be brand-new. What the fuck? Army boots took a beating on a daily basis. Forced marches. Rough as shit terrain. Landing hard after being dropped out of helicopters on far-off mountainsides. Running. Fighting. Kicking in doors. Racing to save a brother's life. Yet the impressions this bastard's boots left were clear and crisp. Not worn. Not worn at all. *Definitely not mine.*

The prints in the damp soil weren't deep, either, considering the size of most men wearing size thirteens. Big boots meant big feet, and usually, big feet meant a big, heavy guy. But these prints were flat. Interesting.

"Stewart," Alex snapped, thumbing the speaker on his cell phone and waving for Grissom to get to his side.

"Boss," Mother spoke up, "I'm watching a black, late model sedan on the frontage road east of Grissom's housing development. It's parked and idling. One person inside, as near as I can tell from the security camera on the front porch across the road. I sent Maverick to check it out. Rory and Ember will be at Grissom's house within minutes. They were already en route when I called. They'll take Tanner and Luke to their place until Grissom's back."

"Thanks," Grissom told her. Ember and Rory were both kids at heart. They'd take care of Tanner and Luke, and they'd make this interrupted Christmas fun. Their son Tyler would help.

"I can't access any satellite footage, not with this stormfront rolling in," she added. "If I could, I'd rewind every last feed and go back as far as I could, for as long as it takes. But that option's out. Can't see through weather like this."

"Know that, Mother," Alex said. "Any other footage you can access? Traffic cams? Doorbell cameras? God knows everybody and their son-of-a-bitching dog's got one."

"No doorbell cameras that give clear images. Axel's backtracking traffic cams on all streets and off-ramps feeding that frontage road. Hopefully, we can catch the plate, at least establish which direction the sedan came from. Then it's just a matter of pinging consecutive traffic cams to catch them, maybe identify them. These people are not omniscient, Grissom. They've made mistakes. It's just a matter of finding those mistakes and intercepting them."

"Tuesday doesn't have that kind of time," Grissom growled.

"Are you sure there's more than one person involved?" Alex asked.

"No, Boss," Mother declared, "just assumed there had to be at least two. One to grab Tuesday and a getaway driver."

Grissom groaned. Not having specific intel wasn't good enough.

"All hands on deck, Mother," Alex ordered. "Tell them who's missing and what little we know."

"Already did. Called in Search and Rescue, too. Figured they owed us one for pulling two of their people from that ravine the last time we worked a rescue with them. Called our local sheriff. Howie's on his way; so's Nighthawk and Tucker Chase's people."

Grissom ran a quick hand through his hair, exasperated and unwilling to wait, like he had a choice. He hated the Swiss cheese his brain had become since the wreck with that FedEx truck. He had no idea who Nighthawk or Howie was, and only vaguely remembered some ballsy guy named Tucker Chase. But all hands on deck wasn't good enough. He wanted the National Guard.

Fighting back the panic crawling up his spine, his gaze dropped to the smooth trail over the thin layer of snow that quietly declared precisely where Tuesday'd been dragged and where she'd been left. Why wasn't she still there? What had this asshat done with her? To her? Deeper prints showed where the bastard's feet had dug into the snow to maintain traction, while pulling her through the trees. Other places clearly showed where his heels had dug in. He'd walked backwards part of the time. Why?

Tuesday wasn't heavy enough that a guy with size thirteen feet would've had to struggle dragging her. Could it be the kidnapper wasn't strong enough? Bullshit! There wasn't a man or woman on The TEAM who couldn't carry a tiny thing like Tuesday. If he were that fool, Grissom would've thrown her over one shoulder, hot-footed it into the trees, and run like a son of a bitch to that waiting sedan. What was the person in that parked vehicle waiting for, if not to secret Tuesday away as quickly as possible? Wasn't that how kidnappings worked?

Or... was she already inside the car? Murdered? Bleeding out? Stabbed? Strangled? Maybe worse? Was the person Mother thought she was watching actually Tuesday's dead body?

No! He shook his mother's ingrained negativity away. Tuesday. Was. Not. Dead. She couldn't be. He'd know if she were. He would feel it.

Then, where was she? Boot prints aplenty danced around the tree. They were dug in deeper in some places, overlapped and crisscrossed their own paths everywhere. But there was only the one drag mark in, nothing leading toward the sedan. There were no tread marks on any part of the smoothed trail that had brought her here, except for two rounded impressions, one on each side of that trail, about two feet from the base of the tree.

While Alex gave Mother stern marching orders, Grissom dropped to his knees and looked closer at the evidence in the thin layer of snow. Whoever took Tuesday had preplanned. He'd come prepared, and he'd dealt with her as soon as he'd gotten her out of sight. But he hadn't killed her. There were no signs of struggle, and Tuesday would've put up one helluva a fight. If she'd still been alive…

Pissed at the possibility that she wasn't and denying it every time the notion hit his brainpan, Grissom looked up at the tree, to the rope lying over the lowest branch, then back to the round holes at each side of Tuesday's last location. Elbows, damn it. Those depressions were where she'd stuck her elbows into the ground. But...

No prints. No signs anywhere that told him she'd gotten to her feet or stood beneath the tree. But there… Right there. On the other side of the tree's wide trunk. Overlaying several thick tread marks left by her attacker's boots, were a deep set of smooth-soled size-seven prints left by—what could only be Tuesday's baby-blue moccasins. The ones she was wearing this morning.

Thank you, Jesus! Grissom licked his dry lips, his mind spinning but no longer from panic. The smooth trail ended at the base of the hemlock, but the slipper prints began with two very distinct depressions, both side-by-side, as if she'd—

He looked up again. How had she climbed this tree without leaving prints at the base of it? What'd she do, fly? Or… had her abductor strung her feet first and upside down, her butt against the tree trunk. That was why the rope. Damn the bastard!

Her prints began where she'd jumped to the ground, a distance of at least twenty feet.

"I'll kill him," Grissom hissed. His woman was strong, damn strong. But she would've had to pull herself up, in a tuck, then somehow grabbed the rope that had probably been tied around her ankles. She'd hoisted her full body weight up and past that damned branch. It made sense. Then she sat up there and untied the rope.

The image of Tuesday sweating and cussing on that branch made Grissom proud as fuck. His woman was unstoppable when she was angry. An over-protective mother bear who'd had no problem ending Maeve Astor, the diabolical black widow spider from hell, who'd killed how many men? How many children?

Which explained why her footprints weren't near the base of the tree. Because his beautiful, crazy woman had jumped. She was injured, in no shape to fight, much less accomplish all she had, but she was headed back to his home and she was fighting mad.

Okay then. "Boss! Get your ass over here. Found Tuesday's tracks. She's on her way home. To my place."

Pushing to his feet, Grissom followed the woman he adored. Tiny crimson beads in the snow told him she was still bleeding but running, following those gawddamned Army issue boots leading back to his house. To his sons. Damn. He had to get there first.

Alex ran alongside, both of them charged with enough angst to blast a rocket to the sun.

"This was never about Tuesday, Boss. Someone's after my boys," Grissom explained, his lungs on fire, pissed that he'd left them alone. Two little guys who trusted him, only him, to keep them safe. Who'd been told to never open any doors. Which might keep them safe. They had no idea how to shut off the alarm. Not like that meant much to Luke. He was too young to understand. Too bull-headed and too stubborn. Too much like his old man. And now, the jackhole who'd hurt Tuesday wouldn't hesitate to break windows or doors. Or heads.

I left them alone. What was I thinking?

Of Tuesday. That was who.

Run, damn you! Run!

Too late. A raucous shriek blasted over the trees. His alarm. His only line of defense had just been breached. Someone was in his house, after his boys. Tuesday had just been a distraction, and Grissom fell for it.

Must! Run! Faster!

Chapter Twenty-Seven

"You bitch!" Pamela hissed the second Tuesday landed on Grissom's rear deck, her fists clenched and so, so ready for battle. Her bare feet were sore from running since she'd long since ditched her slippers. Bare soles and ten toes had more grip. She was poised and focused, weaponless, but ready to strike first and ask questions later. If only that alarm would shut up or turn off. How long was it going to blare like a runaway freight train?

Pamela, on the other hand, didn't seem affected by the noise. She was armed with a small caliber pistol and waving it at Tanner.

"You're alive," Tuesday deadpanned loudly, her head spinning from the over-exertion of the run. She was fairly sure Pam had given her a concussion with that brick. The intense noise didn't help, but no way would she let Pamela McCoy hurt Tanner or Luke. If this miserable excuse of a human being thought she stood a chance of kidnapping Grissom's boys…

Guess again. The only way this deadly confrontation would end was with one of them on her knees, and it wouldn't be Tuesday Smart.

"What's it look like?" Pam yelled, tossing short, greasy red hair off her forehead like some sweaty dancer from that '80's movie, *"Saturday Night Fever."* Her weapon was aimed at a defenseless six-year-old. "'Course, I'm alive. I come back to get my son, so keep outta my way!"

"Son?" Tuesday asked just as loudly. *Not sons?* Man, that alarm was going to be the death of her.

"Yeah, *son*. You deaf or something? Look at 'em, why don'tcha? Which one of these shits do you think is mine?" *How about neither of them.* "Sure ain't the little bastard who takes after his lazy-assed father."

"These boys are not bastards," Tuesday asserted over the intense ringing in her skull.

"That one is." Pam pointed her chin at Tanner. "But Luke's mine, and I'm not leaving without him."

Tuesday hadn't seen Pam's explosive reveal coming. Not in her wildest imaginations had she suspected Luke wasn't Grissom's biological child. Not once. Sure, she'd noticed the differences in the boys' appearances, but kids from the same parents often looked dissimilar.

Now that she had Mommy Dearest to compare with Luke, her brain did the math. He could've only inherited his strawberry blond baby-hair and those sparkling cherub-blue eyes from two parents with the same red-hair slash blue-eye genes. He had the same fair complexion as his mom, although Pam's face was more wrinkled and her skin was sallow and slack. Pam was a drinker and a smoker, probably a drug addict, and every last bit of her self-abuse showed. Didn't matter that her split ends were bright lobster-red. Her roots were the same soft coppery tones as the baby-fine hairs covering Luke's head.

Mother Nature's laws of genetics were hard fast rules, not suggestions. Not up for votes. Ordained long before mankind lifted his bleary, entitled eyes out of the primordial swamp and decided to walk upright. They were as undeniable as the laws of gravity and the speed of light. You didn't have to believe in them for them to be real. They. Just. Were.

But Luke wasn't Grissom's child? The thought had never entered Tuesday's mind. Since the moment he'd collapsed in her hotel door, in Puntarenas, Grissom had done nothing but love both these boys. He'd never treated one better than the other, and his love showed everywhere. While riding horseback in Maverick's field. At Cakes and Honey's. On the mantle. Upstairs in the loft. Under the tree. When he'd hoisted Luke on his shoulder while he and Tanner dragged back the tree she'd chosen. And every moment in-between.

The more concerning question was: *What's Pam on now? Booze? Pills? Crack? Meth?*

"He's mine!" she screamed, stamping her foot like a woman deranged.

All of the above?

"I thought you were with your boyfriend when his plane went down," Tuesday offered more calmly.

Tuesday had no idea what these boys had been told about how their mother died, or if they'd been told anything. Regardless, this was not their battle. They were children and this was adult business, and somehow, Tuesday was once again in a standoff with their evil witch of a mother.

"You thought wrong!" Pam shrilled. "Bastard thought he could screw me over once he was back on his home turf. Well, I showed him. Watching him pat that bitch's ass when he helped her aboard was the last straw. I had enough of his two-timing lies."

Pot meet kettle.

Pam was obviously unhinged. Her pupils were black, enlarged like wide-open camera lenses meant for nighttime photography. Fireworks. Lunar eclipses. Meteor showers. Fun stuff like that.

Where, oh, where was Grissom? And how had this mean-spirited woman breached his security system? The brick laying just outside the deck door couldn't be how she'd gotten inside; the glass doors weren't broken, not even cracked. The crowbar tossed aside on the deck hadn't been used, either. There was no damage to the sliders. None at all. All evidence pointed to the charming little boy holding that goody bag. Luke. Grissom's three-year-old. He must've remembered the four-digit security code. He'd let his mother in.

"So what'd you do, Pam? Decide to stay behind, miss the tour, and…?" *Do something as cruel to Estes as what you did to Tanner? Sabotage his plane? Kill him and everyone with him? Just because he made you mad?* Tuesday had no idea how someone like Pam could be smart enough to do that.

"Ha!" Pam's head jerked back again in what might be a sign of a nervous disorder, as hard as it rocked her balance. "Used my knife, what'd you think? Stabbed a few holes in his wing. Dumb shit didn't know he was losing gasoline when he took off."

"That would work," Tuesday hummed to herself. Wings on most small aircraft were gas tanks. Susceptible and exposed, out in the open. Ready targets waiting for a deranged, jealous woman to come along.

"The dick put that slut in my seat! My! Seat!" Man, this woman could scream. "He set her ass up front, right beside him! In the fucking cockpit! You bet I killed him. Killed her and the fools with him, too. What was I supposed to do? Sit in the back like a nobody? After I paid his way home? Let him get away with treating me like a whore?"

Tuesday almost answered, *'You mean after you stole Grissom's sons and his hard-earned paycheck.'* But her migraine was pounding a drum solo in time with the blaring alarm, and poor Luke was listing to one side. His eyes were closed and bits of whatever treat Pam had given him were sliding out between his drooling lips. "What did you give him?"

Pam turned coy. "Something he likes. Gummies. They're his favorite."

"Uh-uh! She gave him poison, Miss Tuesday!" Tanner yelled from where he stood behind his brother, both boys still in their Christmas pajamas. "She told him not to give me none. Said it was only for good boys and I'm—"

"You're worthless!" Pam screeched. "Never were good for anything! I brought that treat for Luke, not you. They're to keep my baby calm until I get him out of here!"

My baby? Like hell. "No!" Tuesday yelled over the din of the raucous alarm. "You gave these sweethearts to me, and I'm not giving them back. You need to leave, before Grissom comes back."

"I'm already here," Grissom growled behind Tuesday. His hand on her shoulder should've released the tension running through her like flaming det cord. It didn't. If anything, his presence made everything worse. He stepped around Tuesday, closing in on Pam with both fists clenched. "What have you done?" he barked.

"Drop the weapon, Pam," Alex ordered. "It's over."

"Or what?" she spat, her pistol still pointed at Tanner. "You'll shoot me? In front of my sons? I don't think so."

"Try me." Alex's voice turned deadly calm.

Everything was happening too fast. Grissom had turned into a charging bull, and the pistol in Pam's hand was the matador's red cape. Something snapped deep in Tuesday's gut.

Tanner and Luke needed their dad more than they needed her.

Grissom needed to get his baby boy to the ER.

His. Son. Not Tuesday's son. Never Tuesday's child.

This was why she'd survived when her mom, dad, and Freddie hadn't. For this moment. For this right here and right now. This was why she'd ended Maeve Astor, not the other way around. All those deaths had brought Tuesday Smart to this precise day and time. To this very second. She was only alive so Tanner and Luke would always have their dad.

So be it.

Tuesday burst off the balls of her feet and plowed past Grissom, elbowing him aside and out of her way. With one shoulder lowered for maximum impact, Tuesday collided with her target, digging her clenched fingers into Pam's throat, while she fought to get that pistol out of her fist.

"Get off me!" Pam shrieked, jerking backward.

Like she thought she could take on the mother bear Tuesday had become?

"No! Tuesday, no!" Grissom bellowed.

"Miss Tuesday! No! She's gonna kill you!" That was Tanner. Bless his pure little heart.

"Son of a bitch!" Alex roared.

But the wheels were already in motion, and Luke's future was sure. Tuesday understood everything now. Her life had always been forfeit, and that was okay. She'd never be a mother, but she could perform this one last motherly act. It would be her ultimate pleasure to die for the people she loved.

Before Pam could change directions and fire, Tuesday pulled her in for a smothering hug. A hug too tight and too close. A hug too personal to allow the demented woman to move, much less aim with precision. Pam couldn't see past Tuesday. The pistol was trapped between them. If it went off now, it would kill her or Pam. That was the only way to save everyone else. It was the right thing to do.

BOOM! The handgun jerked against Tuesday's ribs. She felt the impact. A scorching finger of death ripped through her flesh. She felt the burn. She smelled the coppery scent of singed flesh and blood. Her skin. Her blood.

Like the insane freak she was, Pam cackled, "I got you, bitch!"

She thought she'd won.

Guess again.

Seconds raced by before it dawned on Pam that she'd missed her intended target and Tuesday wasn't going down. That her shot hadn't gone wild, but neither had she hit Tanner or Grissom. That she'd underestimated the woman she was up against. That this truly was a fight to the death—her death. That Tuesday now had the upper hand.

Still fighting with every last beat of her heart, Tuesday jerked the burning pistol out of her adversary's hand. Panicked, Pam clawed Tuesday's face, hissing like a cat. Aiming for Tuesday's eyes, but missing. Still fighting for control of her weapon.

Not happening.

Tuesday knew Grissom would go for his boys now that she'd cleared the way for him. They were what mattered, not her. He'd put them first, and he'd whisk them to safety like the good father he was. He'd get Luke to a doctor, and he'd make sure Tanner wouldn't see what happened next. And it would happen.

The girl fight of Tuesday's life was on, and her lessons in self-defense were front and center. Pressure points mattered. With Pam still clawing at her face, and for the first time worried her time might be running out, that this crazy woman could still win, Tuesday balled her free hand into a fist and punched the side of Pam's neck, hard enough that her knuckles popped.

The witch stepped back, dazed and gasping.

Tuesday snagged the pistol before it could fall and accidentally discharge. Ouch, that barrel was hot. Not like she cared about blistered fingers or hands. She was expendable, and her strike to Pam's carotid artery and vagus nerve had done what she'd intended. Pam's eyes were bugged out. The woman was disbelieving to the bitter end that someone might just be meaner and smarter than her. She was still standing, but clutching her throat, gasping for air.

Damned if shock wasn't a really good look on Pamela McCoy's ugly face.

Not taking anything for granted, Tuesday jerked Pam in for one last close hug and rammed her skull into that baby killer's forehead. Tanner's would-be killer collapsed into a whiny puddle in the middle of Grissom's front room, holding her bleeding nose and still unable to breathe.

Funny thing about that alarm. In the end, it ended the battle of Tuesday's life. She backed out of the room and into the cool air on Grissom's deck, her head spinning. She needed to get away from the noise.

By then, Alex was at the front door's control panel, his back to the family room, keying in the code to silence the alarm and let in whoever was ringing the doorbell, probably local law enforcement. Maybe EMTs.

Grissom was on the floor, his eyes closed in anguish, cradling his youngest in one arm, his oldest under his other arm. Tanner was a blubbering mess, his sweaty face buried in his dad's shirt. He wasn't watching, and that was good. He'd be okay now. He too had the best father in the world.

Clarity hit hard, but certain. There would be no happily-ever-after with the emotionally damaged man Tuesday had come to love. Grissom's boys needed him, and he needed them. What they didn't need was more grief and tragedy in their lives, and that would surely come if she stayed. If she chose to put her greedy, self-serving needs ahead of theirs.

Life never worked out like you wanted it to, how well Tuesday knew. She loved these three—enough to let them go. But she had to do it now, while no one was watching. Silently, she eased the slider closed, then ducked out of sight, just as Alex opened the front door and let the first responders in. Grissom was too wrapped up in his boys to worry about her. No one saw her stumble off the deck steps and escape from a life that was never meant to be.

"Goodbye, my sweet boys," she huffed, into what had become a blistering cold day. "Goodbye, Grissom. I'll love you forever. Be good to each other, guys."

And live a long, long time. Let this be my Christmas gift to you guys, to live the rest of your lives in peace and happiness.

Her skull had to be cracked, it screamed with so much pain. The burn in her side pounded as loudly. Pam had shot her, but not fatally, at least Tuesday hoped it wasn't fatal. She was still on her feet. That had to mean something. Unfortunately, the two things she needed to make a clean break, her keys and her phone, were back in Grissom's house.

She stumbled onward, determined to run but barely able to walk. Freddie's gentle counsel came to her on the icy breeze: *Head up. Shoulders back. Never let 'em see you blink. Never give up.*

"I'm not giving up," she told the grandfatherly ghost walking beside her. "I'm giving the guys I love most what they need to live. I'm giving me being gone."

A tear welled in the corner of her eye. Just a few more steps. Then a few more. Until, at last, she was hidden within the sweet-smelling pines of Grissom's tree farm again. Breathing hard but standing. Crisp evergreen scent surrounded her as quickly as the silence of the falling snow muffled the rest of the world. This little forest offered Tuesday the temporary cover she needed. Somehow, she'd find her way out of Virginia. Maybe she'd call an Uber or Lyft if she could get to a phone. Things were easy when you were rich and had what everyone else wanted. Well, almost everything. She was leaving the best part of her adult life behind. The best man and the best boys. But she was doing this for them, and someday, they'd be grateful she'd disappeared.

People thought winter killed, that cold was deadly. Tuesday knew better. Eventually, enough snow would cover her and keep her warm, like a fluffy white blanket. Dropping to her knees, she curled to her injured side and watched flakes kiss the end of her nose. She needed to rest for a minute or two. Then she'd get back on her feet, and she'd leave like she planned. It was better this way. Really. It was.

Chapter Twenty-Eight

It was hard dialing 911 with his hands full and his heart breaking, at what Grissom had let happen to his boys—in their house! Luke had gone stock still in his arms. He was so pale. Whatever Pam gave him was killing him. Alex had her face down on the floor, his knee in her back and her hands cuffed behind her. But the shrew was still breathing and cursing and—!

That was more than what Luke was doing. Damn her!

Maverick hadn't called about that damned black sedan, either.

"Central dispatch, what is your emergency?"

"My son's been poisoned! Send help!" *Send everyone!*

Instead of continuing to rant like a maniac at the end of his rope, Grissom calmed himself enough to relay his address, phone number, and Luke's symptoms. He answered every question the polite woman asked. Luke's age, weight, if he had any allergies, if he knew what his son swallowed. How he got hold of the poison. "I have no idea what he swallowed! I wasn't here. His fucking mother gave him—hell, I don't even know what she—!"

"Candy, Dad," Tanner interrupted, his sweet face masked by tears and sweat. "She gave Luke that bag of gummies over there, and she told him not to share with—"

"Gummies?" Grissom barked. Could it be? Had that lousy excuse of a mother—of a woman!—of a gawddamned human being!—given Luke THC-laced edibles? Jesus!

Tanner pulled out of his father's arm and pried the plastic sandwich bag out of his little brother's rigid fingers. "These icky things, Dad. Mom gave him all these and told him he was a good boy and not to share with me cuz I was a worthless bastard."

Grissom had no more than passed that horrific intel to the operator when Eric Reynolds charged into the chaos and gently lifted Luke out of his hands. Stuffing his phone into his rear pocket, Grissom pulled poor Tanner back against his chest, praying for his baby boy. That there, at what felt like the end of his world, with Tanner tucked in his arms, God would be merciful and kind. That He'd be what Grissom had failed at being—a perfect father.

"She poisoned him. She poisoned my boy." Tears fell and Grissom didn't care. He never should've left his sons alone. This was his fault. All of it.

Calmly, Eric laid Luke on his back on the floor, then adeptly snapped on a pair of surgical gloves. Tilting Luke's head back, he inserted an index finger into Luke's mouth and scraped out a congealed mass of half-chewed red and yellow gummies, along with a puddle of drool. "Could be," he replied noncommittally. "Legalizing pot hasn't made stupid parents any smarter."

Pressing the business ends of the stethoscope around his neck to Luke's tiny chest, Eric cocked his head and listened intently. "I'd give this little guy a dose of Ipecac if I knew for sure what he ingested. That was the paramedics you were talking to, right?"

"Yes," Grissom confirmed.

A shrill siren screamed nearby. What a fucked-up Christmas. He scanned the room and his back deck, searching for the sweet comfort and calm only Tuesday could give. But he didn't see her. She was probably in the kitchen, grabbing bottled waters for everyone, or doing something just as thoughtful. Tuesday took care of folks. She stepped up when others didn't. But not having her by his side or anywhere in sight wasn't like her. "You seen Tuesday, Boss?" *Because I can't find her and I need her. She should be here, damn it. With me.*

Alex still crouched alongside Pam. He'd secured her pistol, a pair of leather garden gloves, and was emptying her pockets. That sight was enough distraction for Grissom to ask, "You find a receipt for the shit she gave my boy? What the fuck is it?!"

Alex shook his head. "Not yet. Give me a second. And no, I haven't seen Tuesday, but she was just here. She can't have gone far."

A receipt for the crap in Luke's system would be helpful, but Grissom knew a piece of paper wouldn't save his tiny son's life. This time, Pam had gone too far. *But where's Tuesday? She should be here hugging Tanner. Hell, hugging me. I need her. We all need her!*

Four emergency responders hustled through the open front door, two medics and two firemen. Howie, the local sheriff, followed. He went straight to where Alex crouched over Pam, while the medics took control of Luke. Grissom sat there in everyone's way, his arms around his oldest son, watching what could be the end of his and Tanner's world.

If Luke died…

No! Not happening! It can't! I won't let it!

His youngest boy's life flashed through his mind. The day Luke was born. Grissom had been there, trying like hell to be a good husband to the deceitful woman who'd brazenly cheated on him. He'd always known Luke wasn't his biological son, sure. Wasn't hard to do the math, not considering he'd been out of the country the ten months before Luke's birth.

Yet never had Grissom felt anything but love for the little redhead. It wasn't Luke's fault his mother was a tramp. Biology be damned. When the nurse handed that perfect, wet, little baby into Grissom's trembling hands—the kid was only seconds old—the purest, unadulterated love had washed over him like an out-of-control grassfire. It had sparked a surge of fatherly endorphins or hormones or—whatever. That was the second time Grissom understood how fierce fatherhood could be. And how damned rare.

He hadn't been there to experience that sense of wonder when Tanner was born. No, he'd been denied the priceless gift of holding his firstborn son, fresh out of his mother's body, on Tanner's first day of life. And now that same innocent boy might be witnessing his baby brother's death. Hell, they both might be watching Luke die.

Jesus! Help me save Luke, damn it! Help everyone!

Hopelessness stormed over Grissom again. *Where is Tuesday?* She'd know what to do and say. She was smart like that. Maybe she'd hustle Tanner out of the room and into a safer, quieter place where panic didn't steal every last breath from a guy. Where there was still hope. Where prayers were still answered.

"Ready to transport," one of the medics reported into the radio clipped on his shoulder. Luke was on oxygen and an IV by then. "One, two, and three," the medic said, as the scissor-lift beneath the gurney holding Grissom's tiniest boy prepared to take his baby away.

Like hell.

Grissom looked one last time for Tuesday. He needed her. Tanner and Luke needed her. Where was she? Was she hurt? Had Pam shot her? God, no. A weapon had been discharged, but after that, everything happened so fast, he couldn't be sure. It couldn't have struck Tuesday, not as quickly as she'd shoved him out of her way and attacked Pam with that damned fine karate chop to the neck. That head-butt of hers was another phenomenal offensive tactic. Good on Tuesday. He'd lost track of her when he'd dived into the fray to take the hit he thought Pam had intended for Tanner. By then, Grissom had been running on pure adrenaline. Even now, a sneaky panic attack was creeping up the back of his neck, making all those tiny hairs stand on end.

He looked up into Maverick's rugged face. Why was Cowboy here? Damn. His house was overflowing with TEAM agents, men and women he hadn't seen come in, all dressed in black denims and TEAM polos, as if this were just another mission and not Christmas Day. He'd been so focused, so lost in the what-ifs of a father losing his child and the woman he loved deserting him in his time of need, that—

"I can't find Tuesday," he told the powerful male hunkered down at his side, instantly forgiving Maverick for not calling about the sedan. "I'm going with Luke. Take care of him until I get back. I mean Tanner. Take care of Tanner for me," he clarified, transferring his oldest into Maverick's beefy arms.

"You bet. Anything you need, brother," Maverick answered, as a tearful Tanner latched onto his favorite cowboy's neck.

Leave it to Maverick to use that word. *Brother.* It meant so damned much to the unwanted son Grissom had always been. A brother at his side growing up would've been damned nice. But now? Maverick had just thrown Grissom the lifeline he hadn't realized he needed.

"But Dad, I want to stay with you," Tanner whispered, even as he settled onto Maverick's knee.

"I know, Scooter, but there won't be enough room in the ambulance, and..." *I've got to go.*

Grissom damned near burst into tears at the decision he was making, to leave Tanner and Tuesday behind. "You gotta find her for me, Maverick. Find Tuesday. I don't know where she went. She was right here, but then, she was gone, just gone..." His voice trailed away as his gaze scrolled over the hectic scene in his house one last time, searching for signs of blood. The only blood he saw was still gushing out of Pam's ugly, whiny face, and...

Damn it! Now Tanner would have questions. He'd think his dad lied when Grissom said his mother would never hurt him again, that she was gone for good. Why the fuck was Pam even here? How could she be in his house? Why wasn't she dead? How the hell was she still alive?

Grissom's jaw cracked as it shifted to one side in his big dumb head. If Pam hadn't been in Estes' plane when it went down, then who was? Some woman who looked like her? Was this one of Pam's elaborate schemes to destroy everyone

Grissom held dear? How had that she-devil even tracked him down? *Shit!*

"She might be outside, Dad. It was kinda noisy in here, and I think she has a headache," Tanner offered quietly.

"Who?"

"Miss Tuesday." Tanner frowned. He didn't understand how frazzled his father was, now, when Grissom needed to man up and be everything to everyone, to be everywhere at once. Now, when panic was storming the fragile hold he had on his control. To stay or go, the eternal dilemma of every service man or woman with orders to deploy. To leave behind the people he loved most. To have to choose between them and all that was good in the world. To fight the evil that threatened everything, damn it. This couldn't be happening again, not on Christmas Day.

Tanner tipped forward and pressed his sweaty hand to Grissom's cheek. "Dad, I'm a big boy now, and me and Maverick'll go find Miss Tuesday for you. Don't worry. We got your six."

Grissom grabbed his six-year-old boy into a tight hug at the manly words of comfort pouring out of him.

"Yeah, Grissom," Maverick added. "Go with Luke and let us guys locate Miss Smart. The medics are waiting. I'll stay in touch."

"Thank you." Tousling Tanner's head one last time, Grissom ran for the door, knowing Tanner would be okay and praying with all his heart that Luke would be, too. Hoping Tuesday hadn't left him. She wouldn't do that to his boys, would she? To him?

Grissom looked back one last time, not sure he was making the right decision. Never sure that he ever had. *Lord help me. Do I stay or do I go?*

Chapter Twenty-Nine

She stared into the blissfully silent white blizzard pouring down on her. Covering her. Hiding her. So peaceful. So white. So many flakes, all drifting like tiny downy feathers. Reminded Tuesday of the time she'd encountered those three beluga whales on her first solo photo shoot in the Arctic. They'd called out to her from a narrow stretch of ice-cold water, chirped and grunted like three friendly pets who'd wanted human company.

Hmmm. Or maybe they'd sensed her paranoia at being left alone in one of Mother Earth's harshest climates.

Whatever. Those whales had followed her for as long as they could, along the edge of the ice shelf she'd walked that day—like comfort animals. Sleek. Pure white, devoted companions. In a world as untouched as them. Who was she kidding? Those three chatty, whistling guardian angels had been as untouched by any man then, as she was now. Still a virgin. Always would be.

Only Grissom *had* touched her. Barely, but—enough.

Enough. Was there such a thing as ever having enough of the one thing you craved more than anything else? Enough companionship? Enough hugs and kisses from the handsome, kindly man you treasured most in your life? Enough home? Security? Money? Tuesday had more wealth than she knew what to do with, but what had it gotten her, all the wise investments Freddie'd made on her behalf? All those portfolios and bank accounts? Trusts? Offshore accounts? Real estate? Plans for a future she didn't want now and hadn't wanted then?

It had gotten her here, that much was certain. Here, on her back, staring Heaven in the eye and wondering what one person's life was worth. Did it matter in the grand scheme of things?

There was no pain and not as much blood as she'd expected from a gunshot wound. Hmmmm. Maybe she was in shock. Or numbed by the cold. She'd fulfilled the last measure of her creation, and yes. She would've liked ending up with Grissom, at his side, in his bed, instead of just being in his guestroom. That would've been a perfect ending.

But it was never meant to be. She'd always known he'd be better off without her. He'd surely live longer. Look at Shane. Look at Heston. They were still alive—because they were safely out of her life. Out of danger. They'd never loved her like Grissom did, and she'd never loved them. Had never even thought what it'd be like to end up romantically involved with either of them. Not like she'd thought about spending forever with Grissom, Tanner, and Luke. It hurt knowing her disappearance would hurt the people she loved most. But in the end, it was happening again. She was losing everything and everyone, this time by choice—to save Grissom and his boys.

She was the reason Pam had come back from the dead. Something about Tuesday attracted evil. She was the common link between her parents' deaths, Freddie's murder, and the heinous murders of Maeve Astor's poor husband and tiny children.

Her. Tuesday Smart. The common denominator of all those miserable, horrible, ugly deaths. Life and the execution of it was always about math and reason. About balance. The yin and yang of things. And logic. Logically, Tuesday chose the ending this time around. No one would die because of her, and the only way to make sure of that was for her to leave everyone she cared about behind, permanently and forever. Then and only then, could Grissom and his boys live.

What a beautiful, peaceful place to die, here in the snow. Alone, like so much of her life. But knowing Luke and Tanner were safe, that they were with Grissom…

Their dad…

The best father in the world…

Well, second to her dad…

Tuesday opened her eyes, not recalling when she'd closed them. It took more effort with tiny crystals of snow welled in her eye sockets and blanketing her face. She blinked to clear the frosty flakes away, pursed her lips, and blew what she could off her face. Lacy evergreen boughs overhead framed a gray, snow-laden sky. The view reminded her of what had once been her favorite hideaway at the far north end of Resolute Bay in Canada—the tiny hamlet of Inuktitut, also known as the *'place of no dawn.'*

A memory of Grissom and his boys tramping through his tree farm—like kids—on their way to choose the perfect Christmas tree rolled over her. Three kids. One extra-large. Two tiny. Laughing. Loving each other so, so much, it brought tears to her freezing eyeballs. She'd shared the very same family outing one wintry day with her mom and dad in Minnesota, back when life was still perfect, and she'd naively believed all people were good.

Tuesday exhaled again, her breath a thin puff of frosty air between her and heaven, content to lie there and wait for her mom and dad, maybe even Freddie, to come take her home. Wasn't that how death worked? The people you'd loved most came to be with you at the end?

Instead, a stranger's face loomed overhead, blocking her view. Whoever he was, the guy dropped to his knees beside her, his dark brown eyes scrolling over the wound in her side, then over her bloodied face. "She hurt you? Damned lying bitch. I told her not to touch you, but" —he shrugged— "things happen, don't they?"

Even as dazed as she was, Tuesday sensed the wrongness in this man. "Do I know you?" she asked, willing her brain to come up with the place and time she might know him from.

The stranger's upper lip peeled back to reveal a mouth of perfectly straight white teeth. Had to be implants, as scarred as his face was. "You could say that. I worked with Fred, your, uh, ex-husband. What he did to you was wrong, and I'm here to set things straight." He extended a gloved hand as if he expected her to simply trust him.

Pursing her lips, Tuesday looked beyond the guy to the gray sky overhead. "No, thanks. I'm g-good where I am." *Cold and dying, but good.*

"You see, that's where you're wrong. You got what I want, and you're coming with me." He tipped closer, too close, until his face was the only thing Tuesday could see. His cheeks and nose were covered with pock marks left from a bad case of acne, possibly road rash. White scars bisected both brows. One trailed over his forehead into his hairline. The other crossed one eyelid and ended high on his cheek. The guy's greasy black hair needed to be washed and his breath smelled of garlic, tooth decay, and booze. His leather trench coat was unbuttoned, its sides tossed behind him like a marauder's cape. He was her idea of a typical New York mobster.

"No—!"

"Yessss," he hissed, his fist cocked, ready to strike. "I'm the guy you're gonna marry soon as I get you back to the city, so shut up. Fred cheated me by dying like he did. But that don't matter, cuz everything he left you is gonna be mine now. And it'll be legal."

He struck hard then, his fist another brick to her face, this one with sharp knuckles and a bolt of thunder that knocked her head back. Closing her eyes, Tuesday took the hit. Her poor nose was mashed and bleeding. Her upper lip was cut and swollen. This was her. Who she was. The eternal loser. Tuesday Smart, forever destined to be alone. But this creep was also her last chance to make sure Grissom and his boys lived. A somber thought flickered through the burgeoning haze in her head. *'Darn. I ruined Christmas.'*

Chapter Thirty

Grissom was so damned angry at his ex-wife that he wanted to kill her. Illegal or not. Smart or not. He wanted Pamela dead. What she'd done to the little boy she'd claimed to love more than Tanner was unforgivable. She'd poisoned Luke! With a bagful of 'treats' she'd known the greedy little three-year-old couldn't resist. THC-laced gummies. Damn her!

Thankfully, the ER doctor had been pacing, primed and ready for Luke's arrival. Doc Pratt had checked Luke's vitals, then whisked his gurney down the hall, past the admissions desk, to the ER cubicle where Grissom now stood, stressed, and planning revenge. Pratt transferred Luke to a bed and ordered Grissom to: "Say your prayers. Your son's heart rate's still solid. We may have caught this crap in time. When did he get into your shit? How much did he eat? How long has it been since he ate them?"

Everything about this intense man declared: *'How stupid are you?'*

"About an hour ago, I think. But it's not mine. I have no idea how much he ate," Grissom explained. "I wasn't home. My ex, she gave Luke a bag of THC-laced gummies. She did it to get back at me."

Tossing a disbelieving glare over his shoulder, Pratt snarled, "If you say so."

Turning back to Luke, he barked a string of medical orders into the mic clipped on the collar of his scrubs. As if waiting on standby, several men and women in scrubs hurried into the room and sprang into action. As if they knew precisely what to do. As if they'd done this before. Muscle action. That was what Grissom was watching, all because these folks had performed this exact same rescue too many times in the past. People really were too dumb to live, and he was one of them.

"Relax," Eric murmured in his ear. "Pratt's a good guy, and Luke's in good hands. Don't borrow trouble."

Grissom stared up blankly at the men he'd forgotten had come with him on his run into the hospital. Eric was there. The medics who'd transported Luke waited in the hall. Alex stood at the foot of Luke's bed, staring down at the little guy, his sharp blue eyes fastened on what the medical team was doing.

"What's that even mean?" Tears filled Grissom's damned eyes. "This is my fault. He's my son. What if he—?"

"It means don't get ahead of yourself and start planning a son-of-a-bitching funeral!" It was Eric's firm hand on Grissom's shoulder, but it was Alex who answered. "Your boy's a fighter, Grissom. He's *your* son, and your boys know how to fight. Give Luke some credit. He might be three, but it's your blood in his veins, not his chicken shit mother's. Don't forget that."

Ah, but it's not my blood in his veins. He's not biologically mine. He's—

"And these guys know what they're doing." Alex turned on Grissom then, and damned if those icy blue bolts of lightning didn't pierce Grissom's heart. Fuck. Alex knew Luke wasn't his biological son. How the hell?

But Luke is mine, damn it. In every way that mattered, Luke *was* Grissom's son, and he'd fight to the death before he'd ever let anyone call his boy a bastard or try to take him away.

"Copy that," Grissom whispered. "He's mine and I'm keeping him."

By then, a male nurse had stripped Luke down to his cartoon underwear, while another attached monitors on his little chest to track heart rate, oxygen saturation, and a bunch of other important stuff Grissom couldn't recall at the moment. Placing a hand on Luke's foot, he told his tiniest warrior, "I'm here, Short Stack. I've got your six, and Tanner's waiting at home for you. Fight, baby boy."

Doc Pratt pried Luke's mouth open, tipped his head back to access a straight line to Luke's gut, sprayed something into the tiny guy's airway, and gastric suction began. Grissom cringed as the machine on wheels sucked stomach acid and a shit ton of whole gummies into the clear gray jug on its lower shelf. Whole gummies. Not partially chewed bits and pieces, but whole damned gummies.

His eyes brimmed. The greedy little boy of his hadn't wasted time chewing. He'd guzzled Pam's poisonous treats whole. Nothing else was coming out of his tummy, just thumb-nail-sized blobs of yellow, orange, and green mixed with bile and stomach acid. That had to be a good sign, didn't it?

Splat. Hiss. Thunk. At last, only clear fluid trickled into the jug. Pratt inserted another tube down Luke's throat. He was rinsing the inside of Luke's tummy, going after every last bit of Pam's ugly poison. *He's saving my boy, God, please bless him.*

"There," Pratt said, carefully easing both tubes out of Luke's mouth. The man turned dark, stormy green eyes on Grissom. "You say your ex did this intentionally?" he asked warily, no doubt scrutinizing Grissom for a lie.

"Yes, she's—"

"She's in police custody, Dr. Pratt. In my jail," a gruff male voice stated loudly from the hall beyond Luke's cubicle. "And she's talking, make that screaming her fool head off. Pamela McCoy hasn't shut her damned mouth since I dragged her out of Grissom's house and sat her ass in my patrol car. She's proud of what she did, Pratt. Says Grissom made her do it."

Howie Prince, the local Chief Deputy Sheriff, personally patrolled Alex's gated community. Tall, dark-haired, and strong as an ox, he was every bit as lethal as any TEAM agent. He'd served in Somalia years ago, part of the USMC leg of a joint op that had netted the latest tribal lord. That guy had been an insane dictator who'd killed his enemies with impunity, his own people by starvation.

Sergeant Presley Forsythe stood behind Chief Prince, her shiny black hair pulled tight in a bun, the brim of her deputy ballcap pulled so low Grissom couldn't see her amazing tropical-blue eyes. Was she judging him? Was that why she didn't want to look at him? Was she condemning him like Pratt had?

"I wasn't there," Grissom confessed his most grievous sin without thinking. Everything was his fault. He was worse than his dad. He'd never been around when his boys had needed him most.

"Of course, you weren't there," Howie growled, politely shoving his way into the crowded cubicle. "You were with

Alex looking for your lady friend, the one Pam McCoy has already admitted she bludgeoned with a brick, then dragged into the trees behind your place and strung up in a tree. She claims that was the only way to get you away from your boys, long enough to snatch your youngest."

Pratt acknowledged Chief Prince with a chin lift. "Good to see you, Howie. All the evidence you'll need is in the jar. Yours for the taking. Only wish you could send that woman to hell."

"All I'll need's your signed statement, Gary, but thanks for the offer," Howie replied.

Grissom glanced at the stern police officer. "Thanks for your quick response, sir. Without you—"

"My response, nothing. You and Alex are the heroes today." Chief Prince slapped Grissom's back. "Take care of that little guy, and if you need anything, anything at all, you call me, hear?"

"Yes, sir, I will."

Everyone except Pratt and a nurse stepped out of the cubicle. Doctor Gary Pratt leaned his butt against the counter alongside Luke's bed. The nurse cleaned Luke's mouth, wiped a damp cloth over his face, and then dressed him in the tiniest hospital gown Grissom had ever seen. The sight of his baby boy in that great big bed, alone, without Tanner to squabble with, choked Grissom's heart. He'd almost lost his sons today. *His* babies.

God, where's Tuesday? No man should have to face his sins by himself. Once again, she'd rescued his boys because he couldn't. He needed her, damn it. To hold him up and tell him everything was going to be okay. With her by his side, he could believe. Might even be able to forgive himself. Grissom dashed a hand over his face before his eyes betrayed him.

But Jesus, where is she?

"We see a lot of THC poisoning these days," Doc Pratt said quietly. "Too much. People are careless. Their kids watch them take this crap, then they leave it laying around and joke like it's Mommy's or Daddy's favorite candy. Kids think all gummies are candy. Why shouldn't they? They look like gummies in candy aisles at any grocery store, and they come in clever, colorful bags. But I've never heard of anyone trying to kill their kid with gummies before."

"She's sick and she's damned mean," Grissom answered. "But it's my fault. I wasn't there. I should've been."

"Let me guess, messy divorce?"

"No divorce. Not yet. I was told she died in a plane crash last month. That's what the Costa Rican Coast Guard said. Didn't think I'd need to divorce a corpse."

Doc Pratt adjusted the wire spectacles Grissom hadn't noticed were perched on his nose until then. "They didn't demand DNA to confirm the body?"

"Guess not. Hell, I was recovering from a motorcycle crash. Barely convinced my boss to let me travel."

Pratt cocked his head. "She took your son—?"

Grissom held up two fingers. "Sons. She took Tanner and Luke out of the country without my permission. But once she got there, she and her boyfriend decided they had no use for them. Especially Luke's big brother. Pam always hated Tanner and made sure he knew it. Poor kid's got PTSD worse than me." *And I'm going to have a full-blown panic attack if you don't get out of here real soon.*

Doc Pratt must've noticed Grissom was close to coming undone. "How'd you get them back?" he asked more kindly.

"A woman, an American woman... Tuesday Smart..." *God, I miss her.* "She witnessed Pam's boyfriend abusing Tanner. Bastard was dangling him off a third-story balcony. If he wasn't already dead, I'd... I'd kill him! B-but right away, Tuesday ran up those three flights. She didn't have to, but she saved Tanner, and... and Luke and..." Beads of sweat dripped from Grissom's hair, down his forehead and temples at how close he'd come to losing his boys that day. Both of them. If not for Tuesday...

Where is she?

Panic spiked. Talk never accomplished a damned thing. Especially now, when Grissom was back at square one. When he'd come close to losing one of his sons again. *Jesus, what kind of father am I? Why's this shit keep happening to me? To us?*

"Go on," Pratt prodded.

The soothing tone in his voice snapped Grissom back to the here and now. "Yeah. Right. I, ahh..." *Where was I? Oh, yeah.* "Tuesday just happened to be there that day. She confronted the bastard. Just ran up the stairs and ordered him to let Tanner go. That she'd kill him if he dropped my boy. My wife got pissed. They had a screaming match..." Which undoubtedly was Pam screaming more than Tuesday. "...and Tuesday... and she..." Anyway. "Pam told her to take my boys, that she didn't want them. Tuesday never hesitated, just assumed the care and feeding of my sons from that moment. She loves them. But Doc. I... I don't know where she is."

Grissom looked around the tiny cubicle, more aware than ever that the woman he craved most in his life wasn't at his side. Worse, he had no idea where she'd gone; if she was injured or hurt or just mad that he'd put his boys in danger again. A panic attack was imminent, its ghostly fingers tiptoeing up the back of his neck, waiting to strangle him. To unman him.

"I'm keeping Luke overnight, maybe two days tops, but just for observation," Pratt continued, motioning toward the little guy in that great big bed. "We dodged a bullet here, Mr.—"

"Grissom. Grissom McCoy." *Luke's shitty old man. Mom was right. I'm just like my dad. Good for nothing.*

"Grissom." Pratt bobbed his head respectfully. "You need to understand that Luke's not out of the woods yet. THC poisoning is risky with children, more so when they're under ten. I'll send everything in that jar to our lab to be sure, but most edibles contain more than the recommended dose for adults. Ten to fifteen milligrams of THC instead of two point five. More than half the calls to poison control centers these days involve THC edibles, and most of those calls involve children between the ages of three to five. Those kids are the most at risk, and I hate to tell you, but your son chugged more than a handful."

"What should I watch for?" *Because I'm not going anywhere.*

"No need to worry. We'll monitor him until you take him home. Seizures, low blood pressure, hallucinations, nausea and vomiting, trouble breathing, heart arrhythmias, weakness, and poor coordination are just a few warning signs. In a couple minutes, our trauma team will transfer him to ICU. You're welcome to stay with him. Do you have any questions? Any concerns? Anything I can help with?"

Grissom licked the side of his mouth. Concerns? He had a ton, but where to begin? Which one to ask first? Every last nerve in his body was standing on end, and he had nothing with him to combat the monster he was about to morph into. He needed Tuesday, damn it. How could she do this to him? Just leave without a word? She, more than anyone, knew how much he and his boys loved her. What was wrong with her, to up and walk away like she did?

Pratt's eyes were still on him. The man's mouth was moving. He was talking, but Grissom had disconnected from reality like he had back in the damned looney bin, the name he still couldn't remember.

Just as his throat tightened, just as panic sealed his fate and dumped a shitload of more stress down his gullet, a heavy hand slapped his shoulder. "We need to talk," Alex barked.

"Not before I get an answer from Mr. McCoy," Pratt interrupted quietly.

"Answer to what?" Grissom had to ask because he'd been lost in his stupid head and once again, not present, like he should've been. But with Alex's firm hold—a hold that told Grissom again that the world's best sniper had his six, his reeling brain came back online. It was right then reminding Grissom the truth about Tuesday and her genuine love for his boys and, by default, him. Her instant kindness for people in need, like Persia that evening in his kitchen. Her smile. The way she blushed when they'd talked about sex. Her lack of experience. Her virginity. Her inner beauty.

"I asked if you're going to track down the woman who saved your son and marry her?" Pratt asked. "Because I sure would."

"We gotta go, Grissom." Alex's palm and fingers were now hard on the back of Grissom's neck. "There's something you need to hear."

Grissom maintained eye contact with Pratt, as he backed out of the cubicle into the hall with his boss. "Absolutely, Doc. I'm going to marry Tuesday, and I'll invite you to our wedding."

Pratt nodded as if he'd gotten the answer he wanted. For a moment, Grissom felt relief. Until Alex bit out, "Pam has an accomplice. Are you staying here or are you coming with me to locate your woman?"

"What?" Grissom damned shrieked. "An accomplice? Who?"

His angst nearly drowned him again. *What do I do? Stay or go?*

Chapter Thirty-One

Tuesday came to with a splitting headache and a foul taste in her mouth. Not fish and garlic, more like motor oil, dirt, and…. Her nose twitched. Gasoline? Yup, that was the other nasty flavor coating her poor tongue. All came from the rag wrapped around her head and stuck in her mouth, ugh. The ground beneath vibrated and she was sure that came from tires against pavement. Which meant she was in the creep's car, going somewhere she didn't want to go, trussed up like a fatted goose, and that guy—what *was* his name?—meant to kill her. But he'd do that after he married her. Why not? She'd been married to Freddie for some reason she didn't quite understand and had never questioned. Only Freddie had never been unkind.

She didn't mean to make a sound, but a groan got away from her, and the moment it did, the guy reached over the driver's seat. He patted her thigh like the good dog she wasn't. And didn't intend to be. Despite her precarious situation, Tuesday was thinking clearer now. Still ensnared in this gangster's get-rich-quick scheme, true, but she'd been in worse predicaments before. She was certain she had a concussion. Her head pounded and she was sick to her stomach. But lying there in knots—once again—she had time to plan, and plan she would.

First: she'd take advantage of this one-way drive to who-knew-where to rest and recharge.

Second: she'd play this Neanderthal once they arrived at their final destination, make him think she was weak and delicate, act like the poor little rich girl everyone thought they saw.

Third: she'd strike when the opportunity came. She might not be blessed with a family, but she'd honed plenty of survival skills during her long, dark days in Antarctica and on the lonesome Serengeti. Passersby never looked deeper than artificial appearances anyway, which was why she'd purposely fashioned a feminine mystique that hid her stronger side. The side she only revealed when might equaled right. Grissom had seen her strength the night they'd almost made love. Tuesday let the memory warm her as she lay there and plotted. Just thinking of him lent her strength and courage. Soon, she'd rise up and surprise the heck out of the nefarious thug driving her away from all she held dear. Very soon.

Chapter Thirty-Two

Grissom drove like an ass and… He. Did. Not. Care. Barreling eastward in the TEAM SUV Alex had arrived at his house in, he and his boss were on the tail of some guy from New York City. Sal Moreno, an associate of a Mafia don who thought he ruled the world. *Guess again, asshole. You take my woman, and you're going to die. All of you.*

"Slow down," Alex interrupted Grissom's inner rant.

"Why? You know something I don't? Where is she? Is she hurt? Where's Moreno taking her? Why the hell did he take her? What's he got to do with Pam?"

"Maverick's been tailing Moreno's sedan since he pulled away from that frontage road."

"And yet he let Moreno take Tuesday?" Grissom bellowed, growing more enraged by the second. "He didn't do anything to save her from that asshat?"

"Son of a bitch, give it a rest, will you? Maverick never had a clear shot, and Moreno's our only lead. Right now, Howie's grilling your ex to establish the connection between them. We'll get Tuesday back today. You'll see."

Grissom pressed the phone icon on his steering wheel and ordered, "Call my boss." Which got an exasperated huff from Alex. Also got the cell phone Kelsey had answered ten minutes earlier. She and a few TEAM wives were sitting with Luke. He'd been moved out of the ICU to a quarantined room on the same floor, within reach of Doctor Pratt's team of specialists. His stats were good, and he'd come to, asking for his dad. Which had damned near ripped Grissom's heart out of his chest when he'd heard that, him not being there for his little boy. His baby! Again.

But he'd had to choose. Stay with Luke like the over-protective bear he was and trust Maverick to find Tuesday. Or trust his baby boy's care to Kelsey and her band of TEAM wives, and hunt down the bastard who'd taken Tuesday himself. Hardest decision of his life, but Grissom knew he'd made the right choice.

"Hi, Grissom," Kelsey answered quietly, cheerful despite the circumstances. "Luke's still asleep, but Doctor Pratt just popped in. He couldn't wait until you called back so…"

Grissom heard muffled giggling in the background.

"…but he said to tell you things are looking up. Of course, we didn't know you'd be calling so soon."

More giggling.

"Are you ladies laughing at me?"

Alex huffed, "You think? You called less than five minutes ago."

"Oh, heavens no," sweet Kelsey replied. "We're just talking and reliving some of the traumatic events us girls survived. You know, like getting shot and falling into the White River on Mount Rainier. But you don't remember that, do you?"

"No, sorry. Sure don't. I think I was there…" *Somewhere.* If only he could remember.

"You were there the day we took Michael Keane down," Alex cut in gruffly. "In those repurposed shipping containers east of the Jefferson Memorial, remember?"

"I… I don't. I'm sorry, ma'am, err, boss, but… fuck. I don't." Grissom could feel Alex's eyes drilling into the side of his head, but the truth was out. His memory was shot. His one and only source of income, working on The TEAM, might be, too.

"Don't use that word with my wife."

"Oh, sorry, shit. I mean—"

"Shut. Up." Alex bit out with venom. "She's my wife, a lady."

"I know, Boss, I just—"

"It's okay. Honest, I've heard it all before. We both understand what you meant, Grissom, don't we, Alex?" she asked.

Alex, on the other hand, had turned into a pissed-off bear. "Don't use that language around my wife ever again. Understood?"

"Copy that, but Boss—"

"But what!"

"Tell me, please, what else I can't remember."

"Good idea, Alex. Talking to Grissom might help both of you. Bye now." With that cheery sendoff, Kelsey disconnected.

While Grissom concentrated on traffic, Alex stared at the dash. It took a minute before he finally turned toward Grissom. For the rest of the drive to the Ronald Reagan Washington National Airport, Grissom learned how Kelsey had been targeted by a sniper during the Stewarts' vacation in the Northwest last fall. How she'd been shot and had fallen into a raging river, then been quickly rescued by a ruthless cabal run by the now deceased Secretary of State Tristan Obermeyer. As well as Michael Keane, also deceased, the man

Obermeyer had promised the US ambassadorship to Ireland, and the still-missing Wirths, old man Lancaster and his son Miles, both connected with the Irish Mafia in Boston. According to the press, neither had been seen since the FBI took out Obermeyer and Keane. Judging by Alex's tone when he mentioned the Wirths, Grissom knew there was more to the story.

The more Alex explained, the more ragged Grissom's emotions grew, until he blurted, "Why'd I crash my bike? Were you there that night, too? Was I drunk? Because I don't, can't remember shit."

"You were roofied," Alex said bluntly. "Your counselor thinks it'd be better if you remembered things on your own. But I don't give a shit, and you need to know, damn it. Everything. They found scopolamine in your system that night. The bitch you married tried to kill you. I know because that's the same night she trashed your house, took your sons, and fled to Central America with Estes."

Scopolamine? Shit.

A mighty thunderclap rocked the SUV as Grissom's brain blinked off-line. Scopolamine was known on the streets as the zombie drug. While it had sound medicinal value when used as an anesthetic, others used it for its mind-altering, hallucinogenic properties. Scopolamine rendered an unwilling victim susceptible to total mind-control, followed by a rock-solid case of amnesia, that made it impossible for law enforcement to catch the real villain. A man under its influence became a tool to commit murder, rape, even suicide. All it took was a couple drops in a guy's drink and he became a zombie. Hookers in big cities across the world, New York City, Paris, and Rio de Janero, used scopolamine to divest foolish businessmen of their wallets, cash, credit cards, and identification. It was a damned dangerous drug, known to cause respiratory failure, hallucinations, and heart attacks when the victim was overdosed.

Pam had meant for him to die that night. He'd married a gawddamned cold-blooded killer. She'd abused and tormented Tanner. Might've killed Luke, the son she'd claimed to love. And now she was behind Tuesday's disappearance. His brain couldn't take anymore. Knowing this was all his fault sent the SUV swerving to the shoulder, kicking up a cloud of dust and spraying gravel.

With mere seconds to spare, his muddled brain came storming back online with a vehement, *No! More!* Pam *had* failed. Tanner and Luke *were* safe. Grissom *had* survived, and he was pissed as fuck!

He righted the SUV in the nick of time, avoiding bouncing into the field beside the highway. Damned if Alex wasn't staring at him like a son of a bitch when the joyride ended. Those blue eyes of his were sharp as daggers, cutting through Grissom. Seeing everything. For once, he didn't mind Alex's razor-sharp scrutiny. He had nothing to hide.

"We good now?" Alex clipped sarcastically.

"I remember," Grissom admitted, quietly processing everything he'd just recalled. Not only the horrific things that had happened to Kelsey, but the anguish Heston Contreras had endured when he'd thought he'd lost London, his soon-to-be wife, to that asshat Obermeyer and his gang of rapists. How Obermeyer had used London and several other women, for target practice. Grissom's fists clenched as he recalled the rage boiling out of Alex when Kelsey'd gone missing in that glacier-fed river. Then was found—by Alex—but not expected to live. Then was drugged by some woman working for the Wirths in the hospital's intensive care unit. She'd been in damned rough shape.

Grissom remembered the desperate hunt for London. He'd been inside one of Keane's repurposed shipping containers. Grissom knew precisely what happened to the bastards who'd dared target London. He also knew what had happened to Obermeyer, Keane, and the Wirths. He knew where a couple of them were buried. Only wished he'd been the one who'd taken them out.

"I remember everything, Boss," he semi-repeated. "Including the drink Pam poured me the night I rear-ended that truck. She'd acted all sorts of coy, and honestly? I thought it was beer. Thought she was being nice. But it was apple juice. I almost tossed it in the sink. Should have, but I was dumb. Thought maybe she'd changed. Nope. I do remember her asking me to run to the market for… something. Don't recall what, but she… She knew damned well that I'd take my bike. Hell, she might've told me to crash it for all I know, Boss."

Alex had his cell phone in one hand, his other hand cupped over his ear, while talking into his headset and thumb-dialing a number. "Thanks, Maverick. We're a mile or two out," He turned back to Grissom. "'Course she tried to kill you. That's what Doc Windhall believes, too. Moreno's in the Ronald Reagan Washington National Airport parking terrace."

He brought his phone to his other ear. "Shut down whatever plane Sal Moreno's boarding, Mother. Do it now. He's most likely bound for New York City." Alex paused a second. His jaw tightened. "You don't have to tell me. I know most private jets fly out of Leesburg, but Maverick followed him to Reagan. Son of a bitch! Stop arguing with me and keep Moreno on the ground! Stop every outgoing flight if you have to. That son of a bitch has Tuesday Smart!"

"Yes, Boss," Mother snapped through their common frequency. "I'll let you know where to intercept Maverick. Tuesday needs us, and she damned well needs Grissom."

"And *I* need her," Grissom admitted to everyone listening, "and I'm going to marry her." They might as well all know.

Grissom and Alex had just squealed rubber on the eastbound loop feeding Ronald Reagan National Airport when Maverick's growl came over their earpieces. "He's in parking lot two." Which meant Moreno had booked a flight to New York City on American, Alaska, Delta, JetBlue, or United Airlines.

"That doesn't make sense," Alex hissed "How's he think he'll get Tuesday on board flying commercial?"

"He drugged her," Grissom hissed. "That's the only way to control her, by doping her with something that'll still let her walk and talk and… Fuck! Want to bet Moreno used scopolamine!"

Grissom couldn't bear to think what else the bastard might've forced her to do.

Maverick must've been right on Morena's ass as quick as he yelled, "Let her go, Moreno! Drop the weapon!"

Moreno's reply came back garbled and hollow.

Grissom kicked the SUV to its limit.

"Faster!" Alex gripped the suicide strap overhead.

"I said let her go!" Maverick barked again. "She's been shot. She's bleeding, and she needs medical attention. Do what I said! Do it now!"

She's hurt? Shot? Grissom hadn't thought Pam had hit anything with that wild assed shot. Surely not Tuesday, not as brilliantly as she'd fought Pam after that weapon fired. Tuesday hadn't faltered in her well-handled offense, not once. She'd all but pushed Grissom out of her way to knock Pam down. That head butt of hers was a stellar tactical move. But she'd been hit?

"You do, you son of a bitch, and you'll die!" Maverick bellowed.

Grissom recognized the steel in Cowboy's tone. Things in the parking garage were escalating. Jesus, he hoped his teammate was as good a shot as everyone said.

Maverick had no more than promised retribution when gunfire erupted over the connection. Grissom slammed the brakes to the floor. The SUV drifted sideways, blocking the north entrance to the garage before it stopped rolling. Grissom was out the door, both pistols from his double holster drawn, and ready to kill. He and Alex sprinted onto the ground-level floor. It took seconds to scan the place. No Maverick, tail lights, or signs of police action.

"Where's the fuckin' stairs?" Grissom yelled.

Alex nodded to the nearest corner where red-on-black Elevator and Exit signs blinked over a steel fire door. Several people exited quickly, running past him and Alex.

"Where are they?" Alex asked the harried group.

"In the northwest corner," an older woman replied, pointing towards the north wall of the garage. "Two men and a woman. Hurry. She's bleeding, and the creep says he's gonna kill her if that other guy won't let him go!"

"Like hell!" Grissom answered.

Alex grabbed the doorknob to the stairway, but instead of throwing it open, he forced Grissom to a dead stop. "We do this right. I'll take the shooter, you go to Tuesday. She needs you, so you be there for her, understand? Go straight to Tuesday, no one else. Comfort her. Keep her safe until this is over. Just her, understand?"

Another gunshot boomed from upstairs. "Shit, Boss, I know. I know! Let's go!"

"Grissom." Alex had a ton of steel in his tone.

"Okay, yeah, yes, I heard you. You'll take Moreno. I'll take Tuesday. Got it, now move!" Grissom was dead on his boss's ass all the way up to the next level's steel fire door.

Leaning a hefty shoulder into the heavy metal, Alex eased the door open just wide enough for him to look into the parking lot. Damn it. When Alex was sure the way was clear, it was his nine-millimeter SIG leading Grissom out of the stairwell and into rows of parked vehicles.

An incoming Metro train rumbled on the tracks overhead as Grissom burst into the lot. Metro PD sirens screamed close by. The heavier whine of fire engine sirens signaled they were close, too. Just not there yet. Rounding one of many concrete support columns running east to west under a low concrete ceiling, he finally caught sight of Maverick's broad back a couple dozen cars down. He was in a standoff with a dusky-skinned male in a black leather bomber jacket. Cowboy's stance was taut, his shoulders wide. Both arms were extended and his boots were positioned to fire.

Sal Moreno was no match, his only ace-in-the-hole the dazed human shield in front of him. *Fuckin' chicken shit.*

Grissom dodged left, keeping Moreno in sight, drawing the kidnapper's attention while keeping Alex in sight at his right. His boss had become a shadow among the pillars, slinking from one to the next. Always advancing. Closing in on Maverick without being seen. How a man as big as Alex could pull off sneaky subterfuge like that was a spectacular asset in Tuesday's favor. With every foot closer he drew to the showdown, Grissom kept walking, drawing Moreno's attention, keeping the asshat's focus on him.

Maverick bellowed again. "Don't make me shoot you. Let her go."

Grissom's world narrowed down to just Tuesday and Moreno's weapon, a stubby, break-open, thirty-eight special stuck upward in the soft hollow under her jaw. Rosewood grip. Stainless metal finish. Two-and-a-half-inch barrel. Held by a jackass who wasn't going to live much longer. One discharge from that stubby pistol would send either a thirty-eight special or a three-fifty-seven magnum caliber round, upward through Tuesday's throat, tongue, soft palate, and sinuses, into her brain. She'd be dead before her body hit the ground.

Moreno had a handful of her hair wrapped around his fist, keeping her head tipped back and her chin up. She had to be drugged as spacey as she looked. Her green eyes were fixed on nothing but dead air over her head. He'd flex-cuffed her hands behind her back. She was no longer the gutsy woman Grissom had, just hours earlier, worked with to keep his wife from killing his youngest son. This Tuesday was either too weak to fight back or she'd given up.

"Tuesday," Grissom called out, needing her eyes on him. Needing her to know he was there. That she wasn't alone. "I'm here, love. I've come to take you home."

Moreno snarled something, but Grissom only had eyes and ears for the woman he adored.

She didn't respond, damn it. Didn't even blink that she'd heard him.

Panic whispered, *"Loser."*

"What the fuck did you give her?" Grissom shrieked, his patience unraveling, despite Alex's stern warning minutes earlier.

"Why should I tell you?" Moreno bellowed. "You guys aren't cops. There's no way I'm leaving without this bitch, so get outta the way. Frederick Lamb's widow's my ticket outta here, and yous guys are gonna get her killed if you don't let me pass. You think I won't end her?"

"No way that'll happen," Maverick declared from behind Grissom.

Grissom hadn't realized he'd bypassed his teammate and gotten as close to Moreno as he was. His pistols were still up, both trained on Sal's ugly face, but the jerk kept dodging behind Tuesday, making a solid headshot impossible. There'd be no chance of a body shot either, not with Moreno jerking her back and forth like he was. *Where the hell is Alex?*

"Tuesday. Love. Look at me." Grissom tried again, desperate to get through to her. "Luke's in the hospital, sweetheart. Kelsey, Judy, China, and Persia are watching over him until you get back. He's going to be okay, so is Tanner. He's with Rory and Ember at their house, with Tyler. My boys need you, Tuesday. Everyone's waiting for you to come home."

Not even a blink, damn it.

"What'd you do to her?" Grissom bellowed. "If you hurt her, I'll—!"

"I ain't the one who shot her!" Moreno bellowed back, shaking Tuesday like a limp ragdoll again. "That crazy ex-wife of yours did! She wanted this bitch dead, but all I want is what's mine, the money Lamb owes me. We had a deal, him and me, but he went and got himself killed. I'm supposed to be a billionaire, not chasing that wife of yours."

"Pam McCoy hired you?" Maverick asked.

Grissom knew what he was doing, asking pertinent questions, unraveling the mysteries behind this disastrous day, and gathering intel while he could. Before Alex ended Moreno. Giving Alex time to get in position.

"Your ex-wife? Hire me?" Disbelief contorted Moreno's ugly face. "I wish! I coulda used the cash, but that bitch said she was dead-assed broke, sos I been tracking this one" —he jerked Tuesday's head back farther still— "since she got back from Costa Rica. Mrs. Lamb here's the one with cash. Almost lost her when she went to the Hamptons. Don't know how she got away from me, but that's when I seen your wife casing Jeff Lamb's place like I was. Figured maybe she knew something I didn't sos I bought her a couple drinks and—"

"You and Pam McCoy decided to kidnap Miss Smart and force her to marry you?" Maverick barked. "Why? So you two could live happily ever after you killed her?"

Moreno's shoulder lifted inside his bulky jacket. "We was going to let her live. Honest. All I want's what's coming to me, and to get that, this bitch has to marry me, soon as yous guys—"

Tuesday's head fell back on her shoulders, and—*CRACK*! Her sneak attack happened so fast and was so unexpected, Grissom nearly blinked and missed the back of her skull smashing Moreno's ugly face.

"You bitching whore!" he shrieked, blood gushing down his chin and neck. Both hands went for his nose. Big mistake. That was all the world's top sniper needed to—

BOOM!

One shot.

Came out of nowhere.

Echoed like a cannon under the low ceiling.

Moreno's beady eyes blinked at the sudden impact of the nine-millimeter round Alex had just sent through his cranium. Blood, bone shards, and brain matter whooshed into the air behind him. His fingers stiffened. His body jerked. Rivulets of red streamed out of his mouth. More trickled from the hole between his eyes. His revolver clattered to the floor and he dropped to the ground.

Without Moreno holding her upright, Tuesday's knees buckled. Grissom dived for her, catching her before she landed on Moreno. Hurriedly, Grissom holstered his pistols, then tipped her forward and sliced the flex-cuffs with the blade from his boot sheath.

Maverick stepped between Grissom and Moreno, securing the dead man's revolver.

Alex had a finger in his ear, cursing at some poor soul to send a "son-of-a-bitchin' ambulance!"

Grissom's need to hug Tuesday was squelched the moment she fell limp against his chest. Tiny beads of sweat dotted her forehead. Her arms were clammy, and her coloring was pale. Too pale. Her poor feet were bare and bloody. Worse, the dark red stain on her hip.

He tipped her into the crook of his arm to get a better look, desperately searching beneath her shirt for that wound. Too quickly, his fingertips connected with a sodden streak above her hip bone. Moreno hadn't done anything to stop the bleeding. Not so much as a fuckin' Band-Aid.

"Grissom?" she asked breathily, her eyes glazed, not focused, still not seeing him. Her pupils were so big, the black squeezing out the green. She was going into shock.

"I'm here, right here," he answered. Ripping his t-shirt over his head, he used it to cushion her head before he laid her flat on the concrete.

"I've got her," Maverick cut in. His trusty blow-out kit, first-aid for combat trauma in a molle bag, was already open, its insides spread across Tuesday's abdomen.

"Thanks, sure, yeah," Grissom answered automatically, his brain spinning with all the terrible ways this damned day might still end.

Lifting her shirt, Maverick tipped forward on his knees and applied a healthy dose of powdered Quik-Clot to that ugly wound, then followed up with a thick layer of hemostatic dressing. "Keep her talking," he ordered, pressing his big hand firmly over her wound, "while I get her stable. Medics are nearly here. Give her something to live for until they show."

Sick to death that he was breathing the scent of her into his heart for the last time, Grissom lowered his lips to Tuesday's ear and said, "Tanner and Luke love you, and right now they're scared you're going to leave them. It's Christmas Day, and you're the best present they've ever had. You're their mother, damn it. You can't leave them, you can't!"

"Easy," Maverick murmured.

"You don't understand," Grissom bit out. "I can't lose her."

"Then tell her that, man. Be honest but gentle. Wake up and smell the roses before it's too late." Whatever that meant. Grissom didn't know Cowboy's story, only knew those stormy blue eyes of his were earnest as fuck.

Alex squatted beside them, his cell still in his hand. "She needs you, Griss. Tell her that for starters."

But does she? Could a woman of the world, one so damned beautiful that it hurt to look at her sometimes—especially when she'd smiled at him like she thought he hung the moon—truly need a guy like him? He'd believed so until she'd vanished out of his house like she had. Before she'd run away. But now, Grissom wasn't so sure.

Nonetheless, he pressed his lips to her forehead and commanded her to, "Breathe, Tuesday. Breathe for Tanner and Luke, and for the lost little girl who's been running away from life ever since she lost her mom and dad. Yes, life's hard as fuck sometimes, but you damned well better breathe for me, too, because I am not letting you go. Hear me? Not ever. Man up, girlfriend. Marry me and decide who you—just you—want to be for a change. Stop doing what you're told. Stop taking the easy way out. Stop hiding and breathe, damn it!"

Maverick might've been the one who growled, but it was hard to tell since both apex predators at his side did a lot of growling. All Grissom had eyes for was Tuesday's chest lifting with her first full inhale since Moreno let her fall. "That's my girl. Breathe, just breathe," Grissom purred, so damned proud of her for being brave enough to try. "That's all you've got to do. Just breathe and let me take care of everything else. Just breathe."

Chapter Thirty-Three

Ooomph! "Miss Tuesday!" Tanner cried as a big, warm hand that couldn't possibly belong to a child his size cupped her cheek. "I found her! Dad, I found her!"

Am I dreaming?

"Tanner? No," she murmured, not believing what she was seeing. Tanner and his dad, leaning over her? Kneeling beside her? Where'd they come from? This wasn't how it was supposed to end. They shouldn't have left Luke, not just to find her. He might be dying. "No, no, no. You guys should be with Luke," she wheezed, her heart beating unreasonably hard in her ribcage. "Go. Please. He's important, not me. Go. Leave me. Just—"

"Shut up and breathe! I'm not leaving you!"

Wow. That's harsh. Doesn't sound like Tanner, either.

Tuesday didn't get to finish what most needed to be said, when Grissom's warm, wet mouth clamped over hers and he started breathing for her. Breathing life and warmth into her. Hot tears rained over her cheeks with each forced inhale. But they weren't her tears. They were Grissom's. Maybe Tanner's too. It was hard to know for sure…

Someone else had her arm tucked under his. Easing back from Grissom, she turned to the earnest, dark-haired man on his knees beside her. Whoever he was, he had a bag of fluid tucked up high under his other arm, and he'd just inserted a needle into the underside of her wrist.

"Don't worry, ma'am, me, Grissom, and Maverick gotcha. Everything's gonna be okay." But then he turned and yelled, "Medic! Over here, please hurry!"

Sure didn't sound like everything was going to be okay…

"You're hurting her, Eric. Take it easy," Grissom snapped.

Oh, Eric. That's who he is.

"All I've got's saline, brother, but it's not enough. She's lost too much blood, and EMTs don't carry it. We've got to move fast or we're going to lose her."

You're going to lose me? I'm dying? Oh, yeah. The people she loved most needed to live in peace. *So I ran off and—*

A bluster of gruff, hurried orders and quicker reactions overrode her best-laid plans that now felt like mistakes.

With one manly swoop, Grissom lifted her up, while other hands—so many other hands—helped him hoist her away from the cold embrace of this concrete tomb. Then she was floating on air. Grissom was there and, as much as she wished he hadn't found her, Tuesday was relieved he had.

Every other man in her life had left her behind, in one way or the other. Unwillingly, maybe, but gone was still gone, and she'd been so darned lonely most of her adult life. But this—THIS—was love. In action. Jolting action, maybe. Harshly spoken, yes. But so welcome. Tears flowed like rain at the tender way these warriors handled her. At the deadly urgency in Grissom's voice when he ordered, "Don't hurt her!"

A tiny hand crept into her limp, cold fingers. "I gotcha, Miss Tuesday," Tanner whispered, like the tiny angel he was, his voice full of worry and panting as if he were running to keep up with his dad. Or maybe he was flying? That didn't make sense. Little boys couldn't fly. "And we're gonna take you to the hospital, and you're gonna be okay, and so's Luke and me, and we're all gonna be okay and… and…"

She lost track of his dear sweet huffing and puffing over the hubbub of Grissom's rowdy F-bombs. Oh, how she loved that man. He was fierce and so, so angry. Maybe angry with her. But his temper was born of worry and fear now, and every one of those F-bombs was precious music to her heart.

At last, the gurney slid inside the wide rear gate of an ambulance. Blue lights flashed overhead. An army of extra-large men surrounded her, bent over her, and packed her body with long bags of delicious warmth. Eric, that was his name, pulled a warm blanket out of nowhere and covered her from her neck to her bloody toes.

Tuesday lay there, breathing and listening.

"Be careful, damn it!" Grissom barked.

"Then get out of the way!" That order came from Alex.

Men. Always arguing. Grissom mostly, exerting himself, defending her at what might be the end of her life. But what a way to go, surrounded by men who'd fought for their country, and in some infinitesimally small way, for her.

A hand landed softly on her forehead. That guy with dark, curly hair looked worriedly down at her. "Ma'am, I'm Eric Reynolds. I work with Grissom. You're in shock, and you've lost quite a bit of blood. But you're not dying, you hear me?"

Tuesday wanted to tell him, yes, she could hear him. She wasn't deaf. She understood. But Eric's face kept going in and out of focus, like a loose camera lens. She closed her eyes before it made her sick and breathed, "Grissom."

Eric pressed that big warm hand to the side of her face and gently forced her head to the left. To the man she adored. "You're not dying," he told her gruffly, his eyes glistening. "I won't fucking let you. Keep breathing!"

Sweetest F-bomb ever.

"Me neither," sweet Tanner piped up from somewhere… else. Tuesday thought for sure he was there, but it didn't make sense that a little boy would be crammed into an ambulance with these big, angry guys. Most of them didn't know her, well, except through the press, they all did. But most of what the press wrote and said wasn't kind or true or…

Where was I going with this? Tuesday closed her eyes, too weak and too discombobulated to concentrate. Her life had been one long lonely road after another. It'd be nice to stop breathing and let go. Grissom deserved to keep living. So did his boys. The only way that could happen was without her. She was the jinx. The unintentional killer.

Just when despair nestled into her soul, like an unwelcome bedmate, that tiny little boy-hand slipped beneath the warming blanket and grabbed hold of her index finger. "I gotcha, Miss Tuesday," Tanner whispered, "an' I'm not never letting you go. Not no more. You're mine and Luke's, and we're gonna take especially good care of you from now on. Forever!"

That sweet, enthusiastic little boy had to be a hallucination. Or an angel. No way could Tanner be there. But just in case, Tuesday whispered, "I love you, Tanner. Take care of your dad and your brother. I'll miss you guys, but I can't stay. You have to live. Not me. Not any—"

An alarm shrilled in the suffocating back of that ambulance.

"Don't you dare leave me, Tuesday!" Grissom roared overhead. "I mean, us! Me and my boys. You're all we've got!" He was suddenly so much farther away. Fading, at the end of a long dark tunnel that kept getting narrower and darker. "Save her, Eric. Save my woman!"

Tuesday wanted to tell Grissom everything was going to be okay. But the light was gone.

And so was she…

Chapter Thirty-Four

Three Days Later...

Grissom sat watching the woman he adored love on his boys. There sat Tuesday on his couch, Tanner in one arm and Luke tucked protectively under her other. She'd recovered quickly from her escapade with Moreno. After surgery to repair the graze burn just above her hip, she'd spent a day and night at George Washington University Hospital. The next afternoon, Alex had his medical team: Nurse Judy Mortimer, Dr. Libby Houston and Dr. McKenna Fitzgerald-Villanueva, aka Doc Fitz, travel west with Tuesday on his private helicopter to Grissom's place.

And now, it was time for Grissom to face the truth. Not once before or during these past hectic days had Tuesday said she loved him. As hard as it was to swallow, he knew she might never love him as much as he loved her. Why should she? Tuesday was as shattered as he'd been. Him, by the parents he still had; her, by the parents she'd loved and lost. That kind of pain went deep. It didn't just fade away. They were matching bookends with a million unfinished chapters stuffed between them. They were the perpetual yin and yang of life. Too much baggage kept them apart. They might not have enough reasons to meet in the middle.

As brave as she was, Tuesday didn't seem to want to stay, to give him a chance. To wrap her toes over the edge of her own cliff of despair and take the leap he wanted to take with her. Grissom wasn't sure marriage was the best answer for them anymore. He loved Tuesday with every beat of his heart, that much he knew with certainty. But sometimes, most of the time in his case, a guy didn't get what he wanted. Didn't mean Grissom would give up. Just because Tuesday didn't love him today, didn't mean she wouldn't someday.

She'd certainly jumped straight into the fires of motherhood when she'd literally fought Pam and her now-dead accomplice to save Grissom's sons. Without question or hesitation, with a butt load of passion and—love.

It was hard not being included within the circle of her love. He was the problem, the idiot who'd unintentionally pushed her away the day he'd run to save his sons from their mother. In doing so, he'd saved them, absolutely. But he'd unintentionally left Tuesday out. The story of her entire adult life. Awkward and forgotten. Alone. Overlooked. Never able to heal from losing her parents. That loss compounded when Maeve Astor killed her benefactor, Freddie.

Grissom's reaction on Christmas Day had been instinctive and spontaneous, shaped by a father's fear for his children. He hadn't meant to hurt Tuesday by choosing his boys over her. Had never intended her to feel unwanted. But mean it or not, Grissom *had* left Tuesday out of his family circle and it had crushed her. That was why she'd taken off. She'd been saving herself.

It was natural Tanner would run to his dad, not to her. Tanner'd been running to Grissom all his life. What kid wouldn't run to his old man for safety and security, especially after the ugly encounter with Tanner's witch of a mother?

But that simple gut reaction had reinforced the lie Tuesday still believed today. That she was unwanted. An interloper. An outsider. The woman no one saw because she didn't matter enough to anyone. Because no one cared. Somewhere deep in her psyche, she'd decided she was the reason her parents and Frederick Lamb had died; that it was their love for her that caused their deaths. That she'd killed them...

Grissom wished he could go back in time and redo that day. He wished he'd circled her in his arms along with Luke and Tanner. That he'd cried with her while together they held what Grissom considered to be *their* boys. Tuesday surely cared for them, as if she'd always been their mother. But time didn't work that way, and a man had to face facts. Tuesday was going to leave.

Not. Happening. Today Grissom planned to rescue her for a change.

Tanner and Luke had decided to sleep in front of the fireplace tonight. Which meant, at least in Luke's world, that Tanner was supposed to wait on his little brother because Luke kept insisting, "I'm still sick." Which he wasn't. The little guy had rebounded quick enough after having his stomach pumped. But Tanner was the empathetic nurturer, the perpetual big brother, and he seemed to enjoy running errands for his baby brother.

Grissom suspected Tanner noticed how Luke clung to him since he'd come home. He might be a three-year-old tyrant, but Luke had changed into a benevolent tyrant. Maybe because he knew how much his big brother loved him. And how big a liar his mother was.

"Why'd you leave me Christmas Day?" Grissom asked quietly, so the boys wouldn't hear.

She'd suffered a minor case of hypothermia the day everything went to hell. The scorching burn left by the round Pam fired had carved a three-inch trail on Tuesday's left side above her hip. As if her being 'only grazed' calmed Grissom's need to kill the witch he never should've married.

He couldn't even call Pamela his ex-wife. They were still legally married. Not that he wouldn't marry her evil ass all over again. Their union had brought Tanner and Luke into his life. Too bad that marriage decree hung over Grissom like the blade of the guillotine now. A death sentence, that was Pam. Her dying in that plane alongside Estes would've been the best solution to the problems facing Grissom now.

How was it possible for a murderer to get legal custody of his sons? Seriously? Grissom wasn't sure, but the lawyer representing Pam had already served him with divorce papers that declared she wanted full custody. *Damn, damn, damn her.* He dreaded the day he'd be ordered to hand his boys over, couldn't conceive of ever—ever—leaving them with her.

Was there a judge in the state dumb enough to allow it? Couldn't the state understand that Pam would kill Tanner the first chance she got? Even sitting with Tuesday like he was, Grissom planned how and when to leave the country before that day arrived. To hell with divorce court and its tangled web of convoluted laws. Tanner and Luke mattered more than any damned law.

Tuesday cleared her throat, bringing Grissom back to his family room.

"I'm not sure why I left," she murmured, her gaze on her clasped hands in her lap. "In the heat of everything that happened that day, it seemed like... I don't know" —she shrugged— "I was the problem. I was in your way. You were focused on getting to Luke, and if you'd lost him, if she'd killed him because of me, I'd never forgive myself. You adore your sons and, honestly" —she was studying her fingernails, as if she'd never seen them before— "I'm cursed, Grissom. I'm a jinx. Everyone I've ever loved ended up dead, and I—"

"No." His hand came up fast, a spring-loaded STOP sign in her face. "You're not cursed, love, and you're not a jinx. If anything, you're my lucky star, just like the star on that locket Tanner gave you. None of what happened is your fault. You'd never hurt my boys, and you didn't poison Luke. That's on Pam, and you know it. As far as your parents and Mr. Lamb" —Grissom couldn't bring himself to call that old man her husband— "bad things happen, and sometimes lightning strikes the same person twice. You know I love you, and the boys adore you. How can you not see that?"

She licked her bottom lip, and Grissom's eyes automatically tracked the pink tip of her tongue. Wondering how she still didn't understand what that tiny, insignificant act did to him. Until he remembered. Until he saw past the mask Tuesday had learned to show the world. Until he saw the worried little girl who'd been fighting that vicious world for far too long, behind the polished lie of what everyone else saw: a well-educated, sophisticated, beautiful woman. For all of her adult life, Tuesday had pretended to be something she wasn't: Loved.

The silly woman. If she still had no idea how much Grissom loved her, then he hadn't shown her yet, not in the way she needed to believe. In so many ways he had. He'd certainly said the right words. He'd told her. But Tuesday was still so much an inexperienced teenager, not yet a woman. Old enough, yes, but so much had happened in their short time together, they hadn't had time to truly get to know each other. Not as man and wife. Not even as best friends. His brain had just revealed the true Tuesday Smart to him. Grissom needed her brain to take that same leap of faith and see the real him, to fall in love with him.

Without another word in his defense, Grissom slipped a hand around her waist and pulled her onto his lap, within the circle of his thick, man-sized arms, along with her blanket and heating pad. Once Tuesday settled against him, he buried his face in her neck and asked, "May I date you, Miss Tuesday? Would you go out with me, maybe catch a movie, when you're up for it? Asking questions about each other won't ease your mind, but being with me and the boys" —he cleared his throat— "I mean, *our boys*, for more than a couple hectic hours or days, will."

Her head tipped softly against his shoulder. "*Our* boys?" she asked without looking up at him.

"Yes, love. *Our boys*. Do Luke and Tanner look the least bit worried that their egg-donor isn't here? Do you know who they prayed for while you were in the hospital? I mean after we prayed for Luke's trucks, which, by the way, all have names. Sure wasn't What's-Her-Name."

That brought a tiny uplift to the corners of Tuesday's mouth. "Did you know he named the fire engine Kelsey gave him Spot?"

Grissom tipped his face to the ceiling and laughed. "I didn't, but Spot sounds like a name he'd come up with."

"You think we should explain it'd be a better name for a Dalmatian that rides with his imaginary firemen?"

"Does that mean we're getting a Dalmatian?" At this point, Grissom would buy anything for his boys if it made Tuesday happy.

Still not looking at him, she asked, "We'll take them with us? *Our* boys. On our date?"

"Well, yeah." Grissom hadn't considered not taking Tanner and Luke. Leave them with a sitter? Oh, hell, no.

"Then yes, I'll go on a date with you. Tell me when."

"As soon as you and Luke are both able, and we'll go anywhere you'd like. Think about it."

"Cakes and Honey. I'd like to go back to Cakes and Honey."

Which was oddly the same place Grissom was thinking. Cakes and Honey was where they'd first sat across from each other, like a mother and father with two sons. Like they'd all belonged together. "Good choice. The boys love eating there."

"So do I." He could feel Tuesday's body relax and melt farther into his body. She was happy. But was she happy enough to stay?

She cleared her throat. "Was Tanner there that day? In the parking garage? In the ambulance?"

"No, love, but I heard you talking to him."

"He told me he and Luke were going to take especially good care of me, and then you were there, yelling at someone. Eric, I think."

Grissom placed a warm kiss behind her ear. "You told him to take care of me and Luke, that you'd miss us, but you couldn't stay. Why not?"

She breathed, "Hmmm." Just, "Hmmm." No denial. No change of plans. She was still leaving.

Grissom buried his face in her hair. "Don't go, Tuesday. Give me a chance. Give us a chance, you and me."

Her hands curled over his protective arms. Still no commitment. Still no "I love you."

As hard as it was, Grissom accepted her answer, but he also knew better. Tuesday hadn't declared her love for him because she didn't know how to let go of her past and fall into love. She'd only lived with her parents and Frederick Lamb, which were essentially caretakers. Tuesday was wary of getting hurt again, of causing more death. Who could blame her? He, of all people, knew what a misstep relationships could be. Which was why he was taking it slow and only dating Tuesday, not proposing marriage.

"What was in the hand-delivered letter that came earlier? Must've been important. Was the guy who delivered it Pam's lawyer?"

"Yes-s-s-s," Grissom hissed. "She's suing me for divorce, and she wants full custody."

"She can't do that."

"Legally, she's still their mother." Grissom kept his voice low.

"But…" Tuesday sucked in a long, slow breath. "I might be able to help you fight her. I mean… Umm, there's something you need to know, Grissom. Please don't be mad."

He pressed his lips to her cheek and breathed, "There's nothing you could ever do to make me angry."

"I'm… Grissom, I'm" —she coughed into her fist— "I've got… I mean, I'm… I'm rich. I've got money. Lots of it. I could get you the best lawyers in New York City. You wouldn't have to worry. She'd never get Tanner or Luke. She's unfit and she's evil. No judge in his right mind would grant her anything, but just in case—"

He was stuck on, "You're rich?"

Tuesday finally looked up and straight into his eyes. "Actually, I'm insanely wealthy," she whispered. "Stocks, bonds, time-shares, off-shore accounts, real estate, you name it, I've got it. Freddie left everything to me, including an accountant and a very smart financial manager. I divested some of his property after he died, and I gave his businesses to his sons. But yeah." Her shoulders lifted. "I'm one of those rich bitches you see on TV, the ones who never work unless they're making headlines. I could—"

"But you do work for a living. You're one of the world's best nature photographers," he interrupted, like the dolt his mother'd always said he was. Damned if she wasn't right after all. Not once in the past few days had Grissom connected the dots between Tuesday and the billionaire she'd married. He'd known Lamb was a rich son of a bitch before he'd died, but Tuesday?

Of course she was rich. She was Lamb's widow, and Grissom was poorer than shit, and… Damned if a nasty spike of hairy male ego didn't stand up and shake a gnarly finger at him, urging him to dump her. To push off and slink away like the cur he was. Tuesday Smart was a pedigreed AKC winner, a champion with pure bloodlines. He was a stray, *"Lady and the Tramp"* different from her. He was uncollared and unleashed; mangy and uncouth. She was rich damned royalty, could probably hire a hitman if she wanted to, and then pay off a ton of lawyers to make sure she was never accused.

Hmmm. There was an idea worth entertaining. *Not.*

Grissom's belly expanded as much with awareness as with disbelief. The problem Tuesday thought she'd just unloaded on him was obvious. She wasn't happy and being wealthy hadn't ensured power or influence because those things had never been important to her. What did any of Lamb's wealth mean? Nothing, in Grissom's estimation. He'd never been nor would be rich. But he did know what true happiness was: Tuesday and his boys. End of story. Even if he lost the seemingly perfect house he still owed a mortgage from hell on, he'd still have Tanner and Luke, and they'd make do. The three of them would get by, and Tuesday would make four if she stayed. Grissom had started from scratch before; he could do it again. The bottom line was they'd be okay because they'd be together.

So what if she was one of the top one-percenters in the country? The dollars in all those bank accounts she'd mentioned hadn't made her happy, had they? All a smart man had to do was look at her to see she had low self-esteem. Determination, sure. She had that in spades, but the only time he'd seen her genuinely happy was when she'd been with his boys. Or when he kissed her. He was certain he'd made her happy then.

She wasn't snobbish or unkind. Tuesday had more class in her pinkie than all the rich bitches in Hollywood lumped together. What did her being wealthy and him being a poor dumb jock matter?

Grissom put a finger under her chin and tilted her head so he could look into her soul. And there she was—*my girl.* The woman strong enough to put Maeve Astor in the ground. Fierce enough to stand up to Estes. Brave enough to knock the ever-loving shit out of Pam, despite damned near bleeding to death afterward. Just as brave when she'd nailed Moreno full in his smart assed face with the back of her skull. Yet still so fragile, Grissom wanted to wrap her in bubble wrap and update his damned security system.

"Do you think I'm a snob?" he asked, still keeping his voice low and this conversation private.

Since Tuesday'd come home, his brain had settled down. Panic didn't rule him, and it hadn't snuck up on him once. His boys were happier with her in his house. So was he. For the first time in his life, Grissom had a woman whose touch soothed his soul instead of damned it. He wasn't letting her go just because some billionaire had saddled her with cash and maybe debt, too.

Hmmm... He'd have to look into that. Later. Not. Now.

"No, but..." There went her shoulders again. "Money complicates everything." An ocean of weariness painted her words.

"If we let it."

"Do you think...?" Her pink tongue darted over that succulent bottom lip again. She looked over his shoulder at his sons. "I just wanted you to see me for the real person I am, not because I was rich or because I had Freddie's money. I wanted you to fall in love with me, Grissom. Just me."

"I did. And I do see you. You're my girl, and I love you," Grissom acknowledged quickly. "You're the first and only woman I've ever said that to." His chest heaved with the burning question he couldn't and shouldn't spring on her today. Maybe after a few dates. He'd already declared his love. Blame that on his lack of impulse control, but jumping the gun and asking her to marry him like Dr. Pratt had advised? Would that break the fragile trust between them, or would she jump at the chance? Was he what she needed?

"I could pay for lawyers to fight Pam," Tuesday offered again. "Once you're finally divorced, we could, umm…"

Grissom's heart caught in his throat. Was she going to propose? He hoped.

Instead, the doorbell rang and, of course, Luke jumped up from his 'deathbed' and raced Tanner to the door. Damned if that little guy didn't key in the security code, jerk the front door wide open, and yell, "Come in, guys! Daddy! It's Uncle Alex and Aunt Kelsey, and they bringed Lexie and Baby Bradley!"

"I suspected he let Pam in that day," Tuesday breathed.

"Luke!" Grissom said sternly. "What's the rule?"

Luke turned to his dad, his blue eyes wide and his face ashen. "Ahh. Err. I forgot. And my tummy aches, Daddy."

The little fibber. While Alex and his family walked into the front room, Grissom shifted Tuesday off his lap and pointed to the empty spot on the couch beside him. "Come here, son."

Luke walked to his father, his bottom lip stuck out far enough seagulls could've perched on it. "My tummy really hurts, Daddy. Ouch. Owie. Honest. I'm dying here."

Kelsey chuckled at that very adult remark from Grissom's three-year-old con artist. It was funny, but Luke needed to follow rules. With a big breath, he told the Stewarts, "Excuse us, for a minute or two. My son and I need to talk." With that settled, he took Luke by the hand and together they headed down the hall for a father and son reunion.

I knew I should've changed that code.

Chapter Thirty-Five

"Stay where you are," Alex ordered, before Tuesday could get to her feet and welcome Grissom's friends like a proper hostess should.

"Well, if you say so," she demurred, settling back into the corner of the couch where she'd been holed up all afternoon.

Kelsey took Grissom's place beside her. "You're looking better."

"And you're walking. No more wheelchair?"

"I still use a walker at home but Alex still does most of my running around for me."

"You were damned lucky." Setting Bradley on the floor, Alex told Lexie, "You kids go play in Tanner's and Luke's room. I hear Santa brought them a big surprise."

That was all it took for the little ones to scamper away. As they left, Tuesday heard Tanner telling Lexie and Bradley, "We gotta be extra quiet in case Miss Tuesday needs another nap. I don't hafta take naps anymore, but she does. Do you, Lexie?"

Tuesday couldn't catch Lexie's reply, but Tanner's cautionary comment made her smile. He was a unique little boy. So thoughtful.

"It's nice of you to stop by," she told Lexie's parents.

Alex hmphed. "I've got news, but it'll wait for Grissom. How are Jeff and Henry?"

"They're well." Tuesday wondered how Alex knew Freddie's adult sons. "Henry's son Caleb graduated from Harvard last fall, but he decided not to go into law with his father."

"Oh?"

The blank stare from the former Marine sitting in the loveseat across from her confirmed what Tuesday suspected. "You already know Caleb's in South Carolina, don't you?"

"Yes. He's at Parris Island."

"At the Marine Corps Recruit Depot, training to be a Marine. Like you."

"He comes from good stock. He'll do fine."

"I've never met him," Tuesday admitted, "but if he's anything like his dad and grandfather, he's well on his way." She didn't say where Caleb was on his way to, but men like Freddie, Henry, Jeff, and Alex were giants in whatever field they chose to enter. Caleb would go far as a Marine, then, who knew? Maybe he'd go farther than his grandfather and become a trillionaire, like Elon Musk.

"We met your husband a few years back," Kelsey added. "Jed McCormack introduced us at a charity social for veterans. You called him Freddie."

"Yes. Freddie," Tuesday whispered, looking down at her bandaged hand where only her fingertips showed. Her nails were a mess, some torn to the quick, others cracked or broken. Somewhere in her desperate battle with Pam, she'd lost a complete thumbnail. Fighting to the death took a toll, and Pam had left her mark. The single shot she'd gotten off had left a narrow burn on Tuesday's waistline instead of a cut or slice that could've been stitched or glued. Not like Tuesday thought her injuries were important. They were just a few of the many she'd acquired over her years photographing the wilds of Planet Earth.

"Freddie taught me so much," she murmured. "If you've already met him, then you know he was bigger than life. He believed in taking a stand, fighting back, and making a difference. When he hooked me up with Robert Frieberg, he insisted I take a martial arts class before I left the country. He brought in a few of his friends to train me how to shoot, how to infil and exfil when the weather was bad, about situational awareness, hunter-killer teams, fast-roping out of helicopters, and how to recognize all kinds of threats. Most everything Marines do. Freddie thought I was stronger than I—"

"You are stronger than you realize and don't forget it," Alex cut in. "What would Frederick tell you to do if he were here now?"

"That's easy." She looked Alex dead in the eye. "*'Head up. Shoulders back. Never let 'em see you blink.'*"

"And where do you think he learned that?" Alex had leaned forward. His hands were loose, his long, elegant fingers hanging between his knees, and his icy-blue eyes focused on Tuesday.

"Parris Island?"

Alex nodded. "You'll be okay. You've been taught by the best, and you'll be back in the fight before you know it."

For some reason, Tuesday needed to hear that. "Did you serve with him?"

"Didn't get the opportunity, no. We were different generations, but he and his sons are all Marines. I'm not surprised he didn't tell you."

"Why didn't he?" That would've been nice to have known about the man she'd married.

"Because men who return from war don't discuss what they did or saw in combat. They come home, knuckle down, and get back to the business of living. The heroes are the men and women who didn't make it home. Has Grissom mentioned any of his missions?"

"No, and he's not going to start now, Boss," Grissom interrupted from the hall doorway. "They're over, they're done, and we're moving on."

Alex cocked a subtle smile in Tuesday's direction. "Sound familiar?"

She tossed a smile back at him. "Sounds like Freddie."

Grissom took the seat directly opposite Alex, the coffee table between them. "Hey, Kels. What brings you folks to my neck of the woods?"

"You mean your tree farm?" Kelsey asked, her brown eyes sparkling. "Those pines in your backyard are beautiful with the snow on their boughs. They'd make gorgeous Christmas cards if someone were to take a few pictures while they're glistening. I mean, look at that scene out there, people. It's the perfect setting for one of those cheesy Hallmark movies."

Grissom dragged a hand up the back of his neck. "Not happening, sorry. They provide too much cover, and I need a clear line of sight. Once I log off that acreage, we'll be able to see anyone com—"

"You can't cut those trees down," Tuesday cut in. "I have memories out there, of you and your boys singing Christmas songs, right before we found our very first tree."

A no-kidding smile broke through the weary expression he'd worn since she'd come home from the hospital. "*Our very first tree?*" he asked.

That word, *our,* meant a lot to him, Tuesday could tell.

Thank heavens Alex interrupted with a polite '*ahem,*' before the hot flash creeping up her neck went nuclear. "Howie's been interrogating Pam McCoy."

Hearing his wife's name wiped the smile off Grissom's face. He tipped forward, his palms to his knees, his focus switched to his boss. "What now?"

Alex pointed a finger at Grissom. "You married a helluva liar, for starters. That woman wouldn't know the truth if it spit in her face."

"Tell me something I don't know."

"She's insisting that Tuesday was the aggressor in Puntarenas, then again when she stormed this place" —Alex held both palms forward when Tuesday opened her mouth to protest— "Don't kill the messenger. Those are Pam's words, not mine or Howie's. She said you interfered in what she claims was a peaceful reunion with her and her precious sons until you showed up."

"That woman!" Tuesday exclaimed.

"Precious sons, my ass," Grissom growled. "She lured Luke with what he thought was candy to get him to let her in. Jesus, he was holding the half-eaten bag of THC edibles that she gave him when we arrived on scene!" He raked a quick hand over his head. "What about the roofie she slipped me? What about—?"

Alex gave Grissom his chin. "One thing at a time. You're right, though. What Dr. Pratt pumped out of your boy's gut in the ER is all the evidence Howie needs to put Pam away for life. And what Doctor Windhall pumped out of you wasn't a roofie, Grissom. It was scopolamine, and I already told you that. Remember?"

Grissom nodded. "Yeah. I remember. I'm getting better."

Alex continued. "We now have more hard evidence against your wife than she can possibly manufacture against you, Tuesday. But I've got to tell you, Grissom, if she'd poisoned Lexie or Bradley, I would've already sent her to hell. No questions asked. No quarter given."

"I should've done that the second I saw she'd gotten inside my house," Grissom hissed.

"No, Grissom," Tuesday interrupted. "Your boys didn't need the image of their father killing their mother seared into their little brains. They needed you more that day than she needed to die. She'll get hers. Just wait, you'll see."

"But she nearly killed you." He was still so angry.

"I guess I showed her then, huh?" Tuesday said, with more attitude than she'd felt in days.

The handsome smile of Grissom's came back. "I'm so proud of you."

"Get this," Alex interrupted, speaking to Tuesday this time. "Pam also wants you charged with attempted murder and jailed without bail for trying to kill her."

"Me? But she was the one with a weapon."

"Exactly. But Pam's dumbass attorney maintains you became the aggressor the moment you took possession of her firearm."

"I never had possession."

"It was self-defense!" Grissom roared.

"Yes, and Pam fired but only after Tuesday had partial control of her weapon. Tuesday, you never had a solid hold on the grip or trigger, right?" Alex continued as if Grissom hadn't exploded. "That's what burned your palm, right? Just the barrel, right?"

"That's all I could reach." Tuesday held up her bandaged palm. "It burned my life-line off, but I had to stop her, Alex. She would've killed Tanner if I hadn't."

Grissom reached over and put a hand on her knee. "God, I love you."

"That's not all," Alex said. "Pam wants you charged with assault for the neck chop you nailed her with, the one she claims nearly paralyzed her. Good thinking, by the way. Also for doing that 'ninja thing'—her words again, not mine— when you head-butted her and broke her nose, another damned good self-defense tactic."

"All while maintaining partial possession of the weapon that Pam brought into Grissom's house. Just the barrel," Kelsey added.

"Which clearly shows forethought and intent," Grissom added.

"I don't know how you did it, girlfriend," Kelsey told Tuesday.

She turned to Kelsey at that sweet word, fighting tears. "I had to," she whispered, recalling the stark terror on poor Tanner's brave little face as he'd faced his evil mother. "I couldn't let her hurt my, err, sorry, I meant, Grissom's boys."

"*Our boys*, damn it," Grissom growled. "I owe you everything for coming to their rescue, woman. Fu—! I mean, darn. Oh hell, I mean I wouldn't still have them if you hadn't shown up when you did. Both times. Jesus!"

Lowering her head, Tuesday let the tears fall. He made it sound as if a future were in the cards for them, as if his sons were already hers. Oh, how she wished.

Kelsey joined Alex on the loveseat. As soon as she settled on his lap, he put his arm around her, effectively shackling her to him. They made such a romantic couple. Grissom did the same, just moved in beside Tuesday and lifted her onto his lap. She burrowed under his arm, leaned her head on his shoulder, and closed her eyes. The warmth and comfort his body provided was so welcome. As was the tissue he pulled out of nowhere and tucked into her good hand. As were the gentle kisses he pressed to her temple while she mopped her face.

Tuesday wanted what Alex and Kelsey had. All that love…It wasn't hard to see the shine in Kelsey's pretty brown eyes or the careful way Alex held his wife, his hand on her waist. They were a match made in heaven. A rugged beast and his dark-haired beauty. A fairytale come to life.

"So how'd Pam hook up with Moreno?" Grissom asked, while Tuesday relaxed more fully against him. "He's from New York City; she's a tag chaser from JBLM." Joint Base Lewis-McChord, Washington state.

"Like I said, a liar. Despite what Pam swears is true, that Moreno paid her to kill Tuesday and that everything was his idea, we both heard Moreno say she didn't hire him. Why would *he* lie? According to Sal, they crossed paths when he was casing Lamb's son's house, looking for Tuesday, and I believe him. It's not difficult locating Jeff or Henry, not since the press made Tuesday's life public knowledge when they tried her in public for murdering her husband and the Bremmer family. Moreno was only after Tuesday at first, but once he caught up with Pam, she told him you two were together. He figured if he tracked you, Grissom, he'd find Tuesday."

"So Moreno found Tuesday because of me?" Grissom asked.

Alex nodded. "Yes, but Pam's who led him to your address. Once she knew why he wanted Tuesday, they agreed to work together. After he had all of Frederick Lamb's money, Pam convinced him to hire someone to kill you, Grissom. That was her only condition. She wanted you dead. Moreno got Tuesday."

"Pam wasn't prepared for Tuesday though," Grissom said.

"No, Moreno was supposed to wait on that frontage road while Pam broke in and poisoned her boys. Moreno was only the driver. He had no idea Pam even had kids."

"She hit me with a brick," Tuesday murmured.

"You're lucky that's all she did. Airport security at Reagan found an odd bag of tools in Moreno's sedan: several rolls of duct tape, a pack of nylon rope, boning and hunting knives, pliers, garden shears, and a pencil-tipped, propane torch. Pam's admitted she planned to torture Grissom, but just for fun." Alex finished with a huff. "That woman's a stone-cold psycho."

"How'd she get Grissom's address?" Tuesday asked.

"Post Office has his forwarding address. They're not supposed to share information like that, but with enough money, a person's privacy goes out the window," Alex replied.

"She also stole thousands from Mike Estes before she murdered him," Kelsey added. "She probably would've killed Moreno too, if Tuesday hadn't ruined her plans."

Alex nodded. "At first, Howie thought Pam killed Estes in the heat of passion, but then he got in touch with the police in Puntarenas. Seems she emptied Estes' bank account prior to his untimely death, which is premeditation. Add that to what Reagan Airport security found in the trunk of Moreno's sedan, and she'll go down for first-degree murder."

"Good," Tuesday whispered at the same time Grissom barked, "I hope they hang her."

She could only imagine what was running through his mind. He blamed himself marrying Pam in the first place, for putting his sons in danger, and for the abuse she'd heaped on Tanner. But that was what good fathers did. They stood between their children and evil, and when they failed, they blamed themselves.

"Unfortunately, she won't be extradited to Costa Rica. The Puntarena police won't be able to charge her for murder or seize the money she stole because she burned through it traveling back to the States. She won't hang for her crimes in D.C., either. There's no death penalty in Virginia." Slyly, Alex added, "But there is in Florida."

Tuesday wished she could read his mind.

"What's Florida got to do with that witch?" Grissom asked.

"Because Pamela McCoy lied on your marriage certificate." Alex's lips curved into a delightfully wicked smile. "She might've been living in Washington state when you met her, but she was born and raised in Gainesville, Florida. Her real name's Marcia Valentino, and she's wanted for killing an airman from Eglin Air Force Base seven years ago. She accused him of fathering the child she was allegedly carrying, then stabbed the poor guy when he refused to marry her. The motel they hooked up in had just installed a top-of-the-line security system and caught everything. She was charged with manslaughter, but for some reason, the idiot judge who arraigned her released her on her own recognizance. Pam fled the state and changed her name."

Tuesday couldn't believe the wicked twists and turns in that woman's mind. "Was she really pregnant, or was that a lie, too? What'd she do with that baby? Is it still—"

Grissom's hold tightened. "Easy, Mama Bear. Let's hear what else Alex has to say."

But knowing Pam had refused to nurture her children with Grissom, Tuesday couldn't help worrying. Was that other baby another lie Pam told to get what she wanted, or was it real? Was it in a foster home, bereft and left out for the rest of its life, or was it loved and nurtured like every child deserved to be? Worse, did Pam simply have it scraped out of her body after she'd killed the baby's father? Was she that cruel? That heartless?

Stark desolation roared over Tuesday at all the questions. She needed answers and she had the means to make it happen. As soon as Grissom and his boys went to bed, she'd search online and hire someone to search for that baby. She could fund a string of orphanages. That'd be the perfect way to spend Freddie's money. Private orphanages. Maybe private homes for unwed mothers, too. All staffed by people that cared, truly cared for at-risk people, and she'd work there. And, oh yes, a home for men who found themselves with violent spouses or partners. She could make all of it happen. Every last bit.

Chapter Thirty-Six

The day's revelations were precisely what Grissom needed. Somewhere during Alex's descriptions of Pam's infidelities, Grissom made up his mind to rely on Tuesday's inheritance if Pam insisted on a custody battle. He and Tuesday needed to get past their individual fears about them being together. Ego be damned, he'd take the first step, even if it meant allowing Tuesday to use some of her inheritance to make sure Pam never went near his boys again. Like he'd told Tanner so many times: *Anytime. Every time.* That included Tuesday, and it started now.

After Alex and Kelsey left with their kids, Grissom grilled steaks while Tuesday made a leafy green salad. The boys ate in front of the fireplace, like cowboys riding the range, Tanner said. They were finally asleep in their bunk beds, worn out from playing with Lexie and Bradley all afternoon. It was time to make a move.

Grissom looked down on Tuesday, stretched out comfortably alongside him, asleep in his arm. A powerful sense of protectiveness swelled inside. Closing his eyes, he held her as tightly as he dared. She'd insisted on helping with dinner, and them working together over something as simple as preparing that meal, had confirmed everything he already knew. They needed each other, in all things and in all ways. Breathing in her sweet, feminine scent was a gift he hadn't planned on ever having in his lifetime. But he had it now and he wasn't letting her go.

In so many ways, they were alike. She'd conquered a mountain of insurmountable obstacles in her life, yet was still a virgin. He wasn't as pure as Tuesday, but he was inexperienced in other things that mattered. Like love. No woman had ever loved him like a boy or man deserved to be loved and cared for. His dad had, sure, yeah, in his own, stifled way. But tender womanly expressions of love were as alien to Grissom as Martians on planet Earth.

Tucking her close, he lifted up slowly from the couch, and, with the practiced care of a father of little boys, he headed for his room. Make that, *their room*. With one foot, he nudged the door open and aimed for the bed. Sticking one knee to the mattress, Grissom carefully deposited Tuesday against the pillows, then eased his arm out from under her.

He couldn't remember ever having carried a woman before or talking as openly as he had with Tuesday. With her, he could be himself. She treated him the way she treated his boys, with empathy and respect. Every time.

Just as carefully, he crouched to his knees, eased her feet out of her slippers, and unzipped her jeans. Once her long legs were freed from the denim, he stopped and stared, amazed that a woman as lithe and beautiful as Tuesday was in his bed. She could be a dancer as toned and well-muscled as her legs and thighs were.

His cock kicked against his zipper, wanting her. Every male instinct sprang to life. Molten need roared through his veins, and his eyes watered at the intense juxtaposition of a man like him, a warrior and killer, standing so close to an angel. What had God been thinking, to bring a creature full of light into a life that, for so long, hadn't been worth living?

If not for his firstborn, Grissom would've offed himself years ago. He'd been that low, that hopeless, after he and his team had mistakenly killed those boys in Syria. How did a man ever get past such a heinous act? Sure, it was accidental, one of those ungodly fog of war mistakes. But to Grissom, it seemed enormously unjust that he was free to hold and love his sons, while another father grieved. Death had been a constant in his line of work, and now there was the possibility that another child had been left motherless, maybe fatherless, this one through no fault of his. Tuesday was right to wonder if Pam had truly been pregnant when she'd killed that airman out of Eglin Air Force Base.

Quietly, Grissom stepped from his bed to make a call.

Mother answered with a terse, "What do you want?"

She seemed tense so he gentled his tone even more. "Hi Mom, it's me, Grissom."

"I know. I've got caller ID." Mother was in rare, testy form tonight.

"Could you locate the name of the airman my wife murdered in Florida about seven, maybe eight years ago?"

"Why?"

"Because, allegedly, she killed him after he refused to marry her, and, oh yeah, her real name's Marcia Valentino, not Pamela."

"Oh, sure." Mother's tone softened. "Chief Prince should have that information. Hold, please."

Grissom paused, listening to her fingernails work one of her many keyboards. Mother was a complicated woman. If she liked you, she'd do anything you asked. If not, she could make your life miserable. A few agents found ways to work around her. Many did their own research, or they went to Beau Villanueva, Axel Cho, or Ember Dennison for assistance. Grissom still didn't know if Mother liked him or not, but she was helping now. That had to mean he was on her good side, didn't it?

"The man Marcia Valentino killed was Airman First Class Benjamin McGill. He was from Minot, North Dakota."

"If there was a child…" Grissom wasn't sure how to ask.

"You want me to crosscheck physician and hospital records to locate that baby? Is that what you're asking?" Her tone pitched higher. "Why? Are you going to want it when I find it or are you just curious? Because I'm not—"

"I want to know what happened to him or her," Grissom clarified. "Pam liked getting her way, and this may be a wild goose chase, but if it's not…" He turned back to Tuesday, knowing she wouldn't let this motherless child waste away in the foster system. "Yes, Mom, I want that child. I want him or her to be as safe and happy as my boys are. Can you do that for me or not?"

Nothing but the clatter of Mother's nails on her keyboards answered back. Grissom held his breath. She was an all-out genius. It was just possible that—

"Airman McGill was Native American, as in full-blooded Cherokee," she bit out. "Did you know that?"

"Is that supposed to matter? I don't care if he was purple, black, or polka-dotted. Do you know if—?"

"Don't get smart with me. I'm just asking. Some people care, that's all."

"Well, I don't. I just want the child Pam threw away. If there is one." Grissom couldn't see her allowing a pregnancy to go to full term when there wasn't anything in it for her. There were so many ways she could've ended that baby—if there'd been one to begin with. If not, at least he'd tried. But if there was a baby, if Mother could track it down, and if that little one needed a family…

Grissom glanced over his shoulder at Tuesday. Wouldn't she be surprised when she woke up tomorrow and discovered they were going to Florida to adopt that child?

"Got it," Mother breathed. "An infant girl… a tiny, tiny baby girl… Ahem." Mother paused to cough, but all of a sudden, she sounded—fragile? "Yes," she continued, "someone left a baby girl in the Safe Haven drop box at a Gainesville fire station around the same time Marcia Valentino disappeared. I'm not calling that witch Pam McCoy, sorry. Not calling her your wife anymore, either."

"Okay, yes, that sounds about right," Grissom breathed, relieved for the first time since he'd heard about Pam murdering that poor airman. "That's where Pam, I mean Marcia Valentino, was from. Not sure how we'd know for sure that's Airman McGill's little girl, but—"

"DNA," Mother snapped, her clever fingers going a mile a minute. "I've got yours. Now, I've got Pam's, err, Valentino's. Howie got that when he booked her. Just need Airman McGill's and…" Tap, tap. Clatter, clatter. A few more taps then, "That little girl is definitely Airman McGill's, and… look at this."

Grissom's phone dinged an incoming message. Lifting his cell away from his ear, he looked at the photo of a beautiful, bronze-skinned little girl, around eight years old, with bright brown eyes and shiny, long black hair that fell over her shoulders. She was beautiful, dressed like she was, in a fluffy pink dress and holding a gray stuffed bunny by one ear. Another photo hit his incoming box. The smiling airman in that shot was the spitting image of the child who would've, and should've, been his daughter. His little girl.

Grissom's heart crawled up his throat at what that poor airman had lost, all because of Pam's evil trickery. "Where is she, Mom? Is she safe?" *God, I hope so.*

"She is, Grissom," Mother whispered, her voice oddly strained. "Her name is now Rosario Medina. Hector and Adele Medina adopted Rosario within months of her being left in that Safe Haven box. Hector was the fireman who found her. He and his wife are Cuban. They tried for years to get pregnant and now… and now…"

Was Mother crying? "Are you okay?" Grissom asked gently, wiping his own eyes at the miracle unfolding over his phone.

"Allergies," Mother choked. "I've got allergies and it's hay fever time of year and… and it's none of your business."

Grissom let it go. For now. He was as choked up as she was. "The important thing is that Rosario's safe, Mom. Thanks for finding her for me."

A definite sniff came over the connection. "Would you have adopted her, Grissom? I mean, really? Would you have wanted a baby like her, after everything your wife's done to you?"

"Yes," he answered, with a clean heart and full intent. "The one thing I know for certain is that kids aren't responsible for the sins of their parents, and babies deserve every chance we can give them."

"I know," Mother whispered. "I… I just… I just wish…"

"I don't know what me and my boys would do without you, Mom," Grissom said when she stalled. "Thanks for helping me find Rosario. I'm sad I'll never have that little girl in my life, but she's happy and that's all that counts."

"She is. Happy, I mean." Mother's voice sounded so small. "Thanks for letting me find her for you. I… I needed that." The connection went dead, and it was okay. Grissom knew a lot about devils, and the devil riding Mother must be a son of a bitch.

He turned to find Tuesday watching him from where she lay. "Where are we?"

"In *our* room." Grissom made sure to use that explicit, possessive pronoun.

"*Our* room?" she murmured, lifting to her elbows. "Umm, where are the boys?"

"You mean *our boys*?" he asked, emphasizing the direction he needed her to go with him.

A lazy smile lit her face. "I like that word."

"Good, because from now on, this is *our room,* and those two little guys passed out on their bunk beds are *our boys*." Grissom sat his butt alongside Tuesday, then leaned over and rested his forearm beside her shoulder to hold his weight. Sex was the last thing she needed, but a kiss or two wouldn't hurt. "I want to make love with you, but tonight's too soon. We'll wait until—"

"I'm tired of waiting," Tuesday interrupted softly, her finger tracing up his jaw and over the tip of his ear. "I've waited all my life, Grissom. I want us to be together. Now."

He shivered at the sparks her touch left in its wake. Tipping forward, he pressed his mouth over her lips and was lost in the sweetest heaven on earth. Holding this woman soothed his ragged soul, and kissing her reset his inner compass.

"I have something to tell you," he mumbled around her questing lips.

"What?" she breathed into his face.

"Pam didn't lie. There was a baby. She gave birth to a daughter in Florida."

That got Tuesday's full attention. "Oh?" she asked, pushing Grissom far enough back so she could sit up.

"Yes, but she gave the baby up. Not sure precisely when or if Pam's the one who put her there, but that little girl ended up in one of those Safe Haven boxes at a fire station in Gainesville. You know the ones, where mothers can voluntarily surrender their child if they can't keep it, for whatever reason? Her name's Rosario Medina, and look." Palming his cell phone, Grissom brought up the photos Mother had sent.

"Oh," Tuesday whispered, her fingers gripping Grissom's phone and her eyes brimming. She blinked and blinked. "What a pretty little girl. Is that the man who fathered her?"

Grissom nodded, his heart in his throat, thankful this little one had a happy ending.

"They look so much alike. How'd you find her?"

"With Mother's help."

"Aww…" With a sigh, Tuesday let go of Grissom's hand. "Thank you. I was worried about that baby, if it was even real or just another lie."

"Me, too. Also…" He tipped his forehead to Tuesday's. "I've decided to man up and accept your offer to help me fight

Pam. I want you at my side, and I'd be honored if you'd help me keep my boys safe from their mother."

"Does that mean…?" She was holding her breath.

"That I'm okay spending some of your inheritance? Yes, if it's okay with you."

"Yes, oh, yes! Grissom, yes! Thanks for letting me help! Honestly, I hate being wealthy, but if I can use my inheritance to help you, then yes! Thank you so much!" She threw her arms around his neck, pressing her full breasts against his chest. Flattening her body to his.

Her mouth was so close. So incredibly sweet.

"We should wait," he whispered, even as he licked her strawberry lips.

"No. We shouldn't ever wait again. We never know what tomorrow will bring."

"But you've never—"

"But I'm ready, and my side hardly hurts anymore."

"Well…" He hedged, pulling back far enough to peer into those emerald wells of innocence.

Too late. Grissom fell. Headlong. Powerless to stop himself. Smart enough not to try anymore. Awestruck at the beauty in his arms. Tracing the tip of his thumb from her bottom lip down her neck to the gentle swell of her cleavage, he asked, "Promise you'll tell me if anything we do hurts?"

Her fingers delved into his hair and down the back of his neck. "You'd never hurt me. I know that about you. You're a good guy."

"Damned straight, but I'm not stopping this time and things could get rough. You might feel a pinch when we go all the way, maybe more. Let's take it slow and easy."

Her fingers fluttered down his neck, over his shoulders, to his chest. "If you say so."

Grissom looked toward the ceiling, humbled at the trust radiating off his woman. He loved what the warmth of her touch was doing to him, but those words? *'If you say so.'?* He couldn't explain how much they meant to a man like him. Just knew that her body touching his always gentled the monsters in his head like nothing else.

Her tiny fingers and hands, hands that hadn't hesitated to grab onto his sons to keep them safe, were now smoothing over his head and circling his neck. Her hands weren't large enough for her fingers to meet at his nape, but the idea that a tiny thing like Tuesday Smart was putting her life in his hands was a rush. She was so small, and he was nothing but a hairy, coarse oaf, dying to devour and deflower her. Ready to mark her from the inside out as his, only his.

This was another Leap of Faith moment, and the enormity overwhelmed Grissom. As thrilled as he was that Tuesday wanted her first time to be with him, he hesitated. Should he even take this chance? Would he hurt her when he did? He was larger and thicker than most guys, but would that act destroy what they had now? Their friendship? Her feelings for him? Would making love change everything, just because he couldn't resist her? Worse, oh, God, no, would she turn into another… mistake? A witch? Was it him? Was he the problem?

Her wet, breathy kiss against the underside of his scruffy chin brought Grissom back to his senses. Tuesday lay there serene and angelic beneath him. Waiting. For him, for hell's sake. Him, of all the men she could have chosen. Just knowing she was content to wait for him, while he'd allowed doubt to creep in, made Grissom want to crow. She wasn't Pam. Never would be. No matter what he did or how many mistakes he made, Tuesday loved him. She didn't need to say it for him to be sure.

Peering into those trusting emerald depths, his very own private pools of wonder, Grissom knew this was the right time and she was the only woman for him. Tuesday's peaceful acquiescence, her submissive acceptance of him and his decision to go slow, made him the man he was meant to be. Her man.

Grissom tipped forward on his knees until he was nose to nose with the adorable goddess waiting patiently beneath him. "Mind if I take off the rest of your clothes?"

"Not if I can undress you, too," she whispered coyly.

"Absolutely."

It took seconds to get her bare. Then came the difficult part of this coy game. Striving for patience, Grissom laid back and allowed a very naked Tuesday the experience of undressing him for her first time. He caught the indecision in her eyes once she smoothed his t-shirt up and out of her way. He nearly died and went to heaven when she leaned forward, the deep pink tips of her lush breasts brushing his bare stomach while her hands smoothed over his chest like she was touching a treasure. How her mouth formed a perfect O. How she kept licking those wet, strawberry lips. How her thumbs scrubbed his nipples as lightly as an angel's touch. How her eyes sparkled with delight and wonder. How hard it was keeping his dick under control once the naked woman on his bed unbuckled his belt, unzipped his jeans, and clambered to her feet to pull his pants off his long legs.

By then, his balls were blue fucking smurfs. The last thing he needed to hear was when Tuesday said, "You're so big. Are you sure you're—?"

"I'm sure," he answered, rolling her carefully to her back. "I'm damned sure."

Grissom was on his knees to this woman, his ass in the air. So ready. So damned lost in love. His cock was jonesing to get things going. Reaching down, he gave it a tiny sip of the pleasure dripping from her folds, then tipped forward, barely thrusting into her, watching Tuesday's eyes flash with sudden awareness of what they were about to do.

"Are you just going to stare at me?"

Grissom nodded, because words failed as their very first glide-and-slide began. Her body clenched so damned tight around him, strangling his cock, refusing entry. He took a deep breath and backed off. They had the rest of the night to make this work. Plenty of time.

"It won't fit," she whispered. For an untouched virgin her age, one who hadn't touched herself in play or curiosity, of course it hurt.

"It'll fit, trust me. Women have babies and most babies are lots bigger than me. Breathe, just breathe. No rush." Didn't matter that his damned cock had morphed into a steel spike or that she was the one who had set it on fire. Tonight was only about Tuesday.

'Play. This first time has to be good for her. It has to be about play. Just play.'

Lowering to one elbow, he slid his free hand over her breast, tweaking her nipple while covering her mouth with his. Their tongues clashed and chased each other, lighting yet another urgent message that all systems below were go, go, go.

Still, he dallied, intent on taking the worry out of this monumental first. On kissing Tuesday as long as she needed in order to relax; on savoring the miracle of being with this very naked beauty. Carefully, he squeezed her breast, then the other, while the creature of satin, silk, and a bit of sin writhed beneath him, scrubbing her smooth, sleek body against his, urging him to the inevitable.

Her fingers on his scalp tenderly massaged away the dam that had forever blocked the blood supply to his brain. Shivers tingled up his spine as her gentle touch awakened every last one of his nerve endings.

But next she turned into some kind of dominatrix, her nails biting the cheeks of his ass. Grissom damned near squeaked at the sting. He'd never been a fan of the BDSM movement sweeping the world with its lies of physical abuse causing pleasure. The two were diametrically opposed in his book. Having witnessed what women and girls overseas suffered on a daily basis was a powerful deterrent, and lifting a hand against any female had never been a turn-on for him.

But if Tuesday kept up with that back and forth, her fingers soft and sweet on his scalp one moment, then digging into his ass the next, that he could live with. She couldn't hurt a big guy like him. Problem was, he'd come before she did if she kept it up, and that just wasn't right. Time for plan B.

Deserting her succulent breasts, he dragged his free hand down her centerline, over her taut belly to her luscious folds. Like playing with liquid fire helped his control? Hell, no. The scent of her arousal bloomed like roses in his nose. Everything inside of him powered forward.

"Hold on, love," he ordered, his voice gruff and raw.

"Am I ready?"

"Yeah. Ready. Now. Hurry." *I've let you play too long, and damn it, woman, you're good.*

The second her fingers settled over his shoulders, Grissom surged forward. Less than an inch, but damn. His control was shredded.

Her hands slipped down his ribcage, plucking his ribs like piano keys. Once again, those fingers landed on his ass and out came her nails. Digging in. Painfully. Marking him with erotic stabs and pinches he'd never experienced before, and just enough sass that…

"Do it," she hissed, thrusting upward and onto him.

Just that fast, he was balls deep, lost in the deepest, sweetest clinch of his life.

Fuck! Her inner muscles were like fingers, squeezing the hell out of him. She was so damned tight, and he was gloriously deep. He stopped. Tuesday hadn't whined or screamed yet, had just forced him into her body with that one powerful jerk and…

Damned if this tiny virgin wasn't a helluva lot stronger than she looked.

Pulsing with the urgent need to, 'Move it!', Grissom began a rhythmic series of thrusts that took him deeper each time. Pushing in. Pulling out. Slipping just far enough out. Sliding just hard enough back in. Not too far. Not too deep. No sense rushing, despite Tuesday's tendency to explode on contact.

Too bad she didn't share the concept of going slow.

Her thighs were more muscled than he'd expected, especially now, when he could feel the impact of her naked body slamming against his. As slow as he meant to go, her upward thrusts were feverishly brutal. His woman was a natural. Their bodies weren't just coming together, not as hard as she kept banging into him. Smacking against his pubic bone. Her fingernails still tacked onto his ass.

At last. He was through. But what the fuck? Was she fucking him? Was demur little Tuesday Smart one of those legendary Amazonian women come to life? In his bed? Was this determined woman so fierce and so driven, that he was now the weaker sex? *Oh, hell no.*

With one firm fist gripping her gorgeous ass, Grissom got serious. She wanted to play rough? Game on. Growling from the sheer pleasure of being set free, yet still making sure he didn't bump her bandaged wound, he slammed forward, going as deep as he could. Keeping his mouth on her breast, he sucked hard, stretched that cocky nipple, marking her creamy skin and branding her inside and out. Like primal man did to his woman back in the Stone Ages. With fury, lust, sweat, and a fuck-ton of animal passion.

Right on time, too. Tuesday's legs stiffened into planks. Her weeping core became a burning fist of fire, strangling his cock, reminding him that this was how she'd survived all those years of torment and death. By being strong and fierce, by killing him in the best way.

Tuesday'd been honed in the worst fires possible. Somewhere along the line, she'd apparently elected to become one helluva survivor instead of just another whiny victim. Victoriously strong, she'd conquered her attackers, every last one of them. Grief. Death. The extreme solitude of her chosen profession. The almighty FBI with their illicit, illegal outreach. Hell, even that pig, Maeve Astor. Estes. Pam. Moreno. And now…

She was conquering him and her virginity, both in one fell swoop.

"Fuck, yeah!" Grissom hissed, unloading into Tuesday's sweat-slickened body.

The power and energy of their coming together blew his mind. Her body's grip was so damned strong, and her core so phenomenally tight, he could *not* catch a full breath. Not deep enough to get him through the onslaught of aftershocks radiating through her body to his, holding his rigid cock in place, as if it—he—had no will. No choice. Which he kinda didn't. What red-blooded man wanted one?

The sweetest, feminine, "Wow," shivered over his sweaty chest. Balanced on both palms to keep from crushing her, Grissom stared down at the woman he adored, sweat dripping through his bangs and stinging his eyes. What a rush! "For a tiny thing, you're dynamite in bed, woman."

Delight, joy, and a butt-load of womanly satisfaction glittered back at him. Not a hint of red-light stop, stop, stop in sight. Damned if those darling absinthe eyes didn't light up like traffic lights, all sparkly go, go, go. Made a man proud to realize he'd met his match. His one and only. That he, Grissom McCoy, was the first and would damned well be the last man claiming Tuesday Smart. His soulmate. His other half. His true destiny. She was no shrinking violet, and if that cocky smirk of hers meant what he hoped it did, they were headed for one helluva repeat performance.

There was no need to ask if he'd hurt her, and he'd never admit she'd hurt him. She hadn't. She couldn't, not as small as she was. That constellation of tiny, indented crescents she'd marked his hairy ass with were precisely what had pushed him off the edge of worry and right into her. They'd taken their Leap of Faith together.

He offered another breathless, "Again?"

The wide grin that cracked her pretty face was the perfect answer. Tuesday Smart was one helluva dynamo, and Grissom was up for the challenge.

Chapter Thirty-Seven

After her first fantastic orgasm, Grissom had dragged Tuesday into the ensuite bathroom, where he first covered the burn mark on her waist with a large waterproof bandage before they played like kids under the shower. Soapy fingers and hands had explored each other, their mouths hungry for more than food, and their bodies eager for another coupling.

But when he turned her face to the tile and ordered her to, "Spread 'em…"

When he pressed a massive palm firmly to her lower back until she was bent so far over that she could touch her toes…

When he told her, "Grab the backs of your knees. I'm going to fuck you till you scream…"

Tuesday discovered she liked being bossed. She especially liked Grissom pumping into her from behind. The way he took control. Seemed smart since he seemed to know his way around her body better than she did.

The harder they crashed together, the louder their wet flesh slapped, and the deeper his glorious cock went, the more her love for this handsome father bloomed. She didn't think she could manage another screaming orgasm, but he took her there. What she lacked in experience, she made up with enthusiasm and another ungodly growl that made her sound like a woman in the throes of labor, "Gr-r-r-issom!"

"Shhhhh," he ordered, reaching down and pressing a wet hand over her lips.

As if she could. "Gris-s-s-som!" she hissed between his fingers, pleasure exploding through her body like Fourth of July fireworks.

With one final thrust, he filled her with heat. There was nothing better than his version of play. It took the stress out of sex, because, wow. She never knew orgasms could feel so good. Or how much she craved the smile her coming always put on his handsome face. Or how loud he could make her grunt and scream. Grissom made the night exciting. She couldn't wait to do it again, to stimulate the heck out of her cowboy in his bed.

Better yet… *Our bed.* His fingers digging into her hips kept Tuesday balanced. His cock buried to the hilt didn't hurt. Her hair was drenched, the tips of it swirling like silk on the tile floor. She was utterly boneless, limp as a noodle, but her ass was so damned happy. She'd be sore in the morning, but she'd never regret what she'd done with—and to—Grissom.

Especially what she'd done with her mouth. When she'd knelt in front of him and touched her lips to his—there. When she'd kept her eyes on him to make sure he was watching as she kissed the tip of him—there. When she'd opened her mouth and licked up that squeaky-clean shaft. She'd barely gotten a taste when he'd jerked her to her feet and ordered her, "Wrap your legs around my waist. Hurry up. Now!"

Thrilled with the power she had over him, Tuesday had complied in the nick of time, finding herself wedged into a corner of the shower. With her pinned in place, Grissom worked her slick, wet body up high enough, he'd wormed his shoulders under her thighs, and then… *Whoa.*

She shivered remembering how her thighs had clamped over his ears, holding his head and that wicked, wicked mouth of his in place, while she came and came and—

Her body clenched again, reliving every sensation. Thunder roared once more. The blessed friction of his body pounding into hers brought on another blinding, searing orgasm that stole her breath.

Even facing the floor like she was, Tuesday knew her man was smiling. She could feel it in the gentle way his rough hands smoothed over her well-pleased ass. The way his hips thrust forward while those callused fingers tenderly held her in place. They'd given each other something tonight, something they'd never had before, and it wasn't just sex. It was that indefinable *more*, the coming together of two broken parts. The joy of finally being put back together. Of putting each other back together.

It dawned on Tuesday then, standing there naked in Grissom's shower, tipped nearly upside down, staring at the warm water sluicing down her bare legs. At Grissom's much larger bare feet and toes spread behind her thinner, daintier feet. With his very capable fingers tapping her wet, naked skin… It came to her the way the winter sun dawned over the wild Atlantic on bitter cold mornings. Warming the earth. Promising spring, new life, and second chances. Maybe, third chances, too.

"I love you, Grissom," she told him, her heart in her throat. "I love you so much that—"

One moment she was upside down. The next she was wrapped in a delicious bear hug, her chin against his burly chest, staring up at the most beautifully tortured man in the world.

"Say it again," he ordered gruffly. "Please, Tuesday. Tell me what you just said again."

Gazing up at the strongest man in her world, she ran her fingers through the water-blackened bangs dripping in his eyes like ink. This hulky giant of a man was still so much that desperate little boy who never should've had to fight to be loved. All of his life, he'd needed to hear those four simple words. Which was why he'd fought so hard for Tanner and Luke, to keep them from living the shallow life he'd lived.

And she was the thief who'd held her love back from him. Talk about a rude awakening. She'd treated him just like his mother and his wife.

"I said I love you, honey," Tuesday repeated, smoothing those floppy bangs back over his head. Tipping up on her toes, she kissed the end of his nose. "I think it was love at first sight, but I…" How could she explain the fear she'd harbored, that she'd believed she was a curse? A jinx? That just knowing her might've wrecked his dear little family?

"Good, because I love you so damned much it hurts," he growled, his breath hot on her throat as he slathered his tongue over her sensitive skin. "I have for days."

"I should've told you sooner, but everything happened so fast between us, and I—" She couldn't finish, not the way his hands were squeezing her backside. Grissom was possessive as hell, and those thick fingers were branding her as his. Only his.

When he finally eased off, she dropped her gaze to where their bellies pressed together, damming a tiny pool of water between them. "It's just that" —she couldn't risk looking at him— "everyone I've ever loved is dead, Grissom. Mom and Dad. Freddie. Atchison Bremmer. His babies, Toby and Betsy.

Everlee Yeager almost died in the gunfight with Maeve Astor. If I'd stayed with Shane or Heston, they'd probably be dead now too. I couldn't do that to you or your boys. I was… I was afraid."

Grissom's fingers tightened on her hips. "Survivor's guilt, that's what you're feeling. You're no more to blame for those deaths than I am for what happened the day in Syria when I… when I…"

Tuesday molded her wet body to Grissom's as the story of that tragic day unfolded. She watched his expression change as he relived the death of those poor boys. By the time it ended, his warm hazel eyes were cold, staring through her. Not seeing, and that just wasn't good enough.

"I'm sorry you had to go through that," she whispered, gently drawing his attention back into the steamy shower with her. "It's not fair what happened, Grissom, but you would've died for your men that day. That's why you defended them. You didn't know who was shooting at you and your men. You had to take care of your guys. You're a protector. It's who you are. The first thing I ever noticed about you was that you'd die for Tanner and Luke."

"So would you," he murmured, his whiskey eyes so sad, his palm tenderly cradling her cheek.

"Exactly. That's what people who love each other do, honey. On our best days, we're all just doing the best we can, with what we've been given to work with."

"We're a couple jokers, is what we are."

"Why do you say that?"

"Because look at us. You're telling me the same thing I just told you, only in a different way. We both sound like my counselor. She's been telling me to let the past go and live in the present moment for weeks."

Tuesday couldn't hold back a grin. "Then let's live, Grissom. Together. Let's build that sanctuary for abused men, maybe build a few safe homes for unwed mothers and motherless children, and—"

Grissom's mouth covered hers with heat and passion, ending her crazy dreams for their future. Tuesday wrapped her arms around his neck and hung on. By the time they extracted themselves from the shower, they were prunes. Happy prunes.

Now this… was living.

The next morning, Tuesday woke to an empty bed. The delicious aroma of bacon in the air and the noisy chatter coming from the kitchen told her the men of the household were making breakfast.

She hurried through her shower, then dressed in her last clean pair of skinny jeans, a thin red cashmere sweater top, white anklets, and the adorable red Converse tennis shoes Smoke Montoya, another rough and ready guy, had given her last year, in Texas of all places.

The minute she stepped into the kitchen doorway, she smiled to herself. Grissom had his back to her, as she settled stealthily on one of three barstools at the butcher block island. Tanner stood at his side, but Luke was nowhere in sight. Three plates of scrambled eggs, crispy bacon, and French toast, with glasses of orange juice, lined her side of the island.

Forget about this kitchen needing bigger windows. The man at the coffeemaker more than made up for that oversight. Pure bliss. She'd seen Grissom at his worst and was now drinking in the sight of him at his masculine best. He was a magnificent mass of muscle, from those long, lean legs, to his tight, round ass, to his narrow waist, and on up to those wide shoulders that completed the perfect inverted triangle of male perfection. To top it off, those muscular shoulders were wrapped in a black polo shirt that looked painted on. Twin leather holsters criss-crossed his back. A sheathed knife hung in the center of that leather X. This man was dressed for work. So soon?

"Good morning," she said brightly, trying not to let it show that she was crushing on Tanner's dad. At least, to not look like a star-struck teenager. Last night, Grissom had been all cowboy, but today? Weaponized, strong, and deadly? Drool-worthy. Utterly drool-worthy.

He shot a quick but serious glance at her over his shoulder. "Sorry, but Murphy called earlier, and I've got to leave. Haven't needed a sitter since we moved. Might be gone for a couple days. I was wondering—"

"Ask Robin, Dad," Tanner whined. "Please? She'll come, I know she will."

Tuesday didn't care who Robin was. "But I'm already here, sweetheart, and I'd love to stay with you boys while your dad goes to work."

"You'll stay? Really?" Tanner asked, wringing his fingers. He looked back up to his dad. "Kin Tuesday watch us instead of Robin until you get back?"

Grissom turned around with two steaming mugs in his hands. "Robin's the teenager who lived next door at our old place. She used to watch Tanner and Luke for me when" —he shrugged— "well, you know. When no one else was around."

He meant What's-Her-Name. "Of course!" Tuesday nearly squealed. "We'll be fine, won't we, Tanner?"

Were those tears in his melted amber eyes? This poor kid was breaking her heart all over again. Sliding off the stool, Tuesday crouched and opened her arms wide, ready to catch him if he fell. "I need a hug."

Tanner ran to her and flung his skinny body against hers. Trembling, he wrapped his arms around her neck. My goodness, this little guy was scared. His poor heart hammered like the entire percussion section in her high school marching band—on steroids. "He gots ta go, Miss Tuesday," Tanner sobbed. "This morning. Right away. He gots ta rescue some people who got left behind in, umm, Afghanstontun. Dad's leaving, and he says it's real important, but I don't want him to go, and Luke's hiding under his bed so no one kin ever steal him again and..." Tanner sucked in a shuddering inhale. "I don't want Dad to go. Please, make him stay."

That explained why Luke wasn't in the kitchen.

"And you're scared," she whispered, hugging Tanner tighter.

"Uh-uh," he answered through pitiful sniffles, his wet lips against her neck. "You stay too, so Mom d-don't never, ever come b-back. You kin keep us safe. I know you kin cuz you already did. You saved us before. Can't you save us again?"

This poor traumatized child was killing her. Tuesday hoisted Tanner onto her lap and held him. Just sat there in the middle of Grissom's kitchen floor and hugged that perfect little boy as tight as she dared. "Of course, I'll stay. I belong here with you guys and your dad. Right, Grissom?"

The second his dark eyes locked onto Tuesday's, her heart kicked into overdrive. She was so much in love with this bear of a man who, when he smiled, turned into a gloriously, sexy beast. The ultimate tall, dark, and handsome star in her sky. Decisive. Bold. Stronger than anyone she'd ever known. A fierce, deadly fighter who'd die to protect his family. One of those few hard males who stood alone in the night against their country's enemies. One of the few, the brave, the—the best of the best. Smiling at the way she'd butchered the Marine Corps slogan, Tuesday licked her bottom lip, knowing that tiny action would drive Grissom crazy.

"Yeah, about that…" Sliding the last few strips of bacon out of the skillet onto an already full platter, he wiped his hands on the nearest kitchen towel and then rounded the breakfast island. His hazel eyes shimmered like the soft touch he was. "Tanner, go get your brother. I want you boys to be the first to know."

Tanner tipped back in Tuesday's arms and wiped his face. "To know what, Dad?"

Crouching down to his son's level, Grissom landed a gentle swat on Tanner's thigh and said, "Just go, Scooter. Drag Luke out from under his bed if you have to. You'll find out when you both get back."

"Okay. I'm going."

Once Tanner was out of earshot, Grissom leaned his forehead to Tuesday's. "Actually, you should be the first to know. Will you marry me, Tuesday Smart? Will you take my last name and love me and my sons for the rest of our lives? I don't think I can stand to live one more day without you in it.

Neither can my boys. *Our boys.* I give you all that I am, without reservation. Please, say yes."

"Oh, oh, oh…" was all Tuesday could manage. Her throat went dry, but before she let her fears scare her away from this one-in-a-million man, she gave Grissom the rest of her heart and her answer. "I love you so, so much. Your boys, too. Yes, I'll marry you," she replied hoarsely, collapsing into his arms with tears in her eyes.

That was where Tanner and Luke found her, tucked under Grissom's chin, trying not to cry but doing a lousy job of it.

"Oh, no!" Tanner shrieked. "What'd you do to Miss Tuesday, Dad? Did you hurt her feelings again?"

Luke's tiny hands curled into fists. "Say you're sorry, Daddy."

Grissom tipped his head back and laughed. "I guess I did make her cry, but I didn't hurt Miss Tuesday, and I'm not sorry. She's crying because I asked her to marry us. You guys and me. Those pretty tears in her eyes are tears of happiness, and you boys are going to be my two very best men at our wedding."

"You're gonna get married? To each other?" Tanner shrieked, his eyes bright, as if it were Christmas morning all over again.

Luke made it a hundred times more personal. "You're gonna be my good mommy?" he asked, quietly worming under Tuesday's arm and clinging to her like a tiny spider monkey, his legs around her waist and his butt perched on her hip.

Grissom didn't give her time to reply. "Yes, Tanner and Luke," he said, his voice rough. "Tuesday'll live with us from now on. She'll protect you whenever I have to leave, and she'll sleep with me when I'm home."

"Kin she sleep with us when you're not home?" Tanner asked timidly.

Grissom looked to Tuesday for that answer.

"How about you kids sleep with me when your dad's out of town?" she asked. "There's plenty of room in his bed and I'll get lonely. It'll be fun."

"I'll keep you safe," Tanner asserted, his chest puffed out.

"I kin, Too-Day," Luke mumbled. The traumatized little guy was sucking his thumb. Darn that foul biological mother of his!

Grissom snagged Tanner and cuddled him tight. "Honestly, boys, I don't have all the answers. But somehow, I'll make sure you never have to see your other mother again. I already changed the security code. Only Santa can get in without it, and he has to come down the chimney. I'd like to see your other mother do that."

Tuesday could tell Grissom was trying hard to change the tone of this serious conversation.

"You mean our mean mother?" Luke asked, still so quiet that Tuesday couldn't help patting his back. "She can't never get inside here no more? Promise?"

"That's right, sweet baby of mine," Tuesday crooned. "That mean woman's in jail."

"And that's where she's going to stay for the rest of her life," Grissom declared.

"Promise?" Tanner whispered, shaking so hard it brought tears to Tuesday's eyes.

She pulled him into the new and improved McCoy family huddle, and Grissom quickly settled Tanner on his thigh. "Like your dad said, we don't know all the details yet, sweetheart, but your other mother" —man, how she loved saying that— "will never see you again.

Tanner's cheeks puffed with a big, "Good, cuz I don't ever wanna see her again neither."

"Me too," Luke whispered, his fingers twisting a knot into the neckline of Tuesday's sweater top. "She made my tummy hurt, and sometimes at night, I get ascared, and I hafta climb into Tanner's bed with him. And sometimes, I have a accident and I cry, but just a little."

Tanner laid a brotherly hand on Luke's shoulder. "I don't mind if you sleep with me every night. We fit pretty good in just one bed, even when you bring all your trucks. I got lots of room, and I don't mind helping you get into clean pajamas neither. I even know how to change sheets cuz Dad taught me."

Tuesday heard Grissom's sharp intake of air and his whispered, "Fuck."

"And Tanner told me that somethings scare the crap out of all us guys," Luke continued as if he wasn't breaking his dad's heart by revealing how traumatized he'd been. "And sometimes, us guys know what's scaring us, but sometimes, we don't know, Daddy. But he told me he'll always listen to me even when I'm crying. Every time. Anytime."

Tuesday tipped her nose into the curve of Grissom's neck where it joined with his shoulder. He was struggling to contain his feelings. She could feel the vibration of his heart cracking down deep in his chest. The words Luke had just said were important. Grissom knew them from somewhere; might've said them to Tanner, maybe more than once. And Tanner had wisely passed them to Luke, in his three-year-old hour of need. When monsters came lying and screaming in the middle of the night. When the closest person he had to cling to was his big brother.

Grissom buried his face in Tuesday's hair, hiding his tears like the tender-hearted man he was. With a soft growl, he wrapped his arms around her and the boys. *Their boys.* Together they sat in the middle of the McCoy kitchen floor. Holding each other. Holding each other up. Just being there. For each other. Like a family.

Chapter Thirty-Eight

Six days later

Man, he was tired. Home again, safe and sound, and feeling like a TEAM operator once more. Grissom dropped his gear inside his front entry and keyed in the new code to activate his security system, a string of numbers so long Luke wouldn't be able to remember them. The little guy was smart, but he'd learned his lesson. Poor Luke was skittish now. He jumped now whenever the doorbell rang.

This mission had been an easy, quick in-and-out to spirit thirty-plus Afghan HVTs out of their now-Taliban-controlled country. Among them Arzad's granddaughter Najela, her husband, and children. Arzad, a longtime friend of Alex, was already in America, having escaped Afghanistan months earlier. The others were Afghan friendlies who'd risked their lives helping American soldiers in the war against the Taliban. Tonight, they were safe and on their way to becoming American citizens.

God bless Alex. He never had any trouble telling the cancel culture media where to shove their toxic political agenda. With President Adams' knowledge, he'd already funded several clandestine forays into Afghanistan, in the name of humanity, never politics. The press had a field day when they discovered that a private defense contractor, the same man who'd recently been tagged to become the country's next Vice President, achieved what the US military failed to do. People were all that mattered. Not politicians. Alex still served America, not himself. Grissom wished more Americans were like him.

Locking his gear with its firearms, ammo, and assorted weaponry in the reinforced entryway closet, Grissom's nostrils flared. His stomach growled. *What is that delicious aroma?*

He came to a full stop in the middle of his family room, overcome by how different his house felt. How good. How sweet. There was no tension in the air. No underlying current of fear or drama. No little boys' stilted silence, either. The most amazing sound drifted down from the loft. Grissom had never heard it before. He cocked his head to be sure he wasn't dreaming.

Tanner's giggling? The rumble of a sloppy raspberry being blown into some little guy's neck or tummy joined that breathtaking giggle. Tuesday had to be the maestro behind that heart-stirring music. Because that was what his boys were making—the most beautiful music a father could hope to hear.

"Do it again!" Luke chortled so hard, he coughed and choked a little, but then said in a hoarse voice, "You're making me laugh, Too-Day! I wub it!"

'*I wub it, too,*' Grissom thought, standing there frozen, like an idiot.

He looked to the loft, speechless. He hadn't showered while he'd been gone. There hadn't been enough time, but he was damned tempted to run upstairs and hug everyone before he hit the head. His boys would be happy to see him, and of course he'd brought a few trinkets for them. Not from Afghanistan, there were no souvenirs there worth dragging home. But from the first 7-11 store he came across on his drive home from Joint Base Andrews, where the Air Force C-130 that brought everyone home landed.

Common sense prevailed. There was no way he would crash this party until he'd washed the grit and stink of Afghanistan off his skin and out of his hair. He needed a trim and a shave. Toothpaste and mouthwash would feel damned good. Clean, fresh-smelling clothes wouldn't hurt. He headed for his room, kicked out of his work boots, peeled his t-shirt over his head, and dropped everything outside the bathroom door, in a smelly pile he might have to burn later.

His homecoming took an unexpected turn when he closed the bathroom door and was treated to the lacy red bra dangling off the hook behind the door. His cock twitched with delight. Well, well, well. Looked like Tuesday had moved in. The army of delicate bottles, a pink crystal atomizer, a hairbrush, and cans of mousse and hairspray decorating the vanity made his smile wider and his cock harder. The pink, poofy bath sponge hanging by a ribbon from the shower faucet broke the house. Hot damn. He'd never experienced this simple act of feminine sharing before. Made him feel like he was already married—again. To the right woman.

Lifting his face to the ceiling, he whispered to The Man Upstairs, "I owe You one."

Once in the shower, he cranked the tap to extra hot and commenced lathering. His beard was itchy and too long to be comfortable. It needed to be trimmed and washed down the drain. He had his face in the shower spray when a puff of cool air hit his backside. Just when he thought life couldn't get any better, Tuesday stepped into the spray with him and closed the frosted glass panel behind her beautiful bare ass.

"Welcome home," his very naked woman whispered, pressing her luscious body into his open arms and trailing her fingers over his chest.

With his blood on fire, Grissom cupped her full breasts and buried his face between them. "I've missed you," he muttered, kissing and nipping those succulent tips, kneading them into rigid peaks before he sucked them into his mouth.

"I can see that," she groaned, arching back, effectively shoving her tits down his greedy throat. "And them? Did you miss them, too?"

"If you mean these perky girls" —he gave each nipple a full-mouthed bite— "hell, yes, I missed all of you. Are the boys occupied for a minute or two?" *Or more.*

"I told them I was checking on dinner, but they know you're coming home today."

"I can do quick. Can you?"

She lifted her eyes to the ceiling. "Honey, I can do anything you want or need me to do."

Grissom reacted instantly. There was a frantic, hedonistic rush of slippery fingers and hands sliding over bare skin, followed by a frantic clashing of greedy lips, tongues, and teeth that nearly drowned out the noise of the shower.

His eager hands mapped the salacious curve of her breasts, her narrow waist, and finally, her lush hips. Digging his slippery fingers into the smooth plush cheeks of her ass, he backed Tuesday into the corner under the spray. She was wet, hot, and ready. He was charged to the max and hard as granite. There was no stopping. No reason to.

Surging forward, Grissom breached her core in one slick, sure thrust. As before, Tuesday's body crashed against him.

Her eager mouth inhaled his soul, and her luscious body swallowed his cock, to the hilt.

He gasped at the fierce suction of her most intimate muscles on his manhood. The rush!

She was soft and warm and so damned willing. Like him, she was every bit a warrior. Digging her nails into his ass. Thrusting forward, slamming against him nearly as forcefully as he was powering into her.

The viciously sweet agony of pleasure raced up his spine. Too soon. Too fast. He needed to slow things down. He hadn't intended to rut like a damned bull the minute he got home. Not with her still healing. But— "Sweet Jesus!" he hissed, then followed that with a hearty, "Fuck! I'm… I'm…"

"Then come," Tuesday ordered, as if a dominatrix truly was hidden in that sleek, sexy body. Clutching him with muscles that felt like ten demanding little fingers. Stroking him. Urging him to the finish line. He was nearly there. Taking that Leap of Faith again, with seconds to spare when—

Her pelvic muscles contracted, squeezing him so tight that Grissom shot every last one of his lost dreams into the slick heavenly body in his hands. Deeper. Farther. Until he had no idea where his body ended and hers began. They came in a single throbbing heartbeat. One divine creature. Endowed with the power to create life. Blessed with enough grace and love between them to parent a child. To bring that child up with tenderness and devotion.

Her legs and belly quivered with tiny aftershocks, as he emptied himself, remembering too late they hadn't used protection. Certainly not restraint. But knowing he'd fucked up—in the very best way—made Grissom smile. The mere thought that her flat belly could soon be round with his baby, instigated his horny ass to thrust forward again and again. To go deeper. To nail her harder, in case he missed his target the first time around.

"I love you, woman," he growled at the angel staring at him with hazy emerald eyes and the cutest loopy smile on her strawberry lips. Her legs were still spread wide and her plump ass was wet and warm in his very capable hands. She was now held up entirely by just the press of his body and his cock. This sweet thing kept surprising him with her strength.

Like the sultry siren Tuesday had no idea she was, she ran her long, elegant fingers over his head, raking his dripping wet hair out of his eyes. Grissom looked down at the delightfully plump breasts flattened against his pecs. Men were such beasts of burden, built out of muscle, bone, and one-track brains. They were built for endurance and war.

But women were so much better, full of tears and love, the purest nurturers in the world when they were made right. While men conquered nations and built enormous machines that crossed oceans, canyons, air, and space, only women, like the sexy lady hugged up against him now, could save frightened children and breathe life back into war-damaged men. Even now, sodden tangles of long brown wet hair drizzled between them, delineating her curves, accentuating her lavish pillowy breasts, and hardening her nipples into diamond points of perfection.

"The boys won't stay upstairs much longer," she whispered, gently scrubbing both hands over his head.

Grissom blinked the water out of his eyes, so damned in love that it hurt. "I… I finally have everything," he murmured, his heart close to breaking at the miracle this woman had wrought in his life. Sure, he'd had a handle on providing for his sons before he'd met Tuesday. But the one thing he'd never been able to give Tanner and Luke was the beautiful emerald heart shining down on him from the corner of his shower.

Relaxing his grip on her ass, he slid Tuesday down his undeserving, rugged male body, to her feet. "I don't know how I've survived without you, love. We should've talked about birth control a long time ago, but I'm not sorry we didn't. I'd be one happy son of a bitch if I just got you pregnant."

"If *we* just got me pregnant," she corrected him, wiggling her tiny tummy against his much wider belly. "I'm pretty sure it takes two to make a baby. You want to start using birth control?"

"Hell no. Look down, woman. What do you see?"

She took a half step back and dropped her eyes. "I see us. Joined in love and play. I see a man who's ready to play."

"So you're okay if we get pregnant?"

Tuesday looped her arms around his neck. "Play later," she said with a sly shrug. "If we don't hurry and get dressed, the boys will come knocking, and then you'll have some explaining to do."

With one last long loving look at the woman who'd changed his life, Grissom stepped out of the shower and grabbed the nearest towel. "I'm just a man," he teased, pinching her nipple before he whipped the towel over her head, wrapped it around her, and pulled her in for another kiss. "Here, I'll help you dry—"

"Oh, no, you don't," she shrieked, darting out of his reach. "Get dressed," she ordered, winding that towel into a whip and sending it straight back at him.

He turned to dodge the impact, but—*SNAP!* Damned if she wasn't as good a shot with that towel as he'd heard she was with a pistol. She'd made sharp, stinging contact. On his ass!

"You hit me, woman," Grissom growled, as threatening as he could while grinning.

"Then hurry!" she teased, winding that damned towel into another whip, ready to smack his ass again. "*Our* boys are dying to see you. If you hurry, we can surprise them before they get curious and come knocking."

"You think you're getting off that easy? I don't think so." Grissom easily overpowered Tuesday. Tossing the towel over his shoulder, Grissom hoisted her still naked butt up off the floor and mashed her against his chest. "You got a lucky shot, but that's all it was, luck."

"Wanna bet?" Her bright emerald eyes so damned gorgeous.

This woman was Venus come to life in his arms. He'd no more than stopped speaking when she nailed him with a slick, wet kiss of forgetfulness. Fuck, she tasted good. It took a full moment before Grissom had his senses back enough to ask, "What's cooking? I mean, besides us."

"Enchilada casserole. Tanner made a green salad to go with it, and Luke honey-buttered the scones. You hungry or something?" she teased.

He'd never seen the sassy side of Miss Tuesday Smart before, but he was loving it. She was a brat, an adorable, sexy brat who wasn't afraid to be the happy, contented woman in all of her just fucked glory. Delectably, sinfully sweet. A naughty brat maybe, but his brat.

"I'm always hungry for you," he growled, his body hardening to make love with this woman again. But she was right. His sons needed him, and he needed to get his hands on them. So, while Tuesday dried her tantalizing body, then twisted her wet hair into a ponytail, he trimmed his beard, brushed his teeth, and watched her in the steamy mirror the entire time.

The teasing way she smiled back at him was to die for. She knew he was watching, and the mischievous emerald glints in her eyes dared him to engage. In what, he had no idea… until she wiggled her ass into her panties and jeans. The woman was one helluva Playboy Bunny, standing there half-naked. As seductive as a stripper, she nestled her girls into her bra cups, then lifted a white shirt off the doorknob and—

"Hold up. New duds?" Not like he'd seen much of her wardrobe before, but the shirt hanging off her fingertips did not say New York City. "Where'd you get that?"

"What? This old thing?"

"Doesn't look old to me. In fact…" He purposefully brushed the backs of his fingers over those brimming satin cups to the shiny brass snaps running from the crisply ironed collar of said shirt, over the white, embossed yoke, and down to the tails. "This is pure western. You've been horseback riding? Without me?" *With Maverik? I'll kill him.*

She hung her arms around his neck like a lasso, mashing his hands between their bodies. Which served his purpose. Grissom squeezed the full cups of her bra, enhancing her already dynamite cleavage. If they kept this up, they were never leaving the bathroom.

"The boys and I went riding every day you were gone. Maverick set me up with a dappled gray mare, and, oh, yeah, I found a counselor, too. Ms. Ashlee Peyton. She actually called me, looking for you and your boys, wondering why you missed your appointment."

"Damn. I forgot."

"No matter. I took the boys in to chat with her after she called. Tanner and Luke jabbered like two little magpies. I think that surprised Ashlee. But I didn't go in with them for their session. I figured they'd talk more openly without me, so I stayed in the waiting room."

"They don't usually say much."

Tuesday nodded. "That's what Ashlee said. I talked with her afterward, just to let her know you'd be back for your next session."

"Come with us?"

"I was hoping you'd ask. I'd love to, as long as it's okay with the boys."

"They'll love having you there. You're family. Get used to it."

They dressed, then hurried to the back stairs, where Grissom took the steps two at a time. He couldn't wait to get his boys in his arms again. But he stalled at the top step. Stunned. Speechless. Tears in his eyes. Tuesday had done it again. She'd told him she'd take his family's portrait, but this—

She'd turned his plain, unadorned loft into a photographic essay of love. Portraits. Dozens of portraits. Still shots of him with his boys. Close-ups that had him wiping his eyes. Silhouettes taken against the family room's high front windows. Intimate shots of him and his boys when he hadn't known she'd been working. The resident photographer, Miss Tuesday Smart, had performed a miracle Christmas morning.

She'd blessed this empty old house with spirit. The McCoy spirit.

Several of Tanner's drawings were professionally framed and positioned in their own separate gallery, complete with display lights mounted above them. The silver metal frames matched the jets he loved. She'd included the F-35 and F-16 pilots' autographed, glossy eight-by-elevens. Luke had his own separate gallery of the crayon drawings he'd drawn Christmas day. How could Grissom ever thank Tuesday for capturing these memories? For making Tanner and Luke feel important?

Luke noticed him standing there shell-shocked and silent. "Daddy!" he squealed, beating feet straight into Grissom's arms. He knelt to catch his baby boy as Luke collided with him. "We been busy! I missed you!" he shrilled, peppering Grissom's face with sloppy kisses, his arms tight around Grissom's neck and squeezing tighter.

"I see that," Grissom breathed, so damned emotional he could cry. Could, nothing. He was.

"What's a matter, Dad?" Tanner asked, his voice tight with worry.

Grissom held out an arm for his anxious oldest son to join him and Luke. "I'm just happy," he managed to choke. *I'm so damned happy.*

Tuesday's fingers were light but firm on his shoulders. She was the glue he hadn't realized his family needed. She'd made them a family. Her family. All he'd done was buy a house, but she was the one who'd filled it with love and made it home.

Happy was such a small word.

Chapter Thirty-Nine

Three months later

"I don't wanna be late! Hurry, Luke! You're gonna make me miss everything!" Tanner yelled from the kitchen. Dressed in a mini-tuxedo, he was the sweaty, anxious ringbearer for today's prestigious event, and he was taking it seriously.

"I coming," Luke grouched, his red-and-blue striped tie hanging loose around his little neck. "Daddy says I hafta leave Spot home, but I don't wanna." He glared at his father, as he climbed up beside Grissom on the couch. "Spot's never seen a wedding. He wants ta come, too."

Damn Taylor Armstrong for telling him that no ring bearer worth his salt was ever late. The poor kid had never watched the microwave clock like he was watching it today. Heston and London were finally getting married, and they'd chosen Maverick's barn for the ceremony and reception, and Tanner for their ringbearer. The rustic place was decorated to the rafters, and every last one of those Percherons' manes were braided and they had ribbons woven into their tails. Made quite a sight in the pasture.

Grissom snagged his youngest and settled him on his lap. "You can bring Spot, but he'll have to stay in the truck once we get there."

"But Daddy—"

"Luke." One word was all it took for Luke to comply. He wasn't the bossy little guy he'd been before What's-Her-Name poisoned him. Grissom wasn't sure his youngest understood that she'd tried to kill him. All of his life, Pam had made him believe he was her favorite when she wasn't capable of loving anyone but herself.

For the first time in their lives, Grissom and his sons had futures worth looking forward to, and that future was bright. After engaging with three (Tuesday had more) high-powered New York City attorneys, What's-Her-Name's bully lawyer had backed off her ridiculous demand for full custody. Like a leopard changing his spots, he then went one better and convinced Pam to relinquish all parental rights. She'd never wanted her sons—or her daughter—anyway. To her, children were just tools in her already overflowing arsenal of spite and hatred.

With assistance from Frederick Lamb's sons, Tuesday now possessed architectural plans, the necessary permits, and licenses to build her dream. Grissom was at her side the afternoon they'd (mostly her) purchased the derelict farmland between The TEAM's and Maverick's properties. There they would build *Home Away from Home*, an assisted living center for men in need of a break or escape from their abusive wives or significant others. Marriages today were complicated, not always between a man and a woman. Her unique center would accommodate any man who needed a way out of a relationship, better coping skills, mental or medical care.

He still had to reach out to his dad. Soon. Not today.

She'd insisted on paying off Grissom's mortgage, too, but that was where he'd drawn a hard line. Her funding worthwhile projects made her happy as a clam, but providing for his wife and family was Grissom's job, and that job made him happy. The bank might own ninety-nine percent of the home they lived in at the moment, but pay for it he would. Between the sale of his house in Crystal Spring and the nice bump in salary he'd just received for a mission well done in Afghanistan, that mortgage would be paid off in no time. They'd celebrate the momentous achievement then.

Just thinking of growing old with Tuesday calmed the hell out of Grissom. He'd never known true peace until he'd dropped into her life that day in Puntarenas. He honestly wouldn't have connected with her after that, until, once again, she'd run pell-mell into a pasture full of *giant horses* to save Luke's life. That was what she did best. Tuesday saved lives. Grissom's included.

Which brought him back to his family room, where he was tying a proper Windsor knot in his youngest son's tie. Until Luke breathed, "Wow. Mama, you look bee-uuu-tee-full!"

Mama? That was a first.

Grissom looked to the doorway where Tuesday stood half-in, half-out of the hall doorway. Luke was spot on. She was—wow. Sinfully gorgeous. There were no words to adequately describe the radiant beauty twisting a chunk of chestnut brown in her fingers. No two ways about it. Wearing a mint green (she'd called it celadon), off-the-shoulder gown (she'd called that a dress?), she was a goddess beyond compare. Name one. Aphrodite. Diana. Freyja. Artemis. Venus. Didn't matter if they were Greek, Roman, or Norse. Nothing on Earth or in Heaven compared with the woman gazing wide-eyed at Luke.

"You are so-o-o-o purdy!" He clapped, bouncing his little butt on Grissom's thigh. "Tanner! Come see Too-Day!"

Of course, Tuesday went straight for the little tyke whose words had jump-started her heart and knelt at his feet. "You called me Mama."

"'Course!" Luke chirped. "Me and Tanner decided we're gonna call you Mama from now on. Is that okay?"

Tears fell as Tuesday gathered Luke into her arms on the floor and told him, "Oh, my heavens, yes, sweetheart."

Tanner collided with the twosome, burying his face in Tuesday's neck and whispering, "I ain't calling you Miss Tuesday no more. You're the best Mama in the whole world."

Grissom sat alone in the corner of the couch, listening to his youngsters. They didn't like Pam much now. She'd hurt them, and their trauma was fresh. But the day might come when they'd forget and they might want more information about her. Might even reach out to her. Grissom hoped not, but he'd do everything in his power to facilitate a safe meeting. Hopefully, they'd be grown men by then, confident, and mature enough to understand that not all women made good mothers.

These last months had taught Grissom what true love looked, sounded, and tasted like. The love Tuesday had readily given away to two lost boys in Costa Rica, had come back to her a thousand-fold. Tanner and Luke adored her.

Destiny might be real, but love had it beat. Grissom didn't need to make this tender moment about him. It was enough to sit there and covertly wipe his eyes while the woman of his dreams loved on *their* sons. Luke's calling her Mama proved Grissom's point. He fingered the velvet box in his pants pocket. Tuesday already belonged to the best family in the world—his—and soon the whole world would know because she'd be wearing his ring and his name. Luke's shiny silver nut, the ring he'd given her Christmas Eve, was in the velvet box in Grissom's other pocket. He'd had it engraved with three words: *Anytime. Every. Time.* He figured he'd let Tanner and Luke teach her what it meant.

What's-Her-Name had chosen poorly. Love did conquer hate, and Grissom was watching it in action. Bullies the world over should take notice. His girl Tuesday Smart, soon to be the much-adored Mrs. Grissom McCoy, was in the house.

And she was fuckin' dynamite.

The End

Thank you for reading Grissom and Tuesday's story!

You are the key to this book's success!

Please tell other readers why you liked Grissom
by leaving an honest review
at the retail site where you purchased it.

Recommend him to your friends. Lend him.
Most of all, enjoy him!

Other Irish Winters' best-selling series:

In the Company of Snipers

Alex
Mark
Zack
Harley
Connor
Rory
Taylor
Gabe
Maverick
Cassidy
Adam
Lee
Ky
Hunter
Eric
Jake
Seth
Beau
Renner
Beckam
Walker
Jameson
Tripp
Shane
Heston

Deuces Wild
King of Hearts
Joker Joker
One-Eyed Jack
Ace

Hearts and Ashes
Smoke
Ash

SOBs Novels
Angel
Assassin
Vaquero
Damned

To keep up with my new releases, giveaways, and actionable intel, sign up for my spam-free newsletter at IrishWinters.com.

About the Author

Irish Winters…

…is a best-selling author who, when she isn't writing, dabbles in poetry, grandchildren, and rarely (as in extremely rarely) the kitchen. More prone to be outdoors than in, she grew up the quintessential tomboy on a dairy farm in rural Wisconsin, spent her teen years in the Pacific Northwest, but calls the Wasatch Mountains of Northern Utah, home. For now.

She believes in making every day count for something, and follows the wise admonition of her mother to, *"Look out the window and see something!"*

Connect with Irish online:
On Facebook: https:/www.facebook.com/author.irishwinters
Or at http://www. IrishWinters.com

www.ingramcontent.com/pod-product-compliance
Lightning Source LLC
Chambersburg PA
CBHW051000210726
48287CB00004B/1314